KNOW MORE LIES

Chris Gray

The Book Guild Ltd

First published in Great Britain in 2021 by
The Book Guild Ltd
9 Priory Business Park
Wistow Road, Kibworth
Leicestershire, LE8 0RX
Freephone: 0800 999 2982
www.bookguild.co.uk
Email: info@bookguild.co.uk
Twitter: @bookguild

This work is entirely fictitious and bears no resemblance to any persons living or dead.

Typeset in 11pt Adobe Garamond Pro

Printed on FSC accredited paper
Printed and bound in Great Britain by 4edge Limited

ISBN 978 1913551 841

British Library Cataloguing in Publication Data.
A catalogue record for this book is available from the British Library.

Special thanks to Colin and Big Steve from Aberdeen for their support — I couldn't have done it without you fellas! And to my two best friends — you know who you are.

CHAPTER 1

The time I leave home to go to work depends on when my shift starts. Today, I'm on a 10 a.m. to 6 p.m. gig, so I will leave at 8.45 a.m., walk down to the main road and get picked up by a colleague. They will drive to an industrial estate about ten miles away, park up and we'll enter an enormous warehouse, owned by a company called 'Coopers'.

Coopers is a logistics firm that undertakes all manner of things from storage, distribution, assembly and quality checking. As I enter the facility, the fob I swipe triggers the online system, notifying management that I've arrived. I'll enter the staff locker room and change into my work gear of boots, overalls and a hi-vis vest.

Today, I've been assigned to pick orders for distribution. This is probably my favourite task as it allows me to roam around the warehouse and make banal conversation with colleagues.

My manager's name is Derek, although we call him Des. This makes about as much sense to me as calling someone Bob when their name is Alan.

Des and I share a cordial relationship as I put in an honest day's graft, seldom take time off sick and I'm never late for a shift. This is in stark contrast to some of my less conscientious colleagues, who will royally toss it off at every juncture.

Take Imelda, for example; she has famously never worked a day after a bank holiday weekend. We all know she's been on the lash as the thick idiot posts paralytic updates of herself all over social media. The last bank holiday posting was a video of her attempting to down three pints of lager consecutively before having to stop after one and a half pints to projectile vomit into her aquarium.

The day after a bank holiday, Imelda would no doubt wake up shaking like a shitting dog and have to fabricate some non-drink related illness to excuse her from coming into work. She's now on her last warning; so is Ismail, but his disciplinary issue followed a fight with Wayne, a forklift truck driver who alleged he'd spotted Ismail eating a Ginsters Cornish pasty whilst he was claiming to be observing Ramadan. Hearing this accusation, Ismail grabbed Wayne around the throat and started to throttle him. Apparently, he was turning blue and was seconds away from suffering oxygen starvation before Big Linda intervened and saved his life. According to warehouse legend, she slapped Ismail so hard he swallowed and nearly choked on a filling. At his disciplinary hearing, Ismail produced from his wallet the filling in question which he rather revoltingly managed to retrieve, believing it would support his case. Alas, it didn't.

When I'm on this particular shift, I generally stop for something to eat around 3 p.m. We get a strict forty-five-minute break and there's a staff canteen available if you haven't brought in your own grub. I don't bother with a packed lunch as I can't be arsed to make it and anyway, they always remind me of school trips, which I hated.

Today, I'll order sausage, beans and chips. Sally, who works in the canteen, fancies me and I might have been interested in her if she wasn't thirty years my senior, circa eighteen stone and only has one working eye. She's like a fat, saggy-breasted cyclops with homemade tattoos. I've also noticed her tongue, slightly disturbingly, comes to rest about an inch outside of her mouth giving the impression she's preparing to lick a plate clean. Which, she may argue, is a useful skill for someone working in the catering industry.

Still, I shouldn't criticise her too much because when I ask for sausages the dirty cat always adds an extra banger to my plate. What follows is a predictably smutty comment as Sally speculates on the size and quality of my meat. Her remark is followed by her best attempt at a seductive wink. That's a wink from her good eye. I'm not certain her other eye is capable of such a trick; it appears to be an open wound which, a bit like the hole in the ozone layer, is gradually getting a little bigger by the day.

I'm going to have to be careful of Sally at the next Christmas party as she's been known to wander around after a couple of pints of Babycham and brandy with mistletoe taped to her nipples. Judging from the state of her knockers, I suspect the mistletoe comes to rest on her kneecaps, so the kiss, for anyone mad or pissed enough to indulge, will be a kneeling-down affair.

I smother my chips and sausages in brown sauce, tomato ketchup and mayonnaise before finding somebody to sit with.

I spot Bangkok Bob reading his newspaper and go over and join him. Bob's not from Bangkok, but he's visited the city more times than the King of Thailand. He openly partakes in sex tourism and will happily regale all manner of sordid stories at the slightest nudge. The prompt he receives from me today is, "Have you ever done a ladyboy, Bob?" The fuse is lit and then boom! Off he goes providing me, and anyone else who is listening in to the conversation, with unimaginably explicit details. Upon reflection, asking Bangkok Bob whether he has ever indulged in a ladyboy is akin to asking Tiger Woods if he's ever used a putter.

He's a fascinating character (that's Bangkok Bob, not Tiger Woods) and I don't know what most interests me about him. Perhaps, it's the graphic details he provides when describing his lurid sex acts or that he's totally comfortable sharing his experiences with absolutely anyone, regardless of whether he knows them or not.

I'll complete my shift at 6 p.m., clock off, get changed and gratefully accept a lift home.

Upon arrival, I shall immediately make my dear grandad a cup of tea. We'll sit and have a chat about my day at work. He likes the stories; the gossip; the updates on the staff and he takes great pride that after a rocky start to my working life I'm now gainfully employed.

I'll make sure my hands, face and everything else is washed and clean before I leave the warehouse. I don't want to be bringing muck into Grandad's home because he's ex-military and likes everything to be shipshape. There will not be a speck of dirt anywhere on my person and that's the strange thing, really, because, for all intents and purposes, it won't appear that I've done a day's graft or even stepped into a large industrial warehouse.

And that's because I haven't.

I've never completed a full day's work in my twenty-three years and the Cooper's warehouse story is like most things that are going on in my life – just one… big… fucking… lie.

CHAPTER 2

If, under some bizarre set of circumstances my life depended on receiving a, 'yes please, mate' response to a question, then I know precisely which question I would choose and exactly who to ask.

"Do you fancy a cup of tea, Grandad?"

"Yes please, mate."

His reply instigates a rasping cough. Two years ago, his fifty years of heavy smoking had finally hunted him down and he was diagnosed with emphysema. His cigarette diet should have gone from thirty a day to zero but the crafty old soldier still helps himself to the odd one when I'm out of the house. He thinks I'm oblivious to it but I know where he hides his stash. When I discovered them I considered challenging him, but as he's dodged bullets in Northern Ireland, the Middle East and the former Yugoslavia, never knowing on any given day whether he would make it back to the barracks, I guessed he knew one or two things about managing risk.

Shortly after the diagnosis, when he claimed to have given up smoking, I'd asked him whether he was ever tempted to have the odd puff. When he replied he wasn't, I found it easier to look him in the eye knowing we were not being completely truthful with one another. Now, of course, on the Top Trumps of fibs, you could justifiably argue that telling a little porky pie about having the odd drag on a cigarette wouldn't beat a card which reads someone has awoken every workday for the past two years and pretended to attend a job that doesn't exist, but a lie, is a lie, is a lie. Or at least, that's what I like to think.

In my micro-world of spurious employment, I was again starting my shift at 10 a.m. Beforehand, I would be picked up by a fake person in their bogus car and a fictitious day at work would ensue.

I'd be able to furnish Grandad with the specifics regarding my employment as one of my two best mates, Nails, actually worked at Coopers. He would provide me with all the details I needed to embellish the story; an important component in the lie-telling process. Long ago, I had discovered when presenting someone with a fib, the more details you provided the less likely they were of ever suspecting you of fabrication. There was, however, a strict caveat to this – a golden rule of lying, if you like – and this was to never and I mean *never*, exaggerate. The moment the lie becomes even remotely unbelievable is the point where you invite doubt to the party. It was a skill I'd perfected; ergo, I was able to drift through life throwing lies around like confetti without anyone noticing.

Nails was in on the Coopers lie I told to Grandad. The periodic sweetener of a few beers provided him with a timely reminder of just how critical it was to keep a lid on this delicate little jar of deceit.

I felt compelled to lie to Grandad about my spurious job as a couple of years ago it felt like I was getting backed into a corner. As my period of unemployment lengthened, I was starting to see the disappointment and frustration etched over his face. I was finding this awkward and emotionally draining given the special relationship we shared.

The closeness of our bond had evolved rapidly after he and Grandma had selflessly plucked me from a nightmare scenario and provided me with a most precious gift when I needed it most.

When I was eight years old, I lived in a chaotic and destructive home; parented by a volatile father and a passive mother who had literally had the life beaten out of her. It was a toxic relationship and, in retrospect, one that was only ever going to end in tears.

Those tears arrived and flowed on my mum's birthday when my less than generous father offered to take her out for a meal. Dad picked her up from work, as planned, only, in his wisdom, he'd been in the pub all afternoon before getting behind the wheel three-thirds pissed.

They never made it to the romantic country pub. Instead, Dad indiscriminately swerved his car into an oncoming HGV. Mum was killed instantly, whilst he didn't have a scratch on him. Emerging from the burning wreckage, he legged it across the country fields and into hiding, eventually handing himself in after his money had run out.

He was sentenced to five years in prison for 'death by dangerous driving' but served only two and a half before he was released for good behaviour. I never saw him whilst he was in prison and I haven't seen or heard from him since his release.

On that fateful night, I was collected by the feds before being taken into foster care. That was one hell of a fun-packed evening that I'll fondly remember. It was as if the captain of life's lucky dip team had visited and dropped off a lifetime's consignment of bad fortune in one evening. In the drunken swerve of a motor vehicle, I had lost everything.

Realising I was heading into a care home, Grandad unselfishly cut short the last period of his military career, returned home, and he and Grandma took me under their wing. They had lost their daughter and I suspect they couldn't bear to see their only grandson pass through the care system, a process where a male contestant has a twenty-five per cent chance of serving a custodial sentence during their adult life.

So, they collected me and my belongings from the foster home I was staying in and I moved in with them. They never spoke of their son-in-law, my dad, and I never talked about him either. Despite the obvious inconvenience of having to raise an emotionally damaged child, they treated me like a prince. God bless them both. I remain forever in their debt.

Seven years ago, Grandma, another heavy smoker, started to cough up blood. Within six months she had died. Her passing had a terrible effect on Grandad and me. I was never academically gifted, but her death was the icing on my disastrous educational cake. GCSEs? Failed the lot. College? Dropped out. Even when I found a job, I couldn't keep it. I became a government statistic; one of the troubling long-term issues that no Downing Street administration wishes to dwell upon. I was yet another ill-educated young person swilling around the system doing nothing.

During this time things became a little fractious between Grandad and me. He was a hardworking ex-soldier, so to see his grandson bumming around in his bedroom all day was beyond his comprehension. During our slightly heated discussions, I blamed my lack of progress on Grandma's death. I'd bolt on losing Mum and not seeing Dad to my argument, but deep down it was all a smokescreen. The reality was I didn't have the stomach for work.

Eight hours a day, every day, every week, every year? You can fuck that for a game of soldiers. I was confused as well; I mean, what type of work was I going to do? I had no trade, no qualifications, no training. I would probably end up flipping burgers for minimum wage. No, it wasn't going to happen.

After one heated discussion too many, I decided to take matters into my own hands and that's when I started to engage in a spot of jiggery-pokery. It kicked off with some low-end pilfering of goods from supermarkets and high-street stores which I would flog in the local pubs. Soon after, the operation was expanding into something a little more sophisticated. Now I had all manner of petty scams on the go, with each income stream delivering a trickle of tax-free cash allowing me to have a few quid in my pocket and be able to support Grandad with his bills. The tricks were all small-time, low-level and petty. Consequently, there wasn't a police officer in the city who would bother to give me a second of their over-stretched, under-budgeted time.

Having established a network of scams, I then decided to manufacture the Coopers story. I had a solid income and the number of scams I was engaged in required me to be out of the house for a good many hours. The fabricated shift work angle allowed me to match my spurious working hours with when I was required to be out and about ducking and diving. The details I was able to glean from Nails about the people and job at Coopers which I drip-fed to Grandad was the creamy head on a deliciously pulled pint of lies.

I made Grandad his cup of tea which I'd perfected to his exact preference; Yorkshire teabags; one level teaspoon of sugar and the achievement of an extremely specific mucky brown colour.

"Here you go, Grandad, you'll enjoy this one."

He was continuing to cough heavily as I placed his mug on the little table at the side of his armchair, and I returned to the kitchen to prepare my breakfast. Next to selling nicked gear, my other major passion was eating. When I was not scheming a scam, I was fantasising about food. To put this into perspective, we aren't talking *Masterchef* style, Asian fusion, á la carte nosh. *Au contraire!* This is genetically modified, loaded with salt and sugar, processed junk.

I decided breakfast was going to be a tin of low-grade ravioli, served in pitta bread with grated cheese and mayonnaise. It didn't disappoint. I washed it down with a can of Irn-Bru, let off a force 9 burp and then made Grandad his second and final mug of tea.

"What are you going to have for your lunch?" I asked him before leaving.

"Cheese sandwiches."

"Do you want me to make them for you before I go?"

"Bless you, it's a kind offer, but I'll see to it. You get yourself off to work, you don't want to be late."

He was right about that; I didn't want to be late. But not for the work he thought I was off to do. Instead, my most profitable income stream, dubbed by Nails as *Crackheads R Us*, was open for business.

Crackheads R Us wasn't a complicated business model, but it was mighty effective. It involved a client base of half a dozen seasoned local drug addicts who could only possibly subsidise their £200 per day habit through a life of crime. They would prowl the city in search of bounty before contacting me when they had something to sell. Given I'd been dubbed 'Bottom Dollar', this might provide a clue as to the amount I gave them for their loot. When they contacted me, it was either because they had exhausted their more lucrative purchasing options or they wanted a guaranteed quick cash transaction. That's the beauty with drug addicts: once they start clucking, they will do literally anything for money.

When they needed a hit and had something to sell, I would be contacted by text message. We would arrange to meet and I would carry out a full inspection of the item. Assuming all was in order, I would offer them – well, yeah, they were right – bottom dollar. There would be much protesting about my offer but I'd always make the point of having the dosh in my hand to tease them. It's like a woman showing a red-blooded fella her cleavage, and trust me, these fuckers drool at the sight of hard cash. In their world, money equals drugs and drugs equal no more 'clucky-clucky'.

I had received a text message about an hour ago and was on my way to meet a prized client. The first deal of the day looked odds-on to be closed within forty minutes and I was eyeing a quick fifty-quid profit.

But this client was no big-shot business tycoon, she almost certainly didn't have a LinkedIn account and it was unlikely she'd be applying to go on *Dragon's Den*. For this was an altogether different type of corporate beast: a volatile trader who would fuck you over in a second for a dime.

I was on my way to meet Candy.

Candy was a long-term crack cocaine and heroin user who had a face like someone had sucked the air out of the back of her head. She couldn't have weighed any more than seven stone and didn't have a tooth in her bacteria-infested mouth.

She was in a bad space, the bottom rung of the ladder, a place from where I doubted she would or could ever return. For some inexplicable reason, Candy would always walk quickly as if she were late for an important meeting. Her little twiglet legs would motor her along like Sonic the Hedgehog on amphetamines. As she marched, she would often stop, turn around and indiscriminately hurl vile abuse at someone who had made the mistake of befriending her.

I was guessing Candy wasn't her real name, but then I could be wrong. After all, she had it tattooed on her neck. It couldn't be ruled out that she was once high on crack and decided on a name change and tramp stamp in one spontaneous, life-changing act. The tattoo would be a painful reminder of her new identity when she'd returned to the land of the sober.

According to Candy's text message, she had a PlayStation 4, two controllers and one game for sale. I assumed the game was in the console when she'd nicked it, as this is generally how it works.

I had arranged to meet her at a bench that I knew on the outskirts of the city centre which was gorgeously adorned by overhanging tree branches. The view of the nearby canal and towpath added to the ambience. I would like to think Candy would arrive a little earlier to appreciate the beauty of her surroundings. Perhaps she would gaze out at the distant buildings of the city silhouetted against the sun and marvel at how wonderful life was. Alas, it's fair to say her opening gambit didn't support this theory:

"Where the fuck have you been?" she cursed.

"Easy, Candy. I have things to tend to in the morning," I replied. "Wow! You have got a nice glow. Have you just come from a Bikram yoga session?"

Sarcasm could be added to selling gear and food as my passions in life.

"What the fuck's that?" she snarled.

I'm guessing that was a no.

"Never mind. Right, what have you got for me?"

"Here you go," she said, unzipping her jacket and removing the PlayStation and controllers.

"Oh, come on! You haven't even brought a bag for it."

"Who do you think I am, fucking Morrisons!"

"I'll tell you what, rather than a bag, why don't you throw in a fucking sandwich board with 'look at me, I'm carrying nicked gear' plastered across it?"

"Can't you stick it in your jacket?"

Little did Candy know she was being played. Buying and selling stolen gear was a game, and I moved my pieces in a strategic and formulaic fashion. I was the buyer, and from the get-go, I'd like to establish that *nothing* about the purchase was quite right. I'd sow doubt and negativity into the mind of the seller and never let them think I was pleased with the proposed deal because it would affect the negotiation. No bag – bad move, Candy. If this were a tennis match, then I'd just gone 15-love up.

"Do you know if it works?" I queried.

"Yeah, I've tried it, it works fine," she replied, impatiently hopping up and down.

She was clucking big-time, meaning she needed to score and would have to accept a lower offer.

30-love.

I probed further: "Oh right, so what game's in it then?"

"What?"

"The game that you said was in it; the one that would have appeared on the screen when you tested to see if the console was working."

"Yeah, what about it?"

"Which game is it?" I snapped.

She obviously hadn't tried the console to see if it worked. She'd probably only nicked the fucking thing about ninety minutes ago and was hardly going to risk hanging around the person's house to undertake a full quality assurance test. But I loved asking which game was in the stolen console because you always, and I mean always, received the same answer. I could almost mouth the words as she said them.

"Erm, *Call of Duty*," she finally responded.

I nearly laughed out loud.

"Which version?"

"The one with the ghost zombies."

"The one with the what?" I replied with a sarcastic chuckle.

"Oh, fuck off!"

40-love.

I removed hard cash from my pocket, twenty pounds' worth to be exact, the sight of which was a dirty little trick to play on a rattling drug addict.

"Shit! Guess what? I've only bought twenty quid," I announced, masking a grin.

"You bastard, we agreed thirty."

"You suggested thirty on the text message, we never agreed to it. Anyway, you haven't even brought a bag."

"What the fuck can I buy with twenty quid?"

"How about a Bikram yoga session?"

"You know what I mean. Fucking Bottom Dollar, you tight-fisted cunt!"

"Okay, let's leave it then," I taunted with a shrug.

"Yeah, let's leave it. Go on, fuck off!"

I turned and slowly walked down the towpath whilst counting in my head, knowing that I wouldn't get to ten, maybe not even to eight.

"Fuck it, twenty quid then!" she bellowed.

Game, set and match, and I hadn't even reached three! Blimey, maybe even I'd underestimated how desperate this cat was to be topped up.

The transaction was completed, and to rub salt into her needle-infected wounds I produced a large bag from my pocket.

"Candy, as ever, it's been a pleasure. You make sure you enjoy the rest of your day because it's important."

"Why don't you stick that PlayStation up your fat, sweaty arse!" she ranted.

"I'm guessing now's not a great time to ask for a receipt?"

"Swivel on this fucker!" she said, giving me a middle-finger salute.

She then turned on her heels before her little motorised twiglet legs hit full throttle and she exited along the towpath, randomly chuntering to herself as she did.

When I get an opportunity, I must give Candy some lessons on how improving customer service can maximise profits.

Buying stolen gear at knocked-off, 'take it or leave it', prices is one thing, but to make an enterprise successful you need a fertile customer base to ensure cash flow remains healthy. This is where my multi-faceted approach provides me with an advantage, as I not only sell products, but I also speculate on future deals. I'll find out who's skint but has their son's birthday coming up; whose television is on the blink or who got shit-faced at the weekend and accidentally flushed their iPhone X down the toilet. Information in this game is key, and if there's market intelligence out there to be collected then I grab it with both hands and pop it into my wallet.

In this instance, I don't have a ready-made private buyer but I need to offload these goods quickly. Why? Well, there are two reasons: firstly, the PlayStation is as hot as a chicken vindaloo. I have no idea from whom Candy stole it. She's an addict and they will nick from absolutely anyone. For all I know, she could have taken it from under the nose of some mad bastard drug dealer who, as we speak, is pounding the streets of Leicester with a baseball bat wrapped in barbed wire looking for the person who is carrying a bag with his games console in it. Secondly, never rule out after having brought the goods from Candy that she, or one of her associates, wouldn't try and steal them back – it's been known.

We aren't dealing with the Samaritans here.

Instead, I'll take the safe option and pay a visit to the second-hand, eBay, stolen goods, car boot sale king of the East Midlands, Smelly Nelly.

Nelly's a massively overweight forty-something with a serious personal hygiene problem. This fella properly stinks like he's rotting from the inside. He has long greasy hair that's progressing towards the self-cleaning cycle of dirtiness, fingernails with about half a centimetre of vile decomposing filth under them and teeth resembling Victorian tombstones.

Given I wasn't planning on sleeping with Smelly Nelly, I overlooked such matters and took our profitable relationship at face value.

Smelly's house was a place of extreme fascination. If hoarders were to have a dedicated monthly publication showcasing the absolute best of cluttered properties, then Smelly's premises would be featured as a colour centrefold souvenir edition. He could barely open his front door such was the collection of meaningless junk he'd amassed.

The other interesting thing about Smelly was he was always at home. You would have thought just occasionally he might be out – perhaps doing a spot of shopping, signing on the dole or maybe even on a date with a similarly revolting character – but no, Smelly was always in and, as such, a phone call announcing my intended visit was never required.

Recently, he had instructed me that upon arrival to chez Smelly I should knock three times punctuated by short intervals. This signalled that stolen goods were at his front door, as opposed to the feds or, worse still, environmental health.

I liked to irritate him by prolonging the intervals between knocks. Today, I childishly left a good ten seconds between knock two and three. The door was suddenly flung open and a huge waft of stale body odour finally escaped his house and took grateful refuge in my nostrils.

"What are you acting like a cunt for? It's three knocks with quick, fixed intervals!" he greeted.

"Good morning, Smelly!" I greeted him with fake enthusiasm.

Oh, that was the other thing: no one who knew Nelly hid the fact he smells like a rotting carcass in July and he didn't bat an eyelid at his nickname. In fact, thinking back, I'm fairly sure that's how he'd originally introduced himself to me.

He gesticulated for me to follow him into the trading hub of his business empire – his squalid kitchen. As I entered, the putrid aroma of decaying food made me instantly nauseous. I surveyed the area and then engaged in a favourite hobby of mine where I would try to piece together his last few meals. Congealed mince in the frying pan left out on the stove might suggest spaghetti bolognese; traces of pilau rice all over the cluttered worktops would strongly indicate a curry; oh, and hang on, that weird oddment of carpet on the floor is actually an old slice of pizza.

"What are you going to try and sell me?" he enquired with a sigh.

"State-of-the-art gaming console, two controllers, one game and it's all brand new. You'll get an easy hundred and fifty for this lot," I declared as I removed it from the bag.

Smelly then performed his usual technical procedure for any electrical item that was being offered to him – he plugged it in to see if it worked.

I was slightly relieved to find out everything was in order, but my real interest was establishing that the games disc in the console was the ever-popular *FIFA 19*. If only the hapless Candy had known this then she may have scored herself an extra fiver.

"Fifty quid," he announced, almost randomly.

"Eighty?"

"Sixty?"

"Seventy-five?"

"Sixty-five?"

"Seventy-three-fifty?"

"Seventy?

"Done."

He then reached into his pants and brought out a roll of cash. Bloody hell, I thought, I could end up with hepatitis from one of those twenty-pound notes. He counted out the money and handed it over.

"Any chance of a fried breakfast whilst I'm here, Smelly?" I asked with more than a twinge of sarcasm.

"No, you've Bob Hope. I'm a terribly busy man, so I'm afraid you'll need to fuck off."

It appeared from this rather gruff response that Smelly had been taught at the same finishing school as Candy.

Having nearly tripped up on the way out on a consignment of trowels, spades and a couple of bags of potting compost. (Please tell me he's not planning on opening a garden centre?) I exited his house with the rancid stench of decaying food battling with Smelly's putrid body odour, in a winner-takes-all play-off situation to determine which smell could make me feel the queasiest.

But it takes more than a foul stench to contain my elation after completing a business deal. I strolled down the road cock-a-hoop because whilst thirty-five million people slaved away at honest, tax-paying, national insurance-contributing jobs, I'd made a quick, cash-in-hand fifty quid for the sake of a text message and thirty minutes' walking.

Every time I made money it gave me a rush. I would stomp down the street like the King of the World, sometimes raising both hands in the air, nodding repeatedly and shouting, "Fucking get in there!" And frankly, if anyone saw me, I wouldn't give a damn. Instead, I would offer them a high five, maybe double forefinger pistols and, if they were lucky, a cheeky wink with the doff of an imaginary cap.

I didn't have to be fluent in the language of belly rumbling to know when mine was demanding some processed, high-fat, nutrition-free grub. I was heading into town, which meant every fast food restaurant, café or bakery was in play.

Beforehand, I decided to pay a visit to 'Goodwill', a charity shop in the city centre. Charity shops had become rich pickings, as I'd established a few angles where I could make money.

Firstly, you'd be surprised at how many people donate their unwanted designer gear. Unfortunately, charities have become wise to the usual big-name brands like Armani, Ralph Lauren and Gucci, so even a half-witted volunteer will spot them from a mile off. However, some expensive but lesser-known designer brands can slip through the net. It wasn't unusual to pick up the odd C.P. Company jacket, Balmain T-shirt or Ma Strum sweatshirt. These are all brands that will shift on eBay for good money or, even better, get sold on down my local boozer. This was my charity shop income stream number one.

In addition to this, I had established an excellent rapport with many of the staff working in these shops, and as I purchased a fair amount of stuff from them they appeared to have me down as a salt-of-the-earth-type fella. Little did they know that having gained their confidence I was engaging in charity shop income stream number two, which was, at best, a little crude. This involved me pretending to want to try on a cheap item of clothing whilst having the more expensive one draped underneath and out of view. In the changing room, I would then put the expensive piece on under my jacket, exit the changing room and purchase the cheap rag for pennies.

This item would then be used as stock and this is where income stream number three would come in. Let's imagine I had spotted a blue designer-labelled sweatshirt for sale. I'd then go home and put on my blue cheap garment before returning to the shop where I'd try on the expensive item, switch the two garments before exiting the changing room announcing something like, "It's a bit tight on my heavily muscled shoulders," to the assistant, before placing back on the rack the cheap shit I'd walked in wearing.

The key to these scams, as I have already inferred, but cannot stress enough, is gaining the confidence and friendship of the staff. To accelerate this process, it always went down well to go the extra mile when the opportunity presented itself. I'd offer to help with something heavy that needed moving; maybe drop some doughnuts in for a staff member's birthday or remember their names and little boring details about their personal lives that I could raise during our tedious conversations.

As I slowly walked past Goodwill I could see my favourite, most gullible charity employee, Ethel, was working a shift.

Ethel was a softly spoken Irish lady in her late sixties and about the loveliest person you could ever wish to meet. Having spotted her I immediately walked into the shop.

"Hello, my angel!" I announced.

"Hello, Robbie, how are you love?"

"All the better for seeing you. Come here."

I exercised my usual modus operandi of giving her a nice big hug and a smacker on the cheek – she loved it.

"Ah, bless you," she responded.

"Now then, Ethel, do you have anything that'll tempt me to part with my hard-earned cash?"

She then began to waffle on about a fucking Crown Derby jug that had been donated like I was a collector of pottery or something. I stopped listening to her and started to browse through the racks. My bargain radar was now firmly attached to the top of my head as I sifted through the debris of moth-balled clobber.

Aye, aye, what have we here then? A Lacoste sweatshirt, decent nick, genuine, which would easily fetch £30 down the boozer. I checked the price tag to see if they had spotted the designer label. Yes, they had – £35. Bollocks! Still, the nasty little sweatshirt on the next rack priced at £3 would make an excellent cover. I then headed off to the changing rooms with the Lacoste sweatshirt concealed under this rather tatty piece of menswear. By the time I had exited, the designer sweatshirt was being worn under my jacket, whilst the tatty old rag was draped over my arm. Admittedly, wearing an extra layer was making me a little warm, but a person must make sacrifices in the name of profit.

"I'll take this one, Ethel, it'll do for when I'm pulling the weeds up in the back garden," I said, handing her the wet dog-smelling sweatshirt.

"Lovely, that'll be three pounds then, please, Robbie."

"Here's a fiver, and I want you to keep the change because it's for charity."

She stopped in her tracks and shook her head with glazed eyes. "It's because of acts of kindness like this, that I enjoy working here so much."

"Ethel, it's my way of saying thank you. I'm only sorry that I can't donate more." Even by my standards, the level of bullshit I was engaging in was gloriously despicable. "You take care, love, I'll see you soon."

"Thanks, Robbie, all the best."

And that was it, job done and I'd made a safe twenty-five, maybe thirty, quid profit. It had been a lucrative morning's work and my reward needed to be some sort of meat, wrapped and baked in pastry. I'd decided it was steak bake time, actually, two of them, drenched in brown and red sauce, and served at the royal palace of bakes, pies and sausage rolls. I was heading to the jewel in the crown of hot pastries, the Weight Watchers nightmare, the single best food place in town for the last three years, as voted by me. I was en route to Greggs bakery.

The double steak bake beano I enjoyed was supplemented by the mandatory sausage roll. Not having a sausage roll when you visit

Greggs is as contemptible as not yelling, "Fucking get in there!" after you've swallowed your first gulp of beer for the week.

I then perched myself on one of the many town hall square benches and soon found myself entranced by the bizarre behaviour of a fella who looked to be off his head on a so-called 'legal high' drug.

In his narcotic-fuelled wisdom, he was attempting to climb a lamp post, which in itself wasn't so bad, except whilst dressing that morning he'd decided not to bother with either a belt or underpants. As he was ascending the lamp post Mr Gravity had intervened, and his trousers and pants had gathered around his ankles, exposing all body parts south of his waist. To his credit, he was cunningly utilising his trousers as a climbing support, enabling him to make reasonable progress. That was until he had spotted someone he recognised, at which point he stopped, shouted and then waved. Interestingly, the person he had called out to simply waved back, seemingly unperturbed that his friend was inexplicably at the top of a lamp post and could face serious injury if he should fall – which, of course, he did. A combination of the waving motion and him losing what was probably a tenuous grip resulted in him clattering down the lamp post into a crumpled heap.

As I was trying to wipe the pastry fat from my hands into the strangely non-absorbent wooden bench, I contemplated an interesting question: why were legal highs lawful but cannabis wasn't? Cannabis makes people very chilled out and a bit hungry, whilst some of these legal highs appear to transport people to a different planet and have them acting like a person with a very bad sense of humour was operating their brain and body parts.

Sadly, I didn't have time to ponder further because, having sent a text message to Nails asking if he fancied an after-work pint, he had done his usual trick of ignoring my question and starting his own peculiar and, in truth, annoying text conversation.

Nails acquired his nickname at school as he was the toughest lad in the playground. This may have had something to do with the fact that at eleven years old he was six foot three, sported a beard and was the only boy in our group who could produce body odour.

There was only one thing Nails liked more than a fight and that was *talking* about a fight. He would spend most of his free time watching martial arts movies, boxing, MMA, WWE wrestling; in fact, pretty much anything involving someone smashing the shit out of somebody else. His text messages were always along the same lines, and he loved to pose subjective and hypothetical fighting questions where he would bizarrely claim to know the answer. Today's offering did not disappoint:

If you had to fight Mike Tyson in his prime and pick any weapon, what would it be?

I won't lie, I found this whole routine utterly tiresome and would do my best to shut it down as quickly as possible. But Nails loved these teasers, and out of a modicum of respect, I would cut him some slack and play along.

In this instance, the obvious answer was a twelve-bore shotgun or some sort of anti-tank missile unit, which I suspect even the hard-as-fuck Mike Tyson might struggle against. But Nails was on to me and before my fingers could type in the answer I had received:

And it can't be a gun, automatic weapon or any sort of ballistic operating device.

Bollocks! I was going to have to fully engage with him on this. Okay, Robbie, think about it for a minute; you'd be no good attacking him with a baseball bat or anything else you'd have to swing because his fat head would absorb the blow and he'd proceed to punch your face until it turned into a mini sandpit.

What about a crossbow? I didn't know how to use one and Nails knew it and would respond accordingly. The very fact that I was now thinking about this in any detail annoyed me more than the actual text message. It meant I'd entered into his meaningless world of imaginary violence. Sod it, I'll fling something out:

Pepper spray.

My phone went quiet as Nails was digesting the answer. Suddenly, I received:

Wrong! Before it had taken effect, he would have pummelled your face in.

Would he, though? As I was challenging his response with a text message, I stopped and deleted what I had typed, as maybe he would claim victory and provide me with a meeting time.

2 more guesses then I'll arrange a time with u 4 a beer.

Wishful thinking. I decided to type in some nonsensical answer to get this annoying thread wrapped up:

Peashooter

Unfortunately, he was having none of it:

If you don't play seriously then I'm not going to meet you.

There was no point in being flippant, I was going to have to work through this.

Chainsaw

You wouldn't even know how to start a chainsaw, let alone attack Mike Tyson with one. One guess remaining…

He had a good point and I should have applied the same rationale that prevented me from submitting the crossbow idea.

Rottweiler

That's not a weapon, I'll exclude that as a guess

Claw hammer?

Wrong. I win.

Well done you – what time for a pint?

5.30

Thank fuck for that! Okay, at least my day had gained some structure and it meant I could head to the usual pubs around Leicester trying to offload this Lacoste sweatshirt. Hold on, though, a new text message had arrived from another member of the 'Crackheads R Us' pyramid selling team. This time it was from a geezer with a heroin problem who goes by the name of Moonlight. He had come into possession of an unlocked iPhone 9 and wanted forty quid cash if he could offload it in the next thirty minutes.

Thirty minutes wouldn't be a problem but the forty quid would. My starting offer would be fifteen notes, which he'd moan about and we'd haggle before we settled on a deal. But there was one thing which has already been settled – I'll get a minimum of seventy nicker for that fucker when I sell it on!

Despite being unable to shift the Lacoste sweatshirt, it had been a profitable day. Moonlight accepted twenty quid and I was in possession of an iPhone which, in this era, was as good as having dollars in your pocket.

I was marching off to meet Nails for a pint at our local boozer, 'The Falcon'. There were always a few punters in this establishment on the lookout for cheap gear. Well, I say a few; to be honest, it was like the TV programme *Bargain Hunt*, with alcohol and a dartboard. It was a regular occurrence for a customer to sheepishly open a plastic bag whilst several sets of eyes would view the contents. Any interested parties would then reach into their wallets or purses before the commencement of haggling.

The Falcon was in the middle of a densely populated housing estate which was neither rough nor posh. Its locals were generally hardworking people, many of whom liked to spend their money enjoying themselves. Therefore, should anyone be interested in purchasing an item cheaper than its retail price, then the Falcon was a place where such discounted items were traded.

As I arrived, I spotted Nails drinking with the third spoke in our wheel, Bod. Bod, whilst being a good mate, was as thick as a rhino's foreskin. Having said that, he did have one major commercial use: he worked in a local Sainsbury's and was trained to use the till. Generally, he would be set to do manual work whilst the women with the fat arses sat at the tills all day, making them even fatter. However, as it appeared that fat people have loads of weight-related time off work he was often drafted onto the tills to cover, and that's when our little scam slotted into place.

Bod would let me know when he was working on the checkout and I would then drop in for some shopping. When I innocently arrived at his till the items I would have in my basket wouldn't *exactly* match the items he would scan. Bottles of Scotch, razor blades, boxes of cat food – basically anything I knew I could shift quickly on the black market – would be slid through and deposited into my bag. We never overdid it; just a couple of items at a time and only ever once a day when he was on a shift.

I would also make a point of shopping at the store when he wasn't working, to avoid ever arousing suspicion.

Of course, when he served me, we became strangers, passing

only meaningless small talk and false laughs. It was beautiful and a lovely little earner.

His kick-back was a few beers, and upon arrival to the Falcon, this was my exact intention. As I approached the table where they were sat I could hear Nails talking to Bod.

"No, you can't pick a gun or anything you can launch a missile from."

Oh, fuck! He was asking Bod the Mike Tyson question. I diverted to the bar, knowing full well what the order was.

Standing at the bar was Tiny Toby, a fella who looked like he'd been through a boil wash which had shrunk him to about sixty per cent of his original size. For no discernible reason, despite being schooled in Leicester, he'd acquired a strange cockney accent, as if he were auditioning for a role in *Oliver Twist*.

"Alright, Toby?"

"Alright, geezer! You packing goodies?"

This was a euphemism for, "Are you selling any nicked gear?"

"I've got a very nice iPhone if you are interested?"

"Negative, amigo. I'm already holding a top-of-the-range piece."

"Apart from that, nothing, unless you want to get involved in an oversized Lacoste sweatshirt?"

"Let's have a look at it?" he asked.

I pulled it out of the bag and passed it to him.

"Yeah, not bad, geezer," he said, giving it a proper once-over. "How much do you want for it?"

"To you, Toby, forty. Cost you a ton in the shops."

"Can I try it on?"

This was a question which left me slightly confused. Why would he want to do that? It was an XL and this fella would fit into Mothercare clothes.

"Erm, yeah, sure," I replied, curious as to how this was going to play out.

He took the sweatshirt and headed off, leaving me to buy three beers and return to the table.

"A baseball bat, but with tungsten nails coming out of it?" suggested Bod.

Oh great, they were still at it. Rather than break up a conversation which was being enjoyed so much by my half-witted friends, I headed off to the designated stolen clothes changing room of the Falcon, aka the toilets. As I walked in, Tiny Toby was trying on the sweatshirt and admiring himself in the mirror. It fell a good eight inches below his belt, meaning it was only about ten inches from the floor. It looked like he was modelling a new line in Lacoste metrosexual wear.

Before, I could say, "We only need to stretch you a couple of feet and that'll look great," he chirped up.

"I'll give you thirty-five for it."

I stared at him for a few seconds, trying to decide whether this was a poor attempt at a wind-up and he would suddenly burst into laughter. Yet, only silence ensued, leading me to conclude he had a mate who was bigger than him and he was simply sizing it up.

"Thirty-five? Yeah, done," I confirmed, still bemused.

He then counted the dosh out and handed it to me.

"Pleasure to do business with you, geezer," he declared.

"I assume you want the bag?"

"No thanks, I'll leave it on."

"What, it's for you!" I enquired, totally puzzled.

"Yeah, of course it is. Who the fuck did you think it was for?"

I was struggling to hold in a laugh. "Yeah, fine."

I left the toilet and joined the lads.

"A bike chain with an anchor on the end of it?" enquired a now-desperate Bod.

"Will you two pack this shit in, please?" I intervened.

"What the fuck is Tiny wearing?" Nails yelled as Toby proudly strolled through the bar with his ill-fitting Lacoste sweatshirt hanging off him.

Someone then shouted across the floor, "Fucking hell, Tiny, it looks like you've just recorded a 'SlimFast' advert!"

"Except, you've not only lost weight, but you've also lost height!" said another wag.

And so it started; the customers in the bar effectively becoming one large organic comedy act at the expense of poor Tiny Toby and his ill-fitting sweatshirt.

"Are you working tomorrow, Bod?" I enquired.

"No, why, do you fancy going fishing?"

"I need you on the till at Saino's so I can move some Fusion razors through for a buyer."

"Afraid not. Did you want to come fishing then?"

"Fishing! I'm a businessman, Bod, not Captain fucking Birdseye."

"Please yourself. I'll be leaving about lunchtime if you change your mind."

I then spied Tiny marching over to me, looking furious. The incessant ribbing he had received from all four corners of the pub had finally beaten him.

"Oi, you, I want my fucking money back!" he demanded.

"You what?" I replied incredulously.

"It doesn't fit!"

"Doesn't fit! You tried the fucker on in the toilet, you mug! If there was a problem with it then that was your window of opportunity to say something."

"Well, I didn't notice it then, it just seemed a bit baggy."

"Yeah, well, tough luck."

"Look at it," he said, whilst pulling a good two feet of material away from his torso, prompting shrieks of laughter from Bod and Nails.

"What a shame when you tried it on that mirrors hadn't been invented. Imagine having one in the pub toilet? It might even prevent cretins from buying clothes that were four sizes too big."

"Alright, so I fucked up, but you should sort me out."

"I can't help you – write it up in your memoirs and move on."

"Come on, Robbie, do me a favour?"

I turned away and took a swig from my beer. "Twenty-five quid."

"What?"

"You heard."

"I bought it for thirty-five, you robbing bastard!"

"You've had it on for a full half an hour, so you've added to the number of previous owners and that affects the sell-on value."

"'Previous owners'! It's a sweatshirt, not a Ford fucking Mondeo!"

"Now you're swearing in it, meaning the whole designer thing starts to lose its credibility."

"You total fucking shithead!"

"One more profanity and it's twenty quid," I added.

"Bollocks to it, give me thirty," he barked.

"Sorry, twenty-five, take it or leave it?"

Toby, in a rage, tore off the sweatshirt and flung it at me.

"Here you go, now give me the twenty-five," he bellowed.

Within two minutes of him giving me the money, I was selling it to some fella in the bar for the full thirty-five quid. As I took the cash I turned to Tiny, waved the notes at him and gave him a friendly, all-knowing wink.

This is a game with no rule book, no conventions and, most importantly, no morals. If you want to play, you'd better be prepared to get yourself bloodied because the gloves were never on. Your tools need to be deadly sharp and you should always have one eye in the rear mirror because when bad fortune blindsides you, she's not intending to blow you a kiss in the ear.

Poor Toby was still an amateur and tonight I could see the desperate weakness in his eyes. I'd taught him a lesson that he would do well to never forget, for if he did, it would once again cost him dearly.

I was walking home from the pub, via the kebab shop, when I received a welcome text message from the DR. The DR didn't to my knowledge practice medicine or hold a PhD (although I suspect he could tell me a few things about narcotics). 'The DR' tag had evolved from his earlier nickname, Death Row.

The reason he received the latter moniker was due to being a tall, rangy fella with a shaven head and some of the most fearsome tattoos I'd ever seen. But these were no works of art, no topless women draped seductively over Harley Davidsons or *Star Wars* characters inked to minute detail. Oh no, these were proper homemade, jailhouse tattoos seeming to depict all manner of his previous misdemeanours.

Death Row had tears rolling down his cheeks, a hunting knife etched into the side of his head, 'LOVE' and 'HATE' burnt into his knuckles, 'REVENGE WILL BE MINE' branded on the back of his neck. This was one tormented character; someone who had witnessed and perhaps administered extreme violence. He looked like a prisoner you would see on a documentary aired on one of those obscure television channels who would be ordering their final meal in a US state penitentiary. You could imagine him being escorted from his cell by a fierce eighteen-stone prison guard who would be yelling, "DEAD MAN WALKING," as the DR would be trailing behind in shackles, moaning that he hadn't got to finish his KFC.

Anyway, Death Row and I enjoyed a civilised business relationship, and our dealings echoed those of Candy and Moonlight. It's fair to say I didn't *quite* take the liberties I might have done with Candy. There was, after all, an underlying fear of him taking umbrage at a derisory offer and removing my large intestines with his prized heroin cooking spoon. By the same token, business was business, and I couldn't have him pushing me around.

I met Death Row near the Leicester City football ground; a ghostly place of an evening when there isn't a game being played. He had six recently stolen jars of extra-large branded coffee which he was seeking to immediately offload.

I gave it all the usual, "Who the fuck am I going to sell six large jars of coffee to?" line when I was already lining up a couple of potential buyers in my head. Again, it was all about gaining an advantage. We closed the deal out at twenty quid. I'd be along to see the lovely Jinxy in the morning to have a complimentary fry-up in her café before I sold her the coffee for forty smackers.

Death Row seemed happy with the deal and we always departed with my customary farewell message to him: "And remember, you make sure to say sorry to the victim's family tomorrow before they fry you in the chair."

He loved it. I could see his little smile breaking as I was about halfway through the line.

I was finally on my way home and looking forward to my nightly chat with Grandad before he headed off to bed. As I was walking up the driveway, I was suddenly attacked. This wasn't an act of physical violence; more I was verbally accosted. The perpetrator was our neighbour, 'Moany Tony'. I'm sure he waits for me and then pounces at the last minute. He appears out of the darkness like some seventy-year-old grumpy version of Count Dracula. But rather than sucking blood from my neck, he prefers to drain the energy from my soul. He'll moan about anything and everything going on in the world. Some people use the phrase 'glass half-full' to describe a naturally downbeat person. In this instance, Moany Tony doesn't even own a glass. I suspect if you were to ask him he'd claim it had been stolen by a pack of Eastern Europeans at the same time they were single-handedly pilfering all of the jobs from the indigenous British population.

I was bracing myself for another serving of well-meaning drivel.

"Alright, Tony?" I enquired tentatively.

"How can anyone be alright with what's going on in South America?" he replied.

"Are you referring to the demise of Argentinian football? I know, and they used to be *so* good."

What I loved about Tony was that you could throw in a sarcastic line and he would ignore it. He wouldn't take offence and accuse you of taking a serious subject lightly. Instead, he would ignore the comment and carry on rambling.

"People trafficking, that's what. It's rife. There are hundreds of thousands of young women each day being packed into containers and brought over here to become prostitutes on our streets."

"Yeah, it's not right. I mean, it's going to put our local hookers out of business."

"It's run by the Columbian mafia. I was watching a report about it on Sky News."

Sky News – of course! He devours it, taking in several hours of assorted news items, interviews and special reports each day. But rather than enlighten Tony with information and knowledge, he uses it to plunge his melancholic mood into deeper and darker trenches.

"They pretend they are taking teenage girls to Britain to find them proper jobs, only they are drugged and forced to have sex for money," he added.

I wonder whether Candy knows about this. With the words 'drugs' and 'sex' in the same sentence, she might very well be inclined to buy herself a one-way ticket to Bogota.

"Yeah, it's bang out of order, Tony. Anyway, best go and see Grandad."

Whenever Grandad was mentioned, Tony would always turn a little sombre. He knew of his deteriorating health and, to be fair, would always ask after him. He would then adopt a voice similar to that of a newsreader when they are interviewing victims of crime.

"How is he?" he enquired compassionately.

For no reason that I could articulate, I would also lower my voice like I was attending a funeral.

"He's managing, but it gets a little more challenging every day."

"Give him my best wishes, will you?"

"I always do," I lied.

Tony then vanished into the darkness. By sucking the positive energy from me he would live another day. He only needed to ensure he avoided the light, garlic and anything bordering on a good news story.

Grandad was sat watching the History Channel, which was one of his favourite pastimes, especially since the onset of his illness.

"Alright, Grandad?"

"Hello, son, you alright?"

"Yeah, good. Fancy a cup of tea?"

"That would be lovely."

"Have you eaten?" I asked.

"Yeah, I made myself something earlier."

I fixed him a cuppa and plated up my kebab. I then joined him in the lounge and we watched a programme called *World War II in Colour*.

"What's going on here then?" I asked, shortly before a huge dollop of chilli sauce dripped from my kebab onto my sweatshirt. Bollocks!

"It's about the fighting in North Africa during the Second World War. Fascinating, it is. That Rommel was a crafty bastard; we did well to see him off."

Grandad's comment had left me slightly puzzled, as 'Ronald' doesn't sound very German. Or was he African? I've been known to get easily confused about things, especially when I'm eating.

"I'm surprised you don't like kebabs, Grandad, they're beautiful," I said as the hot fat from my lamb doner squirted out of the pitta bread and joined the chilli sauce on my sweatshirt. Great! I think I've pretty much ruined this fucker now.

"How was work?" he asked.

"Yeah, good. I was picking orders again today so the time flew by."

"Was Des alright?"

Grandad had never met Des and, come to think of it, neither

had I, but he liked to know the details and he also remembered everyone's name.

"I only saw him briefly. I think he was in and out of meetings all day," I replied, trying to put some flesh on Des's busy, but imaginary, working schedule.

"Whatever happened to the Muslim fella who got into a ruck on the factory floor?"

"You mean Ismail?"

"Yeah, that's him."

"He's been disciplined for it. He's now on his last warning."

"Seems a shame if he's a good worker," he added.

"Yeah, and he's a decent lad, to be fair."

I wasn't sure if Ismail was a decent lad or indeed a good worker because he didn't exist. He was a figment of my imagination. Nails had told me a similar story about Wayne and some fella who was on Ramadan, but I couldn't remember the geezer's name, so I provided Grandad with a fictitious one. In future, I needed to be careful about this sort of thing because remembering the truth is so much easier.

We carried on chatting away for another twenty minutes or so before he became tired and I helped him to his room. I sat on the side of his bed, as he lay, closing his eyes.

"Do you have all of your medicines?" I whispered.

"They're on the side."

"Hold your head up for a second then and let me stick another pillow underneath you."

He didn't like two pillows; he preferred the lumpy flat ones he'd got used to during his time in the army. However, the more pillows he had the easier it was for him to breathe.

I sat and watched him drift off to sleep and as he did I held his hand.

It was nearly time for me to go to bed – a place I dreaded. It's there where I dream; dark, horrible vivid dreams of my past. I dream of the nights Dad would come home drunk and beat up Mum; the time I spent in a foster home and the evening the police arrived to tell me Mum was dead. These dreams would never go away; they would visit at least once every two, maybe three nights and, whilst slightly deviating in detail, the narrative was always the same.

I would wake up feeling lost, helpless and lonely. I would suffer from severe anxiety until I plucked up the courage to turn the light on. I would then sit bolt upright in bed and hyperventilate.

I was secretly scared of the world and what it had forced me to see. I wouldn't want to go back to sleep as I knew I would return to the nightmares, and it was here where I stared into the eyes of my demons. Sometimes I would cry and want it all to end, and when I did, I would feel like that petrified, vulnerable eight-year-old kid all over again.

CHAPTER 3

In my spurious world of work, I was once again getting picked up at 8.45 a.m. in readiness for what I imagined to be an arduous 10–6 shift. In reality, I had received a text message from Moonlight, who had magically stumbled on five top-of-the-range electric toothbrushes. I nearly asked him if he was tempted to retain one to check whether his dental hygienist noticed a change in his teeth-cleaning routine, but sarcasm and a desperate drug addict were seldom a mix which appreciated comedy.

Having made Grandad his two cups of tea, I was heading into town for my meeting with Moonlight at a newly opened business centre for young entrepreneurs – the back of the Black Lion pub.

As I was passing the Goodwill charity shop, I saw Ethel outside wrestling with a huge bin liner full of donated clothes. With equal measures of chivalry and inquisitiveness, I decided to help her.

"Morning, Ethel, do you want a hand with those?"

"Yes please, Robbie," she said, clearly struggling with the weight and quantity of what was in the bin liner. "Some lovely young man has just left this outside before I had the chance to open the shop."

"That was nice of him," I replied. "Let me take them in for you."

I lugged the bin liner, which looked like it might rip with the weight of the clothes, into the shop. On opening the bag, I was astonished to see it was full of top-notch designer brands, and I'm talking the real fucking deal! There was a Tom Ford sweatshirt, Versace coat, Vivienne Westwood jeans, Gucci jumper; my God, there must be twenty grand's worth of gear in here! Even on the second-hand stolen designer clothes market, the yield could be anything between three to five thousand pounds.

Right, I needed to think quickly! Here was an amazing opportunity which I had to grab with both of my filching hands. I dropped the crammed bin liner in the small storage area at the rear of the shop and then hatched about the crudest plan ever. It had the sophistication of a discounted Co-op suit, but it might just work!

I immediately telephoned Bod who, I knew from our conversation last night, was off work and wouldn't yet be out fishing. His phone rang and rang and rang until finally, he answered with that distinctly 'I've just woken up' voice.

"Bod, it's me, listen, I need you to get up, get in a cab and get your arse down to Goodwill," I whispered.

"Why?"

"There's a massive load of designer gear that's been dropped off and I need someone to help me steal it."

"Who?"

"You, you fucking dummy!"

"What will I have to do?"

"There's only some old dear working here, so I need you to get a cab and text me when you're close by. I'm then going to distract her. You're going to walk into the shop and pretty much in front of you will be the black bin liner full of clothes."

"Then what do I do?" he queried.

"I want you to try on all the items and then nick only your favourite one."

"Which favourite one?"

"I'm joking, you idiot! You'll see the bin liner in front of you, then you're simply going to pick it up and leave with the fucker!"

"I'm not sure about this, mate," he replied, sounding understandably concerned.

"It'll be like taking candy from a baby! Get the cab driver to pull up outside, and when you've grabbed the bin liner, get straight back in the taxi and take it back to your house."

"What if someone sees me?"

"With a bin liner, coming out of a charity shop! No one will think a thing. Listen, if you do this job, once I've sold the gear, I'll give you a grand."

"A grand!" he replied, with considerably more interest.

"A thousand smackeroonies, mate! Think about it."

"Fuck it, I'm on my way! I'll order an Uber now."

"Good lad. Remember to text me when you are close by."

"Will do."

I ended the call and went back to the storage room, where Ethel was milling around.

"Do you want me to put this stock out in the shop for you, Ethel?"

"Yes, that would be good of you."

I bent down to pick up the bin liner, mindful not to tear the plastic, and in doing so present bird-brain with a problem when he arrived to steal it.

"Actually, you'd better not, love. It all needs to be gone through and priced up. I'll wait for Keith to get here. Just leave it where it is," she said.

"Okay," I replied.

Shit! This had presented me with a problem; how the fuck was I going to get the bin liner back into the shop without arousing suspicion?

"It's time to open the shop, it's well after nine-thirty," she announced.

"Yeah," I said, quickly trying to fathom out how I was going to make this work.

I walked back into the shop and started idly browsing stuff until I worked out a plan.

Once again, another piss-poor strategy was cobbled together, but I was getting desperate and it was time to go for broke. I sent Bod a text:

R u on ur way?

Thirty seconds later, a reply:

Yea. B there in 10.

Change of plan! Wen u arrive the bag is in the storeroom, oppo the entrance door. I'll try and distract Ethel. If u c her, act like you're just shoppin until I manage to get her out of the way and then u can nick it.

Ok.

And don't forget the 2 min text warning

Ok.

I then nervously loitered around the shop until finally the text landed and I'd received confirmation he was en route. It was time to execute my plan, and I removed a sweatshirt from one of the racks and took it into the changing room.

"I'm trying this on, Ethel."

"Okay, love."

I removed my jacket and jumper before pulling on the charity shop sweatshirt which was deliberately small for me. At this point, I manoeuvred it so it wouldn't go over my shoulders. My head was stuck and I pretended my shoulder had become contorted.

"Ethel, Ethel!" I cried out.

"What's up?"

"Could you come into the dressing room? I've managed to get myself stuck in this bloody sweatshirt."

As Ethel made her way into the dressing room, I knew this was my window of opportunity and I needed to seize it.

"Look what you've done," she remarked sympathetically.

"I know, I thought it would fit me, but I can't get it off and I've pulled my shoulder. I think I've gone and aggravated an old cricket injury. I once fielded the ball and as I threw it back I heard something snap and it's never been right since. That was the last game of cricket I ever played. A promising career was down the tubes because of a freak accident. My grandad says if it wasn't for the injury, I might have gone on to be the next Frankie Flintoff and play against the West Indies in the Ashes."

Of course, I was just jabbering, using deliberate timewasting tactics, buying time and hopefully providing Bod with extra valuable seconds so he could complete his mission.

Ethel spent at least three long minutes trying to help me whilst all the time I was resisting taking off the sweatshirt, claiming I could hear the fabric pulling. I was periodically letting out rather pathetic shrieks of pain due to the imaginary aggravation I was causing to my bogus long-term shoulder problem.

Meanwhile, I could hear the shop door open – surely this must be Bod? After a couple of minutes, I'd decided the deed had either been done or he'd bottled it and there was another customer in the shop. I managed to release myself from the sweatshirt, thanking Ethel profusely for her assistance.

I left the changing room and returned the item to the rack. My phone then beeped.

Dun it. On my way home!

Fucking get in there! The boy Bod, who ordinarily claimed the dunce's hat, had scored the goal of the month!

"Right, Ethel, thanks again for your help, I'll be on my way," I said, whilst gently massaging my undamaged shoulder.

"Robbie, did you move those clothes that were dropped in this morning?"

Shit! She had noticed they were missing, meaning the time of theft had been established and it was when I was in the shop.

"No, why?" I replied innocently.

"They've gone," she added, sounding concerned.

Okay, I need to play this with a straight bat otherwise I'm going to get in trouble. I walked into the storeroom.

"I left them there," I announced, pointing at the spot.

"I know you did," confirmed Ethel, who was now looking decidedly worried. "I wonder where they could have they gone?"

"And you're sure you didn't move them?"

Even as I asked this question I had to appreciate its stupidity. Obviously, she hadn't fucking moved them, Bod had!

"No, I hadn't touched them because I was waiting for Keith to get here."

"Perhaps the fella who dropped them off earlier had second thoughts and came back for them."

"But he wouldn't know they were in here, would he?"

"I'm guessing it wouldn't take him long to work out if they weren't in the shop then they would be in here."

"Do you think so?"

"I reckon that's what happened, Ethel. Look, I wouldn't worry about it, love. Let's pretend the bin liner was never dropped here. I certainly won't tell anyone," I said, giving her a wink.

"Do you know what? I think someone stole them when I was in the dressing room with you."

Shit! It felt like the heat was getting ramped up and suddenly Ethel had turned into Inspector fucking Morse.

"No, no, no, I don't. I think you'll find it was the geezer who dropped them off. I wouldn't worry about it," I added, as I was starting to worry about it.

"I'm going to have to tell Keith, though, because he's the manager."

"I wouldn't. You might get yourself into trouble." I cautioned.

"I know, but what will happen if the gentleman who dropped

the clothes off comes in to see how many of them have been sold? He might think I've stolen them."

"No, no, no, no, no, Ethel. No one would think that of you."

"I've got Keith's number, let me ring him," she commented, her voice trembling as she reached for the phone.

"Are you sure about this? I think you're making a mistake."

I then realised who was making the mistake – it was me for trying to talk her out of ringing him. I needed to do the exact opposite and in doing so deflect any possible suspicion.

"No, you're right! Call Keith and tell him what's happened. Do you want me to watch the shop for you?" I asked, adopting my best attempt at a supportive and sympathetic look, which involved me raising one of my eyebrows whilst drawing the other closer to my eye.

"Would you? I feel like it's all my fault."

I could see Ethel was in tears. Bloody hell, what have I gone and done!

She went into the storeroom and rang Keith. I was desperately earwigging, trying to find out what she was telling him. She shortly returned looking a bit happier with herself.

"Keith said not to worry because it wasn't anyone's fault."

"Of course, it wasn't!" I said, knowing it was actually all my fault.

"But he has asked me to call the police and report it."

Shit!

"Yes, yes, the police, that's the right thing to do," I lied.

"Would you mind waiting around and watching the shop whilst I telephone them?"

"No problem, Ethel. Don't ring the 999 number, though, because it's not an emergency. Call 101."

"Who?"

"101."

"Who's Juan O'Won?" she asked.

"No, the number 1-0-1."

"101, okay."

And off she went. 101, that'll sort it! The Old Bill would view this as nothing more than a minor theft from a poxy little shop. There's not a chance in hell that the feds will bother to send anyone around to investigate; they're way too busy chasing after kids who are taking machetes into their infant schools to carve up teachers. They will allocate a crime reference number and effectively close the case.

About ten minutes later she reappeared.

"Everything alright?" I enquired hopefully.

"Oh yes, he was a very helpful young man."

"What did he say?"

"He gave me a crime number that I've written down. I'll give it to Keith when he arrives."

"I would."

"I hope I've written it down correctly," she added, now rattling on about it.

"Good, right then, I need to crack on. Sorry about what has happened this morning."

"He said on the phone there's an officer in town and he'll be calling in. He asked whether you could wait around because they'll no doubt want a statement from you."

For fuck's sake, a statement!

"Yes, that'll be fine, Ethel. I haven't got anything else to do and I'd like nothing more than to support the police with their investigation."

About thirty minutes later a police officer attended the shop. Thankfully, this wasn't a seasoned, hard-nosed, big-drinking detective; rather a civilian in a uniform who was typically overly friendly and wet behind the ears. I had no problem convincing him I was a regular customer who was in the shop helping Ethel carry a heavy load. Ethel herself talked about what had happened and made it clear there was no possible way I could be implicated in the theft. She spoke fondly of me, emphasising my friendly and helpful nature. It felt like the angry seas were calming.

I gave him a brief one-page statement and laid it on with all the usual, 'if there's anything else I could do to help, Officer' bloody bullshit.

I even made him and Ethel a cup of coffee. In fact, if I'd been any more helpful he would have invited me to the next police recruitment day.

I eventually left the shop, walked around the corner and then called Bod.

"Where are you?" I asked.

"Back at my house with the bag. Why haven't you called?" he complained nervously.

"The Old Bill turned up and I had to give them a statement."

"Oh, shit!"

"It's fine, he believed every word I told him."

"The clothes can't stay here, Robbie, my mum will find them."

"No problem, I'll take them home. I'm getting an Uber now, so I'll be at yours in ten minutes."

I had a slight problem. I needed to get the gear back to my house without Grandad seeing me, as he thought I was at work and it may appear a little odd when I randomly walk through the back door. Even as I was seeking a resolution to the problem, I was formulating another simple but brilliant plan. You see, I was a cunning bastard when I wanted to be.

I summoned an Uber, called at Bod's house, collected the gear and then, with the cab driver's engine still running, returned home. As I walked through the front door I called out, "Only me, Grandad."

"You're home early – is everything alright?"

"Yeah," I answered as I popped my head around the lounge door. "I've gone and split my trainers at work. I've had to come home to change them."

"So, you're not stopping?"

"I can't, there's a bloke outside from work who's giving me a lift back in."

The crafty old sod was after a cuppa!

I dumped the gear in my bedroom and went back downstairs. "Right, I'm off. I'll catch you later."

I left and headed back into town. I tried to call Moonlight but there was no answer. I'm guessing I'd missed out on the consignment of toothbrushes and they had been sold elsewhere. Still, I was staring down the barrel of my best-ever score. Even after I gave Bod his grand, I would make two, maybe three thousand quid. This had been a cracking day, and one worthy of a rumbustious knees-up. Within twenty minutes, I was in the Falcon having a pint of lager and a celebratory bag of Branston pickle-flavoured Mini Cheddars with Bod.

"Do you know when I'll get my thousand quid?" he queried.

Fucking hell! The gear hadn't even been unpacked and he was already on at me.

"As soon as I've sold all the gear, Bod."

"When will that be?" he probed.

"Unfortunately, my crystal ball is in for service, so, without being able to look into it, I don't know."

"You will get a move on, won't you?"

"I'm not sure, actually. I was thinking about storing them to see whether I can work the 'vintage clothing' angle in another thirty years' time."

"You know what I mean,"

"You aren't going to nag me about this every ten minutes, are you?" I snarled.

"I was only asking."

"I told you at the time, I'll give you a grand *when* the gear's been sold."

"What, when you've sold the *entire* lot? Every piece of clothing?"

"Oh, fucking hell! I'll tell you what," I replied, getting visibly irritated with him. "Once I've sold a grand's worth, I'll give it to you. Then maybe you'll stop breaking my fucking balls about it."

"I'm only asking."

"Yeah, well, go and ask fucking the barmaid for two more pints, I'm parched."

As he stood up to go to the bar, Tiny Toby walked in.

"Hey, Tiny, come over here," I called out.

"That's the look of a geezer who might have something juicy he wants to sell," he said, approaching the table.

I lowered my voice and beckoned him forward. "I've dropped a big score, mate. A raft of Premier League, Top-of-the-fucking-Pops designer gear. I'm talking thousand-pound jackets, six hundred-pound sweatshirts, three hundred-pound pairs of jeans, the lot, and they're all available at once-in-a-lifetime prices."

"Where's is it then?" he asked.

"Let's just say it's being checked into my warehouse as we speak."

"You own a warehouse!" he shrieked.

"Shhh, we need to keep a lid on this. I want you to only approach your tried and trusted mates. Tell them there's some top-notch gear being flogged and you're the middleman. For every item I sell to your crew, I'll kick you back a score. But I need you to keep it away from anyone who might snitch because there's some serious heat on this one." I looked at him and winked. "Know what I mean?"

"Alright, tell me when you're packing the gear and I'll have a look at it. You've got my mobile, haven't you?"

"I sure have. And remember, Toby" – I looked both ways around the pub – "tried and trusted mates only."

I arrived home, eager to have a good plough through the bounty so I could assess the full extent of its value. As I was walking up the driveway his face appeared from out of the darkness from over the fence. Fucking hell, it was like living in a three-bedroom semi-detached house in Transylvania.

"Alright, Tony?" I asked, masking the slight scare he'd given me.

"I was, until I saw the news."

Oh, for fuck's sake!

"Don't tell me the government have done a U-turn on offering free porn subscriptions to pensioners?"

"Iraq."

"Who?"

"Iraq. What a mess it's in. I'll tell you what, they might just as well have left Saddam Hussein in charge."

"I thought he was still in charge. When did he retire?"

"Rival factions; all different religions that hate each other. It's coming to a boil and you know what will happen then, don't you?"

"A game of rock, paper, scissors to sort out who gets what?"

"They'll all get in their little rubber dinghies and head over here. We'll be inundated with them and, as usual, we'll do nothing to stop it."

"I'll let my grandad know they're on their way. He might want to prepare the spare bedroom."

"I saw him earlier; he doesn't look too clever, does he?"

"He's alright, he has his bad days," I answered, in a slightly prickly manner.

"When you came home earlier, what did you have in the large bin liner you were carrying?"

Bloody hell!

"Just a bunch of old work clothes," I replied, trying to remove the guilt from my face.

"What do you mean?" he probed, staring at me with a poker face.

"You know, a load of clothes I'd shoved in my locker at work that I needed to bring home."

"But it was a huge bag, you could barely carry it. Surely, they wouldn't have all fitted in a locker?"

"Erm, well, there were a few other bits and bobs in there."

"What do you mean, 'bits and bobs'?" he interrogated.

"Just stuff, Tony! Nothing very interesting. I'm sorry, I need to go because Grandad will want a cup of tea."

"Alright, I was only making conversation," he added sheepishly before retreating into the darkness.

What was that all about! That's all I needed, some nosey old bastard spotting me with the loot. I'll have to keep my eye on him.

I entered the house and walked into the lounge.

"Alright, Grandad?"

"Hello, son. You okay?"

"Yeah, good."

I sat down on the settee and sighed the sort of sigh that I would imagine working people make after a hard day's graft.

"You take the weight off your feet. How was work?" he asked.

"It was alright."

"What did they get you doing today?"

"Erm, I was assembling parts for a load of washing machines."

"The stuff these companies do these days! I remember when warehouses were no more than goods in, goods out."

"Times have changed, Grandad. What are you watching tonight?"

"A programme about German U-boats. Tough times down in those submarines."

"I'll make you a cuppa in a minute – I just need to nip upstairs and sort out some gear."

"Would that be the stuff Tony said he saw you bringing in earlier when you came home to change your trainers?"

I was in my bedroom sifting through the gear. It was an incredible array of mega-expensive designer clothes. As each label presented itself I was using eBay to provide a second-hand guide price. One garment had 'Buy It Now' for £995; another piece showed the best bid was £250; even a plain-looking T-shirt by Vivienne Westwood was going for £200. It was a veritable jackpot! Who in their right mind would donate this stuff to a charity shop? Maybe it was fake gear? No way! You could tell it was kosher from the quality of the material, the stitching and the incredible detail.

Ethel said she only saw the back of the bloke who dropped off the bag. Maybe it was a woman? Perhaps she had caught her fella cheating and this was an act of revenge whereby his beloved wardrobe ends up at the last place on earth he'd be seen dead in?

It would remain a mystery, but whatever the background circumstances, I was the benefactor. I folded some items neatly into a pile and placed other more expensive ones on coat hangers. My wardrobe was now bulging. I was barely able to retrieve my very modest range of Sports Direct-purchased tracksuits.

Alas, all the gear was very slightly small for me, all except a gorgeous Gucci leather jacket. According to the internet, the RRP of a similar one was £1,600. Good God, who pays this sort of money?

I tried the jacket on, and whilst a little snug around my fast food-loaded tummy, it was generally a good fit. Fantastic! I would wear this as a showpiece garment. I would give it all the 'it'll cost you sixteen hundred quid in the shops, yours for four hundred quid and tell your mates because there's a lot more where this came from'. This will be a great way to get the party started.

It was a major score and it could provide me with the capital to move up a level. Maybe my days of trading with the likes of Candy and Smelly Nelly were numbered. Having said that, I wondered what Nelly would make of this consignment? He had previously never turned his blackhead-infested nose up at anything I had offered. Maybe eliminating him from my list of buyers was a tad premature. I decided to call around this geezer's house tomorrow and tell him what I was holding and whether he had any interest in getting involved in the supply chain.

With my new, first-class, fully reclining beds, all-the-Champagne-you-can-drink Gucci leather jacket on, I was heading out to meet the DR. He had dropped me a text explaining he'd come into possession of a Henry vacuum cleaner. I can only assume he had woken at some ungodly hour clucking for drugs, headed out looking for loot and stole Henry from some poor unsuspecting cleaner who would no doubt face disciplinary action for allowing the item out of her sight.

I told him I could only meet him on a road close to Smelly Nelly's, as I wasn't going to drag Henry halfway around town for the sake of twenty quid.

The one thing I love about doing business with drug addicts is they are always, and I mean always, on time for the buy. It could be argued they probably don't have to worry about a diary clash with another business meeting, but it's a useful trait and one I appreciate. Sure enough, Death Row was waiting at the bottom of a back street, conspicuously out of view on a small plot of wasteland.

Oh dear, he really did look a sorry sight. His face was a pallid, tormented mess. He was huddling his coat around himself like it was his morning duvet and he appeared to be quivering like a slapped arse on a sumo wrestler. I needed to be careful here as I didn't want to be lighting his fuse, otherwise, in a couple of hours my severed head could end up being discovered by a dog walker.

"You okay, mate?" I greeted him.

"Yeah, yeah, yeah, yeah, yeah," he replied, in a distressed state.

"Let's have a look at Henry then."

He passed over the vacuum cleaner. It was in decent nick; there was a bag in it and I did not doubt for a minute it worked.

"Yeah, looks alright. I'll give you twenty quid for it."

"Thirty, mate," he tersely responded.

"I can't give you thirty. I'll flog it for thirty. There has to be a margin in it for me."

Of course, I would be selling it for more like forty, but he didn't need to know that.

"No, no, no, thirty, mate, I need thirty quid."

This geezer was desperate.

"Look, as a favour, I can give you twenty-five, mate, that's my final offer."

He grabbed my arm. "You don't fucking get it, do you!" He was spitting as he was talking; I could see the anguish on his face. "You will give me thirty fucking quid for this bastard vacuum cleaner – have you got it?"

The image of my decapitated head being licked by a friendly Labrador then flashed through my mind.

"Okay, mate, chill the fuck out! Thirty quid it is. But you owe me one, alright?"

"Yeah, mate, look, I'm sorry. I'm in a bad way; I don't feel well."

"I get it, but it's not my fault," I replied as I peeled off the thirty quid. "Here you go. Stay safe, will you?"

He took the money and walked off. After ten or so steps he stopped and looked around at me. "Thanks, man," he called out. And he meant it.

The whole episode put a chill down my spine. Death Row was approaching the bottom of a very dark pit and I couldn't help but feel sorry for him. Sometimes we're prejudiced, but maybe we have no right to be. At some point in his life, something terrible had happened and I strongly suspected whatever it was had occurred during his childhood. His only crime was trying to escape his inner demons; to shut out the memories; to stop hating his abusers, and I knew exactly how that felt.

I cradled Henry like a tired child and made the short walk around to Smelly's. My slightly disturbing intervention with the DR prevented me from indulging in any shenanigans with the three knocks and I applied only the customary practice.

"Ah, a Henry, I like those," Smelly announced after opening the door.

"Yes, good morning to you, Smelly. I'm very well, thank you. May I come in?"

He turned and walked down his stinking, congested hallway. I followed him to his bacteria-plagued kitchen where our business would be conducted.

Before this commenced, I carried out my usual assessment of the congealed food spread around various plates, pots and pans and attempted to assemble Smelly's meal diary. The first clue was obvious: he had treated himself to full English breakfast, as the frying pan was on the table with a knife and fork sitting on the remains of egg white and some bacon. He'd evidently decided not to even bother plating it up and had eaten it straight from the pan. Did this man's efficiency genius know no boundaries?

Smelly then took Henry from me and began his examination.

"I'm starving. Is there any chance I can finish off the breakfast you've left in the frying pan?" I asked, struggling to complete the sentence without laughing.

"Yeah, help yourself," he replied, as he took Henry through to the lounge for a thorough quality assurance test.

Bloody hell, he thought I was serious! One mouthful of that muck would have probably sent me into a convulsion. Within an hour, I would have made Death Row look like Rosemary Conley.

I could hear the whirring sound coming from Henry. He was alive and well and about to make me a tidy profit.

"Yeah, it works," announced Smelly, just in case I wasn't familiar with the sound of a fully functioning vacuum cleaner.

"Top-notch gear, these Henry's. Forget all this Dyson bullshit, people prefer a brand they can trust. I also think hoover bags provide a sense of security that you don't necessarily get with your more modern—"

"Just shut the fuck up with your sales patter, will you? I'll give you thirty quid for it."

"Fifty."

"Thirty-five."

"Forty-five."

"Thirty-seven."

Thirty-seven – what the fuck? He had thrown me!

"Erm…"

"That's thrown you, hasn't it?"

Efficient and perceptive. This fella's multi-skilled.

"No. Forty-two."

"Thirty-nine."

"Done."

I had been, for a pound!

He then reached into his pants and handed me thirty-five pounds in notes before picking four one-pound coins up from a little pot sitting on the worktop. The thought of the rancid bacteria he'd passed on to me very quickly dulled the pain of being outmanoeuvred during our haggling.

"Now then, Smelly, do you have any interest in purchasing some top-of-the-range designer gear?"

"Fakes, I assume?"

"No, all kosher."

"What type of designer labels are we talking about? Nike, Adidas, that sort of thing?"

"Oh no, mate! I'm talking Gucci, Valentino, Vivienne Westwood, high-end gear, worth a lot of money. This is Premier League trading."

"Please don't tell me you've got hold of the clobber that was stolen from that charity place yesterday?"

Fucking hell! How did he know that?

"What charity place? What are you talking about?" I asked in a panicked state.

"Didn't you read about it?"

He walked into his lounge before bringing in a copy of yesterday's *Leicester Mercury* which led with the headline:

My chest tightened; I couldn't think straight.

"No, I've had this stuff for a while," I said, desperately trying not to look guilty. "What's happened here then?" I queried as I began to read the article:

This morning, Tom Needham, from Leicester's top rock band Lazarus, donated a collection of designer clothes he had worn on the band's last tour. He had dropped the clothes at a local charity shop, Goodwill, in Leicester city centre only for a heartless thief to steal them minutes later.

Tom was hoping the donation would boost the charity's flagging fortunes. "I didn't want to make a big thing of it, so I dropped the bag of clothes off before the shop opened. Most of them were clothes designed by various London fashion houses and all the stuff was worn on our last world tour. I was hoping Goodwill would be able to raise several thousands of pounds from the sale of them. I'm gutted about the news."

My eyes scanned the rest of the story.

Police have disclosed they have CCTV footage of a man leaving the shop at about 9.40 a.m. and he appeared to be getting into a taxi. They have appealed for the taxi driver and any other witnesses who may have seen the man, to come forward.

"Fucking hell!" I cursed, suddenly realising the enormous swamp of shit that Bod and I were in.

"Stealing from charity shops – it's out of order, mate. I'm no saint, but really!" added Smelly.

"Yeah, bang out of order."

"Anyway, you were saying?"

"Erm, it's a mixture of gear, you know, erm…" I couldn't think straight, let alone finish my sentence.

"I could be interested. Why don't you bring it around and I'll have a look?"

Bad vibes had saturated my brain and it felt like they were seeping out of every fucking guilty pore of my charity-stealing body.

"Right, I need to get going," I declared, becoming anxious and desperate to get out of his house.

"Didn't you want to finish my breakfast?" he asked before I quickly departed.

I sent a text message to Bod, who I knew would be working at Sainsbury's.

I need to speak to u very fucking urgently!!!!!

I was marching into town when I realised I was clothed in one of Tom Needham's very distinctive jackets. He had no doubt been wearing this same garment at Glastonbury or some other festival, parading it on stage in front of millions of adoring fans.

I dived into the first newsagent, bought a couple of items and a five-pence carrier bag. When out of sight, I removed the jacket, folded it neatly and put it in the bag. Typically, as luck would fucking have it, it began to spit with rain. The bad-luck gods were having their fun with me. At this rate, Tom Needham, escorted by the entire cast of *In the Line of Duty* would walk around the corner and ask me what I was carrying.

I continued walking into town. When I was about two minutes away from Sainsbury's, I received a response from Bod.

I'm on my break. R U in town?

Yea. I'll b there in 2. B at the back door

I messaged back, quickening my stride.

What have you got me in to?!!!!

He was right to be worried and correct to accuse me of dragging him into this mess. As I approached the rear of Sainsbury's I could see he was outside the door waiting for me.

"What's up?" he asked, looking worried.

I took him to quieter spot around the corner.

"We're in a bit of bother, mate. Have you seen yesterday's *Mercury*?"

"No, why?"

"It turns out the gear we nicked was dropped at the charity shop by the lead singer of Lazarus."

"Who, Tom Needham?"

"Yeah, that's it. It was on the front page; the press and the Old Bill are all over it."

"Why did he drop his clothes off there?"

"Apparently, he thought Goodwill was a dry cleaner."

"Did he?"

"If you're going to be a fuckwit about this, then we're in trouble! He was donating the fucking stuff."

"That's good of him."

"I know that's good of him, you fucking moron! Unfortunately, everyone thinks that's fucking good of him, which is why you and I will become Leicester's public enemy number one if we're caught."

"How will they know it was us?"

"No reason, Bod, only CCTV footage of you coming out of the shop with the bag and getting in a taxi."

"And you telling Tiny Toby about a big score of designer gear last night," Bod added.

"Oh, shit!" I raged.

"And then telling him to let everyone know about it," he added.

"I should have known the minute you got involved that this was going to happen," I snarled unfairly.

"What are you on about?"

"I should have done the job on my own."

"It's hardly my fault!" he snapped.

"Okay, okay, let's just deal with the CCTV."

"They will take one look at it and see it was me," he said.

"Why would they do that? You aren't exactly Reggie Kray, are you? You've never been in trouble with the feds for anything, so unless you were wearing your Leicester City top with your name on the back of it, how will they know it was you? Oh no! Please tell me you weren't wearing your Leicester City top with your name on the back of it?"

"Of course I wasn't. Well, I was, but I had my jacket on over it."

"The good news is, you're a non-descript, run-of-the-mill, boring fucker. I suspect the CCTV footage will be grainy, so I'm not sure they'll get you on that. The problem is the taxi driver. Where did he drop you off?"

"At home, obviously!"

"Yes, I know that, but was it at the bottom of the street or around the corner, maybe?"

"No, right outside the door."

"For fuck's sake, Bod!"

"The bag was heavy, wasn't it? I didn't want to drag it down the street."

"What about the cab driver?" I asked.

"What about him?"

"Would you recognise him if you saw him again?"

"He was an Asian fella."

"That's a spot of good news. We've narrowed it down to ninety-nine per cent of cab drivers in the city. Hang on a minute, you took an Uber, didn't you?

"Yes, that's right."

"Then your account will have all of your trip details on it."

"Brilliant! Where do I find my account?"

"I'm guessing on your Uber app, maybe under the section titled, 'My Account'!"

He pulled his phone out and I had to wait for the blubbering idiot to unlock it and find the Uber app. Meanwhile, I received a text from Nails:

If Anthony Joshua had a street fight with Conor McGregor who would win?

Oh, fuck off!

I put my phone back in my pocket. Meanwhile, the future captain of the Eggheads was still pissing around.

"Have you found it yet?" I questioned irritably.

"Yes, I'm on it," he finally announced.

"Go to the 'Your Trips' section. His details will be in there."

He continued messing around before announcing, "You're right, here we are, the driver drove a Volkswagen Passat."

"Great! But who is he?"

"Mohammed Zahir."

"Click on his name and see if it takes you to a contact number," I suggested.

Bod tapped away. "It describes him as a 'very friendly individual'."

"Bod, I need to contact him to see if he'll take a bribe to keep his mouth shut, not date the geezer."

"It says here, 'It was lovely to meet Mohammed, he drove well and we had a nice friendly chat.'"

"What are you on about?" I snapped.

"It's a passenger review."

"Fucking hell, he only gave someone a lift home; that review sounds like he was providing marriage guidance counselling. Honestly, who writes this shit?"

"I think that one was me."

I turned away, shaking my head. "This is exactly what I am talking about. The one time I need you to keep your head down and you do the polar opposite and effectively put Mohammed forward for cab driver of the year."

"Do you reckon he'll snitch on me?" he asked.

"I don't know. Looking at Mohammed's photo, he strikes me as more of a porn-surfing dude than a *Leicester Mercury* reader."

"So, what do we do now?"

"You need to go straight home, collect your passport and money, say goodbye to your mum, and tell her we're going to escape to Brazil."

"What!"

"Nothing, mate, we're going to do nothing. If you happened to get nicked, deny everything. You haven't got the gear, so you'll be okay."

"I knew I shouldn't have got involved in this," he proclaimed, with a guilty little boy's face.

"I know, I know, I know! But you *are* involved, so stop banging on about it. Let's just see what happens."

"I'd better get back to work," he announced before trudging off.

I knew if they arrested him I would also be nicked shortly afterwards because the first thing the feds would do is to check his phone records and it was all there, laid out neatly in front of them. We would be paraded like US prisoners of war in Iraq. The whole of Leicester would turn against us and I'd spend the rest of my life, after a spell in prison, saying sorry.

But what concerned me the most wasn't what would happen to me; the fine I may receive or the prison sentence I might serve. I could take all of this on the chin. My big worry was just how ashamed Grandad would be of his only grandson whom he had sacrificed so much for.

CHAPTER 4

In life, you can only control the controllable. Grandad told me this when I was a kid. In the situation with the charity shop theft, there were several variables I had no control over; like the taxi driver telling the feds where bird-brain lived or someone recognising him from the CCTV footage.

One variable I could manage was ensuring Tiny Toby didn't connect me with the theft. I headed down to the Falcon, optimistic that I would bump into him, as I don't think I had ever been in there and not seen him.

I arrived, ordered a pint and took a seat. After a few minutes, one of the regulars, Casino Kev, came over. Kev, whilst being generally a decent bloke, has a ferocious gambling habit, hence his nickname. He also bears a passing resemblance to the footballer Eric Cantona. However, I suspect that's where the similarities end, as I'm inclined to think the ex-Manchester United player isn't a fruit machine addict and doesn't play the pub game 'Spoof' on a Sunday lunchtime for a quid a go.

"Alright, Robbie?"

"Alright, Kev."

"A little bird tells me you might be shifting some top-end clothing?"

Bollocks! The cat was now royally out of the bag and having a shit in the Falcon beer garden.

"I had a few pieces, mate, but I've flogged them on. Sorry."

"But Tiny said you hadn't received them yet?"

"He's mistaken. I'd taken delivery last week."

I needed to make sure any association I had with dodgy stolen designer gear pre-dated the charity shop theft.

"Alright then, mate, stay lucky," he ended before returning to the bar.

This was a lesson learned and I needed to stick to this story.

My then phone beeped. It was another fucking stupid message from Nails.

I've floored you with the AJ / McGregor question. Wanna know the answer?

'Wanna know the answer?'! It was like he operated in a parallel universe where he could play out hypothetical scenarios and then share the result with his friends who lived on planet Earth.

I was in the process of texting him some expletive-ridden message when Tiny plonked himself down next to me.

"Alright, geezer," he effused in his usual mockney accent.

"Alright, Tiny, how's tricks?"

"They'll be all the better when you show me this gear you were talking about. I've already got a few bites on the end of my fishing line."

"Yeah, well, about that, there's been an update, to be honest."

"What's that then?"

"It's gone, mate. Some fella's had the whole lot. One price; deal done; goods sold; cash in my back pocket."

"You said you hadn't yet taken delivery of the merch?"

"You know how this market works, mate. It changes quickly. I did have the gear, but there was no point showing you it until my number-one buyer had declined it. As it happens, he didn't. Not to worry, there will be plenty more where that came from."

I was positioning this nicely. At some point, the heat on this gig will have completely burnt itself out. I could then venture into the market and flog the clothes whilst being beyond suspicion.

"That's a shame," he said. "Hang on a minute, what have we here then?"

Like a ninja, he swooped and snatched the plastic bag I'd concealed under the table.

"No, that's—"

"That's one lovely jacket, that's what this is!" he said as he quickly whipped it out of the bag. "Fucking Gucci! Are you sure you've shifted all the gear?"

"It's a fake, it isn't worth shit," I said, desperate for him to put the fucking thing back.

"Good-quality fake, I know that much. I need you to put me onto your contact."

He then stood up and held it against himself, and as he did, Casino Kev was returning from the toilet.

"Haven't you learned your lesson, Tiny? His stuff's not going to fit you."

"Come and have a look at this, Casino. Look at the quality of it."

I was tugging at the jacket, trying to retrieve it, whilst Casino was tugging the other way, attempting to get a closer look at it.

"Yeah, this a nice piece of leather," Casino added.

"Can I have it back, please, I need to go," I desperately asked.

We were then joined by a third party, someone I knew only as 'Cowboy', due to the quality of his brickwork. Cowboy was a tasty geezer with massive hands and fingers the size of Fyffes bananas.

"Nice jacket," said Cowboy. "It looks like the one the bloke from Lazarus wore at the gig he played up the road."

Bollocks!

"How would you remember? You were pissed up and asleep under one of the trees," interjected Tiny.

Oh great, they were all at the gig!

"I've seen the footage on YouTube," Cowboy remarked.

"Right, sorry, fellas, can I have my jacket back, please? I need to get home," I said, wrestling the jacket from Cowboy.

Casino then aggressively grabbed my wrist.

"He's having a look at the fucking jacket, now get your hands off it," he hissed.

Bloody hell, the party had suddenly turned sour.

Cowboy inspected it and tried it on. "Yeah, nice piece," he commented.

"Let him have it back," Tiny generously said.

Cowboy took it off and handed it back to me. I was dry-mouthed and more than a little shook up.

"Are you flogging it then?" queried Tiny.

"No, mate. I've already got a buyer. Anyway, I must dash."

I legged it out of the bar and out onto the street. If that lot find out I'd nicked Tom Needham's clobber then they'll fucking lynch me. They were that sort of crowd. There would be no police, no judge or jury, only a bad fucking beating around the back of the pub. I'd seen people with the bruises and heard of others who hadn't ever dared return.

I left the pub realising I'd narrowly dodged a bullet. But I was streetwise enough to know it was highly likely that another would soon be loaded into the 'get Robbie Howard' gun and next time I may not be quite so lucky.

I was on my way home and frankly pleased to enter an altogether calmer haven after what can best be described as a troublesome day. I would immediately put this bloody Gucci jacket in my wardrobe and then make Grandad a cuppa.

I was carefully constructing the lies I would regale to him in terms of my bogus day at work.

As I entered the house, I heard conversation coming from the lounge.

"Here he is," Grandad announced.

Fucking hell, who was he talking to? I immediately took a right turn into the kitchen and shoved what was surely a cursed jacket into the cupboard under the sink before nonchalantly walking into the lounge to see who was there. I was, of course, fully expecting it to be a police officer.

To my surprise, it was a casually dressed man in his late forties, maybe early fifties. He greeted me with a smile and stood up to shake my hand.

"Robbie, this is a reporter from the *Leicester Mercury* who wants to have a chat with you. Sorry, I've forgotten your name."

"Sean Egan, but everyone just calls me Egan. Nice to meet you, Robbie."

His accent was thick Irish and harsh like his handshake. His grip was firm, facial features chiselled and he wore a hefty scar above his left eye. He was just the other side of six foot and dressed sharply.

"Nice to meet you," I replied.

How the fuck did the *Leicester Mercury* get my address?

"Sean wants to talk to you about something that happened yesterday, mate – you didn't mention anything?"

"Didn't I? Sorry, I thought I did," I lied.

"I'm surprised you didn't, Robbie. It was quite a thing that happened. It made the frontpage headlines," Egan added.

"Frontpage! Bloody hell, what happened then?" asked Grandad.

"I'll let this young man explain later. In the meantime, Robbie, perhaps you would be so kind as to make me a cup of tea and we can chat in the kitchen?"

"Yeah, no problem."

"Will you excuse us, Mr Howard? I've interrupted you for long enough. You get back to your war documentary. I've seen it, it's very good."

Egan followed me into the kitchen and closed the door behind him. There was something discerningly confident about this fella.

"I am happy to talk to you, Mr Egan."

"Just Egan," he said.

"Okay. I'm just interested, how did, erm… how did you get my address?"

"Well, let's just say I'm an investigative journalist, so I have my sources."

"Okay, yeah, fine," I replied. "I'm happy to talk to you about what happened."

"Are you comfortable going on record?"

"What do you mean?"

"Provide me with your name and details and allow us to quote you in the paper?"

"I'd rather not. I've nothing to hide, but my local pub is full of fellas who will be quizzing me about it for ages."

"I understand."

He took out his notepad and a pen.

"I'll scribble some notes and refer to you in my column as 'a source'. Are you comfortable with that?"

"Yes, fine. As I say—"

He held his palm up to me. "Don't worry, I get it."

"How do you take your tea?"

"Actually, I'll pass. I've had enough caffeine for the day," he replied. "So, tell me your version of what happened yesterday."

"I was walking through town on my way to meet a friend and as I passed the charity shop the lady who works in there—"

Egan looked at his notepad. "Ethel?" he interrupted.

"That's right. Ethel was struggling to carry a bin liner of stuff that someone had left on the doorstep of the shop, so I went over to help her out."

"That was good of you."

"I know Ethel because I go into Goodwill quite a lot."

"What for?" he explored.

"To see if there are any bargains. Sometimes people drop off nice items of clothing."

"Do you buy them for yourself or do you sell them on?"

"I buy them for myself."

"Sorry, carry on with the story."

"Yeah, so I carried the bag in for Ethel and she asked me to drop it in the little storeroom at the back of the shop."

"Then what happened?"

"I offered to put the stuff out on the clothes rails for her, but she wanted the manager to go through it first."

Egan stopped taking notes and looked up at me. "You offered to put the clothes on the clothes rails for her?"

I shrugged my shoulders. "Yeah."

"But the clothes wouldn't have had prices on them – how would you have navigated around that?" Egan enquired. He was very slightly beginning to change his tone.

"I don't know, I didn't think of that," I responded.

"I'm guessing you had seen the contents of the bag?"

"I knew it was clothes," I answered.

"Did you notice it was all designer labels?"

"No, I didn't," I replied, trying not to look guilty.

"What did you do then?"

"I started to have a look around the shop to see if there was anything to buy?"

"But I thought you said you were off to meet someone?"

"I was."

"You'd already been delayed helping Ethel, surely you needed to press on, didn't you?"

"I was running early, plus Ethel was on her own and she was doing something out the back so I offered to keep my eye on the shop for her."

"You're a good man, Robbie. There's only a few like you about, I can tell you that."

"You try and do your bit, don't you?"

"Absolutely. And from when you helped Ethel with the bag of clothes to when you were browsing in the shop, did you use your mobile phone?"

He had properly caught me off guard with this question.

"Sorry?" I asked, stalling, buying myself a bit of time to think of an answer.

"Your mobile phone – did you call or text message anyone in the very small window between helping Ethel with the bag and browsing for stuff in the shop?"

"I can't remember."

"Why don't you check your phone to jog your memory? If you're not sure how to do it then I'm happy to show you."

"What's this got to do with what happened?" I challenged, getting slightly agitated.

"It's just a line of inquiry. If you don't want to tell me, you don't have to."

"I don't want to tell you."

I knew that I'd changed the whole landscape of the conversation with this reply.

"Continue with the story, from when you were browsing in the shop."

I was now having to tiptoe carefully. I was in the presence of a pro-baller. This guy was in control of the conversation. He was setting traps and I felt vulnerable. I wondered whether I should tell him to clear off, but I knew it wouldn't end there.

"I found a sweatshirt and told Ethel I wanted to try it on. I took it to the changing rooms, only when I put it on it got stuck and I wrenched my shoulder."

"Did you? Then what did you do?"

"I called Ethel to the changing rooms and asked her if she would help me take it off. We were messing about with it for a bit before we were able to remove it."

"'A bit'?"

"What?"

"You said you were messing around with it 'for a bit', then it came off?"

"Yes."

"How long is a 'bit'?"

"A minute or so."

"'A minute or so' – what does that mean?"

"What's the big deal?"

"In that 'minute or so', it appears someone entered Goodwill, walked straight to where the bag was and stole it. So, was it a minute or not?"

"Probably two, I don't know, it could have been three. I was trying not to rip the bloody sweatshirt which had got stuck."

"And all this time Ethel was in the changing room with you?"

"Yes."

"Just long enough for someone to come into the shop and steal, without question, the most valuable donation Goodwill have ever received."

"I know, it's out of order."

"What is?" he asked.

"Stealing from a charity shop."

"What did you do then, Robbie?"

"I hung about and helped Ethel with the police after she had called them."

"Did *you* suggest to her that she call the police?"

"Yes."

"No, you didn't."

"I did, I told her to call 101, not 999."

"This was after she had called the store manager. You advised her not to bother calling them. I think you said something along the lines that it was probably the bloke who had made the donation who had come back to reclaim his clothes."

"I was trying to make life easier for her. She was upset they had been stolen."

"She then called the police, so what did you do then?" he asked.

"I waited with her until they turned up."

"Did you do this voluntarily?"

"Yes."

"No, you didn't. You told her you needed to get going. She had to persuade you to stay."

"No, no, no, that's wrong. I told her I would stay with her."

"The fella you were due to meet, what happened to him?"

"I text messaged him and said I would be late."

"Ethel said she doesn't recall seeing you use your phone."

"I did."

"Maybe that's something else she got wrong then."

"I'm telling you the truth!" I snapped.

"I don't doubt it, Robbie. Sorry, sometimes my investigative instincts get the better of me."

"It feels like you're interrogating me."

"Does it? I apologise. We're just two guys, aren't we, having a chat about something that's gone on?"

"Yeah, I suppose."

"So, the police have arrived, you've given them a statement, then what did you do?"

"I went off to meet my mate."

"And where was that?"

"Erm… it was outside of Leicester Cathedral."

"Leicester Cathedral?"

"Yes."

"It was definitely Leicester Cathedral?"

He was on to something, but I had committed myself, so changing my mind would appear suspicious, and in any event, I had no idea what he had up his sleeve.

"Yes, Leicester Cathedral," I replied, showing irritation.

"And yet the CCTV footage shows you leaving Goodwill and turning right heading to Charles Street. If you were going to Leicester Cathedral you would have exited the shop and turned left, wouldn't you?"

Shit! I was snookered.

"Did I? I don't know. I could have walked down Charles Street then taken a left turn."

"Did you or didn't you?"

"Yeah, I must have done."

"So, you did?"

"Yeah."

"Did you meet your friend at Leicester Cathedral or not?"

"Yes."

"Who was it?"

"Just a mate."

"'Just a mate' – what do you mean by that?"

"I'm not giving you his name, if that's what you are getting at. He won't want to be dragged into this. Anyway, how long is this going to last? I have stuff to do," I ranted.

"Your grandad told me you were at work yesterday. He said you work for Coopers in their main distribution centre."

Bollocks! It felt like the heat had been turned up yet another notch.

"Yes, that's right."

"So, if you were supposed to be working there yesterday, how did you find yourself in Goodwill trying on sweatshirts?"

"It was my day off."

"Not according to your grandad, it wasn't."

"He old and ill; he gets things confused."

"He looks perfectly competent to me. He said you woke up at the usual time for a ten o'clock shift. This involves you leaving the house at a quarter to nine and getting picked up, which is what you did. Now, that's quite a thing to do for a lad of your age if you had a day off?"

"I'm not going into it, but I didn't go to work," I replied, lowering my voice.

"But you did tell your grandad you went to work, didn't you?"

"Yes, and it's a long story as to why."

"Why you have told him you didn't go to work or why you've told him that you work at Coopers when you don't?"

"Fucking hell! What's this about?"

"I'm simply trying to get to the bottom of what has happened."

"What do you want from me? I didn't steal the bag of clothes."

Egan slowly walked towards me and whilst doing so raised his forefinger and placed it against his lips, gesturing that he wanted me to be quiet.

"Of course you stole the clothes. It's the worst story I've ever heard. You helped to move the bag into the shop, saw what was in it, rang one of your equally small-time mates, he jumped in a cab, entered the shop whilst you had distracted the old lady and then made off with the bag. After the police had called around and you had given them your bullshit statement, you left the shop, like a snowflake wouldn't melt in your mouth, and probably went around to his house to collect the gear," he said in a hushed voice.

"You're wrong," I replied.

"Do you know what I think?" he asked.

"What?"

"I think the clothes are somewhere in this house. They are, aren't they, Robbie? Come on, tell me, where have you hidden them?"

"I don't know what you're talking about."

"They are in your bedroom, aren't they? Is that right? Have you even gone to the trouble of hanging the clothes up in your wardrobe?"

"Get out of my house! I'm going to ring the *Leicester* fucking *Mercury* tomorrow and tell them about you, coming around here, unannounced, making accusations and getting my details illegally," I fumed.

"I can only apologise, Robbie – as I say, I have a slightly inquisitive mind."

"Yeah, well, let's see what happens when I call your boss and let him know what you've done."

Egan raised both hands in the air, suggesting he wasn't going to push it any further.

"I had better get going," he said. "Robbie, thanks for your time and could you wish your grandad a good night for me. I wouldn't want to interrupt him again."

I followed him out and opened the door, desperate for him to leave.

"You and I have something in common, young man," he announced.

"Yeah, what's that?"

"We are both a little conservative with the truth. You, with your phoney story about your job at Coopers." He then stopped, turned around, smiled and winked. "And me with my little white lie about working for the *Leicester Mercury*."

Bod took a large gulp from his pint, enough for some of it to trickle down his face, which he somehow didn't realise. I watched as it congregated on his chin before dripping onto his mobile phone. Hearing the splash on the screen, he stared at it before looking up at the ceiling like it was letting in beer.

"If he doesn't work for the *Leicester Mercury*, then who does he work for?" he asked.

"How the fuck would I know!" I replied.

"Maybe he's Old Bill?"

"Then why would he pretend to be from the *Leicester Mercury*? If he's Old Bill, he would just say, 'I'm Old Bill', unless he's the only fed in the history of the world who likes to impersonate being a journalist."

"I'm only throwing a few ideas out."

"Is there any chance you can throw out something remotely fucking useful?"

"Perhaps he's connected to the band?"

"That's a better theory. Who, though?"

"The drummer?"

"He's clearly not *in* the band, is he? They are all in their thirties. This fella was more like in his late forties or early fifties."

"I didn't know, did I?"

"But I suppose he could be their manager or something," I pondered.

"They might have hired a private investigator to get the gear back?"

"Again, not a bad theory, Bod. This is better," I said before tugging one of his cheeks as I rose to go to the bar. "You're starting to use your old grey matter."

"What's that?" he asked.

"Nothing," I replied with another exasperated sigh.

I went to buy us another round of beers. As I was standing at the bar, I was approached by Cowboy, one of the aggressors from the other day.

"Alright," he announced.

"Alright."

"About the jacket you had with you the other day."

Bloody hell, here we go.

"Yeah, what about it?"

"Someone was telling me that Tom Needham had dropped a load of togs off at a charity shop only for some scumbag to have them away. Then, a day later, you're sitting in here with a Gucci jacket in a plastic bag and you seemed very uncomfortable when I was trying it on."

"I told you, it was a fake."

"Didn't look like a fake to me," he added sternly.

"Look, I have explained to Tiny, I'd had the gear for ages and it's nothing to do with the stuff that was nicked from Goodwill."

"Ah, it was Goodwill, was it? You certainly know your details."

"It was in the paper!"

He then looked at me as if he was about to lay me out with a punch.

"Now listen to me, boy, in this pub, we don't mind a bit of M&S gear being sold off cheap, maybe the odd bottle of perfume from Boots, even a mobile phone that someone has *stumbled* on in the street, but the second you start pinching off charities, then you have entered a whole different ballpark. Now I'll take your word for it for the time being, but if I find out you had anything to do with nicking these clothes, then you and I are going to fall out. Do you understand?"

"Loud and clear. Now can I get served, please?" I responded, turning away and giving him the impression that I didn't give a toss when I did.

I collected the beers and returned to Bod.

"What was that about?" he asked, concerned.

"Nothing to worry about, mate. Only a fucking nut-job with hands like shovels threatening to fill us in if he ever finds out we were the fellas who stole the stuff from the charity shop."

"How come he thinks it was us?"

"Because it was us and this thing feels like a ticking fucking time bomb! I have got that mad bastard threatening to stove my head in and some total stranger coming around my house giving me the creeps."

"Why don't we go the feds and own up to it?" Bod suggested.

"What, and if we do, do you think the pub psycho over there will call off the cavalry? No, that's a bad move."

"At least we should get rid of the gear," he recommended.

"Where?"

"Just dump it somewhere."

"Somehow it will lead back to us. We could always burn it, I suppose," I suggested, rattling around poor ideas.

"Where?" he queried.

"How about my lounge? Maybe we can do it tonight as soon as my grandad goes to bed."

"We'll have to mind your carpet."

"This is why I'm getting so fucking cranky! I've managed to do a job with the thickest fucking bloke in Europe. Why couldn't you have been working on that day, Bod? If you had, none of this would have happened."

Just then a text message came through from Nails:

The original Terminator vs the original Alien – who would win?

"Fucking hell, I'm going to go ballistic in a minute!" I screamed. "I can't think straight, I am surrounded by fucking cretins!"

"What are we going to do then?" Bod asked, desperately.

I put both of my hands over my face. "I don't know. I reckon the best thing to do is to do nothing. Leave the gear where it is and let's see what happens next. If the Old Bill are contacted by the taxi driver or the Irish fella then they'll soon work out we nicked the stuff and them finding it will be neither here nor there. At least if we get away with it, we might be able to offload it at some point and make a few quid. The unfortunate thing is the gear's as hot as soldering iron and I can't see it cooling down anytime soon."

CHAPTER 5

Despite the passing of a couple of quiet days, I was still jumpy. I wasn't sure who was waiting for me around the corner, who the next text message was coming from or who was about to come knocking at the backdoor. I hadn't been in the Falcon and frankly, I was happy to give the place a wide berth.

I had been out and about and doing the usual deals. I had purchased a brand-new coffee maker from Candy. I'm guessing her barista apprenticeship hadn't worked out and she was provided with a decent leaving present. She didn't realise she was holding a three hundred-pound piece of kit. Actually, she wasn't holding anything, as it was in an ASDA shopping trolley. Anyway, she seemed happy enough with twenty-five notes and I was even happier when Smelly Nelly gave me eighty for it. The trolley ended up in his neighbour's front garden, as I wasn't going to push that fucker around all day.

I had made a few quid and was on my way home with double saveloy and chips.

As I was walking up the driveway, from out of the darkness appeared Moany Tony. For fuck's sake, I was starving and my tucker was getting cold.

"Good evening, Tony," I said in an almost resigned tone.

"Is it?"

"What's happened now? Don't tell me, the entire refugee

population of Syria are on their way over here on a jet ski?"

"Cocaine. Did you know it's easier to get hold of in London than a pizza? There are dedicated hotlines you can ring and they deliver it for you."

"Yeah, we have them here. It's called Domino's. Sorry, you meant cocaine."

"The drugs courier knocks on your door, hands you the gear, then you pay them. It's that simple. No questions asked, no police, no law enforcement, nothing. What have we become?"

"Entrepreneurial?"

"It's like an unstoppable wave of unruly behaviour. People become addicted to drugs, then they lose their jobs because they can't function, then they turn to crime."

"Then they are forced to become politicians and end up putting expense claims in for new bathroom suites and prostitiutes. It's an evil cycle."

"We are witnessing the erosion of society, but no one seems to care."

"No one except you, Tony. Keep on caring because it's making a difference. Meanwhile, I have got a couple of saveloys to get stuck into."

"*Two* saveloys? Why have you brought one for the big Irish fella?"

"What big Irish fella?"

"The one who's sitting in your lounge having a cup of tea with your grandad."

He had returned. Why did I think for one minute he wouldn't? I walked slowly through the door where I could hear him and Grandad chatting away and laughing. It appeared Egan could switch his charm on and off like a bedside lamp.

I popped my head around the lounge. "Alright," I said.

"Here he is! Mr Egan was telling me the news. I'm thrilled, Robbie! A job as a trainee journalist! My grandson, working for the *Leicester Mercury*!"

"Sorry, Robbie, I thought you would have already told your grandad; I didn't intend to steal your thunder. You see, Mr Howard, I could spot the talent in him within minutes of us chatting about that charity shop business. It was the systematic and articulate way Robbie relayed the story. I just had to speak to the editor straight away. 'I've spotted a diamond; we need to hire him immediately,' I explained. Thankfully, we're recruiting at the minute, so he gave me the green light. Robbie, did you manage to leave the job at Coopers on good terms?"

"Have you left already? But don't you have to work your notice?" challenged Grandad.

I was bemused.

"Zero-hour contracts, Mr Howard. I think I'm right in saying you were owed some holiday, so you could leave today, couldn't you, Robbie?" Egan asked, feeding me information like you'd feed a Shetland pony sugar lumps.

What was I going to say? I could hardly say, I haven't left Coopers, Grandad, he's making it all up because the fucking job is made up! The subject of my employment was now an expanding network of lies.

"Yes, I've finished today, I'm all done," I replied, dumbfounded.

"Brilliant! All set for the next chapter of your life. I'm sure it will be an interesting one," Egan added with a wink.

"I'm sure it will," I responded.

"You might need to get used to having him around the house, Mr Howard," Egan said.

"Why?"

"Journalism is seldom a nine-to-five job, I'm afraid, and he can expect lots of unsociable hours. There will no doubt be days when Robbie is here with you. Still, I'm sure he can make himself useful."

"That's fine with me," said Grandad. "He can keep me hydrated with plenty of cups of tea!"

His response and obvious excitement prompted a rasping cough.

"That sounds nasty. I'm going to see whether Robbie will let me have a few of his chips, Mr Howard. We'll be in the kitchen."

Egan walked towards me, put his hand on my shoulder and ushered me through before closing the door behind him.

"What's going on and why are you saying I'm going to be working with you?" I asked, irritated.

"Because you are."

"What?"

"Ethel, the little old lady from the charity shop – you remember her, don't you?"

"Yes, of course, I do."

"You may remember she was quite upset at having a bag of clothes stolen when she was minding the shop."

"She was upset but seemed okay after speaking to her manager and the police."

"Well, she wasn't very okay when it transpired the bag of clothes was donated by Tom Needham and was worth thousands of pounds."

"It wasn't her fault."

"And then it appeared on the front page of the *Leicester Mercury*. A nice colour picture to remind her she should have been tending to the shop rather than helping some shit-bag in the dressing room who was setting up a theft."

"I told you, it wasn't me," I reaffirmed.

"The night after the theft, Ethel had a stroke. She's not in a good way. She's currently in the Royal Infirmary. They suspect she has brain damage. She might not make it and even if she's does, she has a long, painful road to recovery, which could take months and months."

"I'm sorry to hear that," I replied sincerely.

"Of course, having a stroke isn't in any way directly connected with working in a shop where there's been a theft and where she feels responsible for it, but I'm not a believer in coincidences. Are you?"

"I've never thought about it," I replied.

"I'm going to conclude every action does indeed have an equal and opposite reaction. And for every wrongdoing, there will be a victim and a perpetrator."

"I didn't do it," I said.

"Ethel is my mother," announced Egan.

Oh, shit!

"And now my slightly erratic visiting schedule has been upgraded to a daily visit to the infirmary. I mean, I'm her only son, it's the right thing to do; you'd agree, wouldn't you?"

"Yes, of course."

"And such visits are time-consuming. I mean, you have to get there, park up, buy some flowers, walk to the ward, sit with her – you know the drill."

"Sure."

"And it's time I don't have to spare. So, I need to recruit someone to help me out" – he then pointed at me – "and that someone will be you."

"What do you want me to do?"

"Would you be good enough to call into the hospital to see her every day?"

"Yeah, yeah, sure, of course."

"Perhaps I could make you a list of things to take for her and text them through to you beforehand. Would that be alright?"

"Yeah, anything to help."

"You'd do that for me?"

"Of course."

"Despite the fact, you had nothing to do with stealing the gear?"

There was no point in denying it any longer.

"I'm sorry. If I knew this was going to happen—"

"I would have never done it," he finished the sentence for

me. "Yes, don't worry, I get it. We all do stupid things, especially when we're young. But we all need to be held accountable for our actions, that's the thing."

"Are you going to the police?"

He shook his head. "Nope. Look, Robbie, I won't lie to you any longer: there will be no hospital visits to see Ethel, no flowers, no chocolates, no cards or any of that carry-on. Why the hell would I want you anywhere near her anyway? No, as from this evening, you'll work for me. You'll do exactly what I ask of you when I need you to do it. Which is why I felt compelled to kill this nonsense story of you working in the warehouse. Tomorrow evening you will meet me at my place. I'll text you the address at seven o'clock. You will then come immediately and bring every single one of those clothes you nicked from Goodwill. Do you understand me?"

He then proceeded to open the kitchen door and see himself out.

"You haven't got my mobile number," I said.

He turned around, smiled and shook his head. "Tomorrow night, seven o'clock."

I then did something I'd never done before in my life and quite frankly never dreamt I would ever do. I dumped my chips and saveloy. I followed this by sending a text message to Nails and Bod pretty much demanding they meet me immediately in the Falcon. To sweeten the deal, I agreed to buy them three pints each. Within seconds I'd received two virtually identical text messages confirming they would be joining me.

I walked down, somewhat dazed by what had happened. At least I didn't have to continue to lie to Grandad about the Coopers job, but what exactly did Egan have in store for me? It was this question and others, perhaps some relating to hypothetical tough-guy fight-offs posed by Nails, that would be addressed during the ensuing hours.

I walked into the bar, purchased three lagers and grabbed us a seat. Rocky and one half of Dumb and Dumber soon followed and joined me.

"What's gone down then?" asked Bod.

"Nothing too unusual, really," I replied. "Only the return of the Irish fella, who is telling my grandad I quit my job at Coopers—"

"But you didn't work at Coopers," Bod interrupted.

"I know I didn't, bird-brain, but my grandad thought I did. Now he thinks I work at the *Leicester Mercury* as a trainee journalist."

"When did you get that job?" Bod asked.

"I didn't!" I yelped. "For some reason, Egan has made it up and told Grandad that's where I'm now working."

They both started to laugh.

"What's so funny?" I enquired.

"You – a trainee journalist!" speculated Nails with a giggle.

"It isn't so ridiculous. I'm sure I could turn my hand to it. Anyway, I'm not going to be a trainee journalist, because the Irishman – whose name is Egan, by the way – doesn't work at the *Leicester Mercury*."

"So, your grandad no longer thinks you've got a make-believe job at Coopers – he now thinks you've got a make-believe job at the *Leicester Mercury*!" Nail roared.

They both started to laugh again.

"I don't know why you think it's so fucking funny, Bod? You're sitting there like you're in the clear, you little prick. Well, I've got news for you: you aren't. I was forced to admit to Egan earlier it was us who stole the gear."

"Why the fuck did you do that?" he asked, looking decidedly less smug.

"Because he backed me into a corner. This fella's smart, he plays Jedi mind games. God knows what he's going to do if ever he meets you. After one conversation, you'll be serving life in prison for the murder of someone who died before you were born."

"Is he going to the feds?" queried Nails.

"No, I'm sure he won't. It turns out it was his mum who was working in the charity shop on the day we had the gear away and shortly afterwards she went and had a stroke."

"What's a stroke?" asked Bod.

"Medical class is tomorrow, so let's just say it's pretty fucking serious and the old lady is in the infirmary on her last legs. Anyway, he's got a right hard-on for me because of it."

"Well, you can't blame him, can you?" Nails stated.

"I suppose not," I answered.

"If it was my mum, I'd kick your fucking teeth in, and yours, Bod."

"Nice touch, mate. Bod would've been gutted if he'd been left out," I added.

"Is he going to beat me up?" asked Bod.

"I don't think he's going to beat anyone up, but whilst his mum is laid up in the hospital he wants me to go and work for him."

"What does he do?" Nails asked.

"He's told you, he works at the *Leicester Mercury*," replied Bod.

"Why the fuck did I invite you down here, Bod? What possible value are you adding to resolving this predicament?" I fumed.

"I thought you said he did," he replied, embarrassedly.

"No, that was his cover story. I don't know what he does, that's part of the problem."

"He might have a really poncey job," Nails interjected.

"Like what?" I asked.

He took a swig from his beer whilst he searched for an appropriate example.

"Marmite taster."

"Why the fuck would he taste Marmite for a job?" I replied.

"How old is he?" Nails enquired.

"Late forties, fifty, maybe," I replied.

"Worm picker," Bod suddenly announced.

"What!" I replied.

Nails then got himself involved, again. "Crime scene cleaner."

"Great! Here we go, fucking playschool has opened. Go on then, you pair of bellends, get it out of your system."

They were both giggling like schoolgirls.

"Water slide tester," added Bod.

"Cat's-eye cleaner," quipped Nails.

"Biscuit designer," added Bod.

They thought it was fucking hilarious. I rolled my head back and looked up to the heavens, wondering what I had done to deserve this.

"Is there any chance that we could resume the meeting, please?" I asked firmly.

"Sorry, mate, carry on," said Nails, finally drawing a line under the stupidity.

"The other thing I haven't mentioned is he's demanded I take the bag of gear with me to the meeting tomorrow night."

"But it's worth a mint!" Nails noted.

"I know, but I'm going to have to take it."

"Who the fuck does this bloke think he is?" pondered Nails.

"I don't know anything about him, apart from he's persuasive, smooth and very demanding," I said.

"What do you think he's going to do with those clothes? Take them back to the charity shop? I don't think so. If I were you, I'd tell the fella to do one," Nails barked.

"I can't. He'll only return to my house. Trust me, I won't be able to get shot of him."

I watched as Nails took a long, contemplative swig from his beer. "Fifty per cent," he suddenly announced.

"Fifty per cent, what?" I asked.

"I'll get rid of your little problem, but I want fifty per cent of the sale value of the clothes. You boys can split the remainder."

"Where did that come from?" I asked, slightly surprised.

"You've got a problem and I might have a solution. But it'll cost you."

I looked at Bod, who diverted his gaze as he was unwilling to question his offer.

"And how are you intending to get rid of my problem?" I queried.

"He's going to text you tomorrow, right?"

"Yeah."

"Then the three of us will go to wherever he is and I'll straighten it out with him, there and then."

"Do you mean what I think you mean?" I probed.

"Seems to me like it might be the only language that this fella will understand," Nails added.

"You won't get silly with him, will you?" I enquired.

"No, mate. I'll slap him about a bit and that'll be the end of it. Afterwards, you can tell your grandad the *Mercury* pulled the job because of cutbacks brought on due to the internet, then we shall find you another made-up job."

I sat back on my chair. "This sounds like a plan, boys. Bod, are you in?"

"Yeah, definitely! Let's take care of him."

"Okay, so I suggest we meet here at about quarter to seven tomorrow night. When he texts me his address we'll get a cab over there and we can sort this twat out, once and for all," I declared.

I raised my glass and the other two lads clinked it.

Problem solved.

As the evening drew to a close, we left the pub together. When Nails departed, I suddenly felt a surge of pride. He was a beast of a man: tall, lean muscular build and very quick. A man designed solely by the good Lord for combat.

I called out to him, "Hey, Nails, you're not going to be bringing a weapon with you tomorrow night?"

He stopped walking and turned around. "You say weapon, I say finisher."

CHAPTER 6

I'd taken the opportunity of having a lazy day at home as I didn't have to pretend I was heading to the warehouse for a bogus shift.

I sat with Grandad and watched a programme on the Desert Rats. I'd noticed the increased regularity of his coughing. I periodically enquired if he was alright but, like the true soldier he was, he never once suggested anything was amiss.

I'd made up my mind that I would eventually explain to him that the role at the *Leicester Mercury* wasn't working out. Thankfully, Coopers had offered me back my old job, so desperate were they for my return. In my fictitious world of work, I had become a dream employee.

I began speculating about how this evening might play out. I'd seen Nails in fights at school. As the playground tough guy, he wasn't short of competitors, but he never gave them an inch. He could finish a fight in a couple of moves: the odd punch, a kick to the stomach or a shoulder throw he'd perfected on Bod and me. I'm not sure his competition was ever elite class, but he'd certainly proved himself and had remained undefeated.

By early evening, I'd showered, changed and made my way to the Falcon. Was it too premature to consider that should we get Egan out of the way then this might leave Bod and I in the clear? We'd heard nothing from the Old Bill and there hadn't been any follow-up stories in the *Leicester Mercury*. Who knows, maybe in six months I could begin to flog the clothes?

I walked into the bar and bought a round of beers before I noticed the lads had turned up.

"Nails, have you brought a tool with you?" I asked nervously.

"I certainly have."

He took a slow careful look around the pub before opening his jacket. He showed me a few inches of a heavy bike chain he'd taped to the inside of his coat.

"In case he pulls something out. Otherwise, I'm not intending using it," he whispered.

"Go careful with that fucking thing, mate. You're a big lad and he's no spring chicken. I suspect you could do him some serious damage."

"Don't worry, I know what I'm doing."

My phone then beeped:

The old Starlight night club, Wharf Street. I'll leave the door open for you.

"We're in business, boys. Showtime! Let's get the cab ordered."

I'd learned from Bod's previous error and instructed the taxi driver to drop us several streets away from Egan's club, ensuring there was no direct connection between what might go on at this venue in a few minutes and us.

It was an ugly, run-down end of town at the best of times and it was ghostly quiet as we walked along the street. A couple of local Middle Eastern fellas stood outside of doorways smoking and staring suspiciously in our direction.

"Okay, this is how we are going to play this," I stated as we walked. "Let's assume he's on his own. I'll tell him it's no-deal with the gear and he can stick his demand of me being his slave up his arse. If he's having none of it, that's when you step in," I said before turning towards Nails.

"Roger that!" he replied.

"What do you want me to do?" asked Bod.

"Can you hang around the front of the nightclub handing out flyers?" I suggested.

"What flyers?" he retorted.

"Fucking hell! Just stand with us. If we need your help I'll let you know," I added.

"When did this place close?" asked Nails.

"I'm not sure I've ever known it to be open," I responded.

"What are we going to do if he's got a firm with him?" asked Bod.

"That's when you might need to get involved," I answered.

I looked at him and could see he was worried, but then again, so was I. What the fuck were we walking into? We were like three blind mice. In the next five minutes, we could all get our heads kicked in or worse. Why did Egan want to drag me down to some backstreet derelict nightclub? The signs were looking ominous.

"Here it is," I said, pointing at a run-down building on the corner of the street. The 'Starlight' sign was in bits, there was broken glass and debris everywhere and a half-filled skip dumped at the side of the building. There was not a soul around, not even the sign of a car that Egan might have driven down in.

Sure enough, the entrance to the club was partially open. I gestured for the other two fellas to be quiet as I pulled at the heavy old door and began to creep in. The place was in total darkness and had that mouldy smell of an uninhabited building.

"Egan, Egan, are you there?" I called.

The three of us walked in and as our eyes became accustomed to the dark it appeared we were in the middle of an old dancefloor.

"What's going on?" asked a concerned Bod.

"Keep your cool," I replied.

"I don't like it, Robbie. I think we should leave," he advised.

"Maybe we should," I answered.

Suddenly, we were bathed in light and from out behind the bar Egan appeared.

"Well, this is a pleasant surprise! I was only expecting Robbie. How nice of you to invite guests."

"We need to have a chat," I announced.

Egan approached us. "I'm guessing the big fella is Nails, leaving you" – he turned and pointed – "you must be Bod. Am I correct?"

"Yes, that's right," I said. "Now, everyone, be cool, we don't want any trouble."

"So why have you brought the big fella?" Egan asked.

"We've not got the gear with us," I declared.

"I can see that. May I ask why?"

"Because the plan's changed," I stated.

"Changed to what?"

"Changed to your not getting the gear," interjected Nails aggressively.

Egan then raised both hands in a manner suggesting he wanted to calm things down.

"Well, that's not a good start, is it?" he declared.

"And Robbie won't be coming to work for you, whatever the fuck it is you want him to do," Nails growled.

"This has nothing to do with you, so why don't you and mastermind over there go and clear off and leave Robbie and me to sort this out between us?" Egan requested.

"I'm going nowhere and neither is Bod," Nails sternly replied.

The kettle had been plugged in, filled with water and was about to boil – big time. I swallowed hard as fear entered my body.

Once again Egan raised his hands, gesturing for everyone to calm down.

"I would leave if I were you, big fella, and this will be your last warning. You and that silly puppy should get out of my club right this minute or you'll regret it."

Nails then went straight to last base and took the thick chain out of his coat. "Will I?" he threatened.

"I hope you know what you are doing with that?" Egan

queried, with a calm nonchalance suggesting this type of scene was not foreign territory to him.

"I know exactly what I'm doing with it," Nails replied as he stepped forward.

"Come on then, let's see what you're made of," invited Egan.

Bod and I stood terrified as Egan waited for Nails to approach him. Nails had the chain in his stronger right hand and when he was within striking distance of Egan, rather than swing his chain, he jabbed him with his left fist, catching him on the chin. Egan was stunned and stepped back, allowing Nails to land a heavy blow to the side of his head with the chain. After Egan fell to the floor. Nails stood over him, lashing the thick, interlinked metal chunks into his torso, his victim curled up tightly to cushion the blows. He was properly going to work on him.

"Stop, for fuck's sake!" I yelled, grabbing his arm. "He's had enough!"

Egan lay on the floor writhing in pain, blood dripping from his head.

"Don't ever contact Robbie again, do you fucking hear me!" demanded Nails, standing over him.

Egan lay making a low, painful sound.

"Come on, let's go," I said.

We left the club and headed into the city centre.

"Do you think he's going to be okay?" Bod asked.

"Yeah, he'll be okay. Although I bet he'll have a fucking headache in the morning," Nails replied with a smirk. "Still, that's sorted it out, boys. Now, who's for a pint? I'm looking forward to finding out when I'm going to make myself some fucking money."

I arrived home and yet again threw away my fast food. This time it was a chicken balti pie and chips. The violence I'd witnessed had robbed me of my appetite.

We'd gone for a pint after Nails had given Egan a kicking but I was in no mood to talk about how we were going to shift the gear. Instead, I'd promised to meet the lads tomorrow night after I had collected my thoughts and devised a plan.

I sat at the kitchen table with a bottle of energy drink and contemplated what had unfolded.

Witnessing Nails handing out a beating to Egan triggered painful memories and that night in bed the nightmares returned. They were crystal-clear recollections from my past, each so real I could almost reach out and touch them. The details were so vivid: the colours, the faces, the violence and, of course, the terror.

I was at home with Mum playing with my toys in the front room. She'd made dinner and was waiting for Dad to return. As ever, he was late because he'd been to the pub. Mum was in the kitchen waiting impatiently for him, her mood progressively worsening.

Eventually, the front door opened and I could hear him stumble into the kitchen. It was a now only matter of time before the arguing started. I jumped on the settee and put the cushions over my ears – maybe they would block out the shouting? The volume escalated until Dad inevitably turned to the only method of resolving an argument he knew. I heard the screams from Mum as she bounced off the walls. I jumped from the settee and crouched, trembling, whilst watching through the crack in the door. He had grabbed her tightly bound hair in his fist and was threatening her. I saw the saliva dripping from his hate-filled mouth. Blood was trickling from her brow, and a mix of mascara and tears were tumbling down her face. She wore an expression of intense fear as he smashed her face against the wall before storming out of the house.

I ran into the kitchen and to where she lay on the floor. She was curled rigidly in a ball like a beaten animal and was making a heart-wrenching wailing sound. I lay next to her, putting my arms around her crushed body, desperately trying to provide comfort. I could feel her torso shaking with fear. I lay next to her and we cried together.

Despite my freezing-cold bedroom, I awoke drenched in sweat. I checked the time; 4.13 a.m. More sleep meant more nightmares and I wasn't sure how much I could take. I decided to get out of this miserable bed and get showered.

Walking across the landing I could hear Grandad coughing. This hideous sound brought me to a standstill. I popped my head around the door of his bedroom to find him sat upright in bed, wheezing and gasping for air.

"Are you okay?"

He was desperately trying to find the breath to talk. I switched on the light and for the first time in years saw him without his shirt. I was shocked at how much weight he'd lost. As I sat next to him on his bed, I appreciated he was my world and knew that death would shortly come to take him away.

I sat with him for several minutes in silence, holding his hand, before I dared to go downstairs and make him a cup of tea. As I got up, I could see that he'd noticed the sweat on my bed shirt.

"Looks like I'm not the only one who's had a bad night. Did it come back again?" he faintly asked.

"Yes."

"The same stuff?"

"Same as ever," I replied.

He shook his head and sat gasping for air.

"I'm so sorry you ever had to see that. I will never know why she didn't leave him," he whispered.

"Because she was scared," I replied.

"What I'd have given for five minutes alone with him."

"Me too."

I'd arranged to meet the lads at the Falcon to construct a plan of action for shifting the gear. Taking Egan out of the equation had no doubt been a priority but giving Nails fifty per cent now seemed generous. I was adamant that Bod and Nails were going to have to share the leg work, once we'd decided the time was right to start selling, as I certainly wasn't going to do all the hard yards for a miserly twenty-five per cent. I must admit it had crossed my mind that in a world where the word 'receipt' was blasphemous that I could flog the gear and lie about how much I was selling it for. Food for thought if it was clear that they weren't going to add any value to the sales process.

We sat around the table chatting.

"Where exactly is the stuff?" queried Nails.

"My house. I have it tucked away in my wardrobe."

"Is it safe there?" he questioned.

"It should be unless my grandad gets a taste for Versace sweatshirts, which I'm guessing is unlikely."

"Yeah, but it's in your wardrobe. Shouldn't we store it somewhere more secure?"

"I'm open to suggestions."

"Perhaps we could hire a lock-up," chipped in Bod.

"It's a bunch of second-hand clothes, Bod, not the fucking *Mona Lisa*."

"Who's she?" he asked.

"Look, I think the gear is safe where it is. You're the majority shareholder, Nails, so if you want to shift it then be my guest."

He took a long, slow sip of his beer from his pint glass.

"I'll have a think, but in the meantime, leave it where it is."

So actually, the discussion about where the gear was being stored had been a total waste of time. This could turn into a long and annoying evening.

"How much stuff are we talking about?" Nails asked.

"There must be forty items, isn't there, Robbie?" Bod speculated.

"Something like that. There's a lot of it: jackets, sweatshirts, jeans, all sorts," I added.

"When and how are we going to offload it?" Nails enquired.

"We need to give it at least six months," I said.

"Six months! Are you fucking joking – I want my money!" Nails hissed.

"This isn't any old shit we are talking about, mate. This is custom-designed gear which is very distinctive. I made the mistake of parading one of the jackets in here and within a couple of minutes, someone had spotted that Tom what's-his-face had worn it at a concert. We would do well to remember this stuff is still chilli peppers. We've got to let it ice over before we do anything and even then we'll need to be super-careful."

"How the fuck are we going to sell it then?" Nails questioned.

"The gear will never be sold cash-in-hand around this manor. Not today, not tomorrow, not fucking ever and you're going to have to get your heads around that quickly. The second we go down that road we'll have every fed in the city looking for us and before you've even learnt how to spell 'Versace' it'll be game over. eBay's out as well, for the time being; it's way too public. I reckon we need to source collectors, maybe second-hand vintage shops in places like London and New York. Let's see whether they'll take the job lot off our hands with no comebacks."

We were then interrupted by an approaching voice.

"Or you can sell it to me."

We all looked around in unison to see who it was – Egan.

"Mind if I join you?" he asked before he pulled a stool up and sat down.

His face was in a bit of mess with traces of dried blood circling painful-looking wounds.

"What the fuck are you doing here?" Nails griped.

"I'm here to propose a deal," he replied.

"What deal?" I asked.

"First of all, I'll come clean with you; this was only ever about me getting my hands on the clothes. I've been hired by a certain someone, who wishes to remain nameless, but who wants to give you a fair price for them. In return, they'll make sure that any heat you might get from the police will disappear."

"Hang on, so you're telling us the *Leicester Mercury* thing and the meeting last night was just because you wanted the gear?" I asked.

"That's all it was. I tried to get it back for nothing so I could pocket the money from my client, I mean, come on, who can blame me? It was the wrong play" – he then pointed to his face – "and now I've got the bruises to show for it."

"You mentioned a fair price, what are you willing to pay?" Nails enquired.

"A grand, cash, and you'll get it tomorrow. You walk with a grand, I get the clothes for my client, the police lose interest, everyone's happy."

"Your client must be very keen to get his hands on those clothes – why?" probed Nails.

"That's his business. I'm only the middleman."

"Tell him three grand and he has himself a deal," Nails proposed.

Egan smirked. "Just be careful here because you're on thin ice and it's melting quickly. Unless I broker an agreement this evening, I've been instructed to report the three of you to the police and we'll let them sort it out. It's your call."

"Two thousand and you'll have the gear tomorrow," Nails suggested.

"Fifteen hundred and that's his final offer. Take it or leave it. If you counter, I walk."

"Deal!" Nails said. "Fifteen hundred cash."

"Cash! Yeah, I'm not sure a banker's draft will work, do you?" Egan added with a sneer.

"Where and when?" asked Nails.

"Let's try the seven o'clock thing at my club, again. I'll have the cash; you have the clothes and let's get this deal done and dusted, shall we?"

"Sounds good to me, boys, any objections?" Nails remarked, offering it to the floor.

"Fine with me," said Bod.

"And me," I confirmed.

Egan stood up to leave.

"Great, I'll see you at seven tomorrow at my place. And can we all play by the rules this time? I want every item that was stolen and my client knows exactly what was dropped off, so no funny business."

"We'll keep our end of the bargain, just make sure you have the money ready," Nails demanded.

As soon as Egan had left the pub Nails broke out into a massive grin. "Fifteen hundred notes – fucking get in there!" he yelled before he high fived us both.

No wonder he was happy; he was about to pocket seven-hundred and fifty quid, and having done what? He'd slapped around an over-the-hill, middle-age fixer. Meanwhile, Bod and I would only make £375 each despite taking all the risks.

Yes, it would draw a line under the matter, but somehow I was feeling far from satisfied with the proposed outcome.

We'd arranged to meet at my house at 6.30 p.m. During the day I'd purchased three generous-sized bags that we would carry the clothes in.

I'd told Grandad I was having a wardrobe clear-out in support of a local bring-and-buy sale with Bod and Nails coming around to help me deposit the donation. It was a quite ridiculous cover story in so many ways, not least because between us we didn't have an altruistic bone in our bodies. In fact, Bod and I happily steal from charities!

The story was made worse when I heard Grandad rummaging through his wardrobe later in the afternoon to see whether he could contribute towards the donation. He handed over a large stash of mothball-smelling clothes and manky old shoes which

I'm sure the organisers of the bring-and-buy sale would have been incredibly grateful of if there had been any organisers and if such a bring-and-buy sale were taking place.

As I shoved Grandad's donation under my bed and started neatly packing Tom Needham's designer wear into the bags, I marvelled at the level of stupidity of the story I had told him. I needed to consider my tactics more thoroughly; to plan and formulate strategies. I was too inclined to open my mouth and hope something useful might come out when, more often than not, it didn't.

I eyed Bod and Nails walking up the driveway and hurriedly intercepted them before they could knock on the back door. I handed them both a bag to carry before Grandad spotted them and instigated the inevitable small talk. I was being prudent, which, unfortunately, could not be said about Bod.

"Is your grandad about? If he is, I'll quickly nip in and say hello," he suggested in his normal friendly manner.

"No, you fucking won't!" I barked, impatiently thrusting a bag into his hand. "You'll end up blowing an already piss-poor cover story out of the water. Take this fucking bag, do a quick one-eighty and keep walking."

As the three of us armed with our bags departed my house, from out of the darkness the prince of bad timing appeared.

"Who do we have here then? Is it three wise men bearing gifts!" Tony commented.

"Hi, Tony, yeah something like that. We're just dropping some old clothes off," I replied.

"Yeah, where to?" he snooped.

"Erm… there's a charity sale going on tomorrow, so we're dropping them off down there," I answered.

"Which charity?"

For fuck's sake!

"I can't think of the name of it, the one around the corner," I replied. Not for the first time today I was finding the soil of the very deep fucking hole I was digging surprisingly easy-going.

"Which corner?" he probed.

More questions – I cannot believe it! It was like living next door to Inspector Poirot.

"The one on the corner of a junction of roads," I answered, ridiculously vaguely. "Anyway, I'd love to stand here and talk to you for the rest of the month, but we really must get going."

I approached Nails and Bod, who had stopped in their tracks.

"Keep fucking walking, will you!" I whispered.

"He's standing staring at us," Bod commented.

"Well, don't stand there and stare back at him, you fucking moron, otherwise he'll call you over for questioning. Just walk!" I snarled.

Having arrived at the main road, I called a taxi and we leaned against the wall of the post office waiting for it to show up.

"I'll be fucking glad to get rid of this stuff, it's a bad-luck charm," I announced.

"Who do you reckon Egan's client is?" Bod asked.

"Tom Needham," guessed Nails.

"Yeah, why, though?" Bod replied.

"PR, mate. Looks good for the band if he gets his stuff back. It'll appear the Leicester public was looking out for him," he added.

"You might be right there," I chipped in.

"You can't help thinking it's worth a lot more than fifteen hundred quid," suggested Bod.

"Maybe we should re-negotiate?" Nails advised.

"No, no, no, don't go down that fucking road!" I said sternly. "We've done the deal so let's just please get it over the line. Anyway, in about thirty minutes you're going to be seven hundred and fifty quid up so I'm not sure why you would want to jeopardise that."

"He's right, Nails. Let's get rid of this stuff. You heard what Egan said last night: it'll only take one phone call to the Old Bill and we're in trouble," added Bod.

"Well, you two are, I'm not," Nails declared.

"You what?" I snapped.

"I'm only saying that should the feds get involved then they won't be bothering me."

This made my blood boil.

"I can't believe what I'm hearing – we're your fucking mates, Nails! Surely, you aren't suggesting you'd leave us in the shit?" I ranted.

"You two nicked the stuff, I was only helping you out."

I was incredulous. "*Helping* us out! You've helped yourself to fifty per cent, you greedy twat."

"Oi, less of that. I made the problem go away you wouldn't be standing here if it wasn't for me."

"Well, well, well, you've certainly shown your true colours, haven't you?" I added.

"'True colours'! Don't you fucking lecture me! I wasn't the one who stole a load of gear from a charity shop – I mean, who does that shit?"

"Erm, you?" I replied.

"What?"

"You're as much involved in this as we are."

"I don't think I am."

"If what we are doing is so morally corrupt then I'm guessing you're going to suggest we take the gear back to Goodwill in the morning?"

"Yeah, well, it's too late now."

"No, it's not. We can cancel the taxi and take it all back tomorrow. But you don't want to, do you? Because you're only interested in the fucking money."

"Okay, you two, pack it in, here's the taxi," announced Bod.

Nails's comments had made me furious. I held the taxi door open as he got in and for a moment I contemplated throwing my bag at him and walking off.

I wish I had.

We arrived in Leicester city centre and once again instructed the driver to drop us off a couple of streets away from the club. The atmosphere in the taxi had been frosty after our heated exchange.

"We need to be on our guard here because I'm not sure what we're walking into. But let's assume Egan's got the fifteen hundred quid, we'll give him the gear and then get the fuck out of Dodge, okay?" I suggested.

"Yeah, I'm cool with that," Bod replied.

"What about you?" I asked, turning to Nails.

He shrugged his shoulders. "Yeah, fine."

"Are you tooled up?" I enquired.

"I'm carrying a little something in case he's brought in re-enforcements."

"Can you only get it out if he has? You've played your part in scaring this fella so let's just do the deal."

I was concerned that a seemingly straightforward transaction could go horribly wrong and it was clear Nails was getting progressively tetchy as the night wore on.

We walked in silence down the pitch-black street until we arrived at the club. Once again the door was ajar, only this time I noticed the lock was in pieces – someone had broken in.

"Have you seen this?" I worriedly pointed out.

"What's that about?" Nails asked.

"I don't know. Be on your guard, something's not right," I added.

"Perhaps we should go home," suggested Bod.

He was worried. The lad was out of his depth. I suddenly had a really bad feeling about this. What the fuck were we doing here?

"Stay close to me, we'll be okay," I remarked, unconvincingly.

The three us, each with a bag of high-value designer clothes, walked in.

As we did, I could see a television on a stand displaying a fuzzy picture. I dropped the bag and walked towards it.

"What the fuck is this?" Nails remarked as he followed me to the television.

"It's a television," said Bod.

"It wasn't here the other day," Nails added.

Footage then abruptly appeared on the screen of the three of us walking into the club with Egan appearing from the other side of the picture. It was a video recording from our last visit. We watched as Egan had cleverly gestured with his hands to calm down, suggesting he was scared and we were robbing him. He looked an innocent man attacked by three youths entering his club.

Suddenly the lights came on.

"Call it insurance!" Egan yelled.

The three of us turned around as he was walking towards us.

"What's this about?" I asked.

"Take a look at the screen. It's three men breaking into an old nightclub under renovation, threatening the middle-aged owner for money before assaulting him with a bike chain. It was, after all, a very nasty attack inflicted by a man whose nickname might suggest to a court he's no stranger to violence."

"We're just here to do the deal, as agreed, Egan. Fifteen hundred quid, then we're out of here," Nails demanded.

"Sorry, boys, that arrangement is no longer on the table. About an hour after you assaulted me last night I reported the incident to the police. The broken lock on the door as well – I mean, this was clearly a violent and carefully planned robbery. As we speak, the serious crime unit is out searching for you. The three of you are looking at breaking and entering with intent and grievous bodily harm – two very serious charges."

"But I didn't touch you," declared a worried Bod.

"But you didn't help me either, young Bod. You did nothing to stop this thug beating me up in what appears to be an unprovoked attack and that won't go down well in court. No, I'm afraid the three of you are looking at serious jail time, and as for this big lump " – he nodded at Nails – "you can wave goodbye to having Christmas dinner with your nearest and dearest for at least five years."

"What do you want from us?" I asked.

"You'll leave the bags where they are and clear off. Then maybe the police won't get to see this CCTV footage which I'd *accidentally* forgotten about when I reported the crime."

The three of us looked at each other.

"No deal!" snarled Nails.

"Hang on a minute," I interrupted.

"Fuck him, no deal! We said fifteen hundred quid and I'm not leaving without it, and if that means giving you another hiding, then that's what I'm going to do," he said.

Egan started clapping. "Way to go, champ! You've some balls on you; I'll give you that."

"We're holding stolen clothes that you've agreed to buy. You won't want the Old Bill involved in this any more than we do," I said, hoping to broker a peaceful resolution.

"There's some truth there, but there's no record of any deal being done. I mean, who's going to believe you three?" Egan asked.

"We can end this here, Egan. You give us the fifteen hundred or we take the gear back with us. These are the two options; you decide which one you want to take," Nails stated.

"No, I'll stick to option three, if that's alright with you? You leave the bags where they are and leave. Trust me, it's for the best."

"This fucking guy just won't learn his lesson, will he!" Nails cursed, pulling out a wooden cosh.

"Ouch! That could hurt more than the bike chain," Egan remarked arrogantly.

Nails stood where he was, cosh in his hand, ready to attack. Egan took off his jacket, then folded it up slowly and neatly before placing it on the bar.

"Just to manage your expectations, big boy, round two's going to be quite different to round one," he said.

Nails in a fit of rage ran towards him, wielding the cosh. He went to strike him with his right hand, but Egan, in a flash and with reactions that belied his age, intercepted his forearm with his left hand and then wrapped his right arm around Nails's neck, bringing him into his close quarters. He quickly proceeded to deliver a flurry of sickening blows with the butt of his hand into Nails's face. Within seconds blood was spurting out of his nose. Egan then drew his head down and kneed him in the jaw.

He stood back and let Nails limp body collapse to the floor, his face covered in blood. The cosh slowly rolled out of his hand as he lay unconscious.

Egan walked back to his jacket and retrieved a handkerchief from his pocket. Then, with unbelievable nonchalance, he began to slowly and methodically wipe the blood from his hands.

"Fucking hell!" I yelled running over to Nails. I knelt next to him and could hear him lightly coughing up blood.

"Turn him on his side. I could do without him dying on my floor," Egan hissed.

I rolled him over as he was regaining consciousness. He coughed up a large amount of blood and was shaking his head trying to regain composure. He tried to get to his feet before stumbling back over.

"Are you alright, mate?" I asked.

He sat up looking beleaguered, before trying to wipe the blood away from his nose and mouth.

"Bod, will you please get this lump out of my club?" Egan demanded.

Bod approached Nails. "Come on, mate, let's get you home," he said.

"By the way, if I ever see you two again, then trust me the state he's in at the moment will fare favourably with what you'll get next time. Do you understand me?"

Nails climbed to his feet before Bod put Nails's arm around his shoulder. I watched as they staggered out of the club.

"Do you want me to stay?" I asked.

He didn't immediately answer. He walked to the bar, pulled up a stool and continued to wipe the blood from his hands.

"That wasn't your smartest move, was it?"

"I know, I got it wrong."

"In the world you're heading to, mistakes like that will cost you badly and you'll end up getting hurt."

"What do you want me to do for you?" I enquired, knowing I was now at his mercy.

"As we were, Robbie. From tomorrow you'll come and work for me. Ethel's showing no signs of improvement and I'm a busy man so I'll need your help."

"What with?"

"For a start, this place. I'm looking at getting it open next weekend and it needs a coat of paint; would you be okay to do that?"

"Yeah, I suppose."

He laughed sarcastically. "No, this place is just a cover; a way for me to launder money. As from tomorrow, you'll be entering a much darker, volatile and dangerous world than decorating."

"A world of what?"

"*El trafico de Drogas*, as they say in Columbia."

"And what do they say in Leicester?"

"Drug dealing," he replied.

CHAPTER 7

Egan walked from behind the dusty cobweb-ridden bar with two glasses and a bottle of Scotch. He poured generous measures before handing me a glass. Whilst I'd never previously been a fan of spirits, now was most definitely a time for a drop of the hard stuff. I took a swig and grimaced as the alcohol whiplashed my taste buds.

He pulled up two stools from the bar and gestured for me to sit down.

"The drugs market operates on different tiers, with each having a clear point of travel before the next group of people become involved. Eventually, it's sold to an end-user who will either snort, inject or swallow the product. I deal in the penultimate part of this journey."

"Do you sell to drug dealers?"

"We're all drug dealers, Robbie," he replied. "I tend to buy in reasonable-sized quantities, and I purchase heroin, cocaine, MDMA or, if I can get my hands on it, something called *krokodil* – which the Eastern Europeans go mad for."

"What about cannabis?"

"I can't be bothered with it. The same goes for crystal meth, where the quality is questionable, and before you start to spout off about *Breaking Bad*, I don't hold a degree in chemistry."

I smirked.

"Having made the purchase, I contact my distribution network and sell on a first-come, first-served basis. What they do with the gear after that is their business. I have hired muscle which I sometimes call on but, generally speaking, I fly this operation solo and don't have the added burden of trust. Do you trust many people, Robbie?"

"Only one."

"You'll soon come to realise this business attracts some very unpleasant individuals, and do you know why?"

"Why?"

"Because, a bit like you with your small-time scams, drug dealing provides an opportunity to earn money without having to do any real work. The income is tax-free, the hours flexible and there's no clocking in first thing in the morning. In fact, it's very similar to what you are already used to, except the stakes are like the income – much higher. I'm going to show you a world you'll come to loathe. It's a game where you can ill afford to trust anyone and you should always be sure to watch your back because there's an army of parasites waiting to take your place."

"What do you want me to do?"

"I need another pair of hands whilst I'm looking after my mother. It seems only right that those hands belong to the person whom I deem responsible for putting her there – you."

"I wasn't the only one who nicked the gear," I added, desperately trying to dilute my responsibility.

"Did you ever think to ask how I knew the names of your friends?"

"No."

"I didn't think so, and that's because you think you're smart, but you're not. That's going to have to change, and change quickly, because in this game the bad boys will smell the blood of a novice from a mile off and they'll eat you alive." He shuffled forward on his seat and lowered his voice.

"I know it was you who planned the charity shop. You involved

Bod because he was off work and despite him being a bumbling idiot even he couldn't mess up stealing a bag from an unmanned shop. But it was you, Robbie, all you, and that's why you're here and Bod is around Nails's house taking his trousers off before he puts him to bed. You see, I can find out anything I want because I have the contacts, highly technical equipment, money and half a brain – it's a good combination."

"So, you tapped into my mobile phone?"

Egan smiled and took a sip from his glass.

"In a few months, this might all be over. When Ethel gets better our association will be concluded. But in the interim, you will do exactly as you're told, do you hear me?"

"Yes."

"And that means you work as I work. If I say we meet at six in the morning, we meet at six in the morning, and don't even think about being one minute late or there will be consequences."

"Okay."

"If I give you an assignment to complete and you fail, then there will be trouble. Now for the juicy bit – are you paying attention?"

"Yes."

"If you tell another living soul about me and the work you are doing" – he stopped and removed a large hunting knife from his jacket – "then I'll slash your fucking throat open."

He waited for me to acknowledge this.

"Okay," I repeated, taking a gulp.

He pointed the tip of the blade in my direction and I noticed the light reflecting off the highly polished steel blade.

"And if you decide to go to the police and turn me in, trust me I will find out, and I'll only delay in cutting your throat long enough so you can watch me slice your grandad's throat first. Are you clear with the arrangement?"

"Yes."

"I don't intend to pay you, but I'm also not a person without generosity, so if you do a good job I'll consider a suitable reward. In the meantime, I'll leave you to continue with your little bucket-shop scams."

He took another long, slow sip of whisky.

"I'm a demanding person, Robbie, but I won't ask you to do anything I wouldn't do myself."

He then finished his drink.

"I'll call you a cab. You'll next hear from me when I need you. And make sure these bags get back to the charity shop, will you?"

"Don't you want them?"

He sniggered and shook his head.

"What would I want with a load of second-hand clothes? Just make sure when Goodwill opens tomorrow morning that they are on their doorstep."

Like a cursed fucking boomerang, Tom Needham's touring outfits were once again back in my bedroom. One way or another, I would make it my business to finally get shot of them before I had breakfast. The internet informed me that Goodwill opens at 9.30 a.m. I'd book a taxi to take me into town about forty-five minutes beforehand. However, there was no way I was going to risk returning the clothes myself so I'd contacted Death Row and tempted him with the easiest twenty quid he'd ever make. I don't know that for sure, of course, but I'll assume it was.

He simply needed to meet me a couple of quiet streets away, take the three bags to the shop and drop them off. Should he be quizzed about them then the cover story was he'd seen someone throw them out of a passing car. As an avid reader of the *Leicester Mercury*, he'd recognised where they'd come from and did what any kind-hearted citizen would do and returned them to their rightful owner. The last bit of my made-up story was, at best, flaky, as I'm fairly sure Death Row didn't represent the demographic of your typical *Leicester Mercury* reader. In truth, the whole story was fucking rubbish, but I was banking on Goodwill being so pleased to have the gear returned that any subsequent details wouldn't be overly scrutinised.

The DR was more than happy to oblige and we arranged a 9.15 a.m. rendezvous.

The meeting point was a churchyard in town. It's one of those incongruous buildings slapped a stone's throw from the city centre that somehow largely go unnoticed.

Having been dropped off by the cab driver, I struggled with the three bags to the meeting point and was slightly surprised that the usually premature DR hadn't arrived. I took a seat on a bench and waited for him.

After a few minutes of reflecting on what Egan would have in store for me I checked my mobile phone: 9.22 a.m. – where was he?

I tried to call him but it rang off. I then popped him a text enquiring as to his whereabouts. Nothing.

9.26 a.m., four minutes before Goodwill opened and I was a two-minute walk away. Should I risk it myself? Egan said he wanted the gear dropping off before they opened but how would he know?

I waited a little longer for the DR to turn up.

9.36 a.m. I had missed the deadline and was starting to get anxious. It was clear the DR wasn't attending. I didn't want to drop the gear off myself as I was in the shop at the time of the theft. The odds that I would be the person who would then find the gear were so massive that suspicion would inevitably result.

I urgently needed a fixer, someone to seamlessly step in and resolve this awkward situation with guile and efficiency – I decided to call Candy.

Predictably she was in town, and from the tone of her voice and shallow gasps of air being taken, she was walking hastily down the street, away or towards some fella who was no doubt about to receive a hefty verbal broadside.

She agreed to meet me and knew the location. This was no great surprise as I suspect it was the sort of quaint spot she'd used previously to shoot up heroin.

Within a few minutes, her motorised twiglet legs were powering her into view.

"Right, what the fuck do you want me to do?" she hissed.

"I'm good, thanks, Candy, how are you? No, you're right, let's dispense with the pleasantries. Here beside me are three bags of old clothes and I need someone to take them to the charity shop around the corner. That person is you and for your trouble, I will give you twenty English pounds."

"Twenty quid to take some clothes to a charity shop, are you off your fucking rocker?"

"No, it's a genuine offer and I suggest it'll be the easiest twenty quid you will ever make."

My mind suddenly cast to the horrific acts that Candy would no doubt perform for twenty pounds once she started to get the shakes.

"Yeah, okay, fuck it! But one question: why don't you do it yourself?"

"Do you know, I hadn't thought of that. What a brilliant idea! I don't need you anymore so you may as well fuck off."

"Are you being sarcastic?" she enquired, perceptively.

"Let's just say I don't want to."

"And you'll pay someone twenty quid to do it?" she probed, being unduly inquisitive.

"Look, time is not my brother here. Do you want the fucking twenty quid or not?" I asked, starting to get a little narked.

"You look desperate to me, Bottom Dollar. I'm wondering what exactly you've been up to?"

"Take the fucking bags, will you!"

"Whatever you've gone and done, you look pretty fucking keen to get rid of this stuff, and for some reason you aren't too happy to be seen doing it yourself."

"Yes, that's correct, Candy. That's why I'm giving you twenty fucking quid to do it and if you don't take them in a minute, I'll happily give the dosh to another very willing and more grateful drug addict."

"Forty," she demanded.

"You what!"

"Forty quid or I walk and you can try and get hold of someone else to do your dirty work, and I'm going to gamble that you won't be able to."

"You fucking robber!"

"You don't like it when the shoe's on the other foot, do you?"

She was right; I didn't. I was getting a sharp taste of not only my own medicine but also a couple of practically unswallowable tablets.

"Thirty quid, final offer," I countered.

"Thirty-five?"

"Deal – fucking hell!" I exclaimed, clearly annoyed.

I took the money out of my pocket and handed it to her. Her heavily spotted blotchy face was looking smug.

"Thank you very much," she acknowledged, with a wry smile.

"Right, the charity shop is on Rutland Street, it's called Goodwill."

I watched as she strained to pick up the bags.

"Yeah, I know the one."

"No funny business here, Candy. I'm going to be fifty yards behind you. I want to see you and the bags go into the shop, and then you'll leave without them, do you hear me?"

"Yeah, whatever."

"I mean it! If any part of this equation doesn't happen then you and I will fall out."

"Cool your fucking jets, will you! I'll drop them off."

I watched as she struggled with the bags, her little matchstick legs buckling under their weight. She'd advanced about fifty yards before she dropped them to the ground, turned around and shouted at the top of her voice:

"I can't carry the fuckers, they're too heavy!"

I stormed over to her. "You fucking useless idiot! You can't get anything right!"

"It's not my fault they're so heavy."

"Right, I'll carry two bags, you carry the other one. We'll walk to the corner then you can take your bag in, drop it off and then come back for the other two, alright?"

"Yeah, fine, whatever," she snorted.

"Is there any chance you can sort out your attitude? I'm paying you thirty-five fucking quid here for what amounts to little more than five minutes' work."

"I'm sorry, sir, is that better?" she said before I heard her whisper under her breath, "You fucking prick."

At that moment, I finally realised that Candy and I would never have a romantic future together. It was the subtle arrogance and propensity towards impatience she carried around with her which would most likely render any potential relationship troublesome. That and the fact she was a vile little cunt.

We eventually arrived at the corner and I waited whilst she proceeded to make drop number one. She reappeared about a minute later.

"They want to know where I got this stuff from," she said.

"Tell them you found it near the church and you thought they would want it because they are a lovely charity organisation and you're a heart-of-gold skag head. Then get the fuck out of Dodge because I could go without you receiving the third degree."

"Whatever," she replied as she picked up the other two bags.

I followed and watched as she made her way for the second time into Goodwill before reappearing within a few seconds.

Job done! It had been a nice, slick operation with me attracting minimal attention.

Candy then spotted me looking at her from the corner.

"Done it!" she yelled.

For fuck's sake! I shook my head and walked off down the street and as I did I heard a voice behind me.

"Oi!"

I turned around to see who had caught my attention.

Egan. Shit!

"Remind me what the instructions were?" he asked.

"I know, I'm sorry. The person who was due to meet me and take the gear back let me down."

"And I'm guessing, looking at your back-up plan, the person you had arranged to meet was another smackhead?"

"No, no, this geezer was—"

"He was, wasn't he?"

"Yes," I replied in a resigned voice.

"You do remember what we agreed, don't you? About actions being completed on time, in a specific way, to a certain standard."

"Yes, I remember, but—"

"Unless you learn, and learn quickly, then things between us aren't going to run smoothly."

"I'm sorry."

"I'm not interested in apologies because they bore me. I could've let you off here with a warning, but I've decided that you need to fully understand how this is going to work."

"I do understand and it won't happen again," I responded desperately.

"Save your words. I've already put into place your punishment. Remember, Robbie, I need you to work at my pace and to my standards, and if you don't then really bad things are going to happen. Now, if you're quick, you might just get yourself around the corner to Sainsbury's and give Bod the bad news."

"What bad news?"

"That's your punishment. Five minutes ago, I tipped off the police that he was the person who stole Tom Needham's clothes."

I ran the short distance to Sainsbury's and burst into the store. My eyes were scanning left and right searching for Bod. He wasn't on the till so he must be stacking shelves. I marched around the store before spotting him assisting a customer on a self-service check-out.

I dashed up to him. "Bod, I need to speak to you urgently."

He was helping an old lady to pack her food into a bag.

"I can't, I'm busy."

"Please, this is important," I pleaded.

He carried on helping. I noticed a police car had pulled up outside the shop and two uniformed officers got out.

I began to panic. "Bod, for Christ's sake, the feds are here, they've come to nick you!"

He stopped what he was doing as the old lady looked at us in bewilderment.

"What are you talking about?" he asked, looking concerned.

"It's Egan, he's grassed you up, mate. They're coming to arrest you now."

He froze as he saw the policemen walking through the door.

"What I am going to do?" he pleaded anxiously.

"There's nothing you can do. But I need you to do me a massive favour; please don't tell them I was involved."

"But you put me up to the job!"

"I know and I'm sorry, but Egan's got me over a barrel. If I get nicked he's threatening to hurt me and my grandad."

We both looked on as the store manager and the two officers were on their way over to where we were talking.

"Shit!" he exclaimed.

"Own up, tell them you did it, but keep my name out of it, please, I'm begging you."

"You always walk away from stuff."

"Please, Bod. I'm on my knees here. I'll make it up to you."

I turned and walked out of the store. I stood by the window as the three men approached him. The customers, realising there was some drama on offer, started to gather. One of the police officers began talking to Bod and I guessed he was being read his rights. I watched as he was handcuffed and led out of the store. I concealed myself from view as they pushed his head down and he took his seat in the back of the car.

Poor Bod. His only crime was being stupid enough to enter my world. Even if he did drag me into it, he would be convicted, and worse still, he would become a hated figure around Leicester. The man who stole from a charity shop; the fella who cold-heartedly nicked the clothes that Tom Needham had so generously donated.

He'd lose his job, be disowned by his friends, maybe even his family and forever have a criminal record excluding him from a host of future opportunities.

The next five years of his life will be ruined and I would have to accept the lion's share of the blame.

I could only pray he remained strong, loyal and didn't turn me in, because if he did, I would get all of this punishment and a whole lot more.

CHAPTER 8

I had endured a difficult night's sleep. When I did finally manage to nod off the demons revisited; the same uninvited tormentors encouraging me to wake up startled and scared.

I was instantly regretting the text message I had just sent. I should have learnt that if ever there's an element of doubt as to the appropriateness of a message, then the very fact you are considering this is *exactly* the reason why you shouldn't send it.

On this occasion, I was trying to establish whether Nails was okay following his beating, only I couldn't bring myself to simply ask him because that wouldn't be macho enough. Instead, I sent him:

Rock-hard Nails from Leicester v middle-aged over the hill Irishman – who would win?

It was in bad taste and I doubted he would reply. My next text message was to Bod, whom I was more concerned about. Was he still at the police station? Had he been formally charged?

Are you okay mate?

It was the only thing I could think to send, even though I had to acknowledge it was a mindlessly ludicrous question. Again, I doubted he would respond.

As I opened the YouTube app on my phone, it beeped, indicating a message had been received. Had one of them messaged back?

Be ready at 9.36 a.m. outside of your house. I will pick you up.
Egan

Shit! He was immediately on my case. *It* had started.

9.36 a.m. – he was trying to catch me out again. I checked my phone: 8.48 a.m. – plenty of time to get ready. What did he have in store for me? Was this to be my first venture into the intimidating and perilous world of dealing drugs?

I was small-time, a little fish, a back number. I received stolen goods and sold them on. Even if I was to ever get caught by the feds then I'd received a caution at worst. I was now entering an altogether different arena, and from what Egan had described the threat wasn't skag heads like Candy and Death Row. He was doing business with the actual dealers and I got the distinct impression these geezers were naughty.

I slowly started to get ready, having planned to go downstairs, make Grandad his mandatory cup of tea and then leave the house at 9.35 a.m. ready for Egan's pick-up. No, hang on! I can leave the house at 9.25 a.m. and when he arrives I will be waiting for him. Wow! I might have taught myself lesson one in the art of time management.

I'd made Grandad his drink and took it through to the lounge. He was watching the television and tackling the newspaper crossword at the same time.

"Morning, Grandad. Here you go, you'll enjoy this one," I said, placing the mug on the little table beside him.

"Morning, son, thank you. That's a lovely cup of tea."

Bless him, he never fails to thank or show appreciation for anything anyone does for him.

"What have you got on today?" he asked.

"Egan's picking me at nine-thirty, well, let's say just after," I replied. "We've got a story to follow up, but I'm not sure what it is."

I noted the manufacture of this story would be something for me to work on between now and my return home, as no doubt Grandad would want to know the details.

"How's the job going?" he enquired.

"Yeah, it's certainly different."

"Do you think you're going to take to journalism?"

"I'm not sure at the minute, let's see how it goes."

I'm not a betting man, but should Grandad like to offer me odds that journalism *doesn't* become my full-time occupation, then I would be prepared to punt a substantial amount of money.

I waited outside, and sure enough, shortly after 9.35 a.m. a new black Volvo drove slowly down the road and pulled in. It wasn't exactly the car I was expecting Egan to drive. I would have thought a BMW or maybe a Mercedes would have better suited him given his occupation. However, within seconds of sitting in the car, it suddenly slotted into place. It was understated and classy. This fella wasn't about being flash; he didn't have to be; he let his natural charm do the talking. As ever, he was immaculately turned out and I received a whiff of distinctive expensive-smelling aftershave as he shifted in his seat to greet me.

"On time – maybe you are making progress," he noted.

"I was early, I've been waiting outside for ten minutes."

"I like your style – that's your timekeeping, not your clothes. What on earth are you wearing?"

I looked down at myself – hoodie, jeans, trainers. I wasn't going to win any GQ awards, but I had seen worse. "Why, what's up with them?"

"Nothing I suppose, but we need to get you kitted out. I can't have my business associate walking around like he's about to attend youth club. Let's get you some new clothes, I need you looking the part."

"But I haven't got any money."

"I'll take care of it and then take it out of your wages."

"I didn't think you were paying me any wages?" I optimistically asked.

"I'm not. You'll get used to my sense of humour soon enough."

"Let's hope so," I responded, realising my error.

"Clothes, Robbie, they are especially important to a person. They communicate instantly to whoever you are dealing with exactly what you are about, and it doesn't much matter if it's business, finance, IT or a low-life drug dealer like me. A poorly ironed shirt, a scruffy pair of shoes, a tie that isn't knotted properly; if I see it then I know I'm dealing with an amateur.

"My father used to tell me that unless I had a meeting with Giorgio Armani I should strive to be the best-dressed person in the room. Even in this line of work I need people to know I'm serious, worthy of respect and that I won't take any grief from anyone. That's the image I want you to portray, but not like a fashion model or a David Beckham wannabe, rather someone who takes themselves and their business seriously. Do you understand?"

"Yes."

"Never go over the top on labels, but always buy quality. A green sweatshirt with 'Gucci' emblazoned over the front might appear a good idea, but it isn't. It's for classless footballers with more money than sense. Don't go wasting your money in Primark either. The cut of the fabric is poor and the quality of the material non-existent. After a couple of washes, it's ready for the bin. Invest in clothes, be prepared to pay a bit more and then look after them. I own a coat which I paid two thousand pounds for when I bought it twenty years ago and it still looks brand new. Therefore, the current cost of the coat is a hundred quid a year and it's going down by the day. A hundred quid a year – that's two pounds a week. Do you see what I'm getting at?"

"Yeah."

"Start to take yourself seriously and then maybe other people will. Always maximise your chances of success by getting those things right that are within your control. The stuff that's not, well, never lose a second's sleep about them because you won't see them coming anyway."

"I know all about that," I replied.

He entered the multi-storey NCP and parked up. We made the short walk to Leicester's main shopping centre and I followed him into Hugo Boss. Egan, ever-confident, strode up to the counter where a young, keen assistant manager was standing. "Good morning, gentlemen," he announced.

"Good morning. Do you have a pen and paper to hand?" Egan requested.

He bent down under the counter mumbling something to himself before producing the items, which he attempted to hand to Egan.

"Could you write the following down, please?" Egan requested.

"Yes, sir, of course."

"One coat; one jacket; two shirts; two pairs of jeans, one of which should be denim, one black or navy blue; a jumper and a pair of shoes."

Egan waited for him to finish writing.

"Do you have it all?" Egan enquired.

The assistant manager repeated the list back to him.

"I want you to kit this young man out, please. Make sure every item is accounted for, " he commanded before he turned to me. "Text me when you've finished then I'll return and settle up. See you both shortly."

As confidently as he entered the premises was as boldly as he exited. He was charismatic and charming, but at the same time demanding and forthright.

I set about purchasing the items Egan had dictated to the assistant. I wasn't sure about his budget, but I was guessing a man like him wasn't overly concerned with the cost of things.

I remembered what he'd advised and avoided items with large brand names. I kept it simple, but stylish. Everything fitted nicely;

the cut of the fabric was sharp and the quality of the material was superb.

I didn't take long to decide which items to buy and they were gradually being piled up on the counter. The assistant had offered to bag them up, but I thought Egan may wish to cast his eye over them.

Upon choosing the last item I sent him a text message and he shortly returned to the shop. "I wanted to show you what I had brought," I beamed.

He gazed over the pile of clothes. "Is it in keeping with what we discussed?"

"Yes, I think so."

"Then I trust your judgement. Could you choose what you'd like to be wearing now."

"Sorry?"

"Which outfit you would like change into – could you decide then ask this nice young man to snip the labels off? I don't want to have to spend another second with you dressed like an overseas student."

I went through the garments and selected my preferred attire before returning to the changing rooms. When I walked out I could see a faint smile on Egan's face. "That's what I'm talking about. How do you think he looks?" Egan asked the assistant.

"Very smart, sir," he replied.

I couldn't hide my smile.

"Could I trouble you to put his clothes in the bag? I'm guessing he'll feel compelled to wear them again."

The assistant began swiping the bar codes through the till. I watched as it soared in eye-watering increments. £550, £766, £1,010 and still it rose. "One thousand, three hundred and forty pounds to pay, please."

"I assume you're going to apply a discount?" Egan enquired.

"We don't normally apply discounts," came the reply.

"You don't normally apply discounts on single-item purchases, but I'm pretty sure you can do something on what I'm intending to buy here."

"Let me get the manager."

Within a couple of minutes, the store manager appeared. "Good morning, sir. We could provide you with a ten per cent discount on a purchase of this quantity," he suggested.

"I think you can do better than this," Egan countered.

"Ten per cent is the best we can do, I'm sorry."

"When we arrived this morning, there was nobody in the shop. When I returned, there's still nobody here, except young Robbie. I'm guessing your average midweek shopper isn't prepared to spend over a thousand pounds on clothes. So, here's where we are: you'll either give me a fifteen per cent discount or I'll take my money and keep shopping until someone does, and trust me, they will."

The store manager took a breath. "Yes, no problem. We'll give you a fifteen per cent discount."

He fiddled with the till to correct the figures whilst Egan pulled out a wad of cash, which he began slowly counting before politely and charmingly thanking them both for their time, trouble and consideration.

We left the shop; me with a clutch of bags and wearing a fantastic new outfit and Egan, who was over eleven hundred pounds lighter.

"Come on, it's time for lunch," he said.

We walked into a posh-looking restaurant and took a seat before being presented with menus. "Happy with your new clothes?" he asked.

"Very happy."

"Remember what I said: look after them. Keep those shoes nice and buff. Your grandad will explain how to get them looking like mirrors. Once you've worn a shirt, either hang it back up in the wardrobe or put it in the wash. Never iron it with too much heat and don't, whatever you do, get chilli sauce from your kebab on it."

I smiled at his last comment.

"I have got the first job I'd like you to do," he announced.

Shit! Here we go.

"It's nothing to do with business, it's relating to Ethel," he added.

"Sure, what is it?"

"She meets a male friend of hers twice a week at bingo. She's described this gentleman as a bit of a loner; he doesn't mix well, a tad socially awkward, that kind of thing. Anyway, Mum being Mum made it her business to get to know him and they've become friends. By all accounts talking to my mother is pretty much the only time this man makes conversation with anyone. He lives alone, doesn't appear to have any family, doesn't get out much – you get the picture. With her being in hospital, she's worried he'll have no one to talk to, so naturally, I agreed to step in and start my very own befriending scheme. Only I'm not the one who's going to do it; you are."

"What do you want me to do?"

"Once a day, I'd like you to call around his house and see if he's alright; make him a cup of tea; have a chat with him, maybe see if he needs anything jobs doing – you get the drift."

"Yeah, no problem."

"Only don't, whatever you do, mention Ethel, him playing bingo or that I put you up to it. She thinks he'll take it the wrong way and he isn't the sort of person who would appreciate being patronised."

"I see what you are saying, but won't it look a bit odd when a total stranger rocks up at his house, bangs on the door and asks him if he would like some company?"

"You're right. But thankfully you already know who he is so the ice has already been broken."

"Who is it?" I asked intrigued.

"It's your next-door neighbour, Tony."

CHAPTER 9

I was still getting over the horror of being told I was to become Moany Tony's new best mate as I was dropped off at home. I changed back into my scruffs and, in the absence of hearing back from Nails or Bod, headed down to the Falcon to see if either had called in. They hadn't.

I supped a couple of pints before wandering home to see Grandad. I'd decided it would be prudent to explain my intention to go around to see Tony, otherwise it might appear a little odd when the old blabbermouth told him I'd started my daily drop-in service and he knew nothing about it.

I made him a brew before taking my place on the settee. "What are you watching?" I asked.

"An interesting documentary about the Suez Canal," he replied. "We properly got our fingers burnt here."

I didn't have the faintest idea where the Suez Canal was, having only discovered it existed three seconds ago, but, for the sake of being polite, I feigned interest.

At a convenient break in the programme, I moved the conversation. "I was thinking about Tony earlier," I commented.

"Tony who?"

"Tony next door."

"Yeah, what about him?"

"Do you ever feel sorry for him?"

"Not really, why?"

"He seems kind of lonely. No one ever visits him and he always has the problems of the world on his shoulders."

"I've never really given it too much thought. He's an odd one, but his heart's in the right place."

"I was wondering whether I should call around now and then to see if he's alright."

"That'd be nice of you." He then averted his gaze from the television towards me. "This is all a bit out of the blue – what's brought this on?"

"It could be you on your own, and if it was, I'd like to think someone might call in to see how you were."

I couldn't have framed it better. Even on my bullshit scale, this was scoring a perfect ten.

"If that's what you think is the right thing to do, then you go for it. Bully for you, you're developing into a good man."

'A good man': those words suddenly resonated with me. Was I 'a good man'? I was a liar, a tax dodger, a person who dragged his gullible friend into a robbery, a fella who thinks it's okay to dupe an old lady who works in a shop which causes her to have a stoke, and a bloke who doesn't think twice about stealing from charities.

A 'good man'? Don't make me laugh! It was time to finally come clean with myself and admit who I was and what I was about; I was a twenty-four-carat shithead, and that pang of sentiment that was rippling through my body was shame.

Any ensuing melancholy was interrupted by a sudden and violent banging at the back door. It was sort of thunderous door-thumping you knew wasn't the precursor to good news. There would be no smiley-faced representative from the EuroMillions, almost certainly not an envoy from Her Majesty announcing Grandad's surprise MBE or an unexpected box of Spam fritters. Oh no, whoever was the other side of our backdoor had a serious beef and, given my current run of form, the clever money was on it being with me.

"Bloody hell, who's that?" Grandad rasped.

"I don't know, but you stay here, I'll go," I said, making my way through to the kitchen.

As I opened the door I was greeted by a teary-eyed, emotional and highly charged Mrs Bodwin, aka Bod's mum. "What have you gone and done!" she bellowed.

"What are you talking about?"

"My son's been arrested for stealing clothes from a charity and I know you're behind this. So, tell me, what have you gone and done?"

I closed the door and took the conversation into the driveway, hopefully out of earshot of Grandad. "I don't know what you are talking about, Mrs Bodwin," I said, desperately trying to buy some time to I collect my thoughts. "What's happened?"

Tears were rolling down her face. "I'm so ashamed. Lee stealing from a charity shop, what was he thinking?"

"Charity shop?"

"Why are you doing this?" she yelled.

"Doing what?"

"Pretending you don't know what I'm talking about. My boy is hardworking and honest; he would have never done anything like this unless someone like you had put him up to it."

"Honestly—"

"I know it was you, Robbie. I've told him hundreds of times that you're bad news, that you'll end up getting him into trouble, and now it's happened."

"But I—"

"He said he did it on his own, but how could he? There would have needed to be at least two people who stole those clothes and I'm certain the other person was you. Mark my words, whilst there's still air left in my body I'm going to prove it!"

"I don't know what to say, I don't know anything about it."

"You'll be sorry. You've ruined my son's life. He's pleaded guilty and he'll lose his job and it was all because you dragged him into it. You bastard! I hope you're proud of yourself."

"I don't know what to say," I repeated, shaking my head.

"Say nothing because no one believes a word that comes out of your lying, filthy mouth anyway. Now go back in and tell your grandad what's happened. Only you won't, will you? But don't worry, once I get the evidence your grandad and the whole of fucking Leicester will know what a scumbag you are."

She turned around and walked dejectedly down the driveway.

Fucking hell, just when I thought things couldn't get any worse! I needed to decide whether to turn myself into the feds. It appeared the right thing to do. If I did then it might take some of the heat off Bod. I could explain it was my plan and how I coerced him into doing it. But then I had Egan to contend with. He had categorically told me I needed to stay away from the police and out of trouble whilst Ethel was in hospital.

I closed the door and slowly trudged back into the lounge. My shame counter had gone up another a couple of notches and I couldn't even look at Grandad.

"What was that about?" he questioned.

"Erm, it was Bod's mum," I answered in a hushed voice.

"What did she want?"

"She's, erm, she's really upset."

"What about?"

"He's gone and stolen some stuff and been arrested."

"Why is she coming around here?"

"She seems to think I was involved."

"And were you?"

"No, no, of course not."

"What made her think you might be?"

"I don't know, that's the thing. He's pleaded guilty to the police; I suppose she's looking for someone to blame."

"And she's blaming you?"

"Yes."

"Why?"

"I don't know, Grandad. She's upset and acting a bit mad."

"But there must be a reason why she came around here."

"As I say, I don't know," I said with my eyes fixed on the television, desperately avoiding eye contact with him.

"If you've done something you want to talk to me about then now would be a good time," he said.

"Yeah, it would be, but I haven't so I don't need to."

"You swear?"

"Yeah, yeah, I swear."

More bullshit! Utter barefaced fucking bollocks. I had lied so many times that it shouldn't even register yet, for some reason, it seemed to matter more than ever.

Bod's mum on my case; being at the beck and call of a violent drug dealer; Grandad smelling a rat; and having no friends left to fall back on. It felt like the noose around my neck was slowly but surely choking me.

I pulled my quilt a little tighter as I opened my eyes. The amount of light in my bedroom suggested it was still early morning. I noticed the bedroom door I always close before I went to sleep was open. My head slowly moved around until I could see him sitting on the edge of my bed.

"Fucking hell!" I yelped.

He put his forefinger to his mouth and spoke very quietly and slowly.

"Keep your voice down; I don't want to wake your grandad."

"What are you doing here? How the fuck did you get in?" I whispered.

"How does anyone get into a place that's locked when they don't have a key?"

"What do you want?"

"Remind me what we agreed yesterday – what was the job I gave you to do?"

"To call around to see Tony."

"And what did I say about the regularity of these visits?"

"Every day."

"'Every day'," he repeated. "So why didn't you call around yesterday?"

"I was going to start today."

"You were *going* to start today. Why did you think that would be acceptable?"

"Because, because, you didn't say when to start so I thought today would be alright."

"You thought it would be alright?"

"Look, I'm sorry. I'll go around this morning."

"And will this be before or after you've hung up the shirt I bought you yesterday?" He pointed to where I'd removed the shirt last night and left it draped over a chair, half hanging onto the floor.

"Shit! I'm sorry."

"You're sorry – for which part? The visit to Tony's we'd agreed you were to undertake but didn't or the eighty-pound shirt I expressly told you to either put in the washing basket or hang up in your wardrobe?"

"For both."

"'For both'," he repeated whilst slowly shaking his head. "Two things I requested that you do and you've managed to do neither. Is this the way it's going to be?"

"No, I won't let you down again, I promise."

"You promise? But you're a proven liar, someone with a track record of telling untruths even to the person you claim to care about the most. So why would I, a relative stranger, believe for one minute you have suddenly started to tell the truth?"

"I'll prove it to you; I'll do what you ask."

"You know how this works: the last time you messed up poor little Bod ended up in a police cell."

"They charged him and he's pleaded guilty," I said, desperately trying to move some of the heat away from my own shortcomings.

"Good for him."

"I had his mum around here last night on my doorstep in tears. She's demanding I put my hands up to being the man with the plan."

"What did you say to her?"

"Nothing."

"Smart move."

"I'm thinking about going to the feds."

"And telling them what?" he queried sternly.

"That I dragged Bod into it, that it wasn't his fault and I should take the rap."

Egan then grabbed me around the neck.

"You'll do no such thing! You work for me now, do you hear? If I find out you've handed yourself in to the police then, trust me, any punishment they have in store for you will feel like a day out at Alton Towers compared with what I'll do."

I was gagging for breath, trying to remove his hands, but he had an iron grip and his thumbs were heavily bearing down on my windpipe.

"And let your little friend and his mum know that should he decide to give you up then you'll plead not guilty. We'll let the matter roll on to the courts, then shortly before the trial date, the prosecution's main witness, that's Bod to you and me, will mysteriously disappear. At his funeral, you can say sorry to his mum and explain to her that it should be you being buried and not him."

He released his hands from my neck as I gagged for air.

"There are three things you will do today: firstly, sort these clothes out and tidy up your bedroom; it's a disgrace. Secondly, get yourself around Tony's; and thirdly, be at my club at six o'clock sharp."

I sat up in bed examining my Adam's apple for damage.

"When I was a boy living in Belfast, I didn't like the water. Try as I might, I just couldn't learn how to swim. My dad brought me water wings, a life vest, a rubber ring and God knows what, and still I couldn't get the hang of it. On one Saturday, rather than go to the swimming pool in the afternoon, as we always did, he took me first thing in the morning. When we changed I knew something was amiss because he didn't inflate my rubber ring. Instead, he held my hand and we walked past the kid's paddling area until we arrived at the deep end of the big scary pool. I remember looking in awe at the twelve feet sign. That's quite a depth when you're a toddler.

"My dad then very casually picked me up, took me to the side of the pool and threw me in. I panicked like hell; my arms were flailing all over the place whilst I desperately searched for the bar on the side. I was a terrified little boy who thought he was going to drown; thrown into the pool by the one person who I trusted with my life. Eventually, I made it to the side, coughing up water and shaking with fear. He pulled me from the pool and, without saying a word, then threw me back in again. And so it went on until I stopped being scared and I learned how to cope.

"Tonight, I'm going to throw you in the deep end. Only this pool is infested with sharks and they're unpredictable and very aggressive. If you're lucky, I might be able to pull you out before they bite; but if not, well, I'm not sure what'll happen to you."

He then edged closer to me. "It's up to you: you can either start to do what I tell you or you can ignore me and I'll watch you eventually sink to the bottom. It's your choice and I'm not too bothered either way."

He then stood up, but rather than leave he removed my shirt from the chair, and carefully and neatly folded it up before placing it back down.

"Six o'clock sharp at my place, and don't bother to bring your water wings."

I lay in bed feeling shocked about Egan's surprise visit. I was worried, very worried. In Egan's world, whatever it meant to be thrown in at the deep end was going to be dangerous and potentially life-threatening.

I got up and put away the shirt and generally had a tidy-up. He was right: my bedroom was a disgrace with socks and pants all over the floor, trainers littered everywhere and my bedside table covered in soiled plates, empty crisp packets and cans of pop. I went downstairs and grabbed a bin liner before dumping all the rubbish in it. Strangely, within only a few minutes, the place was starting to look reasonably tidy again.

I disposed of the bin liner and made Grandad a cup of tea. I could hear him walking downstairs. I watched as he stopped three steps before the bottom panting for air and hanging on to the bannister. I ran over to him and wrapped his arm over my shoulder.

"It's okay, I've got you." I took his weight and slowly moved him to the lounge and into his chair.

"Are you alright?" I asked.

His mouth was wide open as he gasped for air. He nodded and then grimaced. Poor thing, he was suffering. I put the television on and sat holding his hand.

"I'm glad Grandma isn't here to see me in this state," he whispered.

"She wouldn't have minded."

"I know, but I would."

He was a proud man. We sat in silence and watched the news. When it moved on to the weather I made him another cup of tea and then psyched myself up to make my first trip to see Tony.

I went around to his house and knocked on the door. It was quickly answered and in my most jovial voice, I greeted him. "Hi, Tony, how are you today?"

He looked at me, bemused. "Yeah, fine."

"Right, good. Erm, I was wondering if you needed anything doing."

"Like what?"

"I don't know – perhaps you want a cup of tea making?"

"I've just had one."

"Are there any jobs you'd like me to do?"

"Like what?"

"You know, stuff you might be struggling with."

"Like what?"

Fucking hell! I generally can't shut this fella up for love nor money, but at the one moment I need him to open up he starts to act like I've read him his rights. At this rate, he'll be answering my next question with 'no comment'.

"Is there any chance I can come in and we can have a chat?" I asked.

"I'm off out to the shops in a minute; could you come back another time?"

"Yeah, sure. What about tomorrow, say about ten in the morning?"

"Okay, if you want."

"Great! See you tomorrow then."

I turned and walked down the driveway. For some bizarre reason, Tony was acting coy, a little like a man who had received a visit from a neighbour who generally can't wait to get away from him and now suddenly wants to become his best friend.

Still, I'd carried out the required visit and set up another meeting for tomorrow. Should Egan quiz me about this later then the box had been ticked and my objective completed.

I'd received a text message from Death Row. Given my concern for this man's well-being after our last meeting, I was quietly pleased to hear from him. Perhaps he'd turned his back on the life of an addict and used the thirty pounds I'd given him for Henry the vacuum cleaner to kick-start a rigorous detox programme. Sadly, from the content of his blunt text message, this didn't appear the case. He'd come into possession of five bottles of decent malt whisky and wanted to offload them for forty quid. He knew full well he'd get no more than a score but, like me, he was only playing the game.

I liked buying booze because I had various pub landlords I could quickly sell it on to. In this instance, a swift text message exchange with 'Langy the landlord', the geezer who runs the Knighton Suite bar, confirmed he would take them off me for fifty quid. This should be a quick thirty pounds' profit, which would be a double measure of welcome relief served with ice and a slice given my recent trading distractions.

Inexplicably, the DR had held out for £22 despite my stern warnings that I wasn't keen on anything less than five-pound increments. He was adamant about £22 as if the Chancellor had brought in a new Death Row Add Tax (DRAT?) and that all of his transactions were now subject to a ten per cent surcharge. Still, Langy was good to his word so by the close of trading I'd made a few quid.

As soon as I left the Knighton Suite a stomach-churning fear had started. What was Egan going to have me do that was so bad that even he had warned me to fear the worst?

I was back in my bedroom nervously changing into a Hugo Boss outfit. The uncertainty surrounding this evening was making me restless and irritable. My mind cast back to when Dad would arrive home at night. If he was sober then everything would be fine, but should he be drunk then the evening would wear an altogether different and more volatile mask.

As the front door opened, marking his return home from work, the atmosphere would become tense and hang precariously in the balance. The mere sound of a stagger or a slur and I knew domestic violence would most likely prevail.

I now had a similar sensation. The feeling of being out of control and at someone else's mercy. I was starting to feel nauseous and dry-mouthed. I sat on my bed and took deep breaths. It was going to be alright, I told myself. I'm going to get through this.

It was time to leave. I apprehensively walked downstairs and left without saying goodbye to Grandad. I didn't want him to see the fear in my eyes. I'd decided to walk to Egan's club. Being on the move was better than sitting on a bus or making banal conversation with a taxi driver. I arrived fifteen minutes early and yet again the main door was partially ajar. He was waiting for me like I knew he would – forever one step in front and always pulling the strings.

As I walked in the lights were on and he was sitting at the bar with a glass of Scotch. "Come and join me," he greeted, looking relaxed, but never making eye contact.

I walked over and he handed me a drink. There was no way I was going to decline. If ever I needed some Dutch courage it was now. I pulled up a stool, took a large mouthful of whisky, then another.

"Listen carefully because everything I'm going to tell you is of such importance it may save your life."

Not a great start. I nodded nervously back to him. I was a gibbering wreck and there was no point in trying to hide it.

"Are you okay?" he asked.

"Not really."

"Nervous?"

"You could say that."

"More nervous than when you and your friend stole the clothes from the charity shop?"

I shook my head – back to this, again. He'll never let it lie.

"I'm going to take that as more nervous," he said before he leaned forward on his stool and lowered his voice. "If it's any consolation, when I kept getting thrown in at the deep end, I eventually learned to swim."

I looked at him with contempt.

"I was contacted three days ago by a business associate of mine from Birmingham who's selling heroin. Nothing unusual about that, of course, except in this instance, for no discernible reason, he wanted about twenty-five per cent less than its usual market value. Whilst this isn't a trade known for its charity, I agreed to buy it in case this turns out to be the sale of the century. For insurance, I decided to find out whether there was a rat that needed to be sniffed."

He stopped and took a large swig of his Scotch before turning and pouring himself another generous measure.

"Fentanyl – have you ever heard of it?" he asked.

"No," I replied.

"I'm sure you're aware that when your friends on the street use heroin it's not pure. It's mixed with all manner of substances to make the product go further whilst it's still safe to ingest. However, drug dealers aren't always the smartest people in the world and they certainly aren't great chemists. It turns out there is a bad batch of heroin being sold in the West Midlands and it's been mixed with Fentanyl. Fentanyl is an opiate narcotic, which, when mixed with heroin, becomes lethal if injected. There are six people dead already. Of course, it's a real shame when someone acquires a three hundred pound-a-day heroin addiction, but it's sure great for business. I don't want dead customers in Leicester; I want them alive and buying. Are you following?"

"Yes," I replied, hanging on his every word and waiting for the punchline to be delivered.

"At about seven-thirty this evening a fella is coming over from Birmingham with half a kilo of this gear and he thinks he's going home with thirty-five large, only he's going to be disappointed because I'm not buying it. I'm reasonably sure he's trying to flog it cheap because it's contaminated. He's trying to take me for a mug and I'm not having it. When he arrives this evening, he'll have had a wasted trip because the bad news for him is the deal's off."

He sat smiling at me.

"Okay, what do you want me to do?" I enquired.

"You're the who's going to tell him the bad news."

"What!"

"I'm off to visit my mum. I'm going to take her some flowers, a nice box of chocolates and a bottle of her favourite lime cordial. She loves it for some reason."

"I can't do this; I'll get fucking killed!" I declared.

"Have you tried it?" he asked.

"Tried what?"

"The lime cordial."

"What lime cordial?" I queried, incredulously.

"Roses lime cordial. It's horrible, sweet sickly stuff. If it's ever offered to you, decline it."

"What are you talking about?" I replied, shrugging my shoulders.

"Corey is the dealer's name. He will be meeting you here. He's visited before so he knows where it is. He'll walk straight in and will no doubt be slightly pissed off that I'm not around, but not to worry, you tell him, I'm away on urgent business and you're deputising. Explain, very politely, that you're *terribly* sorry, but he can go fuck himself because Egan doesn't buy contaminated drugs."

"What if he doesn't take no for an answer?"

"He has to. Unless you've brought thirty-five grand with you and want to buy it?"

"What's he going to do to me?" I trembled.

"Well, if I'm going to be honest, I'm not entirely sure. He might give you a kiss on the cheek and leave or he may get annoyed and do something silly. Unfortunately, Corey can be a tad unpredictable."

"Come on, Egan, I'm totally out of my depth here!" I whimpered nervously.

"More than twelve feet out of your depth? Yes, that's the idea, and you can't say you weren't warned. Still, some people need to learn the hard way as it's sometimes the only method to get through to them. Once they've cleared off you wait around for me to come back and we'll have a drink and debrief. Unless, of course, he's decided to kidnap you or something equally as horrible."

"Egan, please, this guy's going to hurt me, you know he is." I was getting desperate.

"Robbie, whatever happens, don't think about running away because I'll find you, that's what I do. You won't believe who I've tracked down today."

"I won't be running anywhere; I've nowhere to go to anyway."

"That's the spirit! You grit your teeth and be a brave little soldier, and with a bit of luck you'll get through this."

He stood up, straightened his jacket and finished his drink. "And don't you let those naughty boys from Birmingham push you around – you make sure you give them as good as you get," he added patronisingly.

As he walked towards the door he stopped and turned around. "Hey, Robbie," he smiled and winked at me, "I bet you wish you had hung that shirt up in the wardrobe now?"

I checked my phone: 7.38 p.m. and there was still no sign of our visitors. Egan had left over an hour ago and I'd had plenty of time to get the script straight in my head, drink some more Scotch and somehow become even more nervous.

I was evaluating the likely outcomes when I heard the faint blast of a car stereo which was gradually getting closer. The bass became thunderous as it stopped right outside the club and then silence before a car door was slammed, then another, then another. Shit! There must be at least three of them. Through the partially open club door, I could make out the movement of figures and hear murmurings.

The door opened and in walked a heavily built black man in his late twenties wrapped in a long leather jacket. His face was mean with a scowl. Two other men walked in behind him, both white: one was menacingly covered in tattoos; the other was seriously built, his tight sweatshirt showing off the curve of heavily pumped muscles.

The black fella looked over to me.

"Alright, bro, is Egan about?" he enquired in a thick Brummie accent.

"He's had to leave urgently on family business. Are you Corey?"

"Who are you?" he replied suspiciously.

"I'm Robbie, I work for Egan."

"How long's he going to be?" he hissed, his scowl becoming ever more threatening.

"He's not going to be here this evening, I'm afraid."

"I assume you're fucking joking, bro?"

"Look, I'm only the messenger here, but Egan told me to tell you that he doesn't want to buy the gear."

"You what!" he answered staring at me menacingly.

"He says he thinks it's a bad batch or something. I'm not sure, but he doesn't want to buy it."

"Are you pulling my fucking chain? Because to be honest, I'm not a man who enjoys practical jokes."

"It's no joke. I'm sorry you've had a wasted trip, but he doesn't want to buy it."

"Fuck this!" he said, looking seriously pissed off. He reached into his pocket and pulled out his mobile phone, fiddled around with it and then put it to his ear. "His phone's turned off!" he shouted. "Now, who turns their fucking phone off when they've set up a deal? Is this geezer having a fucking laugh or what? Now I want you to tell me exactly where he is."

"I don't know. He called me over here, told me you were coming and what I was going to have to say to you and then cleared off."

"You said it was family business – what do you mean by that?"

"I think he said something about his mum not being very well."

"Did you hear that, boys?" he said, turning to look at the other two men. "Egan can't be with us because his mamma is ill!" The three of them started to laugh. "Instead, he left his apprentice to give us the bad news rather than give it to us himself," Corey added.

"As I said, I'm just a messenger."

"I know what you said; I'm not fucking deaf," Corey snarled, raising the aggression a couple of notches.

"Sorry."

"What exactly did he say about the gear?"

"That it was mixed with some chemical, which I can't remember the name of and when someone takes it they die."

"Fucking hell, he's been watching too much *Holby City*! Did he say which chemical?"

"He did, he knew all about it, but I've forgotten."

"We've got a messenger boy here who can't remember the fucking message! What fucking use are you?"

"I'm sorry."

"Answer the question, will you: what fucking use are you?"

He slowly started to walk towards me, and as he did I could begin to see a trail of scars across his face. This fella was a truly horrific character.

"Look, I shouldn't be here, I'm sorry, fellas," I said anxiously and running out of things to say.

"Here's the problem I've got: I agreed a deal with Egan and come all the way over from Birmingham and I'm finding myself talking to some fucking kid who looks like he should be serving quarter pounders at McDonald's, only he's telling me the deal's off and that I've wasted my time."

"I'm—"

"Shut the fuck up, bro!" he yelled. "If Egan thinks this gear is bad, then I'll prove to him it's not."

The two geezers grabbed me and I was wrestled to the floor. One of them rolled up the sleeve on my jacket, unbuttoned the cuff on my shirt and rolled this up as well, exposing my forearm.

"When you come around, be sure to tell Egan how good this

shit is. And also tell him if he still wants it, it's now forty large. I've added a little tax to the price to make up for my inconvenience."

He pulled the bag of gear out and produced a syringe and spoon. "Pass me a lighter," he demanded of the other men.

"I haven't done this stuff before; I might overdose," I squealed desperately.

"Don't worry, bro. I'm going rocket you into space with this stuff. It's going to make you feel like Major Tom."

"Please, don't do this."

He then started to cook it up, the heroin bubbling as it was liquefying. One of the other men then started to tap a vein in my arm. As he did, I could see Corey using the syringe to suck up the fluid. I immediately started to panic and, despite acknowledging the hopelessness of the situation, I began to violently wriggle.

"For fuck's sake, I'm begging you. He made me tell you, I had no choice," I screamed.

"Hold still, bro, I don't want to be slashing open no veins," Corey said, as he moved the syringe towards my arm.

"Please, mate, don't! Please!" I shrieked.

"Tell Egan not to fuck me about ever again," he said as the syringe was about to penetrate my body.

"I wouldn't do that if I were you," came the voice.

I looked up and saw Egan standing behind Corey with a gun to his head.

As Corey looked around Egan edged the barrel of the gun to his forehead. He dropped the syringe as the two other men climbed to their feet in a threatening manner.

Egan nonchalantly gazed over to them.

"Don't move, either of you, otherwise the next thing I do after I've blown the top of his brain off is to shoot you both in the balls."

"Easy, bro, I don't want any trouble. I was just making the point that this gear is cool," Corey said.

"I'm not bothered if it's one hundred per cent pure; you aren't getting a dime for it."

"Come on, man! You're here now, let's close the deal."

"You think it's okay to do this to someone who works for me?"

"I was pissed, bro; I'd driven all this way over here for nothing."

"A two-hour drive at most; it's not the end of the world."

"You could have called me and let me know. I've turned down other offers for it."

"You two get yourselves back in the car," Egan commanded to the two men.

They both hesitated. "Go on, back in the car," he repeated.

They slowly walked off, leaving Corey, who still had a gun in his face, in the club. I got to my feet and brushed myself down.

"You've shown no respect here at all, Corey. This has been poor form."

"Fuck you, Egan!"

"Do you want me to blow your head off?"

"Do what you've got to do, you cocksucker."

"Open your mouth."

"Do I have to repeat myself – fuck you!"

Egan then shot a bullet over the top of Corey's head. The sound of it was ear-piercing, and from the look on Corey's face, he knew it was time to comply.

"Last warning. Now open your mouth."

Corey opened his mouth and Egan stuck his gun into it.

"Here's what is going to happen. You are going to get in your car and drive back to Birmingham. I won't tell anyone about this and neither will you. You will never return here; do you hear me? We won't ever do business again. If you want to make a beef about it and come looking for me, then be my guest. If it's a war you want then a war is what you'll get, but you have a chance here to walk away."

Corey stood up as Egan lowered the gun. "Well, I shall go away and have a think about that," he responded with unbelievable arrogance.

"And get that fucking gear out of Leicester. I don't want any of it sold on my patch."

"That's something else I'll think about."

"You do that. Now get out of my club."

Corey trudged slowly out. His pride had taken a bit of a pounding. Perhaps he was already planning his revenge on Egan? Maybe he was also plotting retribution against me?

Egan returned his gun to his belt and poured us both a drink. After he'd passed me a glass he took a large swig. He then held it out, inviting me to clink my glass with his.

"A toast to the deep end," he proposed.

CHAPTER 10

I was lying in bed struggling to breathe; gasping and trembling; desperately trying to feed my lungs with oxygen. The horror of last night had initiated an anxiety attack. I was vividly recalling the fear I'd experienced as I was being held down, watching as the syringe filled up with heroin, the look on Corey's face, my powerlessness and my fear. At that moment I'd been a boy again, watching his father pulverising his defenceless mother, knowing what I wanted to do to intervene but having neither the power nor courage to do it.

I wrapped the quilt tighter for refuge. I wanted to see Grandad. I needed to hear his voice; for him to tell me everything was going to be okay like he did when he took me away from the foster home.

The sudden buzz of my phone signalled a text message. I was desperate for it not to be Egan. I needed some breathing space; to collect my thoughts and gather some perspective.

Can we meet up today?

It was from Bod. I was pleased the silence had been broken. I messaged back and agreed to meet him outside his workplace at lunchtime.

I dressed and went downstairs before joining Grandad in the lounge.

"Are you okay?" he asked.

"Yeah, fine," I replied, struggling to lift my mood.

We sat in silence for what appeared fifteen minutes, maybe more.

"You're quiet, something is bothering you," he commented.

"A bad night's sleep."

"Do you want to talk about it?"

I turned my head away from him as the tears began to roll down my cheeks. I didn't want him to see me crying.

"Hey, come on, mate, don't get upset."

I desperately wanted to tell him what I'd got myself involved with, to admit the lies that I had told and to ask him for his help; to see if he could pull me out of this swamp. "I'm okay," I eventually replied.

"What's bothering you?"

"Just stuff."

"Is it that business with Bod's mum?"

"Kind of."

"I'm guessing you don't want to talk about it?"

"I'd better not."

"Robbie, if you've got yourself into trouble you know you can trust me."

"You're the only person I do trust."

"Something's biting at you, isn't it?"

"It'll be okay," I replied. I was desperate to avoid putting any of this onto a sick man.

"You know where I am if you want to talk about it."

"Thanks."

It was nearly time to call around to see Tony and it was fair to say I was not in the mood. But I knew I had to do it, otherwise Egan would find out and God only knows what the punishment would be this time.

Tony answered his door almost immediately, like he was waiting for me.

"Good morning, Tony, I'm here as agreed."

He once again cast me a suspicious look. "Do you want to come in?" he asked reluctantly.

"Only if you want some company," I replied, half-willing him to say no so I had an excuse to return home.

"Yeah, fine," he said.

I followed him into his lounge.

"Would you like a cup of tea?" he invited.

"Yes, please. Milk, two sugars."

"Take a seat in the lounge," he instructed.

Sky News was on and, as usual, it was all headlines and drama. Tony walked in with my cup of tea, but not one for himself. It was clear this ridiculous, manufactured situation was making us both uncomfortable. Yet I knew there was no early exit strategy here. Egan was not the sort of fella to say, "Well, at least you tried." I had to persevere and make this work.

"What's going on in the world?" I enquired.

"Trouble in North Korea, again," he answered.

"What are they up to?"

"Testing nuclear weapons. I don't know who they think they are. If I were the Americans, I'd carpet bomb the place and send the diggers in to flatten it."

"That's a bit harsh isn't it?"

"Not harsh enough. If someone doesn't act soon we'll regret it. And have you seen their leader? I mean, how can you trust someone with that haircut? It looks like his mum's done it."

"His mum might be a hairdresser."

"A blind hairdresser if she is. It looks like he gets it cut at the same place Adolf Hitler used to go."

"Blimey, that would make the hairdresser pretty old."

I was pleased he had relaxed and we were chatting away.

Next on the agenda was Russia. He didn't like or trust Putin and that soon developed into the entire Soviet population, who he believed 'had never rinsed communism out of their system and would only be happy if they could reconvene queueing up for three hours a day for a loaf of bread'.

We then moved on to Scotland, which he described as a 'bankrupt shit-pit full of alcoholics and drug addicts who should be grateful they are even in the United Kingdom'.

I was finding his diatribes strangely entertaining. Of course, I couldn't counter any of his theories because I don't follow the news, but I liked how he seemed to have a nugget of information on all the world's most powerful nations. Unfortunately, whilst his point of view was never positive, from the powerful negativity he generated dribbled entertainment.

After forty-five minutes or so I brought the curtain down on our chat and explained it was time to leave. Tony followed me to the door to let me out. I turned to him as I was about to depart.

"Is it alright if I come around again tomorrow?"

"Yes, you are most welcome," he said with an enthusiastic grin.

"Do you want to arrange a time?" I asked.

"No. Call around when you want, I'll be in all day."

"Okay. See you tomorrow."

"I'll look forward to it."

I took a slow walk into town, grabbed two Greggs sausage rolls and hung around the shops before it was time to meet Bod.

"Alright, mate, do you fancy a pint?" I proposed when he arrived.

"Not really," he replied. "I've only half an hour."

We walked around the corner to where it was quiet.

"I pleaded guilty, you know?" he said.

"Yeah, your mum told me."

"My mum!"

Shit! He didn't know I'd seen her.

"Look, mate, she called around my house upset, saying she suspected I was involved."

"I never told her anything."

"I know you didn't. She'd obviously put two and two together."

"You were involved, though."

"I know I was, and if it wasn't for Egan I'd take the entire rap for it, but I can't."

"What's he got you into?"

I suddenly became teary again as my predicament re-surfaced.

"This fucking guy, Bod, he's wrapped me around his finger."

"What do you mean?"

"Trust me, if I get done by the feds for the charity shop gig then I'm not sure if either you or I will live to tell the tale."

"What are you talking about?" he asked looking concerned.

"Your mum was on about dobbing me in to the feds. You can't let that happen."

"But why has Egan got beef with me?" he puzzled anxiously.

"He told me that something bad will happen to you unless I'm kept out of it. Please listen and don't get me involved."

"Why don't you go to the police? Why don't you tell them what he's doing to you and then let them deal with him?"

"Because he's smart and he'll find out and go into hiding. I've seen first-hand what he's capable of, and trust me, it's a long way from the slap he handed out to Nails."

"So, you want me to take all of the blame for this? Wow, thanks, buddy!"

"I haven't got a choice, mate. Are you listening to me?"

"Yes, I'm hearing everything you say. It was a shitty thing we did and I've now got to take all of the blame."

"Once this has blown over, when Egan's gone, I'll make it up to you, I promise."

"I don't want you to," he declared, walking off.

"Bod—"

"I'll take the rap for the charity shop and I'll tell my mum to keep her nose out so you'll be in the clear, mate. That's my end of the deal. Your end is to never contact me again."

"What?"

"You heard me. You're turning your back on me over this – well, I'm turning my back on you forever."

"Bod, don't be like that, we're mates."

"Do you think we are?" he asked.

"Yeah, of course."

He stood there in front of me looking emotional, shaking his head.

"Then this is like the job you used to tell your grandad about" – he angrily jabbed a finger in my direction – "it's just another one of your fucking lies!"

CHAPTER 11

My life used to be a good laugh with practically no hardship and no real pressure. Every day was a series of activities that I wanted to do in an order I wished to do them. Things were changing; the dynamic had exploded and control had been transferred to Egan. I'd become his slave; I was scared of him and afraid of what he was going to force me to do.

I knocked on the door of Tony's house, which was something else he had made me do. Tony once again answered immediately as if he were stood on guard waiting for callers.

"Hello, Robbie, come in."

His greeting was in stark contrast to yesterday. There was warmth in his voice as if he were pleased to see me.

"Morning, are you okay?" I asked.

"I will be once I've had a cup of tea. I assume you'll be joining me?"

"Yes, please."

I stepped into his lounge and took a seat before he came through with a plate of biscuits.

"Milk chocolate digestives; get in there!" I celebrated.

My life had become so miserable that I was applauding any small win.

"You can't beat them, can you?" he added.

He then returned with two mugs of tea. My attention was

drawn to the television. Suffice it to say, Sky News was on.

"What's going on in the world?" I queried, keenly anticipating his take on events. I watched as he revved himself up to tell me. It was like I'd changed the batteries on a Duracell test bunny.

"The NHS – it's on its knees. It's these bloody foreigners coming over here pretending to be on holiday when they only have a few weeks to live and then using our hospitals for operations. It's not right."

"It certainly isn't," I answered, whilst dunking a biscuit. I slowly and carefully removed it from the hot tea. Given my current levels of anxiety, a broken biscuit cascading back into my mug could send me over the edge. The tension was getting too much and I stuck to eating them dry.

The next news item involved the Labour leader who, if I'm going to be honest, I'd never heard of.

"What do you think about this fella?"

"Wanker!"

"Not keen then?" I asked, with a smirk.

"If it were left up to him, I'd be forced to let out my spare bedrooms free of charge to families of refugees. There would be a queue for my bathroom in the morning from here to Syria."

"That's a lot of people. I'm not sure your biscuits would go around them all," I added, before grabbing another handful.

"They encourage people not to work by giving them benefits for this, that and the other. This country was better off before we had a welfare state because people had to work. If you didn't work, you starved to death."

"What about people who can't work because they are ill?" I probed.

"Survival of the fittest – it's the law of nature. I bet you haven't seen an old pigeon waiting to sign on the dole because it's lost one of its wings, have you?"

"I'm pretty sure I haven't, but carry on making your point whilst I try to jog my memory."

"And do you know what happens to them when they do lose a wing?"

"They stop flying?"

"They die. And that's how it should be. If you can't work, then your usefulness is exhausted."

"That's not great news for my grandad."

"He's different because he fought for his country. All military veterans should get a state pension starting the day they aren't able to work."

"What should happen to people who live in countries where there's a war going on – wouldn't you let them in?"

"What happened to the people of this country when there was a war going on back in the 1940s?"

"I'm not sure."

"They stayed put – that's what happened. They rallied behind the war effort. I didn't see my mother trying to hop onto an inflatable raft and paddle out to the Middle East."

"Yeah, I see what you're talking about."

My phone beeped and I excused myself as I removed it from my pocket. As I began to read the text message I felt the blood drain from my head and an acute tightening appeared in my chest.

Meet me at the usual place in an hour.
Egan

I walked into his club full of trepidation. He wasn't a man who met anyone for a social drink. He was a doer, an achiever, a go-getter. When he wasn't executing a plan, it was because he was organising the next one. Every step he took was premeditated, exacting and methodical. His life was a game of chess and most of us were little more than his pawns which, at any time, he would be happy to sacrifice.

He sat at the bar and, despite it still being morning, was getting stuck into a tumbler of Scotch.

"Do you want a glass?" he asked.

"No," I replied, feeling uneasy.

"Take a seat. Are you okay after last night?" he enquired, sounding almost concerned.

"Not really."

"You'll get over it, or maybe you won't."

"And you don't care either way, do you?"

"Not really."

"I know you're going to make me do this stuff but eventually I'll fuck up and it might end up costing you."

"Or it might end up costing *you*."

"Yeah, it might."

"So, what are you suggesting?"

"If I'm helping you out whilst you're looking after your mum, there must be other things I can do to take the pressure off you?"

"'Take the pressure off'," he reflected sarcastically.

"Yeah, you know, errands I can run, shit like that."

"Like taking flowers to the hospital?" He stopped talking and started laughing. "We've been down this road, and read my lips very carefully, will you – no deal! You'll do exactly what I say and you'll do it precisely when I tell you to, and the quicker you come to accept this the better."

This fucking geezer! I now hated him with a vengeance.

"What do you want me to do for you this time?" I asked with a sigh and modicum of arrogance.

He immediately turned and slapped me hard in the face, forcing me to jerk backwards.

"You can pay me some fucking respect!" he ranted.

"What the fuck was that about!"

"Let me tell you something: you will learn and you will learn the hard way, and if you don't then this will go on and on, do you hear me? If you don't raise your game soon, you'll find yourself getting dropped into a hole on a building site before twenty tonnes of concrete come crashing down on your head. And when that happens, who's going to make your *poorly* grandad his morning cup of tea then?"

I ignored him, instead choosing to stare at the ground.

"When I decided what I was going to do to you, my fear was I might grow to quite like you and regret putting you through this. There's no chance of that. You walk around all jack the lad, yet when it comes down to it you're nothing."

I was lost for words.

"Now, listen carefully to what I'm going to tell you."

I again ignored him.

"Look at me!" he screamed.

I looked at him. He stared at me before pouring himself another large measure of whisky. I could see that he was quickly regaining his composure, like a machine which had had its re-set button pressed.

"After what happened last night, I'm short of stuff to sell and I've had to move quickly. I've got a consignment of coke coming in later today and I'm selling on five grand's worth to a new buyer on the St Matthews estate, do you know it?"

"Yeah, I know it."

"What's it like?"

"A rough, run-down place, a no-go area unless you're a local."

"Says who?"

"Says anyone who's been there. It's not a safe place to live and certainly not a safe place to visit."

"Oh well, sometimes you have to dip your toe in the bath to find out if the water's too hot."

"What do you mean?"

"Do you know I was thinking the other day that with my mum in the hospital there's one less volunteer in the charity sector. That's not right, is it?"

"I suppose not," I said, wondering why he had changed the

subject and where this conversation was going to next.

"I'm guessing you're not heartless enough to see charities suffer because of what had happened to Ethel. I mean, it's your fault she can't volunteer anymore so it kind of feels like it's all on you."

"Okay, okay, where's this going?"

"I'd like you to start volunteering for a charity organisation to address this shortfall of labour."

"What?"

"There are hundreds of really good places who are desperate for volunteers who can spare a few hours. You're not going to donate a few hours, though – you'll give them sixteen a week."

"Where?"

"Anywhere you like, except Goodwill. I'm not having you working there as it doesn't sit comfortably with me."

"What do you want me to do?"

"Anything. I'm not bothered. You can work in a shop, pick up leaves, shake a collection tin; who gives a toss, but you will be doing something."

"How do I get a charity job?"

"Good God, you kids! You spend all day messing around on the internet and then ask a question like this. Why don't you go home, put your feet up and think about it? I'm sure you'll work it out."

"Okay, I'll have a look."

Oh dear, my answer had irritated him again and I received another very stern expression.

"Yes, you will, and if I were you I'd start searching sooner rather than later."

"Okay, I will."

"I'm going to give you forty-eight hours to find yourself something."

"Two days! How am I going to do that?"

"It's volunteering work, not a proper job. There'll be no interview; you won't have to send in your CV, get dressed up or any of that carry-on, which, let's be honest, is probably just as well."

"I'll try."

He smirked. "'I'll try' – you fucking useless prick, just listen to you."

"I'll try – seriously."

"Yes, you will because I'm now going to make this much more interesting."

"What do you mean?"

"What time is it?" he asked.

I looked at my phone. "Eleven forty-eight."

"Let's meet back here at exactly eleven forty-eight the day after tomorrow, shall we? And when we do, you will either provide me with the details of your new volunteering job or you'll tell me you've tried, but as with most things in your pathetic life, you failed."

"Fine," I responded.

"It goes without saying that if you tell me you have succeeded then I will be checking the details."

"I wouldn't expect anything less."

"Please don't lie to me, because it'll make me very angry."

"You'll only get the truth from now on," I announced.

"Good! Then I look forward to seeing you in exactly forty-eight hours."

He turned his back on me and took his mobile phone out of his pocket, making it abundantly clear that it was time for me to leave.

I slowly walked out of the club.

"Robbie," he shouted, "if you don't achieve your objective, if you come up short like you normally do, then guess who's going to be the friendly new face walking around the St Matthews estate in three days' time selling cocaine?"

I immediately felt under pressure. Forty-eight hours and the clock was ticking. The horror of having to undertake any sort of work, least of all for no money, had been outweighed by the prospect of being forced into a high-risk drug deal on the St Matthews estate.

I had to make sure this scenario didn't happen. It was way too dangerous. If I were to walk around that estate with drugs on me I wouldn't last five minutes. Then I had to consider the angle with the feds. I would look totally out of place and would be ripe to get pulled over. I'd have a large bag of coke on me; it would be the Monopoly equivalent of landing on the 'GO TO JAIL' square. I needed to bag a volunteering gig even if I was forced to beg.

I was walking hurriedly down the street, desperate to get home and get the ball rolling, when I noticed a well-dressed big fella heading in my direction who didn't seem to be taking his eyes off me. I decided to cross over and he did likewise. I turned and walked in the other direction, only to spot another geezer heading me off.

"Excuse me, mate!" one of them shouted.

I stopped. There was no point running. I once again had to confront head-on whatever was coming down the track.

"Yeah, what's up?" I asked as they congregated around me.

"I'm Detective Sergeant Mathew Wood and this is Detective Sergeant Steve Brydges, Leicestershire CID. Can I ask you where you've just come from?"

"The place around the corner," I answered, deliberately vaguely.

"Which place?" asked Brydges.

"The old nightclub, Starlite Express."

"And what were you doing in there?" Wood queried.

"Doing some work for a mate."

"What sort of work?" Wood probed.

"He's doing up the place so I was helping him to clear some old stuff out."

"Who's your mate?" Brydges enquired.

"What's this about?" I asked.

"We're simply asking you a few questions. If you've nothing to hide, then you've nothing to worry about, " replied Wood.

As with a good proportion of the population, I'd watched one too many documentaries on real-life crime in Britain and I had prepared myself for this moment, albeit not under these exact circumstances.

"Well, unless you give me a clue what this is about then I'm afraid I'm not going to answer any more of your questions."

"Were you with a man called Sean Egan?" Brydges asked.

"What if I was?"

"Were you or weren't you?" he quizzed.

"Yeah, so?"

"And he's intending to reopen the nightclub?" Brydges continued.

"You'd better ask him, that's his business."

"Okay, turn around, this is a stop and search on the basis we believe you may be in possession of illegal substances," Wood stated.

"What the fuck! I've just told you what I've been doing."

I was patted down, forced to empty my pockets and show them my mobile phone.

"What's your name, mate?" Wood asked.

"Robbie Howard."

"Robbie, are you being a silly boy?" questioned Brydges.

"What do you mean?"

"How long have you known Egan?" Wood requested.

"A few months," I lied.

"Where did you meet him?" Brydges added.

"In my local boozer. He was having a pint in there one night, we got talking and he asked me if I was interested in some labouring work."

"What do you do for a job?" continued Brydges.

"Nothing, I'm unemployed."

"How long have you been out of work?" he asked.

"A few years."

"A few years – that's interesting. Do you sign on the dole?" Wood asked.

"Look, enough, alright! I've answered your questions, you've searched me, I'm clean; so are you going to charge me with something or not?"

"Charge you with something – why would we want to do that?" asked Wood.

"Because that's what you do."

"Robbie, you seem like a nice young fella to me, so just be careful that you don't fly too close to this particular spider's web, because trust me, Sean Egan is one man you don't want to get tangled up with," Brydges commented.

"Okay, message received and understood. Thank you so much for the warning," I replied sarcastically.

"Do you need a lift home?" asked Wood. "I wouldn't mind taking a look at where you live."

"No, I'm okay, thanks. I got things to do in town."

Brydges put his big hand on my shoulder. "He wasn't asking you."

CHAPTER 12

Great! To compound my problems, I now had a pair of detectives on my case. They knew about Egan, knew about his club, knew about me and him, knew my name and where I lived. At this rate, I could expect a Christmas card from the Leicestershire CID and an invite to their festive knees-up.

I sat in the kitchen dunking a toasted crumpet into my chicken and mushroom Pot Noodle. I looked at my mobile phone: 12.41 p.m. Forty-seven hours left to find a fucking voluntary job.

I put my head in my hands. Forty-seven hours to find something and I didn't have the faintest idea where to start looking. Bloody hell, what was I going to do? Maybe I could offer my services free of charge to the neighbours and go around and tidy up their gardens? Yeah, like Egan would buy that old shit.

Even this bastard crumpet wasn't toasted properly. The pissing thing was cold in the middle! In a rage, I threw it in the bin, only for it to flick the side and lay butter-side down on the floor. For fuck's sake! I couldn't get anything right. I sat with my eyes closed, breathing in this living hell. A few weeks ago, everything was cool, hunky-dory, nice as fucking ninepence – and now this.

If I didn't get this fucking charity gig I'd have to do the drugs deal which meant I'd run the risk of getting nicked, given the Old Bill's sudden interest in me. I wondered what sentence I'd receive for possession of a large bag of coke. I doubt they would buy the 'it's for personal use only' argument. With the likely size of this stash, I had to be thinking years rather than months.

Right, I needed to be positive and to get my shit together because I had the opportunity to avoid the St Matthews drug cartel. All I needed to do was to sort myself out with a sixteen-hour-a-week gig and the bullet would be swerved. I needed some help, though; someone who might be able to point me in the right direction. I reviewed my list of options: Bod and Nails were avoiding me, so they were out. Candy and the DR were probably unfamiliar with the word 'charity' and I can only ever bear to enter Smelly Nelly's hovel if there was a good chance of leaving with some money.

Of course, it was obvious! I needed to tap into the font of all knowledge, the future *Mastermind* champion and would-be British international diplomat. There was indeed one person who could guide me through this predicament.

Within seconds I was knocking on the door of Moany Tony.

"Alright, Tony, I wondered if I could pop in and pick your brains about something?"

For people like Tony, this question is chicken soup to the ego. The chance to impart his knowledge and help someone out, well, it was pretty much what he was put on this planet to do.

"Yes, come in, Robbie."

Things were looking positive. As we sat down, I acknowledged that saying I needed a job in the charity sector within the next forty-seven hours or I'd be forced to carry out a life-threatening drug deal probably wouldn't go down well. I needed an alternative approach:

"Tony, I've been out of work for a while and need to sort my shit out, so I was thinking about doing some charity work."

"If you're looking for a job, check out what Amazon has got available in their warehouse. They can't get enough people, that's why they're having to farm in immigrants."

"I think some sort of charity work might be a bit more up my street."

"But you won't get paid."

"I know, but I need to find my feet in the workplace without having some boss ball-aching me about being late – slacking, talking too much on the job – you know the sort of stuff."

"Okay, I see what you mean."

"The thing is, I don't know where to start looking."

"Have you Googled it?"

"No."

"Come on, follow me, let's see if I can help you."

We walked through to his kitchen to where his laptop was sitting on one of the side units.

"Okay, let's Google 'volunteering Leicester'," he said as he typed it in. "Here you go, Voluntary Action Leicester, they're an organisation who sort all this type of stuff out."

"Sounds promising."

He then went onto their website where the instructions were to enrol my details, which we did. We then searched for opportunities and I was able to register my interest to the relevant organisation who would be in touch with me.

"How long do you think it will take before I hear back from them?" I asked.

"It's the Charity and Volunteering Sector who employ some good people, but they've got a reputation for moving rather slowly."

"What, so it could be quite a few hours?"

"A few hours! No, it could be a few weeks," he declared.

"Oh, fucking hell!" I exclaimed, not able to keep a lid on my emotions. I was in trouble, real trouble.

"What's the rush?" asked Tony.

I puffed my cheeks out. What the hell. I decided I was going to have to tell him at least some of the story so he understood the urgency.

"Imagine for a second I've got something riding on this which is big and important, and I need to get a voluntary job in the next forty-seven hours or I'm in trouble."

"Are you on some weird TV game show?" he enquired with a smile.

"I know how ridiculous it sounds, but I need to bag a charity job like *now* or I'm in deep fucking shit."

"I'm not even going to ask you what you've done or why on earth you need a voluntary job in the next forty-seven hours, but if I were you, I'd spin the wheel."

"What do you mean?"

"There are loads of charity shops in town. I would have a good walk around tomorrow and pop into every one of them and ask them face-to-face if you can get involved."

"Okay, sounds like a plan," I replied, slightly dejected. Cold calling a bunch of charity places involved me being outside of my comfort zone and I wasn't sure I had the confidence for it.

"I'll tell you what, come around here tomorrow at ten o'clock and I'll drive you in and we'll have a walk around together – how does that sound?"

Tony had perceptively noted my lack of confidence and responded accordingly. It was a very generous offer from a man whom I'd previously taken as being a bit of joke when he was proving himself to be anything but. With his offer of support, a dim light was flickering at the end of a dark and, dare I say, dangerous tunnel.

Maybe there was a way out of this after all.

It was exactly ten o'clock in the morning and I was knocking on Tony's front door. I had little over twenty-five hours to land this volunteering gig otherwise I was going to be thrown into the bear pit.

Tony answered with his coat on, car keys in hand and looking like a man on a mission.

As he drove us into town he began a conversation.

"I thought your grandad told me you were working for the *Leicester Mercury*?" he asked.

"Yeah, I am, but it's freelance work, so it's kind of as and when they need me."

"Are you working with Egan?"

"Yeah, that's right. Why, do you know him?" I asked, intrigued.

"We've known each other for a few years, but I wouldn't say I know him well."

"Where do you know him from?"

"From him being around. Do you know, I've not driven into town for ages. Being a pensioner and having a free bus pass means I usually get the number forty-eight. Where do you think I should park?"

"No idea. Is there a car park in the Highcross shopping centre?"

"Let's give it a try," he replied.

Tony parked up and produced a printout from his jacket pocket. On it, he had compiled a list of all the charity shops and associated third sector organisations in the city centre.

"Okay, we've lots of places to hit. I have tried to put them in some sort of order." He ran his finger down the list. "We're at the Highcross, so let's start with Age Concern, which is number eight on the schedule – we'll work down to number sixteen, then we shall do numbers one to seven. How does that sound?"

This fella was all over this in a big way.

"Alright, what we need to do is to put some urgency on this but without spooking anyone, " he continued. "We don't want people to think you're desperate, so I've worked an angle. The story is you're joining the army in six months and between then and now you're looking to gain as much work experience as you can. Ideally, you're looking for somewhere you can start sooner rather than later. If a place gives us the impression they haven't any openings or they have, but there's a long-drawn-out process you need to go through, then we'll park them. We'll only focus on those places who are keen to get volunteers in. Then we'll find out how quickly we can get you something."

"Great."

"I don't mind doing the talking, but at some point, the manager, or whoever is recruiting, may want you to chip in so get ready to turn on the charm."

"Charm is something I can turn on, Tony, don't worry about that."

"If they ask you any specific questions about the army, tell them you'll be doing your basic training first before you hope to join the Armoured Infantry Brigade. They won't know what the hell you are talking about, so they'll buy the story without questioning it."

"The Armoured Brigade?"

"The Armoured Infantry Brigade."

"You seem to know all about it, were you in them?" I asked.

"Do you mean, did I *serve* with them?"

"Yes, sorry."

"No. I was in two Paratrooper regiment."

"Okay," I said, not having any idea what he was talking about. "Did you know my grandad in the army?"

"Not really. I was in Northern Ireland after he had left. Okay, turn right down here, it's on Humberstone Gate."

During the next four hours, we engaged in a very frustrating session. We'd received a bucket load of responses such as: "Can you go to Voluntary Action Leicester, please?" to "We do all of our applications online," or, "You'll need to speak to so and so, but he's not here," and even, "We aren't recruiting any volunteers at the moment."

However, by the end of it, we'd found two hot leads. The British Heart Society had a sign in their window stating they were looking for people to work in their furniture warehouse. I'd left my mobile number with the lady in the shop and was promised their store manager, a fella called Colin Bourne, would ring me. I knew his name was 'Colin Bourne' because Tony insisted I write it down. He also had the lady spell his surname for me. For Tony, it was all about the little details.

The other useful lead was working as a shop assistant in Loros.

The manager, someone called Raj Modhia, would be given my mobile number and I was promised he'd be calling me. We'd been politely warned about Raj's hearing impediment and that it may appear he was shouting down the telephone when he called.

I wasn't as keen on the Loros job or being shouted at by Raj. My preference was the British Heart Society gig. But as I was even less keen on walking around St Matthews with a bag of charlie in my pocket, I needed to keep my mind and options open.

As we were finishing for the day, I received a text message from Death Row, who had come into possession of a decent G-Shock watch. When Tony was in the toilet, I exchanged messages with him and agreed to meet in a back alley in the next fifteen minutes. The joker wanted a hundred quid for the watch when he knew full well he'd be lucky to get a score for it.

When Tony returned I politely declined his offer of a lift home and thanked him profusely for his help, promising to update him on the outcome of the two leads.

I headed off to meet Death Row, and as I turned off the busy streets of Leicester into the little rabbit warrens that network the outer layer of the city centre, I spotted a familiar pair of twiglet legs motoring towards me. From two hundred yards away I could see Candy's head twitching. She was most probably clucking for an injection of heroin and likely to be on a mission to raise the cash for the said illegal drug by involving herself in thievery or some unspeakable act of prostitution.

Upon approach, she still hadn't seen me. I noticed she was rather insanely mouthing words to herself. I'd like to think she was reciting her favoured lines from *Death of a Salesman*, perhaps preparing for a cameo role in a small-budget production. Alas, it was more likely she was re-enacting a drugs-related confrontation with a fellow addict.

"You alright, stranger?" I called out.

She stopped in her tracks. "Hey up, it's Bottom fucking Dollar! What are you up to then?"

"I'm off to DeMontfort University to pose naked for their fine art students."

"You haven't got a tenner you can lend me?" she asked, completely ignoring my response.

"Candy, if I did lend you a tenner, out of spite you'd relocate to the North Pole just to get out of paying me back."

"Hey, I'm honest, I am!"

"Sorry, babes. I do have cash on me but I'm minutes away from opening trade negotiations with the head of the Chamber of Commerce."

"Who the fuck's that?"

"You know him as Death Row."

"You'd better get a fucking move on," she said, "because we've just scored some brown and he was so desperate that he was cooking up behind the church. He'll have shot it by now."

"Bloody hell, the Chamber of Commerce have let their standards slide a bit."

"What the fuck are you talking about?"

"Candy, as ever, it's been an absolute pleasure. You enjoy your skag because you've worked hard to steal the money you needed to buy that gear."

"It was the cheapest bag I've brought in ages," she announced proudly.

"Be sure to post that on Twitter and use the hashtag, Amy Winehouse," I said, as I concluded our rather pleasant chance meet.

I made my way to the arranged meeting point where, predictably, there was no sign of him. Taking Candy's advice, I walked around to the back of the church.

Sure enough, he was slumped against the wall as high as a US drone over Baghdad. The chances of me getting any sense out of him and doing a deal for the watch were now slim. As I approached, I could see his sleeve was rolled up and a syringe hanging from his arm.

"It was the cheapest bag I've brought for ages," Candy had said. Why was it the cheapest bag? Because I'm guessing that the seller wanted to offload it quickly. But why? Because something had been added to the heroin to make it toxic.

Shit!

I bet it was from Corey's batch. Fucking hell, Death Row had probably injected himself with a lethal concoction. I ran over to him and could see he was in a bad way. There was white frothing vomit dripping from his mouth and his eyes had a fixed, lifeless stare.

"Fucking hell, Death Row, talk to me!"

I grabbed his shoulders and shook them; I then slapped his face – nothing.

"Help! Help! Please help me!" I screamed.

There was not a murmur from him. I lay him on his side and thrust my fingers into his mouth, trying to remove vomit from his airway.

"Help! Help!" I yelled.

A man approached. "What's up with him?" he asked, obviously concerned.

"I think he's overdosed."

"Is he breathing?"

"I don't know, I've just arrived."

The man kneeled and place his fingers on his neck, searching for a pulse. I waited and looked on until he turned to me and shook his head.

"I think he's gone," he said.

"Oh, fucking hell!" I screamed. "Candy!"

"What?"

"Candy – she's got the same gear!" I shouted, thinking out loud. "Mate, can you ring an ambulance and stay with him? I need to find Candy. She's about to shoot up the same heroin. It's going to kill her."

"Okay. Yeah, go!" he replied.

I ran at full speed, retracing my tracks whilst trying to work out where she might have gone. There was a hostel nearby for people who were down on their luck so I decided to head down there.

As I approached there was a group of people drinking super-strength lager loitering outside.

"Guys, has anyone seen Candy?"

"Yeah, she's just gone in," replied one of them, pointing to the hostel.

I ran up to the reception desk, where there was a bell. I rang it continuously until some bloke sauntered through from out of the back eating a sandwich.

"Easy with the bell, dude, that's not cool," he announced.

"I need to speak with Candy now, it's urgent!"

"I haven't seen her," he replied, totally disinterested.

"One of the fellas outside said she's just come in."

"She might have done, but as I say, I haven't seen her."

"Mate, look, this could be a life-or-death situation. She's gone twos up on a bag of skag with some geezer who's shot himself up and it's killed him."

"Okay, I'll tell her if she comes down," he replied nonchalantly.

"What do you mean, 'if she comes down'?" I yelled in a rage. "How do you know she's not upstairs shooting it up as we speak?"

"We have fire alarms fitted. The second anyone starts to cook up it'll go off."

"Could you please go up and find out for me?"

"I can't leave the reception unattended."

"Please tell me you're fucking joking?"

"If you're going to use language like that then I'm afraid you're going to have to leave."

"Okay, tell me what room she's in and I'll go and find her."

"I can't let you in unless you're staying here."

This fucking guy – what a total wanker!

I remembered I had her mobile phone number. I quickly called it, but it went straight on to voicemail. This might suggest she'd got herself a new phone. Unfortunately, drug addicts change their mobile phones more often than I change my underpants.

I sent her a text, just in case, telling her not to take the heroin.

I walked outside and stood close to the group who were drinking cans of beer. One of them called out to me.

"Hey, mate, are you looking for Candy?"

"Yeah."

"I think I passed her about five minutes ago heading into town," he said, slurring his words.

"Did she say where she was going?"

"I didn't talk to her."

"Which way was she heading?"

"On to Granby Street."

Granby Street was one of the main roads into the city centre. Fucking hell, she could have gone anywhere and looking for her would be a needle in a haystack stuff. Suddenly my phone rang – Candy!

It was an unknown mobile number – maybe she had changed her phone but had somehow received my text message.

"Hello," I answered.

"Is this Robbie?" a loud voice said.

"Yes, speaking. Is this about Candy?"

"Who?" the voice bellowed.

"Sorry, I thought this was a call about something else."

"It's Raj calling from Loros."

It was the deaf fella who was talking so loudly he could have saved himself a phone call and simply shouted from the window of his office across town.

"Oh yes, thanks for calling me back."

"I understand you called in earlier looking for some volunteering work?" he blasted.

"Yes, that's right."

"I've already filled the post we were looking for, but I will certainly keep your details on file and contact you—"

I ended the call for the sake of my sanity and the health of my eardrums.

Fucking hell!

Should I go back to where Death Row was lying? What was the point? He was dead and there was nothing I could do which would change that. Presumably, his frail body would be collected and taken to the morgue. His next of kin would then be notified. I suspected it would have been quite some time since they'd last received any news of him. I didn't even know his name, where he lived or anything about the poor bloke. I did know he was an alright geezer, and whatever anyone's opinion was on taking drugs, being slumped in a churchyard and suffocating on your own vomit wasn't the last chapter that any human being deserved.

I was checking my phone every two minutes willing there to be a message from Candy, but nothing, nil, nada. I had absolutely no idea how this was going to play out.

One thing was for sure: for Candy to survive she was going to need something which had eluded her during her short and tumultuous life – a big fucking slice of Lady Luck.

CHAPTER 13

It was ten o'clock in the morning and I was once again knocking on Tony's door. Not because I was paying him his mandated visit; rather, he'd become an essential source of support and, dare I say, an unlikely ally.

Tony answered and, detecting my obvious tension, dispensed with the usual pleasantries.

"Have you heard back from Colin or Raj?" he asked, diligently recalling their names.

"I heard back from Raj, who gave me nothing except a perforated eardrum," I replied.

"Nothing from Colin at the British Heart Society?"

This sort of question always irritated me. Why do people need a second layer of confirmation that something hasn't happened? Didn't my first statement cover this and therefore suffice? Chill, Robbie! I needed to remain calm and be respectful. After all, this fella was helping me.

"No." I paused. "Do you think I should ring him?"

"It can't do any harm. Would you like me to call him?"

Tony had once again read my mind. Whilst I strutted around like I had all the confidence in the world, I had a blind spot or blind spots in truth. There were a plethora of activities I felt awkward doing. I was only too aware of this, acutely mindful that my self-belief was only skin deep and what lay beneath were insecurities and fear.

"Yes, please," I replied as we both walked into his lounge.

The clock was ticking and I had under two hours to provide Egan with details of what, where and when I would commence volunteering, otherwise trouble lay ahead.

Tony came in with his mobile phone and a telephone number he had lifted from the internet. I sat and watched as he made the call. Colin was not in, and from the sounds of it the message to phone me back was already on his desk. As the conversation continued, I felt slightly lightheaded. There was an inevitable doom lingering. Tony concluded the call phone and shrugged his shoulders – this was going to go down to the wire.

"Do you want to tell me exactly what this about?" he asked.

I closed my eyes and shook my head. There was no point telling him, and in any event, I was ashamed. How could I tell a man who had given up his time and helped me that this saga had all started with me stealing from a charity shop?

We sat and watched the news in relative silence.

It was approaching eleven o'clock and time to leave. I thanked Tony for his help and walked gloomily to Egan's club.

Maybe the drugs deal had been cancelled? Perhaps he hadn't been able to buy the cocaine? Maybe the buyer had called off? Maybe he had second thoughts about sending a novice to a gig that only a professional should do?

Maybe.

"That's not the look of a man who's succeeded," he said, as I entered the club.

"No, I've failed."

"But did you fail and give it a really good shot or fail because you couldn't be bothered?"

"I tried my best. I spent most of yesterday going around places but it's been tough trying to get anything at short notice."

"Do you have any irons in the fire?"

"Only one," I replied.

"And what's the score with that?"

"I'm awaiting a call back. They are desperate for people and I reckon when the fella gets in touch I'll land something."

"Are you optimistic?"

"Yes, I am."

"What time is it?" he asked.

I looked at my mobile phone, "Eleven forty-five."

"All hope isn't lost. You've got a *full* three minutes remaining. Maybe he'll ring you and save the day," he added sardonically.

I really did fucking hate this wanker. There was no doubt from his body language and speech he was enjoying this.

"Pop your mobile phone on the bar and we can both watch the time tick over. Let's see whether you get a last-minute reprieve."

I snapped. "Why don't you go and fuck yourself, Egan!"

"Good. The first sign you've got some balls, because where you're going later you'll need them."

He leaned forward on his stool and spoke slower and in a deeper voice.

"Now put your fucking phone on the bar."

I snatched my phone from my pocket and slammed it down hard. 11.46.

"Keep your eye on the display – go on, use the power of concentration to will your phone to ring."

Instead, I stared at him. I knew my fate and I wasn't going to start playing mind games with this prick.

"Eleven forty-seven," he announced. "We're into the last minute, and unfortunately, in this game, we don't add injury time."

He continued to stare at the display; meanwhile, I continued to stare at him.

"Tick, tock, tick, tock, tick, tock. Oh look, time's up!" he eventually said.

"Just tell me what you want me to do," I replied, feeling strangely calmer than I had done all morning.

"There's some heat on us at the moment, so it's best we don't meet here later."

"What heat?"

"I've got trouble with the police; they've paid me a visit."

"They stopped me as well when I left here the other day," I explained.

"Maybe that's something in future you might want to tell me about," he responded, sounding annoyed. "Who stopped you?"

"Two plain-clothed feds."

"Was one of them Jem Langley?"

"No."

"He must have just arrived."

"Arrived from where?" I asked.

"Let's assume we've got eyes on us. I will meet you tonight at eight o'clock on Wimbledon Street, which is about five minutes from here. When you arrive keep walking around the block until you see my car. When you do, I will pull in and give you the coke. It'll have an address on it and a contact name. Read the details, then dump the note. I will let the buyer know you'll be with him at eight-thirty. When you leave home tonight, walk, don't get a cab, and when you get close to Wimbledon Street meander around. There are loads of little back streets around there, so if anyone is tailing you, you'll soon realise."

"What if they are?" I asked.

"Get rid of them. Make a few sharp turns, sprint down an alley, jump over a fence – who cares? But leave them behind. If you're running a few minutes late I will wait for you. The police don't know where our rendezvous point is, so provided you lose them then we won't have a problem."

"But once you've given me the coke, I'll have one big fucking problem if I get pulled by them."

"I know, but I've got a fantastic strategy for this scenario."

"What?"

"*Don't* get pulled by them," he said with his familiar smirk. "In terms of the buy, it's five thousand pounds cash. Nothing less. I'm not expecting you to stand there and count it all, but at least count one bundle and work out if the other bundles, when added together, will roughly total five grand."

"Okay," I said, fearing a massive miscalculation and, therefore, a huge fuck-up.

"This is important: only do the deal at the address I give you. If for whatever reason you arrive and get told the venue has changed, then it's no deal and you walk. If they don't have the full five Gs, then it's no deal and you walk; if the buyer isn't there and he's running late and they ask you to hang about, then it's no deal and you walk. That's how I roll and, therefore, that's how you'll play the game as well, okay?"

"Okay."

"Do not under any circumstances ring me. Once you have the gear then responsibility gets passed to you. If events change, then you will decide on the course of action. Your success will be judged on the quality of these decisions. If you can achieve total control under pressure then you'll go a long way in this world. If the deal turns nasty, and I mean *really* nasty, let them have the gear. Make sure you walk away and save your ass but tell them I will come looking for my money, and when I do, someone's feelings will get hurt."

The danger I was likely to face had become a stark reality. I had started to fear the worst.

"If you get tracked by the police then turn a sharp corner and quickly hide the gear somewhere – behind a post box, in a post box, in someone's hedge, on a garage roof, anywhere – and then keep walking. If they don't see where you got rid of the gear then you might be alright. If they catch you after the deal and you have the money on you, hang on to it. When they ask you where you got it from, tell them I gave you it to look after. It sounds odd, but there's not a great deal they can do."

My head was starting to spin. I was bound to fuck this up with all of these variables to process.

"Now for the last bit: when you're on the estate you'll either have a stash of coke or a bag of cash on you which will make you a prime target for the locals. Wear the clothes I brought you, so you'll look reasonably smart. Then I'm going to give you a leather case to carry. If you are lucky, it might appear you've been to a meeting at the community centre."

"What meeting?"

"How would I know! I'm only trying to give you some hope to cling on to," he answered.

Great – even he doesn't fancy my chances.

"You have got a bit of homework to do between now and eight o'clock. I want you to recce the area. I've had a very quick drive around myself and it's an ideal place to lose someone because of all the tight streets. Get it straight in your head, know the terrain, understand how the roads connect up and where your entry and exit points are. Get Google Maps downloaded on your phone and memorise the layout. Then go and have a stroll through the estate. Only once, though; and don't stop and look around, because you'll draw attention to yourself. Take in what's going on, look out for the other dealers, spot where the local lads hang out and have a look for the cut-throughs which aren't on the map. Who knows, you might find something that later tonight saves your bacon."

"What are my chances of pulling this off?"

"Without getting nicked, robbed or beaten up?" he asked.

"Yes."

"Provided you follow my instructions and do your preparation work, then a very good chance. But if you don't, if you go in there ill-prepared and undercooked, then you'll have a serious problem."

"That's encouraging," I replied.

"You had better get yourself off because you've work to do. Don't forget, it's eight o'clock at Wimbledon Street."

As I turned to leave and walked towards the door he shouted over to me.

"Forty-eight hours, Robbie."

"Forty-eight hours, what?"

"From this point, I will give you *another* forty-eight hours to be starting a volunteering job, otherwise you'll be running another little errand for me." He stopped and took a large swig of whisky.

"And let's just say they don't get any easier."

I left the club and headed into town for something to eat. As I walked up the road I saw a man leaning against his car reading a newspaper. It was the sort of thing gangsters do in movies. I knew he would speak to me because this was the world I now lived in. I wasn't disappointed.

"Robbie, do you have a minute?" he asked as he turned to me and folded his paper. He was in his late forties, short brown hair, stocky build and a face that suggested he was probably a bit handy.

"Depends who for?"

"DC Jem Langley from the London Metropolitan police."

"You're a long way from home, aren't you?" I observed.

"When the carp swim in new waters the fishermen have to follow."

"How can I help you?" I asked.

"Take a seat in the car and we can have a chat." He opened the passenger door and I got in.

I could have walked off, but I didn't. Why? Because I was desperate for this nightmare to end and if I were presented with a rock-solid exit plan by the feds, or anyone else for that matter, and I thought it could work then I might be interested.

Langley got in the driver's seat and closed the door.

"DS Wood tells me you claim to be doing some labouring work at the nightclub around the corner which is now owned by a mutual friend of ours, Sean Egan."

"That's right."

"Have you been working there this morning?"

"No."

"Will you be later?"

"Possibly."

"But you don't know?"

"No."

He sighed. "How did you come to meet Egan?"

"As I told the other fed, I met him in a pub. He told me he had bought an old nightclub and he was recruiting labour."

"And when was this meeting?"

"A few weeks ago."

"Has he asked you to do anything besides labouring?"

"No."

"Are you sure about that?" he probed.

"Quite sure. Why, what did you have in mind?"

"What were you doing at the club this morning, if you weren't labouring?"

"Egan wanted me to—"

"Can you stop this right now! I've heard enough and you are starting to make yourself look stupid, which I don't think you are. I work for the Met's Serious and Organised crime unit in central London and I've been tracking Sean Egan for quite some time. He's a Premier League drug dealer – not the biggest, not the nastiest, but he makes several millions of pounds each year. What makes this fella different is the way he operates. Most big drug dealers in the capital are all about being flash, surrounding themselves with muscle, automatic weapons, that sort of thing. Not Sean Egan. He works with two, maybe three associates at any one time. These are highly trained operatives, very loyal, very slick. His operation is watertight; he only buys the best gear and only sells it to selected buyers. If you deviate from the terms of an agreed purchase he will walk away. He can spot us coming a mile off and we think that's because he has at least one high-ranking police official on his payroll. In truth, it's probably a whole network, but I can't prove it. That's the thing, I can't prove anything about him. I don't even think Sean Egan is his real name. I reckon some clever accountant has created him an identity, complete with a driving licence, national insurance number, the whole nine yards. Anyway, he drops on and off my radar at any point depending on what else is going on in London. Then, one day, I think to myself, Egan's gone quiet, I haven't heard his name for a while. When I try to track him down he seems to have disappeared, no one has heard from him, not even his trusted band of associates who have had to start looking for alternative employment. I'll be honest with you, I assumed he was dead, that maybe he'd been involved in a deal that went wrong and he'd bought it off some East European mob boss. Then, out of the blue, what do you know, he rocks up in Leicester and goes and buys an old ramshackle nightclub which he brazenly registers in his name. I'll be honest, this has me scratching my head – I mean, no disrespect, but Leicester? I get him moving in on Manchester or Birmingham, but this place? It's not much more than a dead king being dug up in a car park and a five-thousand-to-one football team, is it? I can't imagine there's a great deal of money to be made here, unless you are going to tell me different?"

"I don't what he's doing here," I replied. "I didn't even know he was from London as he's never mentioned it."

"Okay, answer me this then: do you know if he is starting to deal drugs or not? You can nod or shake your head if you like?"

"I don't know."

"Are you sure?"

I paused. "I don't know."

"Of course you do. I know you know. You know, I know you know. The only thing baffling me is why has he picked you? You're not his type. He never has anyone in his circle unless they are ex-military, probably ex-special forces, and certainly not any one of your age and lack of experience."

"You'll have to ask him when you next see him," I recommended.

"Yeah, I might just do that."

"Can I go now?" I asked.

"You're out of your depth here, aren't you?"

"What do you mean?"

"I can see it in your eyes. You've got yourself involved in something much bigger, far more dangerous than you ever imagined and the lure of earning some money has suddenly come back to bite you on the ass."

"I don't, I can't—"

He put his hand on my shoulder and lowered his voice. "It's okay to be afraid. If you want out of this, I can help you?"

"How?"

"Tell me what he's doing, give me details of a deal he's involved in and we can take him down."

"What, as simple as that?"

"I'll be able to make it happen."

"If it were that easy then why didn't you nick him in London?" I asked.

"Because we didn't get the sniff of an opportunity. Maybe with your help, we can do this."

"What, because I'm weak?"

"Because you're in too deep. Do what I say and I'll nick him and get you out of this before you get yourself hurt."

"You won't because he's too smart. He'll walk away and the next time you'll see me I'll be hanging off the rafters of that fucking nightclub," I said.

"You weren't even on the radar of the local police, so why did you get involved in this, Robbie – was it the money?"

"He made me," I replied. "I'm cornered. I don't think I'm ever going to get out unless I'm in a wooden box."

Langley pulled his wallet out of his pocket and handed me his card.

"If you believe that, if you think this is only going to end one way, then what have you got to lose? My number is on the card. If you want to help me then I can help you. I'm only in Leicester for the next forty-eight hours, then I'm back in London and the reality is, anything Egan does after that is between him and the local plod."

I took his card from him and put it in my pocket. I opened the car door and got out of his vehicle.

"Hey Robbie, mind how you go," he called to me, as I shut the car door.

The smart play was to grab some food and then carry out a reconnaissance of the St Matthews estate, only the conversation with Langley had left me cold.

I needed to get my head straight by talking this through and there was only one person who would be able to assist me – Tony.

I headed around to his house and was sat in his lounge.

"Tony, I need to tell you something, but you have to swear not to mention this to my grandad."

"I think you know you can trust me."

"It's a long story, but because I didn't get the charity job I'm being forced to run, well, let's just call it an *errand*."

"'An errand', that sounds sinister."

"It is."

"Who for? Don't tell me, Egan. What does he want you to do?"

"His business is drugs. I've got to drop a package of coke at a buyer's house and collect five grand."

"Good Lord!"

"That's the good news; the bad news is the drop's on the St Matthews estate."

"Oh dear!" he added in a resigned manner.

"Yeah, I know."

"And when are you planning on doing this?"

"Tonight."

"This is getting worse."

"Tell me about it."

"What time?"

"I'll be rocking up to the estate about quarter past eight."

"Let me get this right, you're going into one of Leicester's poorest estates, under darkness, with five grand's worth of coke on you, at the time when every bad egg and their dog will be coming out to play?"

"I know, but I can't get out of it. Please work with me on this because I *am* doing it, end of. I just need your help with *how* I'm going to do it."

"Okay. What do you need me to do?"

"Egan was talking about making sure I had an entry and exit route planned. I was wondering if you could lend a hand with sorting this out."

"Stay here."

He went into his kitchen and I could hear him foraging. He returned with a map and pen. He beckoned me to the dining table where he laid the map out.

"What's the address of the drop?" he asked.

"He doesn't know yet, he's going to tell me later."

"Where are you meeting him?"

"Wimbledon Street."

"Yes, I know it." He looked at the map. "It's there." He drew a ring around its location. "The good news is it's close to the estate; it's only a short walk from your collection point."

He showed me the best route to the estate from Wimbledon Street and went through the scenarios of where to enter depending on the drop-off address. We then examined the exit points.

"Listen carefully, you'll look out of place when you're on that estate. The local fellas will know immediately you're an outsider and some of them won't think twice about hurting you to get their hands on what you'll be carrying. You know that, don't you?"

I swallowed hard. "I'm going to have the gear in a leather case and I'll be dressed smartly. Egan reckons it might give the impression I've been to some sort of meeting at the community centre."

"It's not much of a disguise, but I guess it's better than nothing," he said. "If I were you before you go in there I'd establish some rules."

"What rules?"

"Pointers which mean you'll act in a prescribed way if certain situations arise."

"Like what?"

"At any given point, you'll either have the coke or the five grand on you."

"Yes."

"Okay, so let's imagine you enter the estate and as you are walking it is clear you have attracted the attention of the locals. Don't look at them, don't return stares, don't draw any further attention to yourself; just continue to walk – that's rule number one. If they start following and are walking faster than you and close by, say, ten yards in twenty seconds then run, and I mean flat out sprint and get the hell out of there – that's rule number two. Rule three, if you get cornered by them, hand the gear or the money over. There's no 'taking one for the team' tonight. Then, at the first opportunity, split. Finally, rule four: if a person approaches and asks something and you can't close down the conversation and he's becoming aggressive, then assume the worst and punch him as hard as you can in the nose. Then run like the wind because trust me, with the amount of adrenalin you'll have flowing around your body, he'll never catch you."

"What about the buy – I'm guessing I will be in someone's house?"

Tony swung around his laptop and went onto Google Maps and the street view.

"It's pretty much all flats, which are three-storey buildings crammed full of people. My money would be on the deal being in a place like this." He pointed at his screen, showing the type of building he was guessing I would be going into. "If it is, then I reckon there will be three, four, maybe five fellas in there with you. You can't do the deal in the corridor for obvious reasons, so once the door slams behind you then I'm afraid you are in the lap of the gods."

I took another deep swallow.

"What time do you need to be at Wimbledon Street?" he asked.

"Eight o'clock."

"Come around here at seventy thirty, I'll give you a lift."

"You don't need to do that."

"I know I don't, but at least you'll get there safely without anyone noticing, which will be a good start."

"Thanks, Tony. I appreciate it."

"This is a bad hand you've been dealt here, kid. I don't know what's going on between you and this Egan fella, but he certainly isn't making life easy."

"I deserve it," I replied. "Trust me, I deserve everything I get."

CHAPTER 14

I slowly dressed into the clothes Egan had bought before sitting on my bed. My chest was tight and I was having to take shallow breaths. Maybe leaving school and getting a regular job hadn't been such a bad option after all.

I walked into the lounge and sat with Grandad. He looked up and greeted me with a smile.

"You're looking smart, son, are you off out?" he asked.

"Yeah. Egan and I are going out to interview some fella who was nearly killed by a drug dealer," I replied, unable to resist making light of the situation I found myself in.

"Sounds nasty."

"At least he lived to tell the tale."

"How's the job going?"

"Let's just say I think I preferred working in the warehouse."

"Why don't you contact Coopers and see if they will take you back on?"

"I'll carry on with this for a bit longer. I don't want to be one of those people who quit things before giving them a proper chance, do I?

"Good lad. That's the spirit."

"Right, I'm off out, Grandad. I'll probably see you later."

I was lonely and lost, and whilst Tony was helping me, I would have given my left arm to have been able to tell Grandad the whole story so I could have received his support.

Tony was waiting for me at his door. He had a folded sheet of paper in his hand which he passed to me.

"I've photocopied the section of the map covering the estate," he whispered. "There are only about twenty or so roads, so wherever you are heading you should be able to find it pretty quickly."

We got into his car and began the short trip to Wimbledon Street. At this time of day, I guessed we would arrive in about ten minutes but I wanted the drive to last forever. I needed Tony to turn his car around and drive me to a place where I could escape this hell. My stomach was churning; I felt physically drained and unable to collect my thoughts, which could leave me prone to mistakes on an evening where one slip-up could prove fatal.

If I was caught red-handed with the gear by the police then the offence would be 'Possession with Intent to Supply'. I'd be sent to prison, and when I was released it was highly unlikely Grandad would still be alive.

"Remember the rules I told you," Tony said.

"Yes, I remember."

"There's one more golden rule here, though, and that's looking after your own safety. If you get caught by the police then trust me, it's better than being cornered by some drug-hungry man wielding a knife."

"Okay."

"If in doubt – run. You're a young fella with blood pumping through your veins so with a twenty-yard head you'll see most people off."

"Yeah, I will."

"Try to keep your head and remain calm. If you do, then you'll get through this. Call around to my house afterwards. I've brought some chocolate biscuits and cocoa."

"I'm scared, Tony."

"I know you are and I know exactly how you feel. If it's any consolation, it's moments like this that'll build your character. In the long term, it'll do you good."

"I brought this on myself. I want to blame that bastard Egan, but I can't because I started it. If I hadn't made the first move I would now be sitting in the Falcon having a beer with my mates; instead, I'm here."

"There's no point in regrets. You need to look forward. Be focused on your objective because if you aren't then your chances of failure hugely increase."

"You're right."

"Where do you want me to drop you?" he asked as we approached the area.

"At the Athena, please."

Tony drove down Queens Street and pulled up outside the Athena, an old cinema which had been converted into a conferencing centre. As the car gently ground to a halt I turned to jelly.

"I can't—"

"You can and you will," he commanded sternly. "Now go and do it."

I exited the car and checked the time: 7.42 p.m. Tony pulled off and we exchanged waves. I sat on the steps of the Athena until exactly 7.55 p.m. and made the short walk around the corner to Wimbledon Street. The road was narrow with tall old factories either side which had been converted into trendy flats. I walked slowly down the street looking all around, but there was no sign of him. I turned the corner and walked quickly around the block until I was back where I had started. I walked down the other side this time, and as I did I heard the soft hum of a top-of-the-range vehicle pull in. I glanced to my left and saw his car.

His window opened and he passed me the leather case which resembled a posh laptop bag. "The address is on the package. Read it, remember it, then make sure you rip it up. There's a peacemaker in the bag as well. It's a loaded Springfield XD. Stick it in the back of your trousers. There are two safety catches on it, but if you hold the gun conventionally and squeeze the trigger you deactivate both of them with the weight of your hand and the pressure on the trigger. Put simply: if you get in trouble, point and pull. When you've done the deal get out of the estate and meet me in the petrol station on the junction of Madras Road and Humberstone Road. I'll be there from half-past eight and I will wait exactly ten minutes before I leave. Have you got it?"

"Yes," I replied before taking the leather case from him.

A Springfield XD – a fucking gun!

I walked quickly around the corner to a patch of derelict land that had been fenced off. I located a break in the temporary barrier, ventured in and found a sheltered spot which was receiving sufficient light from a nearby lamp post for me to be able to sort out what was in the bag.

I unzipped it and could see a package about the size of a large fist of coke. There was a post-it note attached, which I removed. I turned it towards the light to allow me to read the content.

Khally
Flat 16 Dakcombe Street

I repeated the name and address three times before deciding to type it into my phone for safekeeping. I ripped the post-it note into tiny pieces and scattered them in all directions.

I then took out the firearm. It was a chunky-looking handgun which felt heavy and dangerous. I pointed it before placing it in the back of my trousers. I then practised pulling it out and aiming. As I was left-handed, it made sense for it to sit slightly to the left side of my belt. I tucked it in one last time before pulling my jumper and coat over.

I took out the map Tony had given me and located Dakcombe Street. It was right in the middle of the estate – shit! Okay, I need to remain calm. I took three big breaths and tried to settle my meandering mind. I worked out the route I was going to take. It was a straightforward walk which would eventually bring me out onto the main drag, St Matthews way. The most direct route to the drop would be to walk down this road until I arrived at Wharf Street North. From there I would turn into the estate. It was then the third turning on the right. Okay, that was easy enough.

After the deal, when I exited, it became slightly trickier as I had to rendezvous with Egan. I'd have to turn right and follow the road onto Christow Street, walk to the bottom, turn right on Ottawa Street and then second right at what looked a mini-roundabout, which would take me on to Madras Road. Presumably, somewhere down there I would find the petrol station.

Fucking hell, I was never going to remember all this! I could end up looking like a lost tourist reading a map in the centre of a dodgy estate. I may as well have a 'Come and mug me' sign above my head.

Okay, focus on getting to the address and then sort out the exit when the deal has been done. I needed to find Wharf Street North, then take the third turning right, I said to myself as I folded the map back into my pocket.

I checked the gun was secured and tightened my belt just in case.

I was all set to walk into a notorious housing estate carrying five grand's worth of coke and a loaded gun, which I didn't know how to use.

What could possibly go wrong?

I was walking down St Matthews Way, a thunderous dual carriageway and one of the main routes heading in and out of the city centre. I was nervously looking out for my turning into the estate. The three-storey blocks that Tony had shown me on his computer had appeared on my right shoulder. I could hear voices, shouts and the laughter of people I had never met and who would instantly question what business I had on their manor.

What the fuck was I walking into? I was about to be thrown into a world of seasoned drug dealers: fellas who knew the score, who understood the lie of the land and acted accordingly. I was going in blind, an absolute beginner, wet behind the ears and just waiting to be found out.

I stopped walking and realised I was never going to get through this in my current mindset. If I acted like an amateur, I would quickly get found out, allowing my enemies to prey upon me.

Standing on a main road with the blast of passing cars, street lights cascading onto me and only minutes before I entered the most dangerous scenario of my life might have been an odd place to take stock of my immediate future, but under the extreme circumstances, now was as good a time as any.

I had no mother; a murdering bastard of an estranged dad; a grandad who had months, maybe weeks left to live; my only two friends had disowned me; I had no job; the feds were tracking me and I was under the spell of Egan who was controlling me like a puppet.

I cast my mind back to a World War I documentary I had watched with Grandad. They had interviewed a veteran who had survived the Battle of the Somme. Whilst in the trenches, he and the rest of his battalion had been instructed that they would be going over the top in the morning. They would climb out of the trenches and proceed towards the Germans. The high command told them not to be concerned, as weeks of bombing had killed most of the enemy. Indeed, so confident were they, the instructions stated that whilst crossing No Man's Land there would probably be no need to run, such was the unlikelihood of facing enemy gunfire. The men knew better and guessed they would be heading straight into heavy machine-gun fire and most of them would be killed.

The veteran explained the only way he'd endured the battle was by imagining at the point they were told of the planned attack was the moment he had died. What happened thereafter was of no relevance and if he survived it would be a bonus. But by allowing death into his mind he had found a place of no fear.

This had to be my place of no fear. I simply had nothing to lose as my life was heading nowhere. Even if Ethel recovered and Egan cleared off, what then? It would be more of the same – buying stolen gear from desperate skag heads and selling it on to make a few miserly quid. I was nothing, a lost soul freewheeling through life with no meaning or purpose. I didn't contribute anything; I only sucked the blood from society like a parasite. I fuelled the black market, stealing from hardworking people and taking advantage of desperate drug addicts with whom I was in no way superior on the social ladder. The only difference being I had no addiction, except, of course, the habit of being a loser.

I clenched my teeth – fuck it! If I was going down, then I was going down with these drug-dealing twats thinking I was the real deal; that I was someone they would think twice about fucking around with. They wouldn't see my weakness; there would be no obvious chink in my armour. If I was going to be Egan's ambassador, I would act and behave with his self-confidence, his air of arrogance, his forthright, no-nonsense way of cutting through the fat and getting things done. If it wasn't going as planned, he would walk away, and that's how I intended to operate. I committed to stop accepting mediocrity and to banish timewasters.

I continued walking, only slower. I was no longer in a rush and not anxious, but instead, calm and starting to become composed. The next street, Wharf Street North, was my turning. As I walked down, the housing blocks were now on both sides of the road. I passed a Somalian kid on his bike pedalling like hell. He was no doubt in a rush to get home before his curfew. I smiled as I thought back to such carefree times.

I walked past the first turning, then the second, knowing the next turning was the one I needed to take. As I approached, a black man was standing on the corner, sharing my pavement.

He had the distinct look of someone up to mischief. As I walked past, I could feel his eyes burning into me. I continued along the road until I could see I was heading towards a dead end – shit! This wasn't the turn. I must have missed this on the map. I would now have to do a one-eighty and walk back past him. I thought about crossing over and walking along the other side of the pavement but this would only suggest I was scared and vulnerable.

I walked slowly back the way I had come and I could see he had spotted me. He looked once, gave me a hard stare and then turned away. But as I approached, he looked again. There was no way he was going to let me out of his grasp so I decided to strike first. I waited until I was within ten yards of him.

"Hey, mate, can you tell me where Dakcombe Street is?" I asked as confidently as I could.

"Where?" he answered in a heavy African accent.

"Dakcombe Street."

"Turn right here, then first right," he replied.

"Nice one. Cheers, bro."

"What you want down Dakcombe Street?" he queried.

"Sorry?"

"Dakcombe Street – what business you have down there?"

"I'm meeting someone."

"Who?"

I recalled Tony's rules. This fella was showing way too much interest. I needed to be on my guard.

"Why are you interested?"

"You look lost, man. You aren't from around here. Where you from?"

"You're a bit nosy, aren't you?"

"What you mean, 'nosy'?"

"You don't know what nosy means? It's the same as what the fuck has it got to do with you."

I stood there staring at him as he stared back at me. He then sucked air through his teeth and looked away.

I turned and continued walking now, mindful that I had been on the estate for less than a few minutes and the locals had already taken an interest.

I continued along Wharf Street North before turning down the next street, the sign confirming I was at the correct place. Bollocks! I'd forgotten the house number. I took out my phone and as I did I spotted the black geezer was marching in my direction. I guessed he had digested my reply and decided he had acted lamely. He was walking with a strut, trying to act tough; his intent was almost certainly aggressive.

I walked and checked my phone – Flat 16. I viewed the numbers which were on signs outside of the blocks. Flats 8–16 were right in front of me – a result! I could get out of this fella's way. I approached the entrance door and pressed the buzzer. A voice came over the intercom.

"Who is it?" he asked, again in a thick African accent.

"I am here to see Khally."

"What about?"

"Tell him I work for Egan."

I heard the door buzz and click. I pulled it and entered the building. The lobby and the stairwell had an odd sanitised smell, like bleach was covering the stench of something more unpleasant. I walked up the echoing stairs, and as I did, I could hear a cacophony of noise coming from the other flats, which were all no doubt crammed to the rafters.

I stood outside number 16, where I could hear the loud thud of bass from the grime music being played. I knocked loudly and moments later I could hear numerous locks being worked before the door was opened.

An early-twenties black male face appeared.

"We were expecting Egan."

"I'm here on his behalf."

He reluctantly opened the door and I stood and waited next to him as he closed it behind me before applying the locks. I followed him into the tiny, squalid flat which was heaving with the smoke from joints. The man who opened the door beckoned me into the lounge, where there were two other black men, slumped on tatty chairs, both smoking. They eyed me suspiciously up and down before spotting my case.

"Which one of you is Khally?" I asked.

"Khally's coming," one of them said.

"I was told he was going to be here."

"He is coming soon," the same man replied.

"How long is he going to be?"

"Five or ten minutes. Do you want a drink – a Coke or a tea?" he asked.

"No. I'll tell you what's going to happen, he has two minutes to show up or I leave. If you need to text or call him then you do that, but in two minutes, I walk."

"Fucking chill, brother. I told you he's coming, now sit down," said the man who had let me in.

"I don't want to sit down and your two minutes has started."

One of the men picked his phone up and made a call. He was talking for a brief time in a foreign tongue before he hung up.

"He's coming now," he said.

I made a point of looking at my phone for the time. I was fully committed to leaving within two minutes.

We waited in awkward silence. The three men appearing to fix a permanent stare on me, trying to suss me out, as they continued to smoke joints. I watched as they drew long, heavy drags before slowly exhaling the smoke. I tried to act bravely and look back at them. I had anticipated this would be a tough, fearsome gig and it was not disappointing me. I felt totally vulnerable. I was aware they could very quickly bypass having to pay the money and overpower me and take the coke. God knows what they would do when they found the gun.

I tapped my phone. "Thirty seconds left then I'm going."

I knew that leaving this place was going to be very tricky. I was trapped. The door was locked with at least three different mechanisms. One of these guys would have to let me out and I suspect that would only happen if I forced them. Still, leave is what I would try to do. Thereafter, it would be between me, my courage and what they were prepared to do to stop me.

There was a knock on the door. One of them stood up.

"This is Khally," he announced.

He went to the door, opened it and in walked a distinctive, tall, rangy black man wearing a red bandana. Within seconds it was obvious he was the leader. It was the way he moved, gestured and talked. He sauntered into the lounge and greeted me with half a smile.

"Are you Egan's man?" he asked, speaking good English.

"Yes," I answered.

"I have got a problem with the money," he declared.

"What sort of problem?"

"I've only got two Gs."

"Then you're short," I replied. "I have strict instructions from Egan: I either leave here with five grand or I return the package to him."

"Ring him and ask," he suggested.

"Ask him what?"

"Tell him I'll take the gear and sell it in two days. Then he gets the rest of his money."

"No deal and I've been told no phone calls."

"Okay, let me have two Gs worth of gear then you can take the rest with you."

"Again, no deal. Which part of this aren't you getting, my friend? My instructions from Egan were very clear. If I don't follow them, things will be as bad for me as they will be for you."

The man approached me and was well within my personal space. He lowered his head and voice.

"I need this gear, man. I have brothers relying on it."

I looked up and stared deep into his eyes. "I can't help you, now let me out."

He reached his arm across the doorway.

"You aren't going anywhere unless I've taken that coke," he demanded.

I was in fucking trouble. This was my Battle of the Somme developing right in front of me. I was going to give him one chance, then I was going for it and I wouldn't look back.

"Can you move your arm and let me out?"

"Give me the fucking gear, man!" he hissed.

In the short time it took him to say these six words, everything changed. I knew what had to come next and would likely follow. My life would never be the same again. I would not be able to undo the actions which were now inevitable. I was about to enter an altogether more dangerous world. I had been shepherded to the entrance by Egan, but ultimately was crossing over of my own free will.

"Okay, okay." I sighed, took the leather case from around my shoulder and passed it to him. He took it from me, unzipped it, looked inside and took out the package. When his eyes rose back up to the level of my chest he could see I was pointing the gun at him. I moved the barrel to his head.

"Slowly put the package back in the case or I'll blow your fucking brains out," I instructed.

The other three men stood up, surprised and intimidated. I'd shocked them with my ballsy approach and in doing so realised they weren't quite as tough as they may have had me believe.

"Tell your friends to sit down. If they make any sudden movements then my trigger finger might twitch," I directed. I was now relaxed and in total control.

"Sit down, sit down!" he ordered.

They slowly took their seats.

"Here's what's going to happen: you are going to let me out of here and I'm going to go back to Egan and tell him there has been a misunderstanding. You can either re-negotiate a two-grand deal for a smaller package or let him know when you've got the full five grand. Do you understand?"

"Yeah," he replied.

"Don't follow me and don't do anything stupid. If you do and I don't make it out of here, then the next and last white face you will ever see will be Egan's. Have you got it?"

He nodded.

"Good. Now let me the fuck out."

We walked to the door with the gun still on his head. He unlocked it and I slowly turned him around so the gun was always on his head, only I was able to leave the flat without having to turn my back on him.

"If I were you, I wouldn't return here, my friend," he recommended.

"I don't intend to. It's a fucking shithole," I replied, slowly walking down the stairs backwards. "Now go back inside and lock the fucking door," I demanded.

Once I had heard the click of the lock, I turned and bolted. My head was spinning like a fucking fairground Waltzer! I ran out of the block, returned the gun to the back of my trousers and marched down the road. Fuck the exit plan; I would come out the same way I came in and risk walking the extra yards with the gear and a gun on my person.

I was soon back on St Matthews Way and heading towards the main roundabout on Humberstone Road, where I would take the first left and find the petrol station about five hundred yards down the road. Hopefully, Egan would be parked up and waiting to get me the fuck out of here.

What the hell was that all about? I'd probably overstepped the mark but somehow had managed to walk away from a very tricky situation.

I turned onto Humberstone Road and after a minute or so of fast-paced walking, I could see the petrol station. I checked the time: 8.32 p.m. Egan would be waiting. I was about to put the phone back in my pocket when a simple and terse text message arrived from him.

I could see his car in the petrol station with another vehicle parked behind. Blue lights were being reflected from the rear of his vehicle. It was an unmarked police car which suggested he had been tailed.

I turned to walk back the way I came, only I could see two police officers about a hundred yards away walking towards me. Had they seen me doing a U-turn? If so, it would look very suspicious. There was only one thing for it: I had to turn into Madras Road and head back into the estate. I was going to have to return to the lion's den to give myself a chance to escape. I nonchalantly made the turn and, after twenty yards, under the cover of buildings, decided to make a run for it. I was working on navigational instinct as I ran to the mini roundabout at the bottom of the road and then made a left turning. Shortly before the turning, I dared to look behind me where, sure enough, the feds were in full pursuit. They were fifty yards away and closing fast.

As I ran, I unzipped the bag and dropped in the gun. If I had to, I would throw the bag into a passing garden. I sprinted at full speed, guessing the road I was on ran parallel to St Matthews Way. I needed a left turn to get back onto the main road. After ten seconds or so, I could see a turn approaching, which I took and continued to run down. I could see from the large tree at the bottom of the road that I had turned into another fucking cul-de-sac – shit! Egan's words – 'fail to prepare and all that' – were resonating through my skull as I acknowledged I should have done a physical recce of the area as he'd advised. I stopped briefly and assessed the landscape. There was grass surrounding the tree, so surely there must be a way through. I continued running with the faint pointless calls from the chasing feds demanding I stop, echoing down the street. Dogs were barking and the locals were looking from their windows as the pursuit continued.

I ran past the point where the road stopped, through some bollards and up a grass verge, briefly losing my footing on the damp grass, but managing to retain my balance. As I ran down the other side of the verge, I slid and fell, losing vital seconds. I had mud all over my clothes as I scrambled to my feet and re-emerged onto St Matthews Way. I turned right and intended to cross the busy dual carriageway at a convenient break in the traffic and head into the familiar backstreets of Leicester city centre.

The traffic was heavy and I was unable to cross. As I continued running along the road, I looked back and could see the officers continuing their pursuit. I was tiring, eager to catch a breath; years of bumming around had robbed me of any fitness. I continued running up the road, desperate for a break in this fucking traffic so I could cross. I spotted two more officers approaching from the opposite direction. If I didn't cross over soon I would be boxed in. I checked the traffic again and decided to go for it. I ran out in front of a fast-moving car, narrowly avoiding a near-fatal collision. I could hear the prolonged beep of his horn before I safely dodged the vehicle in the other lane. I stepped over the two-foot-high central reservation; some funny little brick construction with soil in it. I checked for traffic approaching in the other direction and observed it was much clearer. However, as I pushed off with my back foot, I slipped on the damp soil and fell violently onto the road. I heard the screech of brakes as a vehicle had U-turned on the other side of the dual carriageway and was now heading in my direction. There'd be short odds on it being a police car, and as I was flailing around on the road, trying to regain my composure, I knew I was seconds away from being arrested.

I dragged myself to my feet and stumbled in pain as I'd twisted my ankle. I looked up to see the car approaching at speed, its back-end wavering as the driver had slammed on the brakes. I managed to avoid a collision but again lost my balance and fell to the floor. As I got up I could see the four officers about fifty feet away, closing in. The driver of the car called out to me to get in. Like an angel on my wings, it was Tony.

I was back at Tony's house, where a mix of relief and fear was making me giddy. Tony explained that after dropping me off he'd parked up and waited twenty minutes before he'd began doing laps of the estate. He knew there would be trouble and thought he might be able to help. How right he was.

"Cup of coffee?" he asked.

"Do you have anything stronger?"

"Will Scotch do you?"

I nodded before taking off my soiled jacket and winced in pain as I removed my shoe and assessed my twisted ankle.

Tony brought in a half-full tumbler of Scotch and a bag of frozen peas. "Here, put these on your ankle, it'll help with the swelling."

"Thanks," I said, taking a large slug of whisky. The ice-cold sensation from the peas provided some welcome relief.

"That was a close call tonight. I assume it all went pear-shaped?" he asked.

"You could say that."

"What's in the bag?"

"Nothing much really, only five grand's worth of coke and a loaded gun."

I looked to see whether my response had prompted a reaction from him, but it didn't seem to register.

"I'll need to hide the bag," he said.

"Why?"

"At some point in the next couple of hours the police will come knocking on the door and I suspect its contents will be on their shopping list."

"Will they find it?"

He smirked. "They will find the bag, but they won't find its contents," he replied before exiting the room with it.

Whilst he was gone I took stock of what had happened. Had

the chasing officers snatched a good look at me? If Tony was right and the feds were going to come knocking then it probably didn't matter. In any event, I was more concerned with my new African enemies. I was guessing red bandana man wouldn't take having a gun pointed at his head lightly. Would he accept this as nothing more than an occupational hazard? Or would he get the hump and seek retribution?

Tony returned to the lounge with a mug of coffee.

"Not joining me on the Scotch?" I asked.

"Not tonight," he replied, taking a sip from his mug. "Tell me what happened?"

I regaled the full story, warts and all, before moving on to the meeting I'd had earlier with Jem Langley.

"A couple of days before this went down I was stopped by a plain-clothed fed who had come up from London looking for Egan," I informed him.

"London?"

"That's where he's based."

"What's he doing here?"

I was mindful Tony knew Ethel, Egan's mother, and remembered Egan had been clear I was not to mention this relationship to him. I needed to tread carefully. One false move and I could be in trouble.

"Family problems, I reckon. I don't know the details, but he's moved his drugs operation up here for the time being."

"Why you, though – I don't get it?"

"What do you mean?"

"Why involve you in this? Giving you a gun, a package of drugs, sending you on to St Matthews under dark; unless you aren't telling me something, then this isn't your scene at all."

I realised that it was time to come clean. Tony deserved to hear the truth, and for once honesty was a place which might provide solace.

"I did something I'm ashamed of," I admitted.

"Do you want to tell me what?"

"I stole from a charity shop."

"That's not a great thing to do, but I've heard worse."

"I stole a load of clothes that were worth a mint from the charity shop where his mum was working. She blamed herself for not preventing the theft, then a couple of days afterwards had a stroke and she's now really poorly. Unfortunately, he blames me for it."

"And this is his way of getting back at you?"

"Yes, and I deserve it."

"How long is the punishment going to go on for?"

"He says when his mum gets better he'll call it off and move back to London."

"What if she doesn't? I've known people who have had strokes and been in care homes for years."

"I don't know; like you, I'm in the dark. But at this rate, it's only a matter of time before I get locked up or killed. I rode my luck tonight big time, but sooner or later I going to come unstuck."

"Why don't you tell him to get stuffed and say you're not doing it?" he asked.

"Tony, I'm telling you this guy's a fucking psycho! One of my mates who is a proper streetfighter went up against Egan and got destroyed. He's icy cold like someone has removed that section of his brain which makes people scared. I'm trapped and there's no way out of this unless I kill the guy." This was the first time I had even thought this, let alone said it.

"I'm not sure I would recommend that," he replied.

"This detective from London has got it bad for him. He's promised me I will be okay if I co-operate with them – perhaps I should?"

"I've known the police and people in the military say things like this, but they couldn't care less about the individual and what happens to them. They are only bothered about getting their man. Do you think this detective would give a toss about zipping up your body bag if it meant he'd taken down Egan?"

"You're probably right."

"It's your call; all I'm saying is be careful."

'Be careful', how could I? Egan had a leash around my fucking neck and was tugging me around in all directions.

"When they come knocking, I'm going to tell them you're flat-out drunk and asleep on the settee. I'll say you went to the community centre to find out about a basketball programme, but before you got there some local lads took exception to you being on their turf and chased you off. As soon as the police got involved you thought the world and his dog was out to get you and bolted. I was there to pick you up because I'm helping you to get a job."

"How do I explain the bag?"

"You carried a notepad to write down any information you might need. You also thought there might be some leaflets to take away with you so the bag could come in handy."

"Fucking hell, even by my standards this is top-notch bullshit."

"They'll never be able to disprove it. Without the drugs or the money, they'll have nothing. They stopped Egan and I'm guessing he was clean. They may very well have a good idea what was supposed to go down tonight, but without any evidence, they'll soon lose interest."

"How come you are so sure they will call around here?"

"There are CCTV cameras all the way along St Matthews Way. After they have lifted my registration number it'll simply be a matter of time."

I turned my attention to a framed picture of a young woman sitting on Tony's mantlepiece. I was pretty certain I hadn't seen it before. I couldn't have done, such was its prominence.

"Who's the girl?" I asked.

"That's my daughter," he replied rather awkwardly.

"I've never heard you speak about her."

"It's because I never do."

"Why?"

"We fell out a few years ago. She left and has never returned."

"What was the fall-out about?"

"Her boyfriend."

"What about him?"

"Rotten to the core; he's a bad 'un and I could see it a mile off. I pleaded with her to dump him but she wouldn't, so eventually he split us up."

"And was he?"

"Was he what?"

"As bad as you said he was?"

"Worse. He was a drug dealer, and a stupid one at that. He even stole from his own gang. When they found out he had to go into hiding."

"When did you last see him?"

"I hope she's happy. She's my only daughter. She's all I've got and I've lost her."

"Why don't you get back in touch with her and try to sort things out?"

"Too much bad blood and too many things that can't be unsaid. I need to let her go."

"What about her mum?"

"She died a fortnight after giving birth to her. I brought her up on my own."

"This is really sad. What's her name?"

"Zoe, Zoe Grace. She never had a mum, something you know all about."

"I had one for eight years, and a dad, but lost both in the turn of a steering wheel."

"Have you ever seen your dad since he was released from prison?"

"No. I'm not sure I would even recognise him."

"I bet you would."

Our conversation was interrupted by a firm knock on the door. We looked at one another, knowing full well who had arrived.

I stood close to the door, enabling me to listen to the

conversation whilst being out of sight. It was Detective Sergeant Mathew Wood who had called alone. After the mandatory introductions, he cut straight to chase.

"Your vehicle was seen this evening on St Matthews Way picking up an individual who was being pursued by police officers. We believe this person to be your next-door neighbour, Robbie Howard."

"Pursued by the police? I don't know anything about that. Robbie went to the community centre to find out about a basketball programme and when I drove down to collect him he was running out of the estate looking distressed. I ended up having to stop my car in the middle of the road to pick him up."

"You say he went to the community centre?"

"No, he intended to go to the community centre. On his way there some youths had spotted him and took exception to an outsider being on their patch. They threatened and then chased him off the estate."

"Well, let's see whether he corroborates that statement, shall we?"

"I'm sure he will."

"I'll be calling next door in a minute to find out."

"I wouldn't bother."

"Why?"

"Because he's in my lounge."

"Your lounge?" he replied, surprised.

"Yes, it's a room that connects with the hallway."

"Go and get him then," he said sternly, evidently unimpressed with Tony's sarcasm.

"I'm afraid he's in no fit state. He was so terrified after being chased by a group of lads packing knives that he's drunk too much whisky and out cold on my settee."

"How convenient," Wood said.

"Given he's been drinking my twelve-year-old single malt, I consider it to be very *inconvenient*."

"Why are you protecting him, Anthony?"

"Call me Tony, and I was only protecting him by getting him off that estate."

"We have reason to believe he was there dealing drugs."

"You're kidding, right? You actually think there's a white fella mad enough to go on to that estate alone and deal drugs?"

"That's what our informant is telling us."

"If he was, then I don't know whether he should be arrested or awarded the Victoria Cross for bravery."

"Is that the bag he took with him?" Wood pointed at the leather carrier which Tony had left not so subtly against the coat stand.

"Oh yes, so it is."

"Can I take a look at it?"

"Do you think it will help?" Tony asked sarcastically.

"Just pass me the fucking bag!" Wood snapped.

Tony handed him the bag, which he opened before delving around, pulling out a notepad and pen.

"Ah good, I told him to take those with him because you never know when you're going to need them, do you, Detective?"

"Well done, you've managed to get yourself involved in this investigation, *Tony*," Wood said, exaggerating his name. "And make no mistake about it, if we find out he was there dealing drugs then you'll be charged with being an accessory to a crime."

"Yeah, well, good luck trying to prove that one."

"When Robbie sobers up, do tell him we'll be having a little chat, won't you?"

"What, about the basketball programmes going on at the St Matthews community centre?"

"Stop being a fucking clever dick."

"I think it's a role at least one of us should take."

"He's managed to get himself hooked up with a fella who's going to lead him down a dangerous path that I don't think young Robbie is going to be smart enough to get off."

"Like a yellow brick road for drug dealers?"

"When you're standing in the visitors' line at the prison, make sure you remember this conversation."

"I'll recall it word for word. Now you have yourself a lovely evening."

Tony closed the door, turned to me and lightly puffed out his cheeks.

"I think I will have that glass of Scotch," he said.

CHAPTER 15

I woke up after only a few hours' sleep feeling decidedly edgy. I'd moved on from trivial matters like whether Smelly Nelly would give me a fair price for a second-hand Nintendo to being armed with a weapon and sticking it in the face of a dangerous drug dealer.

I was running out of time to land a volunteering job, and that useless idiot from the British Heart Society still hadn't bothered to call me. If he didn't ring soon then in all likelihood I would be roped into another assignment allocated by the ever-generous Sean Egan. He was like a sadistic gift that never stopped cruelly giving. The danger of the first errand allocated had somehow been trumped by the second one. God only knows what he would have up his sleeve next time.

I was surprised not to receive a text or a call from him to see how the St Matthews gig had gone down, but then again it was him all over. He was an all-knowing, volatile and unpredictable character.

Then there was Candy – I had still received no word of her. She was, without doubt, a vile, unscrupulous little shit, but I had witnessed the fate of Death Row and I didn't want her to have suffered in the same way.

I now had dangerous enemies, the feds were trailing me and the small matter of a gun and package of cocaine which I needed to return to its owner.

The vibration of my phone alerted me to an incoming text message. It was Egan.

I've come round to collect my gear

Presumably, he meant he was *coming* round. In which case, I needed to get up and retrieve it from Tony. My ankle had eased up a little, but I still had to hobble downstairs, from where I could hear voices. I sighed and shook my head, disbelievingly. It was Egan and Grandad sat in the lounge having a nice friendly fucking chat! The cheeky twat had dropped around, acting like some long-lost uncle.

"He seems to be doing okay, Mr Howard, he's certainly learning a lot," I heard him say as I approached the lounge.

"Here he is," announced Grandad. "Mr Egan was just saying how pleased he is with your progress."

"I'm so glad," I replied, fixing Egan a stare.

He looked back and winked. "Yes, the boy is certainly doing okay. I mean, you have to test them a bit, don't you? You have to find out what they are made of and take them outside their comfort zones just to see how they react."

"You certainly do," replied Grandad, who was getting enthused about the conversation.

"Right, Robbie, I wouldn't mind a coffee, and I suspect your grandad would like another cup of tea, so I'll give you a hand."

"I wouldn't say no," Grandad added.

We walked into the kitchen and Egan closed the door behind us. "Do you have the gear?" he asked sternly in a hushed voice.

"It's next door; Tony's hiding it for me."

He was clearly irked by this news. "Tony's hiding it! How did you get him involved in this?"

"I was chased off the estate last night by the Old Bill and Tony picked me up. If he hadn't I would now be in a police cell, so he's done us both a favour."

"Is he cool?" he enquired, seeking reassurance he wasn't going to snitch.

"Yeah, he's cool. The feds took his registration number and called around his house when I was there and he fucked them off. Anyway, what happened to you?"

"The police were probably tailing me when I left the club. It's no biggie; they've got nothing on me and they didn't know anything about the sell."

"It went tits up. Khally didn't have the five grand."

"I know, he messaged me. You pulled out the gun and stuck it to his head, didn't you?" he asked with a smile, as if he respected what I had done.

"I had to; he wasn't going to let me leave. There were four geezers in there with me; even if I had got out of there with the cash, I'm not sure I would have managed to get off the estate."

"But you did get off the estate. Maybe you aren't giving yourself enough credit."

"That estate is a fucking minefield."

"Trust me, I've been to more dangerous places," he added.

"What's next? I mean, I'm no nearer to getting this fucking volunteering gig."

"Khally says he's got the five grand together."

"And?"

"And, if you don't get anything within the agreed timeframe then you will be going back to finish what you've started."

I went cold. "You're seriously sending me back to see a bloke whose head I pressed a gun against and threatened to blow out his brains? I'll never get out of there alive."

"He needs his drugs, I'm sure he'll be fine."

"Yeah, you're probably right," I replied sarcastically. "I might even call around a bit earlier and take a double pepperoni pizza for me and his crew and explain how holding a gun to his head was nothing more than a little misunderstanding."

"Or you can start a volunteering job and then you don't have to go at all," he said with his usual smugness.

"Why are you doing this to me?" I asked desperately.

"If ever I need a reminder, I just take a look at my mother laying in the hospital bed."

"She wouldn't have approved of this."

"Tick, tock, tick, tock; at least this time you'll know your way around the estate." He turned to walk out, before stopping. "Don't worry, I'll collect the gear from Tony. I might need to impress upon him the need to keep quiet."

"Tony's sound, he won't tell anyone. You don't need to be doing your big brother routine on him," I said.

"You'd do well to mind your own business rather than start to tell me how to conduct mine. And that includes figuring out how you're going to persuade Khally not to slash your throat open when he next sees you," he said, as he was departing. "Which, by the way, when I was on the phone to him earlier, was something he was threatening to do."

Applying the 'what would Tony' do formula to the pressing issue of landing a volunteering job in the next twenty-four hours, I found myself in a taxi heading into town. My first stop was to visit this Colin fella who worked at the British Heart Society and find out what the score was with this warehouse job.

If this gig was a dead-end, then I would trawl as many places as I could, cap in hand, begging them to accept free labour.

As the cab was dropping me off outside the shop, I acknowledged being in a very odd mood; twitchy and irritable to an extent which was alien to me. I felt somewhat out of control of my own emotions, as if I could erupt at any time.

I walked into the shop and waited at the till until some fat woman finally waddled over to help me. Even then, I received only a gormless stare rather than a verbal welcome.

"Hi, I wondered if Colin Spawn was in, please?"

"Do you mean, Colin *Bourne*?" she replied firmly.

Not a great start.

"Yes, sorry, Colin Bourne. Is he around, please?"

"I'll go and find out," she replied in a resigned tone, realising she was going to have to march her fat arse into the storeroom. "Is he expecting you?"

"No, but I did drop in the other day and I was hoping to have received a call by now, as I'm keen to help out in your warehouse."

"Wait here then," she instructed, again without a smidgen of politeness.

I watched as she dragged her massively bloated body at the speed of a blue badge-holding snail.

She finally reappeared, puffing and panting like she'd run twenty minutes on a treadmill set to the 'Everest' gradient.

"Colin's not in at the moment, but I can take your number and ask him to call you."

"He already has my number. What time are you expecting him in?" I asked.

"Sometime later."

"Is there any chance you can give me an approximate time?"

"I was just told 'sometime later'."

"Do you know what 'later' means? Because in thirty seconds, that will be later."

"I don't know."

"But it will be sometime in the future, will it?"

"Yeah," she responded, seemingly incapable of detecting my obvious sarcasm.

Having witnessed horrific domestic violence towards women, I have always despised any act of aggression aimed at a female, but in a minute, I may very well break my own golden rule and smash this fat cunt's face in. I inhaled deeply, desperately trying to regain my composure.

"Given you can't give a specific time, what I'm going to do is come back every ten minutes to see if he's arrived."

"I would leave it a couple of hours."

"That's useful, thanks. I'll wait for two hours and then come back and if he's not here, then I'll keep returning every ten minutes until he turns up. How does that sound?"

"If you want – it's up to you."

"Great, see you later. Oh, can I take your name for reference, please?"

She then did this weird kind of piggy grunt before confirming, "It's Maureen."

"Maureen, many thanks for your help, co-operation and outstanding customer service. And on behalf of the general public and, more importantly, those people who donate to the British Heart Society, can I say just how grateful we all are for everything you do."

She looked at me bemused for several seconds, searching for an incisive response, something appropriate to acknowledge this rare, overstated slab of gratitude she had received.

"Okay," she finally said.

I left the shop and headed straight to Greggs to take my frustration out on a couple of sausage rolls. I sat on a stool in the window, fiddling with my mobile phone and wondering whether Tony's daughter was on Facebook. I opened the app and began to undertake a preliminary search. If she'd got hooked up with this geezer that Tony so disliked she may have registered herself in her married name only. I searched 'Zoe Hamilton', and there were a couple of younger girls who could be immediately excluded. I couldn't be exactly sure of Tony's daughter's age, but she looked about eighteen in the picture, and for some reason, the photo looked about ten years old.

There was someone in St Albans who appeared to be of similar age, but it couldn't be her, as Tony's daughter was quite pretty whilst Zoe Hamilton from St Albans had a face like a kicked-in shit can.

I searched 'Grace Hamilton' – nothing; 'Zoe-Grace Hamilton' – still nothing. It was a dead end.

My mind then reverted to Candy. As I was idling, I decided to call her mobile phone again. The last time I rang my call diverted straight to answerphone and she hadn't responded to my text message.

I called the number and was surprised to hear I was connected and it was ringing. A man with a gruff voice answered.

"Who's this?" he snarled.

"Is Candy there?"

"Who's this?" he repeated.

"I'm a friend of hers. I need to speak to her."

He hung up. A bit like the Facebook search for Zoe and my hunt for a voluntary job – nothing. I felt like Mother Hubbard. It was turning into a frustrating day.

I noted the time on my mobile phone and estimated I had departed the British Heart Society about twenty minutes ago. I decided to stretch my legs, get some movement into this sore ankle and head up to the hostel where Candy was staying to see if I could discover some answers.

I turned off Granby Street and walked up the quiet road towards the hostel. As usual, there was a volatile group of residents hanging around outside, drinking mental strength beer.

I received the usual evil looks as I walked in. Once again, there was no one at the reception so I had to ring the bell. After about thirty seconds the same useless twat who had refused to help me the other day appeared. His vacant look suggested he didn't recognise me.

"Hi, I called in the other day, if you remember, because I was concerned about Candy. Someone thought she was in her room but then another geezer said she was heading into town. I wanted to check if she was okay?"

"Are you a family member?" he asked in a docile manner.

"No, I'm just a friend."

"I'm sorry, but I'm afraid Candy passed away."

"What!"

"She took a drug overdose and died."

"What? When? Hang on, where was she when she died?"

"We found her in her room."

"So, she was in her room?"

"Yeah."

"Do you remember I came here and told you she had probably bought a bad batch of heroin and I urgently needed to tell her?"

"Not really."

"Come on, think back," I said getting irritated. "I explained she might be in her room but you wouldn't let me in. You do remember, don't you?"

"I'm not allowed to let you in. I'm sorry."

"But you could have gone and looked yourself."

"But I couldn't leave—"

"You couldn't leave the reception, could you? Candy died when she could have been saved BECAUSE YOU COULDN'T LEAVE THE FUCKING RECEPTION!" I blasted.

"It wasn't my fault; they're the rules."

"The rules! Are you fucking shitting me? I've been in here twice, and on both occasions, you haven't even been manning the reception, which is why I have had to ring this fucking bell, you moron! That's how much the rules mean to you."

"I think you had better leave."

"You think I had better leave? You useless cunt, you've gone and killed her."

"You are becoming hostile! I'm going to call the police," he threatened.

I turned and walked out.

One of the fellas loitering at the front of the hostel had just returned from the off-licence with a pack of four beers in his hand.

"Hey up, mate, how much have they cost you?" I asked.

"A fiver," he replied.

I dug into my pocket and pulled out a twenty-pound note.

"Here you go, I'll give you a score for them," I suggested, thrusting the note towards him. Three seconds later, despite looking slightly puzzled, he had gratefully accepted my offer and passed me the beers.

I returned to the reception area where the hostel fuckwit was sitting staring at this laptop.

"Oi, mate," I yelled, grabbing his attention, "here's a present from Candy."

I threw the first can of beer at his head. He raised his elbow, which deflected it onto the wall. I'd thrown it with such force it sprayed everywhere upon impact.

I threw a second can as he was running for cover; this hit him on the back. I jumped over the reception and went after him, throwing can number three, then four. Beer was spraying everywhere. He had tried and failed to open the back door and decided to curl up in the corner. I picked up one of the stray cans, which was half-full and fizzing, and threw it at him from short range.

As I turned to walk out, the gathering group, who'd been outside, had congregated at the reception, open-mouthed and relishing the drama. They were probably enjoying a bit of retribution towards a jobsworth I suspected they disliked.

I pulled my mobile phone out and turned towards them.

"Some geezer has stolen Candy's mobile phone, and I'm guessing he nicked it from her when she was dead. Was it any of you lot?"

They turned and looked at each other like butter wouldn't melt.

"Let's find out, shall we?" I rang her number. "If anyone's phone rings in the next five seconds then we'll know who stole it," I announced.

There was silence as I could hear the rings from my phone, but there was no buzzing mobile. Whoever had stolen Candy's phone wasn't in this group.

But make no mistake about it, I was going to hunt down this scumbag because he wasn't going to be getting away with this heartless act.

CHAPTER 16

I settled down with a pint of lager in one of Leicester's less salubrious taverns before returning to the British Heart Society. Thankfully, the lovely Maureen wasn't in attendance. I suspect she was on her lunch break, which I was guessing would be extended so the fat useless cunt could eat the ten thousand calories needed to sustain her through her afternoon shift.

I was greeted by an altogether more affable gentleman who happily went to find Colin Bourne. On this occasion, Colin appeared. He was about fifty, with a gentle stutter and an odd dress sense. Individually each item of clothing he was wearing might have been okay, but collectively it was a sartorial train crash.

"Hello, can I help you?" he enquired.

"I'm hoping I might be able to help you," I replied with a slight injection of swagger. "I came in the other day as I understand you are looking for volunteers to work in your warehouse."

"That's right, we are."

"Did you get the message that I called in?"

"No, I don't think so, sorry. Anyway, you are here now. Do you want to follow me to my office and we can have a chat?"

He led me to the large storeroom at the back of the shop, where he provided an overview of their operation. The arrangement was they collected furniture from donors, pimped it up and then sold it on, offering a delivery service in the process. I completed a couple of forms with him which he said he would send off to head office.

"When do you think I could start?" I asked.

"When would you like to start?"

"Tomorrow works for me," I said, more in hope than expectation.

"You're keen; I like your style. Let me check my whereabouts." He flicked an old paper diary open before running his finger down the page. "Yes, that's fine."

"Brilliant!" I enthusiastically replied.

"Shall we say ten o'clock start?"

I had finally got a result and it was a lesson to me in being assertive. Don't wait for things to happen; make them happen yourself. Colin claimed not to have received my message. Maybe he hadn't or maybe he had but simply couldn't be bothered to call me; either way, if I hadn't followed this up then I would never have heard from him and I would now be booked in for the St Matthews reunion gig.

I arrived home and made Grandad and I lunch. He had a cheese and onion sandwich, whilst I celebrated by gorging myself on six spam fritters. We sat and watched the television, and I noticed his near-continuous cough. Every couple of inhales of breath would prompt a shallow clearing of his chest. I closed my eyes and grimaced. I knew the fateful day was on the horizon.

I had nodded off on the settee by late afternoon and was awakened by a heavy thump on the backdoor. I looked across at Grandad who, given his startled look, had also enjoyed a nap.

I opened the door to be greeted by Bod's mum, who had returned for round two. Only this time she was absolutely pissed out of her skull.

"Are you happy now?" she slurred.

"With what?"

"My son; he's gone and lost his job. They made him resign before they sacked him."

"I'm sorry to hear that," I responded.

"'Sorry to hear that', you fucking scumbag! It's because of you this happened."

I quickly turned and closed the backdoor so Grandad might not hear the conversation.

"Look, I'm sorry. I don't know what you want me to say, but it's not as if he didn't do it."

"He only did it because you made him," she added as she staggered. "You weren't happy because he had a job. You were pissed off because he was getting on with his life so you had to drag him down to your fucking level."

"It wasn't like that."

"He's in court next week for sentencing. I bet you won't be there to support him?"

"He won't want me there; he's made it clear he doesn't want to see me again, otherwise I would."

"You wouldn't. You wouldn't give anyone the time of day, and do you know why?" she asked as she stumbled backwards. "Because you're the son of a murdering dad, and the apple never falls far from the tree."

That was it – she had lit the touch paper!

"I've been very polite to you so far, but you've just overstepped the mark. Let me tell you exactly how the charity shop gig went down. I called your beloved angel of a son when he was off work and told him about the bag of gear that'd been dropped off. I explained it was a two-man job and asked him if he wanted in. He said no, but then suddenly changed his tune when I told him there was a grand in it. There was no hard sell on my behalf, no coercing your little prince into doing something he didn't want to. Oh no, it was all about the money. Like me, you see, he's a greedy little fucker who doesn't care where it comes from. He knew who we were stealing from and he knew what was at stake, but he still did it. Maybe I've got an excuse? I've had no parents since I was eight years old. What's his explanation, Mrs Bodwin? Did you and your husband fall short? Is little Bod a criminal because of his poor upbringing? Are you looking for someone else to blame because deep down you know it's your fault?"

"You haven't a fucking clue what you are talking about," she ranted, masking a hiccup.

"Do me a favour, will you? Just go and fuck off!" I hollered.

"I'm going to get you back for this, Robbie fucking Howard, you see."

As she staggered down the driveway, nearly falling into a couple of unfortunate pedestrians on the pavement, I called out to her, "Thanks for calling around, Mrs Bodwin. Do drive carefully."

CHAPTER 17

I called round to Tony's house to give him the good news regarding my new volunteering position at the British Heart Society.

"What was all commotion about earlier?" he asked.

"It was one of Grandad's ex-girlfriends demanding a handout for his new baby," I joked.

"Was the woman shouting at you about the charity shop thing?"

"Yeah, her son was my wingman. She's trying to lay it all on me, making out I forced him to do it and that he's a guilty party when he isn't."

"You might want to keep your eye on her. You're involved in a dangerous game with Egan and the last thing you need is some noisy, annoyed parent who's looking to throw a spanner in your works."

"You're right. I laid into her as well."

"I know, I was listening in."

Of course he was.

"Look, Tony, I'm sorry Egan called around here earlier to collect the bag."

"It's fine. How did you explain to him why it ended up around here?"

"I just told him straight, told him you picked me up and saved me from getting arrested," I replied. "Did he lean on you with regards to keeping schtum about it?"

"Not really. Why, were you expecting him to?"

"I never know what to expect with him," I said.

We sat and chatted about the news before I found an appropriate moment to discuss Zoe.

"Your daughter, how old is she?" I queried.

"Twenty-six," he replied, making it clear from his body language this wasn't a subject he wanted bringing up again. However, I needed to glean a little more information to continue my search.

"Is she still in Leicester?"

"I've no idea," he answered bluntly.

I took a long, hard look at the picture, trying to remember every detail about her. I still had other social media platforms to check and I would be surprised if she wasn't active on at least one of them. She had distinctive auburn hair and freckles. Her hair may have changed style, and perhaps colour, and, as with most people, she had no doubt put a few pounds on since this photograph, but her freckles were quite distinctive.

"What's going on in the news?" I enquired.

"The mad fella with the funny haircut who runs North Korea is testing nuclear weapons again. He's a loose cannon and he'll end up causing some serious damage – you mark my words."

"If you test a nuclear weapon, don't you end up killing loads of people?" I asked.

He turned and looked at me. "I'm pretty certain they don't test them in places where people live," he replied with a grin.

"What, so like out in the desert or something?"

"There isn't a desert in North Korea, Robbie. He'll test them in the water or inside controlled underground bunkers," he added before he started to laugh. "Did you actually think they were tested by dropping them on cities and killing their own people?"

I shrugged my shoulders, feeling a bit silly.

"I don't know, I didn't think about it."

We continued to watch the news, chat and dunk biscuits. After an hour I got up to leave and moved towards the door.

"When do you start volunteering?" he asked.

"Tomorrow. I hope I make a good impression."

"You'll be fine," he assured me.

I opened the door and there was some mail in the letterbox. I removed and passed it to him. As I did, I glanced down at the top letter: 'Mr A. Hamylton', Hang on a minute! This wasn't the conventional spelling of his surname. During my brief online search for his daughter, I had been carrying out a search armed with the wrong information. I felt a twinge of optimism. Perhaps now I might be able to track her down?

I was lying on my bed messing around with my mobile phone whilst mindful I had other more pressing tasks requiring attention. First up, I sent a message to Egan informing him I would be starting my volunteering job tomorrow. Of course, this was my way of telling him to go fuck himself with regards to forcing me back into the St Matthews bear cage.

His response was to ask for the precise details of the volunteering gig: where it was, the name of the contact, how many hours per week, etc., etc. This guy was such a fucking prick. There were no congratulations, well done, I never stopped believing in you or any of that shit. Instead, it was a terse message suggesting he didn't believe me and he'd be corroborating details.

When I messaged him back with the required information, his response was simply:

Let's see how you go on

Again, no encouragement, no optimism, nothing. This had become an opportunity to prove him wrong and I was determined to take it.

I then moved on to tracking down Tony's daughter. I went

back into Facebook armed with the new search information and typed her name in. A list of people matching this search appeared; however, at the top of the list was the thumbnail picture of someone that looked vaguely like her. I clicked on this image to get a closer look. BOOM! There she was, clear as day. I spent the next forty minutes pondering how to word an appropriate message before sending it off. At least on Facebook, unlike a text, you can see if someone has read the message. If she did read it and didn't respond, then I would at least know this avenue was dead in the water.

It was fingers-crossed time. I hoped that I might be able to thank Tony for his kindness by giving something back.

It was the first day of my volunteering gig and I was up, ready and strangely enthusiastic about going. A few weeks ago, I may have been a little reticent about attending, fearful of making mistakes and loathe to meet new people, but my recent experiences were starting to provide a greater level of confidence and self-esteem.

I was managing my time so I would leave home, walk into town, grab a couple of Greggs sausage rolls before arriving at the British Heart Society at no later than 9.50 a.m. – ten minutes before my start time.

My shift for the first day was a gentle four hours, although, as someone who had never really worked a day in his life, I was expecting this to be more than enough.

I made Grandad his second cup of tea and took it through to him. He was sitting very quietly watching the television and seemed distracted and concerned. I suspected he'd endured another sleepless night; the fluid on his lungs making any prolonged, deep sleep nigh on impossible.

I knelt at the side of his chair and placed my hand on top of his.

"I'm off, Grandad," I said in a hushed voice.

He slowly turned his head towards me until his gaze met mine.

"Okay," he replied, barely audibly.

"Are you going to be alright?"

He pulled a half-smile and winked.

As I walked down the driveway a car pulled up outside. As I approached the familiar face of Detective Sergeant Mathew Wood appeared from the driver's side. Shit! What did he want?

"Going somewhere, Robbie?" he asked as he walked around the vehicle to where I was.

"Yeah, I'm off to work," I replied.

"Work? That's a funny way of putting it. Don't you mean you are off to sell drugs for Egan?"

"No. I have a volunteering job at the British Heart Society."

Wood started laughing. "A drug dealer in the evening, a volunteer for a charity by day – I've heard the fucking lot now!"

"Well, it's what I'm doing and where I'm going, so you can laugh all you want."

"Laugh? Oh yeah, I will laugh when I want. But do you know what really makes me laugh? It's when the joke's on you."

"What are you talking about?"

"Robert Howard, I am arresting you for the assault and battery of Benjamin Clements, a keyworker at the Darwin Hostel. You have the right to remain silent."

The rest of the narrative was as I've heard many times before. A familiar thread of words, which, if I was going to be honest, I had probably done well never to have read out to me previously. I was placed in handcuffs and told to get into the backseat of the vehicle.

DS Wood looked pleased with himself. He knew his strategy to bring Egan and me down had achieved its first milestone.

I was booked in by a polite desk sergeant, who calmly read me the charge before arranging for some mugshots to be taken. I was inclined to ask him whether he was free to undertake some customer service training for Maureen at the British Heart Society but thought better of it.

I was stripped, searched and divested of all possessions before being allocated some less than fashionable sweat bottoms and a top.

When I was offered a telephone call I decided to ring Egan. He might tell me to clear off, but if there was a man who knew how to get himself released from a police cell then I suspected it was him.

"Hello," he answered in a deadpan voice.

"It's Robbie, Robbie Howard. I need your help."

"With what?" he asked, in a tone suggesting I had wasted my only call.

"I've been nicked for assault of—"

"Don't say anything else," he interrupted. "Which station are you at?"

"Mansfield Street."

"Tell them you aren't prepared to answer any questions until your brief arrives, got it?"

"Okay."

He hung up.

I explained the situation to DS Wood, who looked disappointed he wouldn't get his hands on me alone in the interview room. I was then led away to a holding cell.

Several hours had passed before finally the cell door opened and I was informed my brief had arrived. If there was any doubt this had been arranged by Egan then it was confirmed upon meeting him. He was an incredibly well-dressed fifty-something solicitor. He had grey, immaculately cut hair, a suit to match and was well-spoken, assertive and thankfully in my corner.

As I walked into the spartan interview room, where only he and I would discuss my case, he stood up, gestured for me sit down and then picked up his gold pen which was resting on his case notes.

"Robbie, good afternoon, my name is Oliver Franklin-Jones from Franklin-Jones, Goodchild and Thorpe solicitors in London. I have been instructed by my long-term client, Sean Egan, to represent you."

"You've come all the way from London for me?"

"It's a short hop on the train. You've been arrested, but not charged, for a Section forty-seven offence: Assault occasioning Actual Bodily Harm. The allegation being you entered the Darwin Hostel in Leicester and used threatening behaviour towards a Benjamin Clements, an employed keyworker of the hostel. According to the charge sheet, you attacked him by violently and aggressively throwing four cans of beer at his person, despite no provocation and with Mr Clements trying to defend himself from the attack. Now, don't say anything regarding these allegations at this stage. I am simply here to deal with the facts of the case, as I understand them, okay?"

"Okay," I replied.

"The evidence against you is limited to CCTV footage of an individual entering the reception area of the Darwin reception and engaging in an assault, as described. The reason you are here is this CCTV footage was viewed by DS Mathew Wood, who positively identified you as the person in the video. What I have done is prepared a statement on your behalf which I will read to the police when we go into the interview. After reading this statement you will be asked a series of questions by the detectives. You will answer 'no comment' to each question, do you understand?"

"Yes."

"Do not, and I cannot stress this firmly enough, do not under any circumstances feel tempted to offer any contribution beyond this. It's 'no comment' to everything. If they offer you a drink, I will talk on your behalf; if they offer you a break, I will either accept or decline. You say and do nothing, do you hear me?"

"Yes."

"Good, then we are ready to go."

We sat in the interview with DS Wood and DS Brydges in attendance. The details of the incident were read to me, as was the time, date and attendance details for the recording. Mr Franklin-Jones then intervened.

"I have a statement prepared by my client which I would request to read."

I noticed DS Brydges sighed. "Go ahead," said Wood.

"Before I read the statement, can I say I am somewhat surprised there are two detectives in attendance for an interview of a minor Section forty-seven charge. Either Leicestershire police need to review their resource strategy or I'm beginning to wonder whether this arrest amounts to little more than harassment of an individual whom you believe is involved in an associated matter. Certainly, in terms of the evidence you have provided, it shows nothing more than a man, although even that's not entirely clear, so let's say a person, entering a premises, wearing dark and dare I say unremarkable clothes, with no clear view of their face. Come now, detectives, if you are relying on this evidence as your trump card against my client then I think it's fair to say you don't exactly hold a smoking gun, do you?"

"We are pretty certain this CCTV footage is of your client," said Brydges.

"Presumably a fact which can be corroborated by the numerous witnesses who, as we can see on the footage, were gathered at the front of the premises?"

"We currently don't have a witness statement to this effect but enquires are ongoing."

"Goodness gracious! I've seen sieves with fewer holes. I do hope you two know what you are doing. Okay, if you want to proceed, then I am happy to do so. Suffice to say, I will be preparing a letter, once you have released my client, to the Chief Constable noting my grave reservations about the effectiveness of his force and his use of public funding to service the common good of the people of this city."

Both detectives sighed and looked like naughty schoolboys.

Their tactic to bring me in for intimidation, a warning shot across my bows, had spectacularly backfired. Franklin-Jones read out the statement and their questioning lasted no more than ten minutes before DS Wood called a halt to proceedings.

I was returned to my cell and released, without charge, two hours later. As my possessions were handed back to me there was no sign of the two detectives whom I suspected were seriously pissed off at the mauling Franklin-Jones had handed out to them. I needed to be extra careful now. I had tickled the lion under the chin and it was ready to tear me a new arsehole.

I departed the police station and spotted Egan leaning against his car. As I approached he delivered a simple directive:

"Get in," he growled.

"So, let me get this right," he said in a sarcastic tone, "this girl, Candy, had died in her hostel shooting up Corey's bad gear and you took it out on the fella working there by throwing cans of beer at him," Egan said before he started laughing.

"He wouldn't let me in. If he had done, I might have been able to save her life."

"Please tell me I haven't instructed my three-thousand-pounds-an-hour solicitor to travel up to Leicester to get you off a charge which amounts to throwing four cans of Fosters at someone," he said, as he turned the car off the main road.

"It was Tennents Super," I joked.

Even he smirked.

"Three thousand pounds an hour – are you kidding me?" I asked.

"It's the going rate for a sound legal mind, and trust me, this fella will bill me every penny. I'll get his first-class train fare, taxis, even a tenner for his lunchtime coffee and sandwich. It's how the rich get richer."

"I'm sorry."

"So am I. But not about his bill, more about you throwing cans of beer at this man in the hostel – what's that all about?"

"What do you mean?"

"You need to commit yourself. If you thought this geezer deserved a slap because he'd contributed to the death of this young girl then give him a proper slap, teach him a lesson, make him go home and think about what he's done. Throwing cans of beer at him – that's like a rugby-club drinking game."

"Anyway, I've messed up on the British Heart Society gig. I was supposed to be there at ten this morning before DS Tom and Jerry came along and nicked me. I doubt they'll take me back."

"It's a shame you weren't able to call this Colin fella and make up some of your usual bullshit and somehow stall your start day to tomorrow. For once your lies might have got you out of a hole, rather than put you in one."

"I know, thanks for reminding me."

"It's just as well I rang him then," he said.

"Did you?"

"I played the part of your Uncle Egan on the phone."

"What did you say?"

"Robbie is ever so sorry he isn't able to come in today but his grandad's condition has taken a turn for the worst and he's had to go with him to the hospital. But, be sure, he'll be in bright and early tomorrow, keen and eager to start work."

"What did he say?"

"He was fine with it."

"That's a result," I said, relieved. "Thanks, Egan."

"I only intervened because I genuinely believe you are committed to it. Otherwise, I wouldn't have done anything."

"I was committed to it; I was on my way there."

"Good," he said, as the car turned into my road and he parked up outside of my house. "And I hope you continue to show the same level of commitment when you start tomorrow." He then turned to me. "It's important never to do anything half-heartedly. Always give it your best, put everything into it and you might be surprised where it takes you."

"Thanks for the advice," I said, getting out of the car.

"I'll see you at the club at seven," he announced.

"What?"

"You broke the terms of the deal. You should have started the volunteering job today but you didn't so you're going back into St Matthews tonight."

"You've got to be fucking kidding me, Egan!" I yelled desperately.

"I wondered whether Khally was someone who is all mouth or a man of his word who carries out his threats. I'll get to find out later."

CHAPTER 18

I arrived at the club wearing my drug-dealing Hugo Boss attire. Upon entering, I took a moment to appreciate the skin on my neck. I much preferred it taut and intact as opposed to flapping around, having been severed open by a nine-inch blade.

As usual, Egan was sitting at the bar enjoying a generous measure of Scotch. He noted my entrance and checked his watch, making sure I was on time, which I was.

"Fancy a drink?"

"Yes," I replied tersely.

He poured me a double measure, handed me the glass and I necked it, in one.

"Same again, please," I said as if addressing a barman. He took the glass, without objection, and refilled it.

He produced a package of coke from his pocket and placed it on the bar.

"You'll not be needing a peacemaker this evening," he told me.

"Why?"

"Because they will have learned their lesson. This time you'll be thoroughly searched before they let you into the flat."

"What have I got for protection?"

"Nothing. It's a shit-or-bust deal. You'll either come out of there with the five thousand or in a body bag."

"And are you happy with that?"

"I'll get my money one way or another. My only concern is who's going to be looking after your grandad if Khally makes good on his pledge and butchers you."

I gulped back the Scotch. "What's the arrangement?"

"You'll be going in between seven-thirty and eight. Khally knows he needs to be there and don't worry, he will be. He won't miss this for the world."

"Fucking hell – this is madness!" I said, failing to hold back my emotions.

"Five thousand in cash; five separate bundles with a different pocket for each bundle. You will then get the hell out of there and return any way you can: over gardens, through bushes, pole-vaulting fences; I'm not bothered."

"No pick-up?"

"No pick-up. Unless you've booked Tony's taxi's again?"

"I wish I had."

"I bet you do."

"This is nuts, Egan – fucking bonkers! It's like a suicide mission. Why don't you give me Khally's mobile number?"

"What for?"

"I'll get your money for you, but at least let me change the meeting arrangements, shake things up a bit and take some of the advantage away from him. It could be my only chance."

Egan turned and looked at me with an odd grin which I could have mistaken for admiration.

"Okay, I'll send you his number," he said.

I put the package in my jacket pocket.

"And whilst you're doing that, fetch me the gun as well. I'm fairly sure Khally and his boys won't be getting the opportunity to shake me down."

"What are you thinking?" he asked curiously.

"Maybe an alternative plan. I'm going to swing the pendulum back over to my side. If Khally's thinking of turning medieval on my neck then I'll make sure he doesn't get the chance."

Egan's smile grew a little wider.

"And finally, ladies and gentlemen, I think the penny may have dropped," he said.

I wasn't in possession of the leather shoulder bag on the second evening I entered the St Matthews estate. This time the package of cocaine was in my roomy coat pocket with the gun, again, sitting in the back of my trousers.

I entered the estate by the same street as I had done on the first occasion, only I would not be making my way to Khally's flat.

It was shortly after seventy-thirty and the streets were busy with people going about their business. I walked until I was within sight of the entrance to the flat before finding a place to hide. The numerous side alleys to the other blocks provided me with more than enough choice. Once out of view, I called him.

"Hello," he answered.

"I've got a delivery for you."

"Who's this?"

"Who do you think?"

"Press the buzzer and come up," he said, assuming I was outside.

"Not tonight, amigo. This time you're coming to meet me."

"Where are you?"

"Close, very close. Listen carefully to my instructions and you'll get your package; if you don't and decide to do something stupid, then I walk."

"No, no, you come here, cuz, I'm not coming to you."

"Do you want me to walk? I'm happy to do so."

"Whatever," he said, sounding unconvincing.

"Now we both know you can't afford for this to happen. You need this coke, don't you? You need it because those people who buy from you are getting fidgety and you're in danger of losing them. They will soon find a new dealer and by the time you get your hands on some more gear, you'll be finished. So, think carefully before you answer my next question: are you coming out of your flat to meet me or not?"

He paused. "Okay."

"You'll leave on your own. So, tell your boyfriends to play nicely and stay where they are. If they follow behind you, I'm out of here. Have you got it?"

"Yeah."

"You'll leave your block, turn right and then cross over and walk down Mackenzie Way. I'm sure you know it like the back of your hand."

"Of course I do."

"After this, you will make your way to Bushy Park. It'll no doubt be locked but the fence won't prove much of a problem to get over. When you get in you'll stand in the middle of the park. When I see you've done this I'll ring you again, understand?"

"Yeah."

"Leave now. I'll call you when you're in position."

He hung up. A few minutes later I spotted him leaving the block. With the plan I had in mind it didn't matter how far he was in front on me because, assuming he obeyed my instructions, once he was at the centre of the park, he would be a sitting duck.

I watched as he walked down the road, crossed over and headed down Mackenzie Way. My eyes diverted back to the block where two men were exiting and heading in the same direction. One of them gave away his cover by looking around way too suspiciously for him to be doing anything other than tracking Khally and coming for me.

I called Khally. "What did I tell you about your boyfriends staying put?"

"I fucking told them to stay there! What the fuck!"

He sounded genuine. "Call them off. If they aren't back at your flat in two minutes, I walk."

Within sixty seconds the two men were running, tails between their legs, back to the flat. I watched as they disappeared into the block. I was certain they wouldn't reappear, as Khally couldn't afford to jeopardise the deal.

I followed in his footsteps, and as I was exiting Mackenzie Way, my phone rang.

"I'm here," Khally announced.

As I approached the park fence I looked in and confirmed he was exactly where I told him to be.

"Okay, stay there. I'll call you again in two minutes. I assume you have the money?"

"Yeah, I've got it."

I hung up.

I walked around the outside perimeter of the park to the far end which received little streetlight. I jumped over the fence and hid in the trees. I then called him again.

"I want you to walk slowly to the far side of the park," I instructed.

I watched as he turned around and began walking in my direction getting closer and closer until he was within twenty feet. I then instructed him to stop. He turned to see the expanse of greenery in front of him, looking uncomfortably left and right, no doubt feeling vulnerable, which of course he was.

I slowly took the gun out of the back of my trousers, whilst holding the phone to my ear. I waited for twenty seconds or so before I moved.

"Where are you?" he asked.

"Here!" I replied, now stood right behind him with the gun pressed to his back. I saw him shudder with surprise.

"Don't look around, don't say anything, in fact, don't fucking move. We are going to do this deal, but you are going to follow my instructions. Nod if you're okay with that."

He nodded.

"I'm going to pass into your left hand a sealed package. Egan assures me it's top-grade gear. If you don't believe him then undo the tape and try it."

I passed the package to him, which he took, opened before dabbing a little on his tongue.

"Are you happy?"

"That's good fucking coke," he replied.

"If we are going to do more business together then we need to trust one another. Now put the package in your pocket and start to pass to me the packs of money."

I checked the first pack and it seemed about right for a grand, but I wasn't going to count it. By the time the fourth pack was passed to me, I had spotted a figure walking towards us at the opposite end of the park.

"Who the fuck's this?" I fumed.

"He's not with me," he replied.

"Quick, pass me the last one and then get the fuck out of here, it might be Old Bill."

"Are you trying to fucking stitch me up?" he snarled.

"I was going to ask you the same question. If it's one of your boys then I'm going to shoot the pair of you."

"Fuck you!"

"Just pass me the rest of the money and get the fuck out of here," I ordered.

"I'm going to get you back for this; no one treats me like their bitch."

"If it's any consolation, I've enjoyed every second of it."

I took the fifth pack and then hid back in the trees. It was so dark there was no way we could have been seen until the person was within thirty feet. Khally bolted over the fence and disappeared into the night.

I hid behind one of the bigger trees, slowly turning my phone off and waiting for whoever it was to come into view. This wasn't a stranger; this was someone who had either been following me or Khally.

As the person approached, it became clear it was the build of a man. He was looking in all directions. He knew we'd been here but had been too late to stop the deal.

I watched as he fumbled in his pocket, his face still out of view. He removed what must have been his phone and I saw a faint ray of light from his screen as he dialled a number.

"It looks like they've gone," he said, confirming to me he was after us. "I'm fairly sure it was them, but I couldn't get a clear view. If it was, then it looks like the deal's been done."

I took a deep breath and an even deeper swallow.

"I'll have a look around, but I suspect they've done what they came for and fucked off. They could be anywhere. This place is like a fucking labyrinth, and to be honest, I wouldn't mind getting away from here myself."

I watched as he ended the call and placed the phone in his pocket. He was still looking around to see if he missed anything, but it was obvious he had lost interest.

He then started to walk towards me. I crouched at the side of the tree, and as he walked past I slowly moved around the trunk so he wouldn't spot me. He then jumped over the metal fence and out into the street, where the faint streetlights allowed me to identify him.

It was London's finest who had outstayed his welcome and was still in Leicester. The figure who had appeared from the shadows was DS Jem Langley and he had been thirty seconds away from bringing me down.

I returned to Egan's club, where there was an empty used tumbler next to him which he removed and replaced with a fresh one. He poured me a large Scotch and handed it to me.

"I'm always encouraged when I see associates of mine returning from deals without blood dripping from their necks."

"Khally was the least of my problems. He'll return to get his own back on me another day. The issue is with your friend from London who came within a whisker of gatecrashing the deal," I explained.

"Langley?"

"So much for him fucking off back to the smoke."

"Any sign of Wood and Brydges?" he asked.

"No, he was alone."

Egan nodded his head before slowly pouring another drink. He was always one step ahead. I suspect he had planned for the heat he would get from Langley, as he had already planned what he was next going to do with me.

"Where's the money?" he enquired.

I took each bundle out and placed it on the bar. He picked one up and examined it. I guessed he was only too familiar with the quantity of a thousand pounds in used twenties.

'You've done well, Robbie. You've ventured back into the bee's nest and returned with the honey. That's no mean feat for a novice beekeeper."

I placed the gun back on the bar.

"Do you want to keep it? It might be useful should you run into your new enemies."

"No thanks. The only enemies I'm now worried about own shiny badges and handcuffs, and they would just love to catch me with that thing in the belt of my trousers."

"You're starting at the British Heart Society tomorrow; just make sure you work hard and make a success of it. If not, you'll be in on the next job, and trust me, it's juicy."

"Are you cutting me some slack?" I asked.

He turned away. "Maybe," he answered.

He then pushed two of the packages in my direction.

"Here are your wages."

"Two grand!" I couldn't hide my shock or pleasure.

"Spend it wisely. Treat your grandad to a bottle of Johnnie Walker Black Label."

I took the money and placed it in my jacket.

"I'll be seeing you. Be sure to give my love to Colin tomorrow," he said.

I left the club and, as ever, there were no goodbyes, no small talk, nothing. He was a cold fish, empty and heartless. I suspect he was someone who didn't share love with another soul outside of his family.

I arrived home and went straight to my bedroom. I took the money out of my jacket and lay on the bed staring at it. Two grand! I reckon the most money I had ever previously made was maybe three hundred quid from a decent score.

I took a deep breath. I knew I was flying way too close to the sun and it was only a matter of time before my wings got scorched. The only detail I was missing was who amongst the people who were itching to take me down would get to me first. Egan was smart and streetwise; it appeared he had a sixth sense for danger. I was learning fast but was acutely aware of my blind spots. My lack of experience hiking over this unknown terrain would ultimately end in a fall.

When would Egan next be in touch? Might he feel the heat of invading another dealer's manor and retreat to the bright lights of the capital?

As I lay on my bed, I was conscious that the fear I had experienced on Egan's previous missions had dissipated. This evening I had enjoyed the Marmite emotion of a heavy adrenalin injection. I felt controlled and confident in my decision-making. I had, after all, completed this dangerous task, returned to the club with the money and had gained satisfaction from the financial reward I'd received.

What was I becoming?

I remembered I had turned my phone off and quickly switched it back on. Within a few seconds, the notifications came dropping in, one of which was a Facebook message from Zoe Hamylton.

I opened the messaged and scanned it. She had agreed to meet up with me.

CHAPTER 19

For a fella like me who enjoyed a joke, being in an open-all-hours off-licence, buying two bottles of hard liquor before 8 a.m. was too good an opportunity to waste.

As I handed the seventy quid over to the Indian shopkeeper, I pretended to be shaking and politely asked him if he would have any objections to me drinking the first bottle in the shop to 'steady my nerves'.

I must confess to being more than a little concerned at the deadpan answer I received. He confirmed this would be perfectly okay before he enquired whether I would like a glass and a seat.

I declined his kind offer and shortly afterwards was knocking on Tony's door.

"I'm the bearer of gifts!" I announced before he had time to greet me.

"Johnnie Walker Black label! Blimey, have you won the pools?"

I didn't want to spoil the euphoria by asking him what the fuck the 'pools' were, so instead, I handed him the bottle.

"I drank enough of your whisky the other night and it's a small token of my thanks for the help you've given me," I explained.

He looked thrilled. I had time for a cuppa and a chat before I needed to head off to the British Heart Society.

"Tony, I've some important news for you," I explained pensively. "It's regarding your daughter, Zoe."

"What about her?" he answered dispassionately.

"I've tracked her down on Facebook and sent her a message."

"What message?" he answered abruptly.

"I asked her whether she would like to meet me for a drink and a chat."

"To chat about what?" he asked defensively.

"I want to get to know her."

"Why?"

"To see whether there is any chance of me brokering a deal so you two can meet up."

"Why would you go and do that!" he snapped.

"Because she's your daughter and you obviously care because her picture sits in front of you for most of the day. Isn't this reason enough?"

"You have no idea what happened! She'll still be with that bastard and I can't be having it."

"I think you can work around this."

"Do you have any idea how hard it is trying to bring up a daughter on your own? I wasn't a young man either; I'd get all the 'is that your grandad picking you up' when I collected her from school. It was tough, but we had each other and we kept close."

"Yeah, like I know you would. I have no doubt you were a great dad. But I need to understand what happened?"

"Ask her, I'm done with it. I can't even think about what happened because it makes me so mad! Why did you bring this back into my fucking house? How dare you!" he shouted. He stood up in a threatening way, as he was seriously losing his shit.

"Okay, okay! I'm not here to upset you. I'm sorry."

He sat down and put his head in his hands.

I stood up to leave. "I didn't want to upset you, Tony, that was not my intention."

He said nothing.

Sat in front of me was a broken man. I had ignited pain,

hurt and a fair serving of anger. I felt guilty for this but knew my motives were honourable.

"I'm going to leave. I'll call around to see you in the morning."

As I approached the door he called out. "When are you seeing her?"

"This afternoon, after work," I replied.

I paused to see if he was going to say anything else, but as with the communication between him and his daughter for the past few years, there was only silence.

I arrived at the British Heart Society for my delayed first day of work and was predictably greeted at the till by Maureen. I'm guessing she wasn't overly enthused to see me given the enormous yawn she produced as I approached. She did not attempt to conceal it either: no hand in front of her mouth; no weird contortion of her face which some people do when they realise such an act might not be appropriate. No, Maureen almost tried to exaggerate it: her huge gob opening like an oncoming tunnel; her already bulbous eyes appearing to inflate like gigantic balloons. For a second, it appeared like a giant pig was trying to suck me down its throat before her face resumed its usual resting docile demeanour.

"Hi, I'm here to see Colin Bourne," I announced.

"Can I ask what it is regarding?" she replied in a monotone voice.

"I'm starting here today."

"Starting what?" she asked, as her massive fat tongue began to hang out of her mouth. She looked like a racehorse which had been fed a polo mint.

"Starting work."

"Where?"

"Here! I'm starting work here today as a volunteer."

I decided to omit, 'you fucking thick twat' from the end of this sentence for fear this wouldn't be a great way to broker relations with someone who, unfortunately, was now a work colleague.

"I'll go and get him," she announced, letting off a massive sigh in the process.

I enjoyed watching her waddle off. Walking was a massive effort for Maureen. Her fat wobbling thighs appeared to meet above the knees, whilst her cellulite was so pronounced it looked like someone had thrown Artex at the back of her legs.

I decided it would be my private joke to make her do as much walking as I could to enable my time here to be more bearable. I would manufacture errands for her to run and then watch gleefully as she painfully shuffled off to do them.

Colin walked through the rear storeroom with Maureen. Given Maureen's walking speed of about ten metres per hour, he quickly overtook her and greeted me with a warm handshake. Inexplicably, he was wearing an ill-fitting baseball cap. It was like someone had dared him to wear it. It sat on the top of his head as if he were concealing an Easter egg underneath.

He took me through to the capacious storage area where he introduced me to Baz. Baz was one of the few full-time paid employees who worked at the branch. He was a fat forty-something balding bloke, with traces of early 1980s tattoos which had become badly discoloured and a weirdly distorted facial expression which appeared as if he could constantly smell shit.

"Robbie, this is Baz," Colin announced.

"Are you one of those people who have been sent here by the Jobcentre?" he asked haughtily.

"No, Robbie's come here of his own accord. He wants to join the army and is looking for some work experience. That's right, isn't it, Robbie?"

"Yes," I answered.

"Oh, fuck me! You're not one of these do-gooders who wants to 'give something back to society'?" droned Baz whilst gesturing inverted commas.

"Baz, remember what we talked about at your last performance review," Colin remarked.

"I'm fucking sorry! I wouldn't want to offend anyone, would I?" he responded, turning away in disgust.

"Robbie, you and Baz will be out this morning collecting furniture donations. Baz, don't forget, you need to be back here at one o'clock to pick up the sideboard for Mrs Harvey. She needs it dropping off at one thirty prompt, as her son is going to help her move it."

"Yeah, whatever," he grumbled before storming off.

"Right, Robbie, you go with Baz. Enjoy yourself and I'll see you later."

I trotted on and caught up with him.

"He fucks me off sometimes," Baz complained.

"Why?"

"Barking fucking orders and all that. I've been here longer than him; if anything, he should listen to me."

I followed him to the back of the storeroom, where there was a 7.5-tonne lorry parked near the entrance. Baz reached into his pocket, pulled out a fag and lit up. I stood nearby, like a spare part, waiting for him to finish. As various people entered the storeroom he called them over so he could moan to them about being allocated all the worse jobs and being saddled with having to mentor 'useless fucking volunteers' – in this instance, me.

After fifteen long, painful minutes, he finally climbed into the driver's seat and we drove off.

"How come you're not working?" he grunted.

"Long story," I replied. I had taken an instant dislike to this fella and wasn't big on having to converse with him.

"What the fuck do you want to do this for? You aren't even getting paid."

"As I say, long story," I replied, trying to shut down his meaningless twaddle.

"We get volunteers like you coming in all the while. I get fucked off with them, to be honest."

"Why?"

"Because you show them the fucking ropes and then they stop coming; so, they've wasted everyone's fucking time."

"The woman who is working on the till, I've seen her here a couple of times so I'm guessing she still comes in?" I asked, trying to challenge his theory.

"Who, Maureen?"

"Yeah, she a volunteer, isn't she?"

"No, she's gets paid."

"She gets paid – fucking hell!" I sniggered.

"What do you mean by that?" he snapped.

"Nothing," I replied, remembering I knew nothing of the relationships between any of the existing staff. "I just had her down as a volunteer."

"She's worked here for ages."

"Good for her."

"Why is it good for her? What do you mean by that?" he probed.

"Nothing."

"You haven't got your eye on her, have you?" he asked threateningly.

I turned and looked at him, assuming he was joking.

"Are we still talking about the same person?"

"Yeah, Maureen. I wouldn't try anything with her if I were you."

"Why?"

"Because you're sat next to her new boyfriend," he bragged.

I looked at him and he stared back at me with a 'I've pulled the hottest girl in Leicester, so don't you even think about it' face.

"I think it's safe to say you don't need to view me as competition," I replied.

"They always say that, but just to let you know I'll be keeping my eye on you when you're around her."

"I'll bear that in mind and thanks for the heads up."

Little did Baz know he had also just entered my game. Not only was I going to force his fat pig-faced girlfriend to get off her massive arse and walk whenever I could, I would also jab, at every opportunity, his obvious jealous bone by suggesting I was starting to take a sexual interest in her.

I sat back sniggering to myself as I imagined date night with Maureen and Baz. Her fat tongue would be rolling out of her gob as she was eating a two-for-one burger at Harvesters. Across the table, Baz would whine incessantly about the gross injustices Colin inflicted on him at the British Heart Society, namely trying to make him do some work in return for his wages.

We arrived at the first pick-up: a semi-detached house where a kind old lady was donating a table and chairs. In the name of 'showing me the ropes', Baz had me carry all the furniture onto the back of the lorry. Meanwhile, he borrowed the kind donor's toilet, leaving the parting gift of the stench from his huge shit.

After this call, Baz pulled into a layby for another smoke. He had timed this around Maureen's coffee break. I had to sit and listen to him on the phone to her, making out he'd been working his arse off and how much he was looking forward to a pint later.

We did a couple more collections where, again, he left me to transport the donations into the lorry.

It was approaching one o'clock and despite being no more than five minutes' drive back to the store, Baz pulled over for yet another smoke.

"It's nearly one o'clock. Colin said we needed to get back," I reminded him.

"Yeah, I know! I am entitled to a break," he grumbled.

He deliberately took his time and we eventually returned at 1.20 p.m. to the obvious irritation of Colin.

"Baz, where have you been? I told you, we needed to get you loaded up and on the road for one o'clock," Colin moaned.

"Yeah, we were delayed. There's been an accident down Uppingham Road," he said, scratching his balls. "I've driven as fast as I could, you can ask Roddy."

"His name's 'Robbie'. Right, get loaded up and straight off," Colin instructed.

"But I haven't had my lunch!" Baz replied.

"Can't you have it when you get back?" Colin asked, looking frustrated.

"No, because that'll be over six hours without a break and you'd be in breach of the law, Colin. You really should know better."

"Pass me the keys, I'll take it," Colin responded, getting rightly annoyed.

"You need someone to go with you because of the size of the cabinet and there isn't anyone free," Baz added as he was deliberately creating obstacles.

"I can go with you," I suggested.

"But you finish at two o'clock and we won't be back until after," Colin noted.

"I'm not bothered, I'll go with you."

"Good lad! Thanks, Robbie. Right, let's get loaded up," Colin announced enthusiastically.

Baz stared at me, shaking his head as if I had breached one of his laws of the workplace. Perhaps it was the act of actually working which was annoying him. I had been in this twat's company for three hours and had had a bellyful of him. As I walked past, I gave him a wink before following Colin to the storeroom.

Whilst moving this big bloody lump of a cabinet I eyed Maureen floating around the shop.

"Maureen, Maureen," I called.

Once I'd attracted her attention, I gestured for her to approach. She sighed and slowly toddled over with all the grace of a wounded bison.

"Yeah?" she finally said.

"Would you mind moving that plastic cup from the floor, please? I don't want to trip on it," I requested.

I watched as she had to painfully kneel to retrieve an item

which, at worst, I would have trodden on and squashed. She then shuffled back to where she had come from.

Colin and I turned the cabinet around and lifted it onto the tailgate and into the lorry. Colin jumped in the driver's seat and started the engine.

Before I jumped in, I again shouted over to her.

"Maureen! Maureen!"

She stopped what she was doing. I again gestured for her to come over. She did an even bigger sigh before trundling towards me. I stood and watched with an enormous grin on my face and without making any effort to walk towards her.

"Yeah?" she said as she finally walked up to me.

"Thank you for moving that cup for me," I said, barely able to contain my laughter.

"Is that it?" she queried.

"Yeah. No, hold on. Are you free later for a drink?"

"No, I'm going out with Barry."

"Maybe another time then," I replied, as I climbed into the lorry.

I arrived back from the delivery at 2.45 p.m. Colin was most grateful as I had been prepared to work beyond my allocated voluntary hours. It was no big deal and I enjoyed doing a few hours of graft. For once I felt useful and had a purpose.

Mrs Harvey was thrilled to bits with her new sideboard and treated us both to a slice of her delicious homemade lemon drizzle cake. Colin enthused so much about it that Mrs Harvey cut him off an extra slice which she wrapped up for him to take away. I'm sure Colin would have thoroughly enjoyed this as well if he hadn't sat and squashed it when he took his seat in the lorry. I watched him do it as well and, in truth, could have prevented it from happening, but sometimes in life, there is pleasure to be had in watching unfortunate minor accidents play out.

I killed time between finishing work and meeting Zoe by taking a trip to Virginia Chicken, where I ordered a double-fried chicken burger and chips. Quite how they can knock this out for £1.99 was a puzzle to me until it arrived. It was a pathetic slab of steroid-injected chicken, a limp piece of lettuce with diluted mayo rammed into a pitiful soft bap. The chips weren't up to much either; they smelt like they had been fried in Lidl hair conditioner.

As I was ramming most of my meal into an already full bin, I caught a glimpse of myself in the mirror. It's fair to say as someone who was meeting a total stranger I was appallingly dressed. My attire could best be described as 'industrial' and, having spent the day around old furniture, I had a thin layer of dust and fine wood chips all over me.

Still, this wasn't *Love Island*, more an opportunity to sew back together a fractured relationship, and I felt I owed Tony this for all his continued support.

Zoe agreed to meet in a nice little Italian coffee shop, Café Roma, at 5 p.m. In the interests of being chivalrous, I arrived early and reserved us a seat. Soon after 5 p.m., Zoe arrived. She was easy to pick out due to her distinctive freckles. There was no doubt that whilst she had put on a little weight since the photograph in Tony's lounge was taken, she was still a very attractive woman.

She was easy to get on with and had a good sense of humour. We swapped the usual pleasantries before that slightly awkward silent pause in a conversation when both parties know it was time to discuss what they had met up for. I had the running order of this clear in my head beforehand, but now I was sat opposite her, it was kind of going to pieces.

"Okay, erm so, where do I start," I mumbled making a royal pig's ears of it.

"Why don't you start with how you met my dad?" she suggested.

I smiled. "Yeah, that makes sense, doesn't it? Tony, your dad, moved in next door to me and my grandad about five years ago.

I'm not going to lie, at the beginning I had him down as being hard work—"

"Sounds like Dad," she interrupted.

"He was, well, I don't want to sound disrespectful or anything, but every time I would see him he'd be moaning about something going on in the news. It got to the point where I would dread bumping into him and sort of had the feeling he used to wait for me and then lurch out so he could have a moan."

I realised I may have been talking about him a little too frankly. Thankfully, she cracked a smile and seemed okay with it, so I continued.

"But then one day, I was kind of forced to go around his house—"

"'Forced'?" she interjected.

"Not forced, but I felt I should go around; you know, I felt a bit guilty that he was on his own and I hadn't given him the time of day. So, I went around one day to get to know him a bit better."

"You did that?" she asked with a little admiration.

"Yeah, well, you know, I try to do my bit."

I was moving seamlessly into bullshit mode. If Egan were listening in to this, he'd be going mental.

"I'm sure he appreciated it," she commented.

"I thought it was going to be hard work, going around and making conversation with him, but then it was obvious he's a really nice bloke, like really supportive and he gives a toss."

"Yeah, he is those things, for sure. Have you come across his stubborn side yet?" she queried.

"Perhaps not like you have," I answered with half a smile.

"I'm sure he's told you what happened to my mum and her passing shortly after she gave birth to me. We were close, like really close, and he was a good dad, but then I grew up and naturally started to have boyfriends and this is where the trouble started."

"What trouble?"

"From the moment I had my first proper relationship he didn't like it. No one was ever going to be up to his standard. I brought one guy home once and he practically interrogated the poor lad. By the time he left he was a quivering wreck. No wonder I never saw him again! When I started to see Leon, it was no different."

"Who's Leon?"

"The fella I was going out with when Dad and I fell out. It was obvious the relationship was becoming serious. Dad had met him a couple of times and was being unfriendly, as usual. Then one day I came home and he sat me down and told me he had found out a load of stuff about him."

"What stuff?"

"Who his friends were, what he was doing for money, his criminal record; that sort of thing. It's like he had paid someone to dig around into Leon's background. That's when the trouble between us really started."

"Did Tony want you to finish with him?"

"Yeah, he wanted me to dump him there and then. I mean, I was in love with the guy so I wasn't going to do that. It was ridiculous. It became a 'me' or 'him' situation and I objected to it."

"I'm guessing I know who you chose."

"Do you know what? I didn't choose Leon for any other reason than Dad should have never put me in that position in the first place."

"I suppose he was worried about you."

"Then worry, but seriously, would you dump a girlfriend because your mum or dad told you to?"

"It would have been nice for my mum or dad to have told me anything."

"I'm sorry," she replied, guiltily.

"It's fine. Look, it's clear there's a lot of water under the bridge and I can't do anything about this, but I'm wondering whether there is a chance for you two?"

She shook her head. "I don't know. What did he say?"

"The same as you. I suppose the good news is neither of you

has given a categoric 'no', but I do understand the position you are both in."

We talked some more before Zoe announced she needed to get home. She finished her drink before putting on her coat.

"What next?" she asked, as we were ending our meeting.

"I'll go around to see Tony tomorrow and tell him we met up."

"What else will you tell him?"

"That you weren't dismissive of him. That maybe there's a twinkle of light somewhere."

"Will you message me after you've spoken to him?"

"Yeah, of course I will."

Her last question told me everything I needed to know. She still cared, maybe still loved him. Perhaps there was a chance they could be reunited.

I then realised why this mattered so much to me, and it wasn't all about doing a good turn for Tony. I would shortly be losing Grandad and I had no choice in this. My relationship with him would disappear forever and I felt compelled to give another association life and to bring two people back together. If I did, if I could pull this off, then maybe it would make Grandad's inevitable passing slightly more bearable.

It was my second day at the British Heart Society. I arrived promptly at 9.50 a.m. I now found getting to places on time easy, especially if I walked, as I would know exactly what time to leave home.

I eyed the lovely Maureen at the till, pulling her usual resting pig face as she fiddled with her mobile phone. Her tongue was again dangling unattractively out of her mouth, making her look like a ravenous bulldog.

"Good morning, Maureen."

"Morning," she replied with zero enthusiasm, her eyes refusing to divert from her phone screen.

"How was your Harvesters meal?" I asked.

"What Harvesters meal?" she queried as she reluctantly gazed up from her phone.

"I thought you and Baz were going to Harvesters?"

At this point, I realised my error. The Harvesters meal had been my invention; my corrupt imagination had been working overtime and it had somehow faded into reality. I was asking this fat lump about a night out which had existed only in my fantasy world of comedy and therefore, she didn't have a fucking clue what I was going on about.

"Harvesters, what are you talking about?" She shrugged, pulling a piggy version of a face which didn't have a fucking clue what I was talking about.

"Sorry, I've become confused. I sometimes mix up reality for sexual fantasy. You just went out for drinks, didn't you?"

"Yeah," she said, going back to her mobile phone.

"By the way, the sign outside the shop has fallen over. I think it's creating a hazard on the pavement," I announced.

I watched gleefully as her fat legs scuttled to the door only to discover the sign was perfectly upright. Before she had the chance to return and tell me, I was already in the storeroom.

Colin had allocated me to work with some fella called John. John was a retired carpenter who volunteered two days a week. His job was to renovate the donated furniture so it would sell for more money. From the moment I met John, I liked him. He was a brilliant craftsman and would patiently show and explain to me what he was doing. He kept it pretty basic, so I was sanding down tabletops and applying varnish. John explained to me the different grades of sandpaper, when to use glasspaper and what type of varnish to use. It was a real education. Nothing was too much trouble for him; no question was stupid and he worked at a nice pace.

After a couple of hours, I stopped to make us both a hot drink. I went to the entrance of the shop and noted it was empty and Maureen was again buggering about on her mobile phone.

"Maureen, Maureen!" I called out.

She looked at me and I gestured her to come over. She did a massive sigh and I enjoyed watching every painful step she took towards me.

"Yeah, what?" she bluntly asked.

"I'm about to make a hot drink, would you like one?"

"I don't do hot drinks," she replied.

"No? Don't tell me, I bet you drink those high-protein smoothies to retain your curves."

"I only really drink Coke, Lucozade and sometimes Tizer."

"Even down the pub?" I challenged.

"No. Then I drink Bacardi and Coke."

"Single or double measure?"

"Double if I'm in Wetherspoons."

"Why Wetherspoons?"

I noticed Maureen was quite enjoying the attention I was paying her and she was masking a faint grin. I didn't doubt this conversation, as with the invitation for a drink I made yesterday, would be reported to Baz. It would be her way of creating a 'do you know how lucky you are to have me' situation. This was sure to irritate him and therefore something I needed to pursue.

"Because you can double up for an extra pound in Wetherspoons," she said.

"Gotcha."

"You can in the Walkabout as well."

"Can you?" I replied, feigning high levels of interest.

"And the Black Lion."

"Really. Anywhere else?"

She paused for a few seconds. "I think that's it," she finally advised.

"If you think of anywhere else you've missed out, you will let me know immediately, won't you?"

"Yeah," she replied, nodding at the same time, just in case I needed non-verbal communication to confirm her answer. She reminded me of those old-fashioned nodding dogs some people have in their car. Only she wasn't a miniature furry toy, rather an eighteen-stone human pig.

"Oh no, did you hear that?" I announced.

"What?"

"I think I heard the sign being knocked over again."

"It wasn't knocked over earlier," she recalled.

"Oh, but it was, Maureen. And you need to be careful about members of the public tending to it themselves because, unlike you, they haven't enjoyed comprehensive and rigorous manual handling training. Quick! Go now, before there's a fatality!"

I wasn't sure whether she spoke to me or simply made an exasperated grunting sound, but the outcome was she teetered off to investigate whilst I looked on with a satisfied grin.

I made hot drinks, and as I did, Colin walked in and accepted a coffee. When I took it through to his office, I noticed today's puzzling piece of attire was a sweatshirt with an enormous letter 'H' on it.

"Here's your coffee, Colin," I said, placing it on his desk.

"Thanks."

"Nice sweatshirt. I'm interested, though, have you changed your name to Colin Horne?"

"Who?" he replied, a little distracted due to reading an email.

"Colin Horne."

He didn't get the joke, so I tried again.

"I wondered what the significance of the letter 'H' was on your sweatshirt?"

"What letter 'H'?"

"The one on your sweatshirt."

"Yeah, what about it?"

I sighed, massively regretting ever mentioning it.

"I wondered what the significance of it was."

"Erm, my wife bought it for me from a charity shop. I assume it refers to the make," he replied before turning back to his computer.

"What is it then, Hadidas? Or perhaps Giorgio Harmani?"

"Who?" he said as he turned to me again.

"Nothing," I sighed. "I'll catch you later."

"Okay. Thanks for the coffee."

I set back to work with John. The time soon flew by and it wasn't long before Colin was informing me it was two o'clock.

"Okay, thanks, Colin. I'll finish sanding this cabinet and then call it a day."

"He's a good lad," commented John. "A proper grafter. He's not stopped since he arrived."

Colin smiled and nodded.

I finished off the cabinet, popped my coat on and departed. As I walked through the shop, Maureen was talking to a customer and I could hear her telling him we didn't have any bedside cabinets in stock.

"Maureen, there's two in the storeroom. I've been sanding them down this afternoon."

"Yes, but they aren't ready yet," she replied in her usual unhelpful, workshy tone.

I turned to the customer. "Do you need them immediately or would you be happy to wait until they are varnished up?" I asked.

"I'd be happy to wait, there's no rush. Could I have a look at them first?"

"Yeah, of course you can," I replied.

I noted the utter annoyance on Maureen's face.

"Maureen, would you like to escort this gentleman into the storeroom and show him the bedside cabinets?"

"I can't because there's no one here to watch the shop."

"I'll watch it," I responded with an arrogant smile.

"But you aren't trained to use the till," she grunted, desperate to get out of doing any work.

"There's no one in the shop, Maureen. I think we'll be alright."

She let off an almighty groan.

"Can you follow me then?" she griped, as she scuttled out to the storeroom with the customer following her.

When she returned, the customer had confirmed he would like to buy the cabinet, resulting in Maureen having to record his details, which was even more work for her. I looked on in utter delight.

As the customer left he turned and thanked me.

"No problem, sir. Thank you for supporting the British Heart Society; we greatly appreciate your custom," I replied.

Once he had left, Maureen came scurrying over with a face on her like she'd spent three hours in a dental chair.

"We're not supposed to do that," she moaned.

"Do what – offer customers a good service?"

"Show them stock which is in the storeroom."

"What?" I responded, openly sniggering. "Why on earth not?"

"Because of health and safety. If customers go into the storeroom they could get hurt."

"I had been in the storeroom only thirty seconds beforehand. Colin was in his office and John was varnishing a table. There was no one else there. What could have possibly happened to him?"

"He could have tripped or slipped on something."

"On what? The grains which had come off my sandpaper?"

"There are lots of hazards and risks in the workplace which you wouldn't understand because you're only a volunteer."

"You're right, and thank you for your guidance and mentoring."

"I'm going to need to speak to Colin about it so he knows what has gone on."

"I think it's for the best that you do. If Colin isn't made fully aware of all aspects of this operation then there is no way he could be expected to manage this premises responsibly."

"Yes, well, I'll tell him about what you did before I finish work," she groused before dawdling back to the till to continue playing with her mobile phone.

As I was leaving the shop, I noticed Baz marching towards me down the street.

"Oi, I want a word with you!" he barked, as he aggressively approached.

"Baz, how are you? Have you had a busy yet rewarding day?" I asked mockingly.

"Did you ask my missus out yesterday for a drink?" he fumed.

"Yeah, but only as friends," I replied.

"What do you mean, 'only as friends'!" he stormed.

"Well, you said she was going out with you, so I wasn't after a date, just a bit of company."

"'A bit of company' with my fucking missus – are you having a laugh?"

"I think it's important when you start working in a new organisation to get to know your colleagues. I feel it helps strengthen individual bonds and contributes to effective team working. What do you think?"

"But she's my missus."

"Have I stumbled on a trust issue here? Are you suggesting she might be inclined to go behind your back?" I probed.

"She'd never do that; she knows what side her bread's buttered on."

"Then why are you so paranoid about it?"

"Because it feels like you are moving in on another man's girl."

"Oh, trust me, Baz, I wouldn't do that to you," I said, beginning to walk off. I then turned back to him. "Well, not yet anyway."

Before going home, I dropped in to see Tony. We sat having a coffee and a chat as I was feverishly dunking milk chocolate digestives.

"Have you cracked open the Black Label yet?" I asked him.

"I must admit I had a wee dram last night, for medicinal purposes," he replied.

"You're not ill, are you?"

"No, just old," he responded. "How are you getting on with your volunteer work?"

"Yeah, I'm enjoying it more than I thought. I was working with some fella today who was about your age. What he didn't know about carpentry wasn't worth knowing. It was like spending the day with Pinocchio's dad."

"Listen and learn, young man. He's acquired all that experience over years and years, so glean from him what you can."

"I'll tell you what, though, there are some people working there who royally toss it off."

"Welcome to the workplace! Never think for one second it's full of go-getters and grafters because it isn't. I suspect about a third of people you'll meet at work won't be much good at their job, and about half don't fancy putting in a hard day's slog."

"Really, that bad?"

"It's only my opinion. I've certainly met some poor-quality people at work. Not so much when I was in the army, because you couldn't get away with it, but after, when I worked in the glass industry, there were some proper shirkers."

"It's unbelievable that they can be allowed to get away with it."

There was then a short silence, at which point the elephant, which had hitherto been hanging around the kitchen, crept into the lounge, took a seat and helped itself to a couple of biscuits.

"I met up with Zoe yesterday."

He immediately turned a little coy, his body language changed and he slightly diverted his gaze away from me.

"How is she?" he asked coldly.

"Yeah, she's well. She lives about four miles away from here, in South Wigston."

"Good."

"Look, she kind of touched on what had gone on between you two."

"What did she say?"

"Nothing against you, she was open-minded about what had happened, but I think she regretted not seeing you."

"Is she still with *him*?" he enquired.

"I assume so. She didn't say anything. I'm not sure she wanted to tell me, to be honest."

"That's a 'yes' then." He sat shaking his head. "Bastard!"

"Do you mind me asking what he did that was so bad?"

He turned to look at me. "What did he do? Shall I tell you what that bastard did, shall I? He beat my little girl until she was black and blue; he hospitalised her. The first time I visited the hospital, I walked past her bed because her face was so swollen with bruises I didn't even recognise her."

He was becoming upset.

"I'm sorry, mate. That must have been dreadful."

He was biting at his thumbnail. "It's been four years, four long years, and I haven't been able to forgive him."

"Do you think there is a chance for you two to get back together?" I asked.

"Not whilst she's still with him. I mean, why on earth would she stay with that bastard after what he did to her?"

"I don't know."

"It wouldn't be fair on her either," he added, "because if she's still with him then sooner or later she's really going to hate me."

"Why?"

"Because I had decided some time ago that I'm not going to rest until that bastard is in the ground." He then fixed a stare on me. "And I'm going to make it my business to guarantee it happens."

CHAPTER 20

I had spent a long and lonely weekend at home. Beyond Tony, I now had no friends since Nails and Bod had both distanced themselves from me. I had decided against dropping into the Falcon for a pint because of the whole charity shop thing. Bod had been charged with the theft and it was only a matter of time until he appeared in court and thereafter the newspaper. It was, without doubt, not only the most unscrupulous thing I had ever done but also the most damaging.

The only money I had spent from the two grand that Egan had given me was on food shopping for me and Grandad and the two bottles of Black Label.

I had exchanged several messages with Zoe. I'd updated her on Tony's feedback, albeit wisely omitting the bit about his pledge to kill Leon. From her recent messages, I was starting to conclude they were no longer together, but she hadn't confirmed this and I didn't want to ask directly as it may have appeared a leading question. Leading insomuch as this might suggest I was interested in a relationship with her, although frankly, I would accept any sort of relationship with just about anyone right now.

It was Monday morning and I was up, out and ready for my next shift at the British Heart Society. As I walked down the driveway I spotted a familiar car parked on the road. In it sat detectives Wood and Brydges drinking coffee and presumably waiting for me to leave the house.

Shit! What did they want?

I didn't need to be beckoned over; instead, I simply walked up to the car as Brydges climbed out of the passenger seat and opened the rear passenger door for me to get in.

"Robbie, how are you?" asked Wood, with false friendliness.

"Never better, thank you. But more importantly, how are you and how's the coffee?"

"The coffee's great, thanks, but the pastry was even better. We would have bought you one, had we known."

"Known what? I might not like pastries," I replied.

"I bet you do, though, don't you? I mean, who doesn't like pastries? Especially the ones we've just eaten with the icing, the hundreds and thousands and a hint of cinnamon," Brydges said, looking over his shoulder at me.

"The last time you two were here you nicked me for allegedly throwing cans of beer at someone. What is it going to be on this occasion – an issue with the tyre tread on my bike?"

"Your mate, Egan," said Wood.

"What about him?"

"Where is he?" he asked.

"Fuck knows, why?"

"When did you last see him?" Wood probed.

"Last week sometime."

"Have you heard from him? A text message, phone call; anything like that?" he continued.

"No, nothing. Radio silence. Why, where's this going?"

"Dealing drugs is a funny thing, Robbie. High risk, high gain and for so little work. It's why so many people want to do it. But you have to play by the rules. Egan knows the rules better than anyone; in fact, he probably wrote most of them. And he's just broken one of the golden ones: don't go muscling in on someone else's patch. We haven't a fucking clue what possessed him to leave London and set up around here, but it's backfired on him," explained Wood.

"What do you mean?"

"The sharks have been circling and on Thursday night it appears they went in for the kill," added Brydges.

"What's happened?"

"Egan set up a buy, only for a local gang from Highfields to get whiff of it and gatecrash the party. After the deal, they forced Egan off the road, bundled him into the back of a van and that was that," Brydges continued.

"How do you know all this?" I asked.

"Favours, Robbie. We keep certain people out on the streets with a tight leash around their necks so they can help us," Wood said.

"What happened to him after they stuffed him in the van?"

"We know his gear was nicked, but then our snitch was sent out on a job, so that's where the story goes cold. We don't know what happened to Egan after he got in that van. Do you?" asked Brydges.

"I didn't know any of this and that's the truth."

"I'm inclined to believe you," Wood added.

"Do you think he's dead?"

"I would now consider that highly likely," he replied. "He hasn't been seen since. His club is locked up, you haven't seen or heard from him, our source on the street hasn't seen him, so I'm beginning to conclude that there can be only one outcome."

"Fucking hell!" I responded, gobsmacked.

"Since you've been hanging with Egan, have you made any enemies, Robbie?" Brydges queried.

"Is this off the record?"

"Yes, this is off the record," he answered, having received a subtle nod from Wood.

My mind set back to Corey and Khally and the potential threat they posed.

"Possibly," I answered anxiously.

"Any names you'd like to let us know about?" Brydges probed.

"What help would you give me if I gave them to you?" I asked, sensing a possible angle of support.

"After the mauling your solicitor gave us, not a lot to be quite honest," Wood replied.

"Then stop wasting my fucking time!" I raged.

"In which case, I would watch your step very carefully if I were you. Egan came along with a fearsome reputation, but as he's not around anymore I would say this makes you vulnerable," Wood added.

"Brilliant. Do you have any more cutting-edge advice?" I asked sarcastically.

"I do, actually," Wood replied with a glint in his eye. "The next time you go into Starbucks, order the flat white Americano – it's fucking sensational!"

I felt paranoid and uneasy as I made my way into town. I had decided to dismiss Corey as a threat. I hadn't done anything to him and he would know and respect this. Once word of Egan's demise wafted over to Birmingham, I suspected he would do little more than raise a glass.

Khally, however, was an altogether different proposition. He was a local player with his own crew and I had taken liberties with him: pushed a gun in his face, dragged him into a park and treated him like my bitch. He would undoubtedly be a serious problem. Once news of Egan's disappearance had filtered across to St Matthews he would grasp his opportunity for revenge. He would want his boys to watch my suffering and for the street to be told of the violence he had inflicted. Khally would want to remind the drug-dealing world that he wasn't someone to be fucked around with.

If Grandad wasn't around I would probably cut and run. I'd take my chances elsewhere and escape this nightmare.

I wasn't in the mood for four hours' work at some bloody charity shop and I thought long and hard about whether to bother going. I was only doing this because Egan had forced me and yet, I couldn't deny I was getting something out of it: a sense of fulfilment, purpose and structure. I thought about Tony, the help he had provided and what he would say if I didn't attend. This was reason enough to make the effort.

I walked in and Maureen was picking her nose whilst messing around with her mobile phone at the till. Out of curiosity, I wondered whether she would speak to me if I didn't speak to her. As I walked directly past her, she looked up and ignored me.

I walked into the storeroom to ask Colin what he wanted me to do.

"Robbie, come into the office and close the door, would you?" he invited.

"Is everything okay?" I asked.

"Yeah, yeah, everything is fine," he replied. "Only last week Maureen came in to see me and she was a bit upset."

"With what?"

"She said she was dealing with a customer and you told her she should take him through to this area so he may have a look at an item of furniture."

Whilst Colin was dealing with me in a very pleasant way, I wasn't in the mood for this fucking bullshit and I could feel my blood pressure rising.

"Yes, that's right. She was going to tell a customer we didn't have a product for sale, when in fact we did."

"Okay, that's fine. It's only we tend to leave Maureen in charge of sales in the shop."

"Right, so you leave a person in charge of sales who spends all day on her mobile phone and when a customer does come in, she'll happily send them away thinking we don't stock a product when we do."

"I think you're being a bit unfair there, to be honest."

"Do you? Would you disagree with me that she spends most of her day on her mobile phone whilst doing zero work?"

"Look, I don't want a discussion about this, I'm simply asking you to concentrate your time on what goes on in the storeroom and let me focus on what Maureen does in the sales department."

"Yes, fine, Colin. Thank you for bringing it to my attention and you can be sure I will implement everything you have suggested," I replied sarcastically.

Colin proceeded to allocate my jobs for the day which involved working with John. Thankfully, this calmed me down due to John's soft and friendly nature. At 2 p.m. I finished up and exited the rear of the store, where Baz was having a smoke.

"Has Colin spoken to you?" he ranted.

"What?" I replied in an equally unfriendly tone.

"Has Colin spoken to you about how you upset Maureen the other day."

"Yeah, he has actually," I replied.

"Good. If I were him, I would have fucking sacked you," he added.

"Why?"

For the second time today, I was feeling myself getting irritated to the point of feeling unusually aggressive.

"Talking to my fucking missus like that; who the fuck do you think you are?"

"I was telling her how to do her job because unfortunately, she's so fucking thick I don't think she knows," I replied.

"What did you fucking say!" he growled, throwing his cigarette down on the floor and marching over to me.

"I hope she doesn't take it personally, but she's a bit like you: fat and utterly fucking useless."

"Do you fucking want some?" he beckoned, making himself larger like a parading peacock.

"Do you think you'll be alright to fight me on your own, you fat bastard, or do you want to delegate it to someone like you do when you've been given some work?"

He threw a punch at my face which I allowed to connect. He had started the fight and it was a green light for me to do whatever I wanted under the extended banner of 'self-defence'.

'Commit yourself to it' – I heard Egan's words ringing in my ears. Baz bounced his fat figure up and down, fists clenched, waiting to pounce. As I picked myself up, he lurched his cumbersome body at me for a second punch. I ducked this, grabbed his shoulder and then kneed him hard in his balls. I heard the air exhale from his lungs before he doubled over. I quickly picked up a large stick of wood which was resting against the wall and smashed it over the back of his head. The impact was so great the wood snapped. Baz lay on the ground in a pathetic crumpled heap making a murmuring sound. A trickle of blood dripped onto the cemented floor.

I stood over him.

"Have we finished or do you want to get up for some more?"

He shook his head and I dropped the broken end of the wooden stick to the floor.

"What's gone on here?" Colin trembled as he came racing out of the storeroom.

"He's fallen over. It looks like he's cut his head," I suggested.

Colin knelt on the ground.

"Are you okay, Baz?"

Baz rose slowly to his feet, shaking his groggy head.

"What happened?" Colin asked him.

"You tripped over, didn't you, Baz?" I interjected.

"Baz, what happened?" Colin asked again, clearly needing clarification for my less-than-convincing story.

"I, err, I tripped on something and banged my head," he replied, touching the back of his skull with his hand before examining the blood he had removed.

"Looks nasty, Colin. I'd go and get the first aid box if I were you," I suggested.

"Yes, good idea," he replied. "I'm going to get the first aid box, Baz," he repeated in a louder voice, just in case the 'fall' had rendered Baz deaf.

"I think he's heard you, Colin," I said.

Colin jogged off back into the building where I didn't doubt the whole 'What to do in the event of an accident in the workplace' protocol was running through his naturally anxious mind.

"Baz, let me level with you here: if you think for one minute about getting your own back on me then make sure when I go down, I stay down, alright? Otherwise, I swear to God, I'll get up and fucking pulverise you."

I arrived home and was chilling out on my bed. The beating I had handed out to Baz simply hadn't registered with my conscience. He was a bully, and from the minute I'd met him he tried to control me with his aggressive and taunting language.

He was also a thief. He was paid an honest wage by an honourable charity yet did nothing except abuse this good faith by skiving off work whenever he could and bring the rest of the team's morale down with his behaviour and attitude. He got what he deserved. I hope he went home with a splitting headache. I suspected he and Maureen would have spent the whole evening talking about the incident, repeatedly running over what had happened and speculating on how he should react.

I smiled whilst imagining his loss of pride. He acted like a tough guy and Maureen would have thought this of him as well. She would have felt protected, seduced by his fighting tough talk, and yet when confrontation ensued with someone who wasn't going to back down, he was made to look a mug.

He would look into the eyes of Maureen and wonder whether

he had somehow gone down in her estimations. He would have to re-think his entire strategy for dealing with people because when violence had come calling he simply wasn't up to it. He was overweight, old and slow. The next time he squared up to someone this doubt would re-enter his mind.

I'd sent a Facebook message to Zoe asking how her day was going and had also decided it was time to strike against the person who had stolen Candy's phone after she had died.

Some time ago, I had called the number and a stranger had answered. I was mindful I was contacting them again from the same number, but I fancied they wouldn't remember.

I needed to offer some sort of bait; a reason for them to respond and thereafter meet me.

I decided on something which might entice your average scumbag whilst also being open-ended.

I got some cheap gear that I need to flog. U interested?

I had to be careful. I didn't wish to wrongly confront an innocent person whose only crime was the recent purchase of a mobile phone from the cockroach who had stolen it from Candy.

I probably wouldn't hear back, but, as they say, every accomplishment begins with the decision to try.

I then decided to call Egan. If his phone rang then that might suggest that DS Wood's conclusion that he was dead would have a question mark hanging over it.

Nothing! Straight to automated voicemail. Maybe Wood was right. I envisaged Egan and his phone lying at the bottom of some deep landfill site as tonnes of rubbish were gradually poured over him.

As I returned to work the following morning, I was interested to see how this business with Baz would play out. Would he come after me or let it lie? He would be aware that if push came to shove, I would happily humiliate him all over again.

As I walked into the shop, Maureen was stood at the counter once again on her mobile phone despite there being customers who may have needed assistance.

I made a point of standing in front of the counter and staring at her. After a few seconds, she looked up, her gormless face gazing back at me. I held my stare for a few more seconds before walking into the storeroom.

I eyed Colin in his office.

"Morning, Colin, you alright?"

Colin came to the door. "Robbie, do you have a minute?"

Here we go, I thought as I walked into his office and took a seat. He closed the door and immediately I could see he was acting sheepishly.

"Did something happen here yesterday between you and Baz?"

"What do you mean?"

"Did you fall out with him about anything?"

"No, I don't think so. Why?"

"Did you say anything which might have upset him?"

"No, no, nothing comes to mind," I replied, shaking my head.

"Are you sure? I'm starting to wonder whether his so-called 'accident' yesterday was because you two had argued."

"No, there had certainly been no argument," I replied. "Oh, hang on, I did call him a fat useless bastard, do you think that might be it?"

"What did you do that for?" Colin asked with a resigned look.

"Because that's what he is."

"That's very offensive, Robbie."

"It might be, but let's be honest, we both know it's the truth."

"Baz and Maureen came to see me first thing this morning. They were both very upset."

"Why, had you asked them to do some work?" I questioned with a sneer.

"No, they were upset about something that had happened and both of them offered their resignations."

"Wow – what a result! I bet you're well chuffed, aren't you?"

"They said they couldn't work with you anymore and unless you were asked to leave they would resign."

"I'm sure there's plenty of places looking to recruit fat workshy staff, so they shouldn't have anything to worry about."

"They won't be leaving, I'm afraid," he stated firmly.

"Ah, it's like that, is it?" I replied, having quickly put two and two together.

"Robbie, I like you. Despite only working here three times you've demonstrated that you are a real asset to our volunteering team."

"There's a 'but' coming up here, isn't there?" I prompted.

"If Baz and Maureen both leave there will be repercussions; people on the board will ask questions, and knowing Baz, he will give them answers. He will stir things up; he'll say I took the side of a volunteer who had been here for five minutes over them. You understand, don't you?"

"I understand you're a good man, Colin."

"I've no alternative, I'm sorry," he responded, looking genuinely upset.

"Let me ask you one question," I asked. "Why do you put up with them? You can see what they are like: they come in and do the bare minimum, moan their arses off and then go home whilst taking a fat wage in the process – why?"

"I, I, I know I should be stronger with them, I know I should stand up for myself, but—"

"You don't have to finish that sentence. You're a decent man and I appreciate you giving me a chance here. I'm sorry it didn't work out."

"If you need a reference, Robbie, I'll provide you with one. I'll say you were here for six months and you were a good worker. It's the least I could do."

I stood up and offered my hand to him, which he shook.

"Thanks for the opportunity," I acknowledged as I left the office.

I walked through to the shop, where Maureen was still on her mobile phone. She stopped what she was doing and waited to see whether I would leave. If I did, it would confirm that I'd been sacked meaning she and Baz had triumphed.

I boldly approached her.

"Maureen, Colin asked that you see him in the office immediately. He said it was something about accepting your resignation. Whilst you are there, he has told me to watch the shop."

Whatever a combination of stern and confused is, that's the expression Maureen had on her piggy face. I watched her waddle off for the final time, only with a slightly more purposeful gait resulting in her previous top speed of twenty metres a minute being exceeded.

As she disappeared into the storeroom, I reached over the counter and grabbed her prized Samsung smartphone. I violently threw it down on the hard shop floor and joyously watched it smash into little pieces. I stamped on it a couple of times as well; the last of the stamps merged into a left to right grinding movement of my heel, resulting in a satisfying crunching sound. I would like to think somewhere amongst the battered embers of her phone was her SIM card, where all contact numbers, messages and pictures were stored. I hoped she had always intended to back these up on her PC, but because she was so fat and lazy, had never bothered.

I scooped up the pathetic remains of this device and placed them where she had left her phone. I grabbed a small strip of paper and a pen and left Maureen one final note for her to remember me by. The note was left on top of her savaged mobile phone and it simply read:

Now get some fucking work done! Robbie xx

I walked into the city centre, disappointed that my job at the British Heart Society had ended prematurely. For the brief time I had volunteered there, I'd enjoyed the work, warmed to the structure it provided and appreciated John's mentoring. I had learned so much from him in our short time together. What I admired most was how he'd established one specific area in his life where he'd become an expert. It had become his trade, something he'd dedicated himself to over thousands of hours and a vocational area where he'd built a reputation.

I wanted to be like him; I needed to find an area of interest in which I could immerse myself. Something, in the fullness of time, which could become my specialism.

I was en route to Greggs for a double sausage roll and steak bake feast to lift my spirits, and as I did, I found myself walking past a Wetherspoons pub. Whilst claiming it was open early for breakfast and coffee, it was, as ever, already full of full-time, non-working drinkers, despite it only being 10.30 a.m. There was the usual flock of smokers gathered untidily around the entrance, most of whom would consider it perfectly acceptable to litter the pavement with their discarded butt-ends.

I stopped dead in my tracks as if I'd been suddenly anchored to the ground. There he was, as clear as day, standing smoking a cigarette, holding a pint of lager and chatting away to some other fella. The years hadn't been especially kind to him but he'd not majorly changed. He was scruffily dressed and obviously not engaged in any sort of work given what he was doing and where he was.

It was the first time in fifteen years I had seen my father. I'd often thought about this moment. Should I approach him and introduce myself? Maybe thank him for killing Mum and enquire whether prison time had reformed him? Or should I nonchalantly stroll over and wrap one of the metal pub chairs around his dirty murdering head?

I stood and stared from across the road. He was a pathetic creature and a disgrace of a man. He hadn't given me a second thought since being released from prison. No approach, no love and no apology.

I decided exactly what to do – nothing. He had long been dead to me and that's how it would stay. Grandad had lovingly assumed the role of my father and I would not give any of this responsibility back to him. I decided to carry on walking to Greggs and to try to forget about him as quickly as possible.

I stopped for a second, realising that I eat the same old shit, at the same old places all the while. I had seen the pitiful face of my father and I wanted something better for myself. Fuck it! I had a few quid on me and decided to visit a nice café in town. I called in to a very pleasant local establishment, Deli-ish, where I ordered a jacket potato, homemade chilli and a pot of tea. The staff were super-friendly and for once, I saw the value in trying and doing something different.

During my meal, I had received a text message. Ordinarily, I would immediately stop what I was doing and read it as if it were going to disappear. On this occasion, I ignored it and continued to enjoy my food, uninterrupted.

Once I had finished, the waitress collected my plate and asked whether I had enjoyed the food. She was about my age and I had spotted how industrious she was: always on the move, always working, always alert to what needed to be done next in her fast-moving work environment. When she wasn't serving food, taking orders or clearing away pots, she would be wiping down surfaces and ensuring the place was clean and tidy. I observed her to establish whether she would ever sneak a glance at her mobile phone, but she didn't. Maybe it was in her handbag, out of sight and out of reach. I wanted to believe that whilst on her shift she focused all effort on work and only refer to her mobile phone once her shift had ended. I needed to think the likes of Maureen and Baz weren't typical employees and that some people wholeheartedly committed themselves to work.

I eventually took my phone out and viewed the message. It appeared I had acquired a new friend. It may be the scumbag who had taken possession of Candy's phone and this individual wasn't going to pass up the opportunity of purchasing cheap goodies.

What gear you got

Was the reply that I had received to my earlier message.

A gram of brown. I need ££. U can have it for £50

I sent back. This was half the usual street value which I had used as bait. I had run the risk of making it too cheap resulting in them smelling a rat and ignoring me. However, we weren't talking security bonds being offered to a city trader by an imminently bankrupt blue-chip company. This was class A narcs and the client base was ever so slightly different to your average hedge fund manager.

I'll take it. Where U want 2 meet

St George's church. 15 mins. Come alone. If there's a party – I walk

Ok

Smackheads – you've just got to love them! He or she had arranged to meet me despite not knowing who I was, what I looked like or where the gear had come from. When you are addicted to a substance, you stop giving a shit about anything. The window of your conscience gets flung open and all rules, morals and sensibilities are thrown out.

I was five minutes' walk from the church but I was in no rush because I wanted my new friend to be in position before I approached. I would spot them from a mile off. They would almost certainly be deathly skinny, scruffy, twitchy and with a pasty, blotchy complexion. If it was a girl, I would walk on. If there was more than one of them, the same. If it was a fella, I would suss them out, establish how they had come into possession of Candy's phone and then decide what to do.

I took a stroll to the church and checked the time – the fifteen minutes were up. I headed in through the gate and proceeded towards the church doors, which I knew would be locked. As the pathway curved, I could see my new friend, who was a perfect match against my predicted profile. He was anxiously eyeing left and right, twitching, irritable and checking his phone as I approached.

I then realised it was the fella from outside the hostel who had told me Candy had departed and headed into town when I had gone there looking for her. I sighed as I realised I'd been duped. She was upstairs poisoning herself on drugs at probably the same time this weasel was stealing her possessions. He had thrown me off the scent to get me away from the scene, leaving him in the clear. Candy had been but a short distance away from me and, had I have known, I could have entered her room and saved her sorry soul.

"Alright, mate, do you have the fifty quid on you?" I asked as I approached.

"Yeah, yeah, yeah, have you got the gear?" he queried, shuffling around.

"Yeah," I replied.

"Let's have a look then?" he requested.

"I was expecting Candy to turn up, not you."

"Who?"

"Candy, the person whose phone I sent the text message to."

"Yeah, yeah, she sold her mobile to me, but I'll take the gear off you, bro."

"When did she sell you the phone?" I enquired.

"What?" he replied, looking irritated that I was asking questions.

"The phone – when did you buy it?" I asked sternly.

"A few days ago. She owed me some money which she didn't have, so she gave me her phone, innit."

"How long have you had the phone for?"

"I don't know," he tutted. "A couple of days, maybe."

"A couple of days?"

"Yeah. What's with all the fucking questions?" he replied, getting very defensive.

"Was this before or after she died?" I probed.

He shrugged his shoulders. "After, after, it was after."

"After," I replied, laughing. "Think very carefully about what you've just said to me. You're telling me you've brought a phone from someone who is already dead!"

"What the fuck, man!" he replied losing his cool. "Before she died, I mean, before, innit. Are you selling me this fucking gear or not?"

"There is no gear, there's only a parting gift from Candy."

I punched him hard on the nose. He instantly clattered to the floor. I grabbed a clump of his disgusting, greasy, matted hair and smashed his face against the wall of the church. Blood was starting to trickle down his cheeks.

He wasn't making a sound, he wasn't moving; in fact, he wasn't doing much at all.

I reached into his pockets and removed Candy's phone, a packet of Rizlas and about forty pounds in notes and change. I smiled and shook my head. He hadn't even brought enough money to do the deal we had agreed!

I sat quietly next to him until he eventually came around. When he did, he turned and looked at me, wiping the blood from his nose and forehead.

"Why did you do it?" I asked him.

"Do what?" he replied, sniffling.

"Steal a phone from someone who was dying – why did you do it? Why didn't you call for help?"

"I didn't know her. I left my room and saw her door open and she was lying there out of her head. I didn't know she was dying, I swear. I just thought she was high."

"So, you went in and stole her phone?"

"Yeah, that's standard, bro. If you get fucked up at a hostel and you leave your door open then you're going to get your shit nicked. It's happened to me like fucking loads of times."

"What is going on with you people?" I noted despairingly.

"It's the way it is, but I swear, I didn't know she was dead."

"Yet when you found out she was dead you were happy to carry on using her mobile phone?"

"Yeah, well, she weren't going to need it, was she?"

I sat feeling numb and ashamed. I used to buy stolen goods from people like this fella. I was part of the supply chain; I was somewhere embedded in this squalid game. I was embarrassed about everything I had ever done, every stolen item I had ever traded and every person I had ever ripped off. It stopped right here, right now. I was out of it, retired, my spurs hung up and I would never again buy anything that I knew to be nicked.

I took Candy's mobile phone, his money, even his Rizlas out of my pocket and returned them to him. I also pulled out another fifty quid and presented this to him.

"What's this for?" he asked.

"Consider it my retirement present to you," I replied.

"What are you on about?"

"You probably won't listen to this and even if you do, I know you won't do anything about it, but if you can, if someone gives you a chance, escape the life you are living and look for something better, because it is out there."

"I know it is, but every day I get pulled down to the bottom. I've stopped believing, bro. I'm not sure anymore whether I'll ever have the courage to get out," he replied honestly.

"She was okay, you know," I told him.

"Who was?"

"Candy, the girl you stole the phone from. If she'd had a chance in life I think she would have been okay."

"You can say that about all of us," he replied.

I had decided to spend the afternoon trawling the pubs of Leicester having a few quiet beers which turned into a few more. My solitude was broken by a flurry of messages to Zoe. After six pints I was struggling not to be flirty but managed to keep a respectful lid on things.

I visited a local Gala casino, lost a couple of hundred pounds on roulette and then went for a curry. I was aware I'd become a lonely soul wandering in a lost state. I needed to quickly return some structure to my life.

I opted to head home at about eleven o'clock. If Grandad was still awake I would suggest we share a nightcap of Black Label whisky to see what all the fuss was about.

When I arrived, the downstairs was in darkness so I put the kitchen lights on. As I walked into the lounge and approached the lamp to it switch on, I noticed an arm draped at the side of Grandad's chair.

I went cold.

This was the moment I had been dreading. I was about to find him dead.

"Grandad! Grandad!" I called out. There was no response and no movement from the flailing arm.

As my shaking hand fumbled for the switch to the lamp, my heart sank. Having found it and switched it on, I turned slowly around, preparing myself to see his dead body. My eyes fixed a gaze on the subject.

"Egan! Fucking hell, I thought you were dead."

He sat casually with a glass of whisky in his hand.

"So do the police," he replied.

"What went down?" I asked, pouring myself a glass of Black Label and taking a seat on the settee.

"When I was a kid living in Ireland, my mother would constantly go on about Cornwall. She was raised in the area, so she'd romanticise about the bays, the beaches and the little shops. One year, when my sister and I were kids, my dad buckled to her nagging and we holidayed there. We visited a little fishing town called Fowey. Have you heard of it?"

"No," I answered.

"Beautiful place with a lovely little harbour. I recall one day the weather was pleasant and we sat eating a picnic against the water when, all of a sudden, my sister noticed there was a dog stranded in the sea. She was getting all upset about it, so my dad climbed down and fished this poor little thing out. It was a West Highland Terrier which was shaking with fear.

"We took it around the town with us to see whether anyone was missing a dog, but nothing. We went to the local police and made a report and agreed to hang on to it until someone came forward, but no one ever did. So, we took the dog back to Ireland with us. We even called it 'Fowey'. I loved that dog in a way that only someone who has ever owned one would understand.

"Eventually, Fowey grew old, became ill and got progressively worse. Animals come to give you a certain look when they've had enough. They seem to be pleading with you to do something and you feel so helpless. Fowey was giving us that look and we knew it was time. We were just waiting for Dad to make the dreaded appointment at the vets.

"One day, I arrived home from school and found my dad in the back garden. He was terribly upset, like properly sobbing. It was the only time I had ever seen him cry. I assumed the dog was dead, but he wasn't; he was still alive and lay panting on the lawn. I watched as Dad went into his shed and brought out a shotgun. I screamed at him and demanded he told me what he was planning on doing. He looked at me very calmly with tears rolling down his face and said, 'If anyone is going to put our dog to sleep, then it's going to be me.'

"I watched as he walked over to Fowey, pointed the gun at him and ended his life. I couldn't bring myself to look at my dad for months afterwards."

"What's this got to do with you getting kidnapped the other night?" I asked.

"Nothing," he replied. "It's just a story."

"Why not tell me the story about what happened with the Highfields gang? I heard they followed you after a deal, stole your money, kidnapped and then killed you."

"I died years ago; you can't kill a man twice," he said, taking a sip of Scotch.

"What does that mean?"

"The police only know what I want them to know. There was no Highfields gang; that story is nothing more than a decoy. The truth is Khally contacted me a couple of days after you had seen him. He said he wanted twenty grand's worth of gear; he said the quality was so good he couldn't get enough of it. So, we set the deal up and arranged the meet, only he pulled a gun to my head, took the gear and I never received the money."

"What about the kidnapping bit?"

"There was no kidnap. After he took the coke, he left me in the hands of two of his trusted henchman who drove me to someplace out in the sticks where there was a deep reservoir."

"They were going to kill you?"

"I'm pretty certain they weren't planning on giving me kayaking lessons."

"Fucking hell! Are they dead?"

"One of them is."

"And the other?"

"He's fine. We thought it for the best if he stayed at the club for a while until things get sorted out."

"I don't understand."

"He's on my team; he has been for a while. He had tipped me off that Khally wouldn't be weighing in with the money, so the gear stayed at the club and the package Khally stole was nothing more than high-grade, super-duper baking soda."

"What are you going to do with Khally?" I asked.

"How's it going at the British Heart Society?" he enquired.

Fucking hell, I swear this geezer owns a crystal ball. "Oh, so you found out."

"Found out what?" he replied with an arrogant, all-knowing look on his face.

"I got sacked today."

"Sacked from a volunteering job!" he laughed. "Blimey, that takes some doing."

"I fell out with someone there; he's a right wanker. He punched me, so I gave him a kicking."

"Please tell me it wasn't another incident involving you throwing beer cans?"

"Where's this going, Egan?"

"Are you worried?" he asked.

"I'm now immune to worry like I'm immune to you. I've had a gutful of stories about fucking dogs getting shot like I'm sick of stories about kids being thrown into the deep end of swimming pools."

"That's a shame because behind every story there's a meaning. The trouble is you're too stupid to work it out."

"Cut to the fucking chase and tell what you want me to do and where you want me to do it."

"Let's just say you're going to wish you were back volunteering in that wood factory."

"This is going to go on forever, isn't it?"

"What is?" he asked.

"You setting me targets, me failing and then having to do your dirty work for you. It's all a game to you, isn't it? But it's my life."

"You may be feeling unduly pessimistic, but perhaps there's some hope."

"Meaning?"

"Ethel is back at home and making good progress. I reckon I'll return to London in three weeks, leaving you to live out the rest of your life in peace and quiet."

"But there's another assignment, isn't there?"

"Of course there is. You messed up at the workshop, so the terms of the deal are you will pay the penalty."

"What do you want me to do this time?"

"It's all about our friend, Khally. You and I are going to head into St Matthews tomorrow night and we're going to find him."

"And then what?"

"I'm going to make him sorry for what he did. You were going to simply watch my back," he said before taking a large swig of whisky. "But as it's clear your bollocks are now so fucking big, I think it's only right you play a more prominent role in his punishment."

CHAPTER 21

I was contemplating what exactly Egan had in store for me, how was he going to track down Khally and, when he found him, what role was I to play in his fate?

Whatever he had up his sleeve, he knew exactly what he was going to do and there was no point in second-guessing him because not even God knew Egan's plans.

I received a message from Zoe. She was free for a coffee this afternoon and suggested a meet. In the not-so-busy world of unemployment, I was available at the suggested time and our date was arranged. At least this would take my mind off this evening's activities which promised to be extremely high risk. I had the opportunity to present myself to Zoe in a better sartorial light than the scruffy gear I turned up in the other day.

I went downstairs, made Grandad a cup of tea and sat with him as he watched the television. Even when I placed the cup down on his table, he couldn't say 'thank you', without breaking out into a distressing cough.

Some time ago, I had decided to savour every second I spent with him. I had come to realise that life is just one big sand timer. It gets turned upside down from the moment they cut the cord. The only thing you don't know is how many grains are in the glass. The saving grace I had with Grandad's progressive illness was I knew I was going to lose him and when that day arrived, I could at least have no regrets about appreciating the time we had shared.

Sometimes I would stare at him and feel grateful he was still alive. I now pondered fearfully how it would conclude. Shortly, he would have to be admitted to hospital. I assumed he would be put on a respirator of some sort and eventually get moved to intensive care. On the fateful day, I would unwittingly visit and a kind nurse with a sympathetic face would present me the bad news.

He had so little air left in his lungs he could no longer ask any questions about my bogus job at the *Leicester Mercury*. At least I didn't have to lie to him anymore. He would see me come and go and assume I was going to work.

For the past few days, I had even contemplated coming clean and telling him the truth; admitting every dirty deceitful lie I'd ever told. To finally put my hands up and confess that his only grandson, whom he had adopted as his offspring, was a shit-out, a loser, a liar, a thief and someone who would trade with drug addicts and steal from charity shops. But how could I do this? There was no trade-off. I couldn't follow the confession up with, 'but the good news is, Grandad I'm now doing, blah, blah, blah', which might at least sweeten the story. There was nothing to gain from telling him except pain and hurt, and I wasn't prepared to put a frail, sick old man through that.

By the afternoon, I was heading into town to meet Zoe. I was dressed in my smartest Hugo Boss attire with the sole intention of impressing her. We were only meeting for a coffee, but I was looking forward to some company as I'd become lonely and missed having any friends around.

I arrived early and ordered us both a drink. Ten minutes later, I saw a man holding open the café door allowing Zoe to walk in with a pushchair. I wouldn't say I was shocked by this; we had deliberately not shared any personal details in our message exchanges so I had an inkling there was a child involved. Maybe we were both a little embarrassed about our respective pasts to start swapping details. I suspected today was a time for a little more openness and honesty.

I helped her with the pushchair and was introduced to her baby boy, Ollie. He was a little over two years old and seemed perfectly happy in the company of a total stranger.

In terms of any potential romance between us, there would be many fellas my age who would run for cover at the sight of a child. In truth, I might have done three months ago but felt differently now. Perhaps my feelings had evolved from the fear of being alone when Grandad passed?

We were happily chatting away as the conversation slowly drifted on to more personal matters.

"What is it you do for a job?" she asked.

"I work as a trainee journalist at the *Leicester Mercury*."

"Do you?" she responded, clearly impressed. Great! Another lie I would inevitably have to own up to. "How long have you been doing that for?"

"A few months. I used to work in a warehouse, but this job came up and I applied for it and so far, so good."

"What sort of stories do you write?"

"I don't. I shadow one of the journalists, gather up comments, take photos, do research, that sort of thing."

I was off again; the lies were flowing and they rolled out so worryingly easy.

"Are you enjoying it?" she asked.

"Yeah, it's not without its challenges, but it's interesting."

"Is today your day off?" she asked.

"No, I'm working this evening. I'm covering a story and the person we're interviewing can only be seen tonight."

"Is it an important, top-secret story?" she enquired mischievously.

"Not really."

I felt it was time to put the cards on the table; to establish the lie of the land.

"Can I ask you about your fella, Leon?"

"Do you mean my ex-fella?"

"Is he?"

"Yeah, we split up about a year ago."

I received a rush of happiness. I knew I had fallen for her and the opportunity for us to nurture a relationship had just increased exponentially.

"Do you still see him?" I asked.

"Yes, unfortunately. It's a long story, but let's just say he comes and goes, dipping in and out of Ollie's life. It's more disruptive than beneficial, to be honest."

"Your dad tells me he didn't treat you well."

"Sometimes you can't see the wood from the trees, can you? It was a relationship that had gone toxic. Unfortunately, no one bothered to tell me, except Dad, of course, and I had stopped listening to him."

"Tony doesn't like him very much, does he?"

"You could say that."

"Still, if someone were beating on my daughter I might feel the same way."

"I wondered if he would tell you about that side of it."

"He didn't go into the gruesome details, but he painted a vivid enough picture."

"He'll get him back for it, don't worry about that."

"I can see the hatred in his eyes, but I don't think Tony is the sort of bloke to do anything stupid," I stated.

"How much do you know about my dad?"

"Not a great deal beyond you, his interest in the news and his love of tea and biscuits."

"Has he told you he was in the army?"

"Yeah, he said he was in the Paras."

"He joined the Paras but was later moved to a special operations unit."

"What, like the SAS?"

"I'm not sure, I don't think so. But whatever it was, it was top secret and dangerous, although he rarely mentioned it."

"Bloody hell."

"Yeah, you wouldn't think it, would you?"

"More evidence that you should never judge a book, I guess."

"Be careful of him. He can be a nasty, devious, scheming piece of work when he wants to be."

"We are talking about the same fella here, aren't we?"

"One day when I was a kid at school I walked out of the playground to meet him, but before he arrived some weirdo approached me and offered me a bag of sweets and a lift home. My dad called out as he approached and he cleared off. Dad ran after him just in time to get his registration number as he drove away. Three months later I saw that some bloke being pushed around in a wheelchair."

"But you don't know for sure that Tony was responsible."

"After I saw him in the wheelchair, I told Dad and he just shrugged his shoulders. Despite my tender age, I knew full well that he had put him there."

"Blimey! Perhaps it was for the best Leon did a runner from those drug dealers in London before Tony got his hands on him."

"He did a runner from what drug dealers in London?" she asked, looking confused.

"Tony said he'd ripped off a bunch of guys, they were coming after him and he had to go into hiding."

"Leon didn't run off because of any drug dealers in London; he ran off *because* of my dad."

"What!"

"After he beat me up, Dad visited me in hospital. I could see the look on his face and I knew exactly what was going to happen next. I had to tell Leon straightaway otherwise he would have killed him."

"What did he do?"

"What any right-minded person would have done when you get tipped off that an ex-special forces soldier is after you – he cleared off. But not before reporting the threat to the police. He wanted to make sure Dad's card was marked should anything ever happen to him."

"What did the police do?"

"Called around his house and warned him off. They told him exactly whose door they would knock should Leon ever turn up dead."

"Do you think that's the end of it?"

"No, I don't. He'll get to him; I know he will. Leon's been lucky so far, but he's on borrowed time. Only I don't think Dad will get his hands dirty with it now. He's getting on and won't fancy spending the rest of his life in prison."

"What's he going to do?" I asked.

"I'm not sure, but I suspect somewhere deep in his past there's someone who's short of a few quid or who owes him a favour."

"I feel a bit shellshocked, to be honest. Just when you think you're starting to get to know someone."

"Enough about that, what about you – are you dating anyone?" she asked.

"No, I've been single for ages."

"Really? You've got the gift of the gab, I assumed you would have them flocking around you."

"Maybe it's the company I keep," I replied with a smirk.

"What do you mean?" she asked.

"Long story. I suppose I'm a bit like you when you realised you had to move on from Leon. I know I need to make some important changes in my life."

"What sort of changes?" she asked.

Without thinking, I spontaneously dived in headfirst at the deep end.

"Do you fancy going out for a drink with me sometime?" I asked her.

"Sorry?" she replied, suitably shocked.

"A night out and a few drinks, do you fancy it?"

"Erm, well, I'll need to get a babysitter," she replied, royally knocked off her guard.

"Yeah, of course. But is it something you'd like to do?"

She continued to look a little bemused.

"I've not gone out with anyone since Leon."

"I understand, and trust me, I'm every bit as rusty as you are."

"Okay, let's do it! Nice and slow, though."

"That suits me."

I felt a wave of euphoria wash over me. I would be taking Zoe out on a proper date and couldn't be happier. At the end of our time together, I kissed her on the cheek and told her I'd be in touch.

I took a steady walk home with a big grin on my face. With everything else that was going on in my life, this was a narrow ray of sunshine breaking through the dark clouds and I appreciated the respite.

I turned off the main road and walked towards my house. Despite the roads being quiet and the atmosphere almost peaceful, I didn't see or hear them coming. It was a total surprise when I was violently grabbed from behind, my neck placed in a strong headlock whilst a second man bundled me into the back of a van. It was a slick movement, well-practised and no doubt executed many times. Within a matter of seconds, I had thick gaffer tape drawn over my mouth, whilst my hands were forced behind my back before being secured by a plastic tie.

Shortly before I had the blindfold placed over my head, I caught sight of the driver of the van as he peered over his shoulder. I saw the glint of a gold tooth as he smiled at me. He had the look of a man who was satisfied he had captured his target and could exact his revenge. The gold tooth and look of contentment belonged to Khally.

We had been driving for no more than ten minutes before the van stopped and I was led out. I detected the straining of a man before I heard the snap of a metal bolt. A heavy door was opened and I was ushered in. I listened to the scraping of a chair across the floor which I was forced to sit on.

My blindfold was removed and I was surprised to see they had brought me to Egan's club. I had to quickly piece together the jigsaw of what was the actual truth, as detailed by Egan, and what they believed. I had to presume Khally thought Egan had been killed.

A lean, muscular black man was tying me to the chair with heavy-duty gaffer tape. Khally stood staring at me, waiting for him to complete his job. Another man was rifling under the bar, pulling out and smashing glasses from the cabinets as he did. He was searching for something and I had a fairly good idea what.

Once I had been secured to the chair, the man who'd undertaken the taping joined the search party as Khally stepped forward.

"Where's the fucking gear, cuz?" he asked menacingly.

"What gear?" I replied.

He picked up a one-litre transparent bottle and began to violently shake its clear liquid content.

"The gear Egan was going to bring to the deal we had set up. Where is it?"

"God knows. Do you think he'd tell me!"

"Unfortunately for you, you're the only person left alive who might know where it is, so either you tell me or I'm afraid you're going to get hurt real bad," he announced.

Egan had told me he had left it somewhere in this club. But he could have moved it, and if he had, then they would never find it and I'd be fucked. My only hope was the fella from Khally's crew who had switched to Egan's side. Egan said he was lying low and staying here. Would Egan have bolted the entrance door and locked him in? If he was here, would he present himself and save my sorry ass? I was clutching at straws.

"I'm being straight with you; I don't know where the fuck he's hidden it. It might very well be here somewhere, but if it isn't, then I'm all out of ideas," I said.

Khally walked slowly up to me and bowed his head close to my ear.

"Do you know what I have in my hand, bro?" he asked, shaking the bottle. "It's sulfuric acid. My two boys are going to tear this place down looking for the gear. If they don't find it, I'm going to throw half of this bottle over your face. The word is, it stings like a bitch, like the worst pain you've ever felt. It'll melt away your skin; it might even blind you. Then, after I've done this, if you still don't tell me where the gear is, you'll get the second half of it over you. They'll be nothing left of your skin after that. It'll be bare flesh and you won't look at all pretty. Even if you survive, you'll be like a walking fucking zombie."

"I would tell you if I knew. I swear to God. He never tells me anything. I'm his runner, a dogsbody, a fucking errand boy, nothing more."

"You were an errand boy with a gun and a smart mouth, and you seemed to know what you were doing. I think it's safe to say you probably know more than you're letting on," he whispered.

"I don't, I swear. I don't know where he's hidden it, please listen to me!"

"Quieten down, cuz. You're boring me now. Either you tell me where the gear is or shut the fuck up because I'm not someone known for their mercy."

I sat terrified as I watched the two members of his crew ransack the club: ripping up wood panels, bludgeoning plasterboards, crashing over tables; the lot.

There was no sign of his turncoat gang member either whom I thought might be hiding somewhere in the club. However, I had one last card to play and I decided to lay it on the table when all other hope had faded. It was an outside chance and it would probably come to nothing, but nothing is what I had to lose.

After a while, one of his gang walked in covered in dust with a large claw hammer in his hand.

"Fuck all," he announced.

"Have you checked everywhere?" Khally asked.

"Everywhere, bro. There's no coke in this place."

"Arif, stop already and come here," Khally shouted to the other man.

He walked slowly into the room, again debris and dust all over him.

"What's your name?" Khally asked me.

"Robbie."

"Robbie," he repeated, as he wiped the top of the bottle slowly around the skin of my face. "I bet you didn't think when you pushed that piece in my face that it would come to this," he said before again shaking the bottle.

"Do you know what, I kind of knew there wouldn't be a happy ending to this story," I replied, resigned to my fate.

"And you were right," he added, as he unscrewed the bottle top and slowly drew the neck of my bottle so I could smell the acid.

"You don't need to do this; the gear's not here. I would tell you where it was if I knew. Please don't throw that stuff over me," I pleaded.

"I'm almost sure I believe you," he replied. "But I've seen that look before and been proved wrong. Some men will hold on to the truth for as long as it takes. They will swear on the lives of their children that they know nothing but then, after a whole lot of pain, the truth suddenly comes out." He then looked at the bottle before taking a quick sniff of its contents.

"A whole lot of pain is coming your way, my friend. Let me hear what your truth is," he declared.

It was time to make my last play; my final roll of the dice. This was the ultimate shit-or-bust deal.

"Where do you think Egan is?" I asked him.

"Egan?" he chuckled. "Oh, we've taken good care of him."

"Did you see it happen, Khally? Did you see your men kill him with your own eyes?"

"I might have done," he answered.

"You didn't, though, did you? Now ask yourself a question: how would I know that?"

"I don't know. How would you know that?" he asked in a hushed voice.

"You left your two foot soldiers to kill Egan and get rid of the body – that's right, isn't it? But have you seen them both since?" I asked.

"I've had contact with them," he replied. However, I noticed that he had started to look a little concerned.

"What, messages or phone calls?"

"Cut to the chase, bro. What are you saying?" he asked, getting slightly irritated.

"Because here's a thing, I guarantee you haven't spoken to both of them either in the flesh or on the phone."

"What are you getting at?"

"Egan's alive. I've seen him, talked to him face to face like I'm talking to you now."

"Fuck off, you got jokes, man!" he said, turning away, smiling awkwardly.

"He's alive, unlike one of your crew. Two men took Egan away to kill him and let's just say one of them wasn't exactly loyal to you."

"I don't believe you."

"He was working for Egan. He and Egan killed the other fella and since then Egan's been hiding him."

"This is fucking bullshit – you're only saying this to save your ass!"

"You might have heard from the geezer Egan's protecting, you even might have spoken to him, but I swear you'll never see him again."

"Shut the fuck up!" he screamed.

"And you'll certainly never see or hear from the other man because the bad news is he's the one lying at the bottom of the reservoir, not Egan."

"I don't fucking believe you!" he blasted.

"Go ahead and call the other fella who you haven't heard from. I swear you'll not be able to speak to him; in fact, I will bet my life on it."

"Bet your life on it, did you hear that, boys? Okay, let's play that fucking game then, shall we?"

Khally then pulled out his phone, dialled the number and put it on speaker so we could all hear the outcome. If Egan was lying and he answered then I was toast.

As the call was being connected Khally just stared at me. It went straight to automated voicemail.

"I told you, he's dead, and if Egan arrives here later and finds me with my skin shredded then he'll come after you. He's a fucking psycho. He'll kill the three of you, then the rest of your crew, and if he fancies it, he'll have some fun with your families as well."

Khally turned and looked both ways at the men standing either side of him.

"You can take your chances if you want, Khally. You can hang around and try and take Egan out, but you'll fail. If you hurt me then I'll give you forty-eight hours before you, your crew and your family are all dead. If you leave me alone and get the fuck out of Leicester, set up somewhere else, then you might have a chance."

Khally stood, deep in thought, weighing up his options.

"I think we should leave him," Arif said, looking scared.

"You shut the fuck up!" Khally yelled.

He knew he was snookered; he recognised that unless he departed Leicester quickly then Egan would hunt him down and kill him. My big fear was whether, as a parting gift to Egan, he would murder me before he left.

He suddenly put the cap on the bottle of acid he was holding and threw the bottle across the room.

"Fuck it!" he yelled. "You fucking tell Egan, I'm going nowhere. I'm going to wait around for him and he knows where to fucking find me!" Khally barked.

There was then a sudden and ear-splitting blast resulting in Arif falling to the ground with the top of his head blown off. His brains and skull spread across the floor, blood seeping from the other half of his head that was still attached to his neck. Khally and the other man immediately turned around. At the door was Egan with a pistol in each hand. He had come to settle this score.

"He was right, you know, the boy, he was right," he explained as he strolled in. "If you had thrown the acid on him I would have really hurt you over several hours before finally putting you to sleep. I would have paid a Deliveroo driver a grand to have your body dropped at the front door of your family."

"I should have looked after you myself, shouldn't I?" Khally concluded.

"If it's any consolation, you've got less than a minute to regret it. But you're right, your boy Shayan had become a most valuable asset."

"You tell him from me that when news of this gets out, that brother is on borrowed time."

"Oh no, my friend, you can tell him yourself shortly. I put two bullets in his head about an hour ago."

"Why?" Khally asked.

"Because if he can betray you, then he'll likely betray me. If you see him in your afterlife, be sure to let him know it wasn't personal."

I couldn't see Khally's face, but I suspected he would be wearing the expression of a man who knew his fate. He played by the rules of the street and they dictated this could now only end one way. His time had come. All of the people in his life who had warned him that being involved in this business would likely end in him being killed would be proved right.

Egan first shot the other man in the stomach. I watched as he went down, writhing in agony. He then turned his attention to Khally. "Get on your knees," Egan demanded.

Khally followed his orders, and Egan walked up to him and pressed the muzzle of his gun to his forehead.

There was no final speech, no request for Khally's last words, no justification and certainly no apology. Egan just blew Khally's brains out of his head, and from the look on his face, his conscience didn't even flicker.

He then cut me free as the wounded man was still lying on the floor in agony.

"Are you okay?" he asked.

I was simply lost for words; nothing would come out. Egan walked behind the bar.

"Oh shit! They've only gone and smashed all the glasses," he ranted.

A most macabre observation given the two dead bodies on his floor, not to mention a third injured man who was leaving a trail of blood as he was crawling to the door. Egan spotted his vain attempts to escape and dispassionately strode over to him, drew his gun and put two more bullets into his body.

There were a few moments of silence whilst I tried to digest what had happened.

"What are you going to do with this lot?" I asked, pointing to the bodies.

"I guess I'll have to pop into John Lewis tomorrow and buy some replacement tumblers," he replied with a grin and a wink.

Fucking hell, this fella was cold, brutal, seemingly without a soul and unable to feel remorse.

"I'm getting tired of Leicester, Robbie. I don't know whether the locals have warmed to me. Maybe it's time for me to move on," he revealed.

"What, just go, leave, as simple as that?"

"Nearly," he replied with a smile.

"Nothing with you was ever going to be that simple."

"You've one last thing to do," he announced. "There's one final objective I need you to achieve, then I'm out of here and you'll never see me again."

"What it is?"

"You've exactly two weeks to get yourself a job. A proper job, that is, not some temping, zero hours, part-time fucking bullshit gig in Aldi. I mean a properly contracted, full-time job. If you do that then you'll be saved from the last challenge."

"What's the challenge?" I asked.

"Oh, you'll like it a lot. If you thought this was dangerous then, trust me, you had better be wearing a nappy for the next one."

"Fucking hell, what it is?"

"It's best I keep it a secret because once I've told you it'll keep you awake at night."

"Why, Egan? Why do this? I've done everything you've asked of me whilst Ethel was laid up. What difference will it make to you if I get a job or not?" I pleaded.

"I want to make sure you are on the straight and narrow before I depart and that you're not tempted to do something silly again, like steal from another charity shop."

"And if I fail, what then? What's the forfeit this time?"

"If I were you, I'd go hell for leather and land myself a job, otherwise, well, let's just say you'll need a passport and a decent-sized suitcase."

CHAPTER 22

I walked home from the club in a daze. It was like I had just appeared in a real-time action movie. The images, the fear, the bodies, the blood and gore. It all felt surreal.

I needed to talk to someone about what had happened. I had to tell them what I had seen and what I had experienced. I had sniffed the blood of extreme violence and had come within a whisker of suffering unthinkable pain. I required the solace of another human being. I couldn't put this on Grandad; it wasn't fair. But I knew a man who had been no stranger to extremes.

When Tony answered the door, I broke down and had an outpouring of emotion. I couldn't, try as I might, hold back the tears.

"Hey, are you alright?" he asked compassionately. "Come inside."

I sat down on the settee and began to try to compose myself, but my shock resulted in the random spouting of nuggets of what had gone down.

"He killed them all, Tony, all of them."

"Who?"

"Khally and his two boys. All three of them, dead. Bang, bang, bang, like he was playing a video game."

"I assume you're talking about Egan?"

"Egan, it was all Egan."

"What's happened to him? Where he is?"

"Drinking at his club as if nothing has happened. They threatened me, Tony. Tied me down to a chair and they were going to throw acid all over my face if I didn't tell them where the coke was."

"Okay, okay, slow down. You're going to be fine. You've had a bad experience, that's all."

"I thought they were going to kill me."

"Are you going to the police?" he asked.

"No way. I'm right in the middle of this. I was there; I watched it happen, Tony, I saw it with my own two eyes!"

I continued rambling about what had happened. Tony poured us both a whisky and handed me a glass. I was shaking violently so he came over and steadied my hand. I raised the glass to my lips and drank, then drank some more. I rested the glass on my leg and puffed out my cheeks.

"It's over, you're okay, it's over," he said.

I turned to him. "I thought they were going to kill me!"

"I know that feeling, and it'll never leave you, but you'll be okay," he replied. "You're safe now."

I woke up on Tony's settee. The combination of whisky and stress had exhausted me. He was sat in his chair watching the television and looked over as he saw me stir.

"You okay?" he asked.

I sat up and rubbed my eyes. "Yeah, what time is it?"

"Ten o'clock. You've been out cold for three hours," he replied.

"I wasn't there, was I, Tony? It's just something for me to forget about."

He nodded. "Just something for you to forget about."

"I need your help, again," I said.

"Sure, what with?"

"Egan says he's going to be around for two more weeks then he's off. In that time, I've to find myself a job."

He sniggered. "Is this guy a gangster or does he work for the Department of Work and Pensions!"

"Obviously, there's a forfeit if I don't land myself something."

"What's that?"

"I'm not sure, except he says I'll need a passport and a suitcase and I'm kind of ruling out an all-inclusive trip to the Caribbean."

"That could mean anything."

"Yeah, but this is Egan we are talking about, so you just know the gig's going to be hot."

"A job in two weeks? I'll sort one out for you. My friend works in recruitment and they are all always looking for temporary staff."

"He's ruled out any temping work, part-time shit, anything like that. It needs to be a proper job, full-time and permanent."

"Okay, and will he check?"

"Will he check? Are you fucking kidding me! I got bombed out of the volunteering gig at the British Heart Society and Egan found out about it before I even got home."

"I'm not even going to ask you what happened there," he replied, as I realised this was the first he had heard about it. "Okay, let's focus our efforts on getting you a job. So, you need to be starting it in two weeks?"

"I don't think he meant starting it, I think he said I could have received a solid offer."

"So, first things first, we need to sort out your CV."

"What the fuck are we going to put on that? I haven't done anything since I left school!"

"We need to position it slightly differently. Let's put the onus on your appetite to succeed, the skills you have and your potential, rather than highlight what you haven't done."

"That sounds like a start."

"But we need to be smart with the jobs you send off for. You've got two weeks, so we need to be applying for jobs where the closing date is the next day or two. They'll mess about deciding who to interview, then even if you do get shortlisted, you'll need to land the job, and sometimes they even fanny around offering the position."

"This is fucking hopeless! I may as well go next door and dig out my passport," I said.

"Yes, you're right, it's hopeless, let's not bother," he replied, visibly irritated as he poured himself another glass of whisky.

"I didn't mean it like that."

"The only chance you ever have of success is believing you can do it yourself. You might be the only person in the world who does, but if you stop believing, then you will fail."

"I know, I know."

"No, I don't think you do, because you've never applied yourself to anything you've ever wanted. You've never had a goal that would push you beyond what you believed you were capable of and because of that you see anything which appears difficult as being impossible."

"It's only that two weeks doesn't seem long enough."

"You're doing it again! Can't you see you're dropping the barrier of failure right in front of you? Thank God when we send our troops into battle they don't have the same mindset."

I was receiving a right royal telling-off here and I deserved every word of it. I was acting like a weak-willed pussy and it was time to stop. "Okay, fuck it! I'm going to get this fucking job – bring it on! What do we next?"

"Get yourself around here first thing in the morning and let's get the show on the road. We'll write up your CV, get you logged on to whatever these job site things are and let's go for it. You've got all the jabber, so if you get an interview then you have got a chance."

"I have got a chance," I added. "Thanks, Tony, you're a real friend."

The next morning, before I was due to call round to see Tony, as I was sat watching the television with Grandad, I contemplated the true meaning of being a 'friend'. It's a word we all freely band around but how should it be defined? Was it someone who would join you for a pint, meet you for a coffee and a gossip, or did being a 'friend' have deeper tiers compared to those whom you might only bother to refer to as acquaintances?

What struck me was real friends make the effort to help each other in times of need, even when the circumstances of this assistance may greatly inconvenience them. I am sure Tony had better things to do this morning than spend time constructing my CV, registering me for job sites and helping me apply for employment. There was nothing in it for him, beyond, perhaps, some satisfaction should I succeed. His support was a selfless act; his assistance came without a price and was delivered only with goodwill.

I was ashamed because never in my twenty-three years had I done the same for anyone else. Despite not working and having an abundance of time on my hands, I never lifted a finger for anyone. I even made a fuss of making Grandad a cup of tea. Tony had lived next door for ages, a man of maturing years, all alone, and yet I had never once asked him if he needed any help. He would have had days when he was ill, struggling to get out of the house to buy groceries, and he had no one to call on, whilst I had been a matter of twenty yards away, lying in bed, doing fuck all.

And yet when I did ask him for his help, his offer of support was unconditional despite the transience of our matured companionship.

My thoughts then turned to Egan. I realised I was only a small part of his grand plan. I was being used so he may achieve a greater objective. He was in total control of my immediate future. The problem was I didn't have the faintest idea what his plan was and, moreover, how it was going to end.

I called around to see Tony, who enthusiastically sat me down at his dining room table. Overnight and this morning, he had been researching the best job sites, how to construct a CV and searching for jobs that fitted our closing date criteria. I was humbled by his efforts; he had done all of this whilst I had been at home doing nothing. Tony had proved himself to be a dear friend and I would never forget this and forever be in his debt, whatever the outcome of this next fortnight.

We had been working away for well over three hours. My CV was completed and he was firing it across the internet whilst applying for a host of local jobs. We had even applied for a handful of apprenticeships, whatever they were.

We stopped for a tea, taking time out from a busy but productive morning.

"Do you know what you really ought to do?" he posed.

"Go on," I replied.

"Join the army."

I nearly spat my drink out. "Please tell me you're joking?"

"No, I'm being deadly serious. Let me ask you a question: what irritated you the most about the people who you were working with at the charity place?"

"The fact that some of them did fuck all work," I replied.

"Exactly. It got on your nerves because they lacked discipline when you didn't. This is a perfect starting place for the armed forces."

"I can't see it, Tony. Anyway, look at the state of me! I'm not fit enough to get in the army. I get out of breath walking around the block."

"No, you don't. I regularly see you walking into town and then walking back again. That isn't the behaviour of a man who is totally out of shape. Sure, you're carrying a stone, maybe twenty pounds of fat, but you would soon get rid of that if you started training."

"I don't know if I've got it in my toolbox, to be honest. Anyway, I couldn't leave my grandad on his own."

"He won't always be around, Robbie. You know that."

"Yeah, I know. But look, unless the British army is going to swing by here in the next couple of weeks, recruit me, do the medical and then take me on full-time, perhaps we need to concentrate on warehouse jobs, frying chicken and selling energy deals in call centres."

He smiled, turned back to his computer and we pressed on in our quest to find me a job.

CHAPTER 23

I was ten days into my job search and the timer was running down fast. Whatever Egan had in store for me was coming down the track at pace and I probably wouldn't be able to get out of its way. I had received dozens of confirmation emails following the umpteen submissions of job applications I had processed, but so far nothing. In desperation, I had even walked around town handing out my CV to shops and businesses.

I had been summoned, by text message, to meet Egan at the club and had arrived at the designated time to be greeted by him, once again, sat at the bar drinking.

"Good to see you you've bought some new glasses," I said.

"I've only bought a pack of four. I'm don't intend using them for much longer," he replied.

"What are you going to do with this place after you return to London?"

"I'll probably hang on to it for a while. Who knows, they might even invest a bit of money in the area, give it a facelift, make it trendy, then the value of it will go up. It's a tried and tested strategy I've used in London."

"Why put yourself in such danger?" I asked.

"What do you mean?"

"You've made a few quid, so why carry on dealing and hanging around people like Khally? You could have been killed the other night."

"Danger, Robbie. It's a drug, worse than anything I sell. I need it; I have to live on the edge; it's what keeps me alive."

"But you know your luck will run out eventually, don't you?"

"I used up my luck years ago. I'm still breathing because I see the angles. I know what needs to be done and I do it, whatever that entails. If I do get whacked it'll be because I was sloppy, not because I was unlucky."

"So, you're an adrenalin junkie?"

"How's the job search going? I'm guessing in this instance no news for you isn't exactly good news?" he asked.

"You knew two weeks was going to be a struggle."

"I suppose it is given you didn't manage to find a job in the last seven years."

"Let's assume I fail, what happens then?"

"'Let's assume I fail', that's not exactly fighting talk, is it?"

"What's going to happen to me, Egan?"

"A nice little trip over the water to Amsterdam – have you been there?"

"No."

"You'll like it, it's a great place. There's some fantastic bars, architecture, canals, beautiful little restaurants and a world-class supplier of pills."

"What sort of pills?"

"Well, they aren't multi-vitamins, put it that way."

"What have I got to do?"

"You're going to help me bring them back into the country."

I went cold. "You fucking what?"

"It's a three-man job for such a large consignment. We will share the pills up. Your job will be to get your share back here."

"What if I get stopped at customs?"

"Jail time, Robbie, dead simple. It could happen to either one of us or all three or neither of us. It might sound high risk, but it's not that dangerous if you think about it. The pills are odourless and we can cover them with X-ray proof bags which are practically untraceable unless someone stops you and wants to search your bag."

"Then what happens?" I asked.

"Jail time. Are you listening to me?"

"This is fucking mental!" I yelled.

"How do you think this gear gets out onto our streets? There are hundreds of consignments coming in every day. The customs staff at ports and airports are chasing their tails and they know it. It's practically a gimme. They must stop less than one per cent of what's coming in. You just need to make sure you're not the one per cent, and let's be honest, with odds like this, you've got to fancy yourself."

I stood, shaking my head. "So, if I get caught, how long am I looking at?"

"What's all this with the failure again; have you no faith in yourself? You've come this far, haven't you? You've survived Khally and Corey, so a couple of overworked customs officers should be a piece of cake."

"How long would I get in prison, if I'm caught, Egan?" I asked again, sternly.

"Difficult to say for sure. I'd get you a decent barrister" – he turned and nodded to me – "don't mention it, but you'd have to be thinking three to five."

"I'm guessing that's years, not months?"

"Well, it's certainly not weeks!"

"Fucking hell, Egan!"

"I bet you're regretting the charity shop robbery now, aren't you?"

"Don't rub it in, you know I do."

"Leaving poor Ethel in that state, just for the sake of a few quid. That really was a bad day at the office for you and poor Bod."

"Yeah, I know, you don't have to keep going on about it."

He then slapped a copy of the *Leicester Mercury* on the bar. On the front page was a colour picture of Bod arriving at court. "The picture of him reminded me of why I'm doing this," he said. "He got off lightly. I heard he cried like a baby in court, pleading with the judge to be lenient, saying he was a reformed character. I would have loved to have seen it," he explained. "I wonder how his mum felt?"

"What did he get?"

"He escaped prison, received a load of community service and a five-hundred-pound fine. I suspect the real punishment will be all of his friends and family seeing him on the front page."

"Poor Bod," I sympathised with a lump in my throat.

"It could have been you in the picture with him as well. That would have been a nice souvenir for your grandad, wouldn't it?"

"Don't you think I know all of this?" I added meekly.

"You should be grateful, Robbie. What you have been asked to do is far better than being an outcast in your community. I mean, seriously, everywhere Bod goes, he'll be known as the bloke who stole the kind-hearted Tom Needham's clothes from a charity shop. He won't be able to step foot out of his front door without someone having a pop at him. I'm afraid if he's to have any sort of life it's either plastic surgery or relocation to another city."

He was right; me being on the front page would have been unbearable. I could not begin to think of the shame Bod's feeling, and even though I may argue he attended the theft of his own volition, the fact remains had I not instigated it then none of this would have happened.

"What are the arrangements for Amsterdam?" I asked, in a resigned tone.

"I'll let you know the full details, but you'll be flying out of East Midlands airport on your own. We meet the other fella when we are out there. I've booked him on to another flight."

"Okay, I'll wait to hear from you."

"Or, you can get yourself a job and miss the whole trip. It's your choice. We'll fly out the day before your deadline, so I'll give you until noon the following lunchtime to see if you get a result."

"I won't hold my breath," I said.

"No, neither will I," he replied.

I walked into town and without even having to look at my watch knew it was beer o'clock. It was early afternoon and the bar was quiet, allowing me to take stock. I reflected on both the Bod situation and my forthcoming all-expenses-paid trip to Amsterdam. This may very well be my last serious interaction with Egan, but if it ended badly I would experience a long and uncomfortable reminder. If I was to get stopped with a load of pills at the airport and slung in prison then this would surely finish off Grandad. Worse still, there would be no one around to sort out the funeral arrangements. No one, perhaps, except Tony. Yet again, I found myself relying on him.

I woke up my mobile phone and accessed the online *Leicester Mercury* webpage. It was leading with Bod's court appearance and the same photograph which had appeared on the front page of their newspaper.

MAN PLEADS GUILTY TO THEFT OF ROCK STAR'S CHARITY DONATION

It couldn't have been more damaging. I should have been in the picture with him, I thought, sharing the spotlight of shame and maybe supporting him. It was wrong that I had walked away from the social repercussions as well as the court's punishment.

I finished my beer, visited an ATM and then walked around to Bod's house. Despite four people living at this address, there was an inevitability about who would answer. As I knocked I braced myself for the onslaught. I was not disappointed.

"Oh, look who it is!" she screamed.

"I don't want any trouble, Mrs Bodwin. I just want to talk to Bod."

"Of course you do! You'll want to tell him how sorry you are. Well, sorry won't cut it, so why don't you do one? Don't you think you've brought enough shame on this family?"

"I need to speak to him," I persisted.

"He doesn't want to speak to you; can't you get that into your stupid thick head? No one wants to speak to you; you're not welcome around here anymore, not now and not ever; so, do us all a big favour, will you, and fuck off!"

I simply had no comeback to this, so, after a few seconds' silence, turned to leave. It was then I heard Bod's voice.

"It's alright, Mum. Let me speak to him."

"No, don't, Lee! You've nothing to say to him," she yelled.

"It's okay, let me deal with it," he said, walking out of the front door and closing it behind him.

"I saw the *Leicester Mercury*; I don't know what to say," I said.

"Don't say anything because however bad you think this is, trust me, it's a thousand times worse."

"I'm sorry, mate."

"I've had to close down all of my social media stuff. I've got people threatening to come round to torch my house, beat me up, I've even had someone saying they are going to kill me. It's a nightmare."

"Shit, mate, that's bad. Is there anything I can do?"

He suddenly burst into tears. "I wish so much I hadn't done it. I would give anything to go back to that morning, to tell you it was a bad idea, to have gone fishing like I said I was going to do. We were stealing from a charity, Robbie, a charity! What were we thinking?"

"Money, that's all it was. It was the only thing we were bothered about and we didn't give a shit about anything else. Well, it's royally backfired on us."

"On 'us', on *me*, don't you mean?"

"You've taken the worst of it, but this fucking Egan fella's got me jumping through hoops. I was even tied to a chair the other day with some gangster threatening to throw acid in my face."

"What's that all about?"

"It's gone way too far. I can't think straight anymore. I've got one more thing to do which could get me sent down for a long time."

"What?" he asked.

"He's making me bring back a load of pills from Amsterdam. We fly out in a couple of days and I've got to smuggle them in."

"Are you fucking mad?"

"The only way out of it is if I find work. He said if I bag a full-time job then he'll let me off."

"How long have you got?"

"We fly in three days; the deadline is noon on the fourth day, whilst we are out there."

"What sort of game is this fella playing?"

"A game where I'm the only fucking contestant and one that I never wanted to play."

"If I hear of any jobs, I'll let you know. I'm looking myself at the minute, but I'm not sure I'll have a queue of takers right now."

"It'll die down, mate, you'll see. It'll soon be old news. Who knows, the front page headlines in a few days might be about some bloke who gets arrested at East Midlands airport with ten thousand pills on him."

"Good luck with that."

"Yeah, thanks," I replied. "I miss you, mate. You were the one true friend I had. I doubt you'll ever forgive me, but if you do you'll call me, won't you?"

"It's still sore, you know. It still hurts," he replied.

"I know it does, but I think we need each other."

"I don't know, maybe."

I reached into my pocket. "I want you to have this." I passed him the five hundred pounds I had withdrawn from the ATM.

"What is it?" he asked.

"It's your fine money. I want to pay it for you."

"No, mate. I'll sort it out."

"Take it, Bod, please take it," I pleaded with a tear in my eye. "It's the least I can do."

He paused for a second. "I can't."

"You can, please. If you don't I'll only come back and post it through your letterbox."

He reluctantly took the money from me.

"Thanks," he said quietly.

"I'll be off then."

I turned and walked away. As I reached the gate, he called out.

"I reckon a Taser would have done it."

"Done what?" I asked, confused.

"I reckon a Taser would have floored Mike Tyson in his prime."

I smiled as I recalled Nails's text message and the question he had posed. It was a happier time for both of us. We were carefree and enjoying life back then. But since the robbery and the subsequent fallout, everything had changed.

I was woken after another broken night's sleep by the beeping of my mobile phone. The message was from Zoe, who was accepting my invitation for a drink tomorrow night; the day before I was due to fly to Amsterdam. If the trip was indeed to be calamitous, then it would be my last night out for quite some time.

She had booked her usual teenage babysitter but, as she wasn't very old herself, Zoe would have to meet me late afternoon, as she'd need to be home around nine o'clock. I was thrilled she had accepted my invitation. The date was a welcome distraction from the prospect of the Amsterdam trip, which I was now getting anxious about.

Having fired off a friendly text message to Zoe, I was startled as my phone rang.

"Hello," I answered.

"Can I speak to Robert Howard?"

"Yes, speaking," I replied.

"Hi, Robert, my name is Chris Hockey from Encore Recruitment. I am calling about the job application you have sent into us."

I sat up in bed, feeling a little shocked.

"Oh yes."

"We would like to invite you in for an interview and wondered whether we could schedule a time?"

"I am available whenever you like. I'm free today if you have any availability your end."

"Okay, let me check my diary." There was a pause before he came back. "I could see you today. How about three o'clock?"

"That sounds great."

He gave me directions to the office and offered himself as a contact point upon arrival. Fucking hell, my very first job interview! I hadn't a clue what to expect, what they were likely to ask me or what I should take along me. There was only one thing for it: I needed to get changed and head over to Tony's.

Tony guided me through the whole process: the initial and important greeting with Mr Hockey, the questions I could ask at the end and what questions they were likely to ask me. We even researched the company and I made a note of five things I could tell them about their business, should I be asked. I was rusty on my answers, to begin with, but with Tony's excellent coaching, my responses were becoming slicker and more detailed.

By 2 p.m. I was again knocking at Tony's door, only this time wearing my interview attire. It was pretty much the outfit Egan had brought me from Hugo Boss.

"Where's your tie?" Tony asked.

"What tie?"

"It's an interview; you'll need to wear a tie."

"I haven't got a tie," I replied. "Anyway, who wears fucking ties in this day and age?"

"If I were you, I would assume Mr Hockey does, and if you walk in there not wearing one, then you can count yourself out of the job before the interview has even started."

He went upstairs and brought down with him a range of ties to choose from. I selected a plain-coloured one.

"Yes, that'll do you," Tony said. "Put that one on."

"Yeah, about that," I replied.

"What?" he asked. "Oh, don't tell me, you don't know how to tie it."

"I've never worn one, what do you expect?"

Tony stood over me like I was a child on their first day at secondary school preparing something called a 'Windsor Knot' – whatever the fuck that was.

"There you go. Now, whatever you do, don't fiddle with it, otherwise, you'll get in a mess."

I looked at myself in the mirror and felt quite proud, as I appeared for the first time in my life, well, corporate.

"Okay, I reckon I'm all set. Go through the checklist with me again," I requested.

"What's the name of the company?" he asked.

"Encore."

"Address?"

"Twenty-one Millstone Lane."

"The person who you are asking for when you arrive?"

"Chris Hockey."

"Would you like a cup of tea or coffee, Mr Howard?"

"No, thank you, just a glass of water."

"Do you have any questions you would like to ask us?"

"Do you know how long it will before you can let me know the outcome? I may have other job offers, but I would like the opportunity to work here."

"Excellent!" he said.

"Oh, and by the way, Mr Hockey, did I mention to you I have extensive experience in trading illegal drugs, negotiating deals with dealers, stealing from charity shops and ripping off addicts – if you think these might help my prospects of working here."

Tony smiled. "Well, if all else fails, it might be worth a try."

"Okay, it's time for me to leave. Wish me luck."

He put his hand on my shoulder. "Good luck, son. You can do this!"

"Tony, I need to tell you something," I said. "If I don't get this job, Egan's going to make me go to Amsterdam and bring back a load of drugs."

"Okay," he answered, not at all shocked.

"If I get arrested with them, I'll be going to prison. Egan thinks it'll be a three-to-five stretch."

"Then you had better go and get this job!" he demanded.

I puffed my cheeks out. "Blimey, I think I was less nervous walking onto the St Matthews estate with a gun and a bag of cocaine," I said, as I left his house.

I arrived at the interview exactly ten minutes before my designated time. I was sitting in reception before someone arrived to collect me and take me through to Chris Hockey's office. Chris greeted me with a confident, warm handshake. Straightaway, I could see he was a no-nonsense individual who would take no shit from anyone. He was motivated, focused and determined to get the right people around him. Sitting next to him was someone from HR, who was taking notes and occasionally looking up at me with a smile.

Chris wasted no time in getting under the skin of what I had been up to.

"I like your honest CV, Robbie. I found it refreshing. But I need you to explain to me what on earth you have been doing between leaving school and sitting here today."

"I can answer that in one word, Chris: 'nothing'. Certainly, nothing of any note. I could tell you a sob story about being effectively orphaned at the age of eight, being put into foster care or living with my grandparents and then losing my grandma as I was about to take my GCSEs, but that would only be a lame excuse.

"I've lost seven years of my life, and this is time I should have spent building a career. Those years have been and gone, and I cannot do anything about that. The trade-off is, I am determined to make amends, to catch up on lost time, to throw myself with one hundred per cent commitment and passion into a job. I just need to find someone who would be prepared to take a chance on me."

And this was pretty much the tale of the interview. It wasn't about proving to them what I had achieved previously; instead it was about what I thought I could bring to their workplace should I be given a chance.

The interview was concluded by Chris advising they would let me know the outcome via email or telephone by close of play tomorrow. This worked perfectly. If I had landed this role then I would have escaped the Amsterdam trip by the skin of my teeth.

Not for the first time since Egan had turned up in my life, I was relying on a big slice of good fortune to pull me through.

I arrived back home and immediately called in to see Tony. I recounted every question they asked and gave him a summary of my answer. He nodded enthusiastically throughout, suggesting I had done well.

"How do you think it went?" he asked.

"I gave it my best shot. I told them all the things you told me to say."

"Good lad. And when will you hear?"

"Tomorrow. So I should know before I have to get on the flight," I answered, suddenly realising the enormity of what I had riding on this job.

"You've done all you can, Robbie. There's no point worrying about it anymore."

"Tony, if the worst-case scenario happens and I get nicked

coming back in from Amsterdam, then it's likely I'll be inside when it happens."

"When what happens? Oh, sorry, yes, I get you."

"I'll need someone to arrange the funeral and everything that goes with it," I added.

"Of course I will. Leave it with me," he replied, with his usual generosity.

This was a load off my mind.

"Thank you. Someday I'll repay you for everything you've done for me."

"You owe me nothing," he replied. "Just be sure to do a good deed for someone else if and when the opportunity presents itself."

CHAPTER 24

I had been awake since 5 a.m. I suspected one or two key issues would get resolved today, and none more important than whether I had secured the job at Encore.

I'd arranged to meet Zoe in a city centre bar at 4 p.m.; maybe before this, I would have received confirmation of landing the job and have something to celebrate.

I had taken the opportunity of having a chat with Grandad and letting him know that Egan and I had a story we were running and it required us to interview a witness in Amsterdam. I explained that I would only be gone for one night and would return the following evening. I advised that should he need any assistance then Tony would be happy to help. Grandad, forever the old soldier, was adamant he would be fine and for me not to worry.

By 3 p.m. I was getting spruced up ready for my date with Zoe when there was a loud banging at the back door. This could only be one person. I called down to Grandad that I would answer it. I was inevitably greeted by Mrs Bodwin, who had made an unwelcome drunken return.

"Don't you think that just because you paid his fine this makes everything alright because it doesn't."

"I never said it did."

"Do you know last night a load of kids came to our house and threw bags of dog shit at our front door?"

"I'm sorry about this, but—"

"Go fuck your apology, fuck your excuses and fuck you! I know stuff about you, Robbie Howard. I know stuff you don't think I know," she said as she stumbled.

"Look, Mrs Bodwin, what has happened is terrible and I regret it, but you coming around here drunk and causing a nuisance isn't helping anyone, least of all my grandad, who's very ill."

"Give him my apologies, I mean no disrespect. I know he's a good man. What a shame you didn't take after him."

"Can we please let this go? Do you want me to call you a taxi home?" I asked.

"I don't want anything from you, nothing, absolutely nothing, I'd rather walk home than have you buy me a ride."

She walked down our driveway with a silly grin on her face, repeating the same phrase as she departed. It sounded like, 'farewell, Robbie' but she seemed to be putting on some weird accent. Mystified, I closed the door and continued to get ready.

It was 3.30 p.m. and I was walking into town. I had my phone in my hand waiting for the call to come through from Encore.

I was assuming when Chris Hockey said 'by close of play' he meant by 5 p.m., maybe 5.30 p.m., but surely not much later than this?

I arrived at the bar and ordered myself a drink. Zoe walked in shortly afterwards and we found a nice quiet table where we could have a chat. It was great to see her and she was looking gorgeous. We were laughing, joking and swapping tales. She was telling me what her son had been up to, whilst I explained my spurious business trip to Amsterdam. However, the light-hearted conversation ceased as talk, once again, gravitated to her ex-boyfriend, Leon.

"Where's he living?" I asked.

"I haven't got a clue, it's probably local, but to be honest, I'm not sure I want to know," she replied.

"Sounds a bit odd. What's that about?"

"He's born and bred Leicester, but after a year of going out with him we moved down to London and that's when things turned sour," she said.

"Why?"

"He told me he was a sales rep for an IT company. I didn't doubt it for a second: he had a flash BMW, he was good-looking; well dressed, charming. He told me the move was a promotion, but it wasn't. As you know, he was a drug dealer and he moved to London to make some serious money."

"And did he?"

"Yeah, he made some proper money all right, but then, for reasons only known to himself, he decided to start skimming cash from the gang he was working for."

"Did they ever find out?"

"I'm not sure. He came home one night, high as a kite on crack cocaine and clearly agitated about something, and then knocked ten bells out of me. I was in hospital for a month. That was when Dad visited me and when I knew he was going to kill him."

"Bloody hell. When does he see your son?"

"He just drops in from time to time and then disappears again. He'll be gone for weeks then he'll pop back up. It won't last forever, though."

"Why?"

"They'll find him eventually and he'll either end up dead or in prison."

"What happened between you two?"

"We fell out; it was as simple as that. He was a drug addict and he'd get high, turn nasty, then he'd like to beat me up."

"How do you feel when he pops around?" I asked.

"I hate it. I never know who might be following him or whether it's the last time my son will see his dad. Anyway, he called in earlier; he's clearing off somewhere for the weekend and popped around to pick up his passport. At least I can relax a bit."

"This sounds rough," I added before being interrupted by the vibration of my phone. I looked at the display and went cold. The call was from Encore. The balance of the Amsterdam trip would be decided in the next few minutes.

I excused myself and answered my phone in the street. I gulped hard as the outcome of this conversation could be the difference between having a job and serving a hefty prison sentence.

"Hi, Robbie, Chris Hockey. Sorry I've not been able to get back to you earlier, it's been a bit of a mad one."

"No problem, Chris. I appreciate the call."

"Look, we were both impressed with the interview you gave yesterday; you came across very well and I appreciated you'd researched my company and knew what we were about," he said.

"Thank you."

"What does concern us is your lack of experience. We're really busy at the moment, so we have decided to offer the job to a candidate with more experience."

SHIT!

"Okay, Chris. I understand," I replied. I was absolutely gutted.

"You did come second in the process, so we shall keep your details on file and contact you if any other opportunities should arise."

"Thank you. I appreciate your comments and for taking the time to ring me, rather than send an email." The call was ended on good terms and in a professional manner – the product of the Tony Hamylton school of business coaching.

I re-entered the bar feeling numb and brought us another round of drinks.

"Was that a work call?" Zoe enquired.

"Yeah, it was confirmation that tomorrow's Amsterdam trip is definitely on."

"It must be pretty cool getting to travel to cities like Amsterdam for work."

"Yeah, being a journalist certainly has its upsides."

"Fucking hell, are you a journalist now?" came the approaching voice.

It was DS Steve Brydges.

Bollocks!

He had clearly imbibed a few beers and staggered slightly as he approached the table. "I wouldn't believe a word this bloke tells you," he said to Zoe.

"Why wouldn't I?" she asked.

"Do you mind? We're having a quiet drink and you're off-duty, so do one!" I demanded.

"We nicked him the other day, you know, this fella here" – he pointed at me – "but his big-shot drug-dealing mate got him a fancy solicitor to get him off."

Zoe looked at me. "What's he talking about?"

"She doesn't know, does she? Do you want to tell her, or can I? Go on, I'll spin you for it!" he joked, slurring his words.

"I'll tell her. In the meantime, why don't you go and fuck off! Otherwise, that same fancy solicitor will be getting a call from me and I'll tell him I've been harassed by a drunk, off-duty fed."

"Just so you know, Robbie, it'll be me and DS Wood who bring you down. Mark my words, you're going to take an almighty fall. If I were you, love, I wouldn't go making any long-term plans with him, you know what I mean," he said, winking at her. "Now, you kids enjoy yourselves and play nicely."

He turned and left the bar.

"Are you going to explain?" she asked.

"Yes, and I'm sorry."

"For what?"

"For being a fucking a liar! Everything I've told you about me is bullshit. I am going to Amsterdam tomorrow because I'm working for a drug dealer. We are going there to bring back a shitload of fucking pills."

"And the *Leicester Mercury* job you told me about?"

"It's a lie. I don't work for the *Mercury*, I've never worked for the *Mercury*, I don't even read the fucking *Mercury*!"

"Why did you do this?"

"Because it's what I do because it's what I have always done."

"Oh great, here we go again," she remarked, looking like she was ready to get up and leave.

"It stops, though, I'm out. I've finished. From now on you'll only get the truth."

"Yeah, I bet I will," she said, packing her phone into her handbag.

"I will, Zoe, I swear."

"How many times do you think I heard Leon say he'll change and get a proper job?"

"Lots, I suspect."

"As many times as you're thinking, only multiply that number by ten."

"I'll make you a cast-iron, twenty-four-carat gold deal: after this Amsterdam gig, I'm out, that's it. If I'm not, even if I sell half an ounce of fucking weed to some student in a college car park, you can walk, turn your back on me, delete my number, anything you like, but I'm begging you for this one chance."

"Why should I?"

"It's a very long story, but if I get through the Amsterdam trip, if I survive, keep myself out of prison, then I will have learned the hardest, most severe lesson you can imagine, and I promise you, this disgusting, degrading life I have been leading will be over."

"What if you don't get through the Amsterdam trip? It's clear you've annoyed the police and they're gunning for you."

"Then I'll put you to the top of the list of my monthly visitors at the prison," I quipped.

"Why go then? Why not throw the towel in now?"

"Because I have to. I've done something that I'm ashamed of and I'm in debt, only the debt gets wiped if I do this one last job."

"'One last job', again, you'd never believe—"

"How many times you've heard it. I know and I believe you. I fly out of East Midlands tomorrow morning and I come back in the afternoon the day after. If you haven't heard from me by the time you go to bed then assume the worst and I'll promise never to contact you again."

She smiled, then shook her head. "You've one chance."

"That's all I need," I replied.

"I'll tell you what I need," she said with a grin. "I need another drink."

"So do I."

"Make me a promise," she asked.

"What's that?"

"From now on we deal only with the truth – okay?"

I kissed her on the lips. It was our first proper kiss; number two quickly followed, then number three.

"Only the truth," I finally replied.

It was 8.45 p.m. and Zoe's evening pass was shortly to expire. I escorted her to the cab rank, and a most pleasant date was concluded with another kiss and our final embrace of the evening. Without needing to say the precise words, it had become clear our relationship had officially started. At some point, I was going to have to tell Tony about us but decided I would see how my immediate future panned out before I bothered to make any announcements.

As Zoe headed off in a taxi, I decided to have a nightcap before I called it a day. It could very well turn out to be my last drink on home soil for quite some time. The risks associated with the trip were flitting in and out of my head. Was there any possibility the feds could know about the Amsterdam trip? Brydges was adamant they would arrest me but he said nothing specific about tomorrow's gig.

I ordered a double whisky, neat, no ice. Egan's influence was right here in front of me, represented in a glass.

As I gazed out of the window, I saw smokers congregated

outside of the Wetherspoons pub. I looked out for my dad. Would he be in amongst them? Or would he perhaps be somewhere in the pub? I'd had a few drinks and was undoubtedly feeling a little melancholy given what I had riding on the next two days. I knew it was a matter of weeks before Grandad died and then I'd be all alone. Maybe Dad would let me back into his life? Perhaps we could put the past behind us and establish a relationship, even become friends? I acknowledged this was a moment of weakness, but right now I felt vulnerable and unable to fend it off. Was my concern about being lonely, having no family and therefore reaching out to my father such a bad one?

I gulped down my drink, walked across the road and entered the pub. Even though the likelihood was he wouldn't be in here, it was my only connection to his whereabouts. I walked slowly around the pub, looking for his face, feeling nervous should I spot him and not having a clue what I would do or say. I had completed a lap of the bar – nothing. I grabbed myself another shot of whisky and took a seat. Maybe he would come in? Maybe he was in the toilet? Or maybe he was in one of the numerous other cheap drinking holes in Leicester where he'd be getting pissed without giving me a thought.

I had made a mistake. Searching for him had been an error. I finished my drink, departed and made my way home.

I walked through the centre of the Highcross shopping centre and past Cinema de Lux at the same time as a bunch of people who had been to see a film were leaving. I glanced over and noticed a fifty-plus demographic. I chuckled as I concluded it unlikely they had attended the premiere of the new *Captain Marvel* film.

That's when I spotted Ethel.

She was walking towards me with a similarly aged female friend. Egan had said she had been released from the nursing home and was making good progress, but in truth, she looked as fit as a fiddle. She was walking normally and was laughing and smiling with the other lady. I stopped walking and apprehensively allowed her to approach me. My issue was I didn't know if she had worked out or had been told that I was behind the robbery. If she had, it was likely she would give me the cold shoulder, or worse. As I was several drinks in, my confidence was sky-high so decided to test the water.

"Hi, Ethel, it's Robbie," I announced with a welcoming smile.

She stopped for a few seconds as I had caught her off her guard. "Robbie! Yes, sorry, the young man who used to come into Goodwill. It's lovely to see you."

I was thrilled she was being friendly and therefore didn't know I had been instrumental in the theft.

"Have you two ladies enjoyed a pleasant evening at the pictures?" I asked.

"We have, we've been to see *Morse Code*. It was wonderful," Ethel replied.

"Great!" I replied. "Ethel, I understand you've been poorly. It's good to see you looking better."

"Okay, thanks," she said, looking a little confused. "I had the flu about six weeks ago, is this what you meant?"

"I was talking about the stroke you'd had."

Both Ethel and her friend started to giggle.

"I think you're getting me mixed up with someone else," she explained. "Thankfully, I've not had a stroke, or at least I don't think I have!"

"Or maybe you have, but you don't remember. She's forever forgetting things," her friend added, prompting more laughter.

"But, Egan told me you'd had a stroke."

"Whose Egan?" she asked.

I remembered DC Langley telling me that the name 'Egan' was probably an alias.

"Your son, it was your son who told me."

"Did he?" she asked, with a smile. "He would be doing well if he did because I don't have a son."

CHAPTER 25

I woke up with a familiar dull headache and a dry, dehydrated mouth. I checked the time on my mobile phone: 9.32 a.m. By this evening I would be in Amsterdam – shit! My nightmare was to become a reality. My last and only hope of getting a job had come crashing down yesterday afternoon. I now needed to be focused on the precarious task of getting these fucking pills through both airports, avoiding prison and escaping this life forever.

I could hear the faint sounds of voices emanating from downstairs. I opened my bedroom door and listened closer. It was Egan. He was in the lounge chatting away to Grandad like they were long-lost pals. He was no doubt bullshitting Grandad about my progress as a trainee journalist. I was inclined to go downstairs and unload the whole bullshit Ethel story on him. I was struggling to work out his angle but knew it would be calculating and sinister. But I was mindful not to disrupt the flow and avoid knocking him off balance because it probably wouldn't work to my advantage. As it stood, if I successfully returned from the trip with the pills then I was out. I felt inclined to retain the status quo and walk away.

I dressed, went downstairs and walked into the lounge.

"Here's sleeping beauty," announced Egan.

"I was telling Mr Egan that I heard you banging around last night when you arrived home so suspected you'd had a few jars," Grandad said.

"Yeah, I'd had a couple," I replied.

"I hope you have room for a few more this evening," Egan added before turning back to Grandad. "There's some good quality beer to be drunk in Amsterdam, you know, Mr Howard. Have you had the opportunity to visit there?" he asked, with a wry smile.

"We had one or two trips," Grandad replied before pausing to gasp for air. "We used to visit when I was stationed in Germany."

"I bet you did," Egan said before standing up. He gestured for me to go into the kitchen. "I'll not trouble you any longer, Mr Howard. I'll give young Robbie the details of our trip then be on my way. Now, you take good care of yourself."

"Thank you, Mr Egan," he replied, "and thank you for everything you have done to help my boy."

Egan closed the kitchen door.

"He doesn't look too good," he observed.

"That's because he's dying," I replied. "Ah well, not to worry, his only carer will be away this evening and may very well end up in prison, but I'm betting that you aren't too bothered about that, are you?"

Egan snapped. "Don't you fucking tell me what I am bothered about! You know nothing about me. And don't go pulling the fucking sympathy card either. If you were such a warm-hearted, doting grandson, then how did you find the time in your care schedule to go out last night and get pissed?"

"Alright, Egan; enough already! Just tell me what the score is for this fucking trip."

"Listen carefully," he hissed. This guy was seriously upset about something. Maybe even he was getting anxious about this smuggling gig. "There will be a taxi picking you up at exactly two-thirty this afternoon. It's been paid for. Only take hand luggage, but make sure it's a decent size, like a sports bag, and don't overfill it on the way out."

He reached into his jacket pocket and brought out a bunch of documents, which he slammed on the table. "You are flying out from East Midlands airport at five-fifteen. Here are your tickets. When you arrive, get a cab from Schipol airport to Amsterdam Central station. You will be staying for one night in the IBIS hotel which is opposite so you can't miss it. I will arrive separately, go and meet the seller and buy the MDMA. The next time I'll see you will be tomorrow morning at ten-thirty in the Grasshopper bar.

"Where's that?" I asked.

"Trust me, after being in Amsterdam for an hour you'll find it. We'll meet the other fella in a café near the airport and sort out who is carrying what. All three of us will board the same flight home, but we'll have separate seats on the plane. We'll rendezvous outside East Midlands airport after we land and I will collect the pills from you both. Is that clear?"

"Yes, I'm on it."

"Don't go getting drunk or high tomorrow and missing the meet time. If you do, I'll add six months to my stay in Leicester."

"I'll be there, don't worry about that."

"Of course, you still might land yourself a job by tomorrow lunchtime and get out of having to do any of the dangerous stuff," he added with a sneer.

"That's not going to happen," I responded. "Last chance saloon closed its doors yesterday evening."

"Oh dear, well, at least you can say you tried," he replied with his usual arrogance.

He reached into another pocket, removed his wallet and pulled out a wad of Euros, which he placed on top of the tickets and confirmation paperwork.

"Here you go. It might be your last night of freedom for a while, so if I were you, I'd get myself laid. I suspect down those narrow backstreets near the canal, three hundred Euros will get you pretty much anything you fancy."

He slowly put his wallet back in his pocket, and as he did he stared at me. His eyes were mean, mysterious and scheming. He had something left up his sleeve, I was sure of it. There would be one more twist before our association concluded. But, as usual, I didn't have the slightest idea what it was going to be.

I gathered together a bunch of clothes, my passport, the travel documents and the money Egan had gifted me. The taxi would shortly be calling to pick me up and I made my way downstairs to have a final word with Grandad before I departed. "I'm going to be leaving shortly. Are you sure you're going to be okay?"

"Yeah, I'll be—" He began coughing and wasn't able to finish the sentence, so he put his hand up and nodded.

I checked to see if his tablets were to hand should he need them. I then went into the kitchen and made him a cup of tea which I left on the side table. "Thank you," he said softly. "Be careful what you're doing in Amsterdam with Egan," he added, with a smile.

"Don't worry, I'll be fine."

I looked at him and he winked. From outside, there was the beep of a car horn, indicating my taxi had arrived. I kissed him on the forehead.

"I'll bring you a nice bottle of Scotch back."

He smiled and nodded. "Goodbye, son," he very quietly said.

Amsterdam was indeed a fine city, albeit an eye-opener for a twenty-three-year-old. Watching people openly sitting outside cafes smoking weed was a bit of a culture shock. Given how chilled out these smokers were, I might be inclined to legalise it in the UK. It has to be preferable to how some men react after eight pints of Stella.

The Red Light District was also fascinating. Sex was openly for sale in all manner of shapes and sizes. I even walked past one window where a seemingly attractive woman was enticing me into the boudoir by playing with his cock and balls.

Despite Egan's advice, sex was not on my menu. Paying for it wasn't my thing and, in any event, I was way too anxious.

I finished the evening off with a ten-Euro glass of beer in the attractive Grasshopper bar. As Egan had described, it was indeed a stately building in a prominent location. I finished my drink, headed back to the hotel and went to bed.

In the early hours of the morning, I woke up fearful and tense. For some reason, the hotel room was boiling and I was drenched in sweat. I whacked the air conditioning down to the coolest setting before drying myself with a towel. Today was going to be the biggest challenge that Egan had presented. I was going to need to get the pills, which I now knew to be MDMA, out of Holland and through British customs. I realised that I could just as easily be spending the evening in a Dutch prison as a British jail.

I decided before I met Egan that I was going to drink some alcohol and continue boozing throughout this whole episode. I needed to be buzzing with self-confidence, act like I had nothing to hide and in a manner suggesting I wasn't a nervous wreck who was making his drug-smuggling debut. There was no way I was going to achieve this demeanour by being sober.

I drifted back to sleep before waking up with a jolt at 7 a.m. Fuck this! I decided to get up, shower and get my stuff together. I checked out of the hotel and opted for an amble around the canals.

I had been walking through the picturesque backstreets killing time for over an hour. My stomach was churning and I felt lightheaded with apprehension. I had this unusual, dry, almost metallic taste in my mouth, making me even more nauseous.

I found a café and ordered a coffee and double shot of whisky.

I checked the time: 9.31 a.m.

I fiddled with my mobile to see whether Zoe had messaged – nothing. The phone then startled me by ringing as it was in my hand. "Hello?" I enquired.

"Robbie, it's Tony. I'm online having one last sweep for jobs and I think I might have stumbled onto something."

"Yeah, what's that?" I asked with desperate hope.

"There's a supplier of industrial equipment in Leicester urgently looking for people to work in their warehouse. I called the owner of the business, a gentleman called Paul, and he said they are so keen to get people in that if you give him a call and have a chat he might let you start on Monday."

"Fucking hell! Could you text me his number, please?"

"I'll send it to you in the next two minutes. Good luck!"

Upon receipt of the number I called Paul, the owner of Westbury Industrial Supplies. From minute one we got on well and I had established a good rapport with him whilst sounding business-like.

"Look, mate, I have got a heap of orders and I haven't the time to arse about interviewing people. You sound alright to me. Why don't you come down on Monday and we'll put you on a month's trial? Let's call it nine quid an hour and forty hours a week. How does that sound?"

"Yeah, brilliant!"

"If it doesn't work out for me or you, we can call it quits at the end of the month."

"This sounds fine with me. Where are you based?" I asked.

"Thurmaston, a short bus ride out of town. We're on the main road so we're dead easy to find."

It was an unbelievable stroke of luck, and yet again, more timely intervention from Tony. It was my ticket out of this gig and my chance to get away from Egan and finally kill our relationship.

"This sounds great, thanks so much. I'll see you on Monday," I effused.

"By the way, you don't know anyone else who might be looking for a job, do you? I need at least one other person."

"I might be able to help you out. I'll text your details over to a mate of mine and ask him to call you."

"Great! What's his name?"

"Lee Bodwin."

As I ended the call a huge wave of relief cascaded over me. I closed my eyes and slowly exhaled before punching the air in triumph.

"Get in there!" I screamed. The barman looked over and smiled. I immediately approached the bar.

"Another shot of whisky, please?" I requested, passing the glass to him.

"You had good news?" he queried, in pidgin English.

"No. I've had some fucking great news!" I replied. "And now it's time to fucking celebrate! Make sure you have a drink with me."

"No, thank you. It's a bit early."

I threw ten Euros onto the bar. "Well, at least have one on me later."

"Thank you," he replied, gratefully scooping up the note.

I sent a text message to Bod explaining to him what had gone on and that there was a job available if he wanted it. I informed him that he would be working with me and understood if he didn't wish to pursue it. I knew full well this could be a chance for us to rekindle our friendship. Hopefully, he would view me paying his fine and then opening the door to a job as a genuine attempt to apologise for not taking any heat for the charity job.

I sat with a huge grin on my face for fifteen minutes or so, before I received a text message back from Bod.

Called him. I start with u on monday. Thnx M8

It might not have appeared much, but the 'Thnx M8' meant the world to me. These six simple characters were a clear indication that I'd been forgiven and we could start again. This time around, he would find me a far more tolerant and loyal friend.

I simply didn't feel the same way about Nails. I had seen the worst of him in so many ways once he'd become entangled in the Goodwill gig. I believed he had acted selfishly and inappropriately, and I wasn't interested in making amends with him. Not yet, anyway.

I settled my bill and made the short walk to the Grasshopper, where Egan was sitting alone at a table drinking coffee and reading a newspaper.

"Guess what?" I asked as I bounced in.

"You've fallen head over heels in love with a roly-poly hooker and you're about to invite me to be your best man?"

"Warehouse job, Westbury Industrial Supplies, start on Monday, full-time, nine pounds an hour. Fucking get in there!" I raved.

"When did you get that?"

"About half an hour ago. The owner interviewed me over the telephone and offered me the job there and then. You can ring him if you don't believe me."

"What's his name?" he probed.

"Paul, Paul Westbury."

"Where are they based?"

"Thurmaston. Keep going, Egan, try and catch me out if you can! It's forty hours a week and I start at nine o'clock on Monday morning. It's a done deal, mate. Mission accomplished! So, you can go and get some other fucking mug to carry your shit through customs," I chirped, being unusually cocky to him, compliments of the two shots of whisky which had gone straight to my head.

"Fair play to you. Fancy a beer to celebrate?"

"Yes, I fucking do!"

As he walked to the bar, I reflected on what had happened. Thank God for Tony, who had come through right at the death. And fancy me ringing the one job where the owner didn't even bother with an interview!

For once, during this whole saga with Egan, things had gone my way.

I'd had a huge slice of good fortune.

An enormous stroke of luck.

It was unbelievable.

Hang on a minute, I thought. *Maybe this was too good to be true?* I glanced across at Egan as he was waiting to be served. He didn't seem shocked by the job offer – slightly inquisitive, maybe, but certainly not overly surprised.

Why did I suddenly get the feeling I was being played here? I quickly ran over some of the key points of what had happened to me since the robbery: Egan had approached me with the made-up story about Ethel, then I had been forced me to get to know Tony. Egan didn't know Ethel, so his story of Tony's friendship with Ethel had to be a lie. So, what was Egan's real connection with Tony?

I recalled the picture of Tony's daughter which had suddenly appeared on his mantlepiece. He must have known I would eventually ask about her. But what was his motivation?

Tony had admitted to me when we were on the hunt for voluntary work that he had known Egan for a few years but had quickly shut down the conversation when I dug deeper. What was he hiding?

Then I recalled Zoe's words when describing Tony. "Be careful of him. He can be a nasty, devious, scheming piece of work when he wants to be."

The pieces were beginning to fall into place.

Shit! I then recalled Zoe telling me that her ex-fella needed his passport for a trip. Was he the man we were going to be meeting near the airport? Was he the third spoke in the wheel who was earmarked to help bring in the pills? Had this whole episode been orchestrated by Tony so Leon would obliviously creep out of the woodwork, thus allowing Egan to avenge the beatings he had given Tony's daughter?

Finally, I recalled Tony's words when he described his hatred for Leon and the pledge he'd made: "I had decided some time ago that I'm not going to rest until that bastard is in the ground. And

I'm going to make it my business to guarantee it happens."

Had I simply been the cotton used to stitch this fabric together? Had I been played by Egan and Tony to contact Zoe and to attempt to repair Tony's relationship with her, whilst Egan was plotting Leon's demise?

But why Egan? How had Tony managed to secure his services? How had he convinced a successful dealer to up sticks from London and relocate to Leicester? What did he have over Egan that made him come calling when he clicked his fingers?

He returned from the bar with the two pints and also a couple of glasses of whisky.

"I think your news is worthy of celebration," he declared.

"What's going to happen to the pills I was going to take through?" I asked.

"I'll see if the other fella wants to carry them. If he does, I'll pay him more."

"And if he doesn't?"

"I'll probably dump them."

"I thought you were bringing some through as well?"

"Me? No, I'm just the decoy. I'm expecting to get stopped because I always do."

He took a long swig from his beer. "Unless you fancy earning yourself five thousand quid and bringing them through?" he proposed.

"You're kidding, right?"

"No. That's the deal if you want it. It's easy money."

"Unless I get stopped."

"You won't get stopped. I'll get stopped; you'll go straight through. Five grand cash; straight in your hand when we get back. It's sitting in the boot of my car."

"I'm alright," I replied.

"It'll take you a long time to earn five grand with your nine-pound an hour job," he said. "Imagine, you'll be able to take Zoe away on a nice, romantic weekend break."

BOOM!

He had just mentioned Zoe and yet I had never told him about her. Egan had just shown me his hand of cards. "I know the whole fucking plan now, Egan. Everything. I've worked it all out."

"What plan?"

"Don't give me that fucking look, you *know* what plan. I'm just trying to work out whether you've just deliberately let the cat out of the bag or not."

"I'm not sure what you're talking about," he responded. For the first time since we'd met he was unconvincing.

"I think you do. It's all become clear to me now."

"Has it?"

"I might look an idiot, but maybe I'm not as stupid as you think."

"What gave it away?" he asked.

"You just mentioned Tony's daughter, Zoe, and how I was dating her. I had previously never mentioned her or our relationship. And that's before I move on to Ethel. I saw her yesterday looking as fit as a butcher's dog. A quite *amazing* recovery from the serious stroke you said she had suffered. Still, given she's never heard of you and doesn't even have a son, then how would you know if she'd been ill or not?"

"The plan has nearly been executed, Robbie. May I respectfully ask you not to rock the boat."

"The only part of the puzzle I can't work out is why did a fella like you get yourself involved in something like this?"

"What do you mean?"

"Leave London, move to Leicester, nearly get yourself killed by the locals, put me through this and just to help someone else. I don't get it."

"You would have done the same under the circumstances."

"What circumstances?"

"When you were tied to the chair the other night and Khally was about to maim you, imagine if it had been a friend who had risked everything to have saved your life. Would you call that a debt?"

"Yes, for sure."

"So, would I."

"You're paying back a debt?"

"I call it a favour."

"How did that come about?"

"It's a good story, but a tad long."

"I like long stories," I replied.

"Back during the troubles in Northern Ireland, I was brought up on the west side of Belfast which was predominantly a Catholic area. At the time, there was a lot of sympathy in these communities for the IRA. Have you heard of them?"

"Yeah, from the programmes me and my grandad have watched."

"Whilst at university, I became quite vocal about the IRA's bombing campaign. Although the British were doing some pretty nasty stuff in our towns, I didn't think that killing woman and children was the right strategy. I had written articles detailing my reservations for the student union newsletter, attended rallies, that sort of thing. One day, totally out of the blue, I received a visit from a man who, it turned out, was a member of the British Secret Service. They were on the lookout for young Catholic men and women who were potential sympathisers of the peace process and wanted to know if I was interested in joining them. To cut a long story short, I did. They recruited and trained me in London before I returned to Ireland, where I had to worm myself slowly but surely into the IRA. Having succeeded, for years afterwards I became a 'sleeper', which means I didn't communicate with my secret service case handler. Instead, I worked myself further and deeper into the organisation, gaining trust, rubbing shoulders with the right people and eventually demonstrating that I wasn't scared to get my hands dirty with operations.

"Fast forward eight years and I had become a mid-level IRA

operative and was starting to feed back information to the British. It didn't take long before the IRA top brass realised they had a mole and that's when they started shaking people down and letting out bogus intelligence to see where it went.

"One day there was a bomb attack on the mainland and British intelligence had found out it was the work of one of the senior IRA's bombmakers, a man called Seamus Murray. He used to run what was called their 'Nutting Squad'; this was the team they would use to interrogate informers.

"The British wanted this guy dead and the intelligence chief was under pressure to deliver his head to the government. The problem was, Seamus was like a shadow, a ghost, a disappearing act that nobody ever saw. The British would only receive grainy black-and-white pictures of him days after he had turned up somewhere. They could never second guess his daily whereabouts to capture him and it was becoming an issue.

"They decided the only way to get to him was by a sting operation. They would offer the IRA an informant as bait, then wait for Seamus to turn up to interrogate them and then take him out. Unfortunately for me, I was the bait. The British very kindly leaked my role; I was kidnapped and taken to a safe house. They tied me to a chair with the intention of questioning, torturing and then killing me."

"Fucking hell, what happened?"

"The British unit who were staking out the property were told very clearly not to go in, but to wait and call the second Seamus arrived. The unit knew it was a matter of time until they began to torture me and, of course, there was every chance that Seamus wouldn't even turn up. I was stripped naked and strapped to this big wooden chair. There were five other guys in there with me who were desperately waiting for the green light to get their hands on a dirty little traitor. The tools they were going to use were all laid out in front of me. Trust me, it wouldn't have been pretty, and it would have lasted for days and days. It was the last time in my life I was afraid.

"Anyway, I had met the captain of the British unit on a few occasions; he was a good guy. He knew after a couple of hours of me being in that safe house that I was in real trouble. So, he defied orders and sent in the troops to rescue me. The five IRA soldiers were shot to pieces before they cut me free of that fucking chair and dragged me out of there as naked as the day I was born.

"A few nights later, over a couple of drinks, I expressed to the captain that I owed him big time. I pledged that should he ever call upon me to do anything, however extreme, then I would never refuse him.

"It's been called in, Robbie. All this, everything that's gone on. I'm simply returning a long-standing favour."

"Are you going to kill him?" I asked.

"Who?"

"You know who. Are you going to kill him here or wait until we get back to Leicester?"

"I haven't decided yet," he answered.

I stared deep into his cold eyes and knew full well that being indecisive was foreign to him. He was a strategist and a control freak. He knew *exactly* what he was going to do with Leon and when he was going to do it.

We left the Grasshopper bar and walked to Central Station, where Egan flagged a taxi. The trip was taken in silence save for the low volume of a Dutch radio station.

The sight and sound of a thunderous low-altitude 747 confirmed we were close to the airport. The taxi pulled into a sterile-looking new-build industrial estate, with grid-like roads and perfectly organised commercial buildings. He dropped us off at the 'Urban Hotel', a generically named four-storey monstrosity which would undoubtedly be full of expense-rinsing corporates. We walked into the foyer, which expanded into a large restaurant and café open to non-guests. It was busy with people getting stuck into the lunchtime buffet, shovelling mountains of food onto plates, whilst others queued for fresh artisan coffee and pastries.

We found a table away from the masses and took a seat. Egan looked at his watch and then checked his phone. His expression of annoyance suggested Leon was running late.

"Why the two bags?" I asked.

"One for me and one for him," he replied tersely.

"Won't he already have a bag with him?"

"Why don't you leave the thinking to me and just sit back and enjoy the trip home?" he tetchily answered.

It was obvious that upon conclusion of our rather unusual association, Egan and I probably wouldn't be exchanging Christmas cards. Up until two days ago, I believed he did have some love in his heart. He had duped me into thinking he was genuinely bothered about the welfare of his mother, but now I knew the truth. I realised this man was a stone-cold killer. Maybe it was the episode in the safehouse which had changed him? Perhaps the betrayal of the British when he thought he was protected only to be used as a worm on a hook had taken its toll?

I then caught him staring out of the hotel window. Something, or rather, someone had caught his eye. I presumed Leon was on his way.

I looked out of the window and saw in the distance a man in a red and black ski jacket approaching with a plastic carrier bag.

"Can you go and get us three coffees?" he demanded. "Make mine a cappuccino, he'll have a flat white Americano and whatever you want. Go now!" he hissed.

Something had got under Egan's skin. His generally cool, controlled demeanour appeared fractured.

I walked to the far end of the restaurant and joined the back of a queue of ten or so people. I was intrigued to find out what Leon looked like, but from where I was standing I couldn't get a good view of him as there were plants and people forming obstructions. I could make out he had taken a seat at the table and was talking to Egan. His back was turned to me and the rest of the restaurant. I assumed in the spare bag that Egan had bought with him were the pills he would be smuggling into the UK. If Egan was to kill him then I couldn't work out when he was planning on doing it. It looked for all the world as if he were to allow Leon to smuggle the drugs first, before ending his life.

I spotted Leon handling the plastic bag he had brought in. I was guessing these were his personal effects and he would dump them into the holdall Egan was about to give him. Egan had mentioned he was to offer him the chance to earn more money by taking through a larger consignment of pills. I assumed he would gratefully accept this offer. I was guessing Leon's money was running out and another five thousand pounds would be enthusiastically received.

The queue was taking ages as people were ordering all manner of things. Some were even getting chocolate powder sprinkled on top of their coffee in the shape of fucking tulips. Eventually, I was the next person to be served before receiving a tap on the shoulder. I looked around; it was Egan holding out my bag for me to take.

"Come on, let's go," he ordered.

"Don't you want a—"

"Let's just go!" he growled.

I took my bag from him and we left. Leon had already taken off in front of us and was nowhere to be seen.

"Is he on our flight home?" I asked.

"You know he is because I've already told you," he snarled.

"Sorry I asked."

"Did you see him? Did you get a good look at his face?" he asked, through gritted teeth.

"No."

"Then do me a favour, will you? When we arrive at the airport and then get on the plane, can you avoid looking around for a glimpse of him like you're a fucking meerkat! I noticed you doing it when you were in the queue for the coffee. You're drawing attention to him and therefore to us. Just keep your head down and mind your own business. Do you hear me?"

"Yeah, alright. What's with the tone?"

"Shut the fuck up, will you!" he yelped.

He was as tetchy as I had ever seen him. Maybe for once, something hadn't quite gone according to plan. But what was it?

We were following a trail of people making the short walk to the airport terminal. There was the distinctive grating sound of suitcase wheels being dragged across roads and pavements. I always thought people behaved slightly unusually at airports. They seemed jumpy, anxious, perhaps wary of missing their flight, worried about getting stranded wherever they were and not being able to return to the safe comfort of their homes.

Egan eventually broke the frosty silence. "When we get into the airport, I'll check in first and be about ten minutes in front of you. Don't talk or look at me when we are in the queue. You're effectively travelling home on your own. If anyone asks, you met a mate for a few beers in Amsterdam and he's going home on a Manchester flight this evening. Got it?"

"Yeah, fine."

"I'll see you outside of East Midlands," he grunted before striding off in front of me.

I was confused. I wasn't carrying any pills and neither was he, so why was he acting like this? He did mention he had a track record of getting stopped at customs. I could only assume his name would be flagged up on the system given his connections, track record and what the feds knew of his activities. But he was expecting it, so I was unsure why this would cause such angst.

I checked in, took my hand luggage through security and grabbed something to eat in the departure lounge. Schipol airport was an enormous place. There were signs articulating how long it would take to walk to various gate numbers and some of these indicated it could be up to twenty minutes.

I kept a careful eye on the departures board, and as soon as my gate number appeared I walked smartly there, sat in the moulded plastic seats and inconspicuously waited to board the flight. I kept my eye out for Egan and Leon but there was no sign of either.

When we were called onto the plane, I found my seat and jammed my bag in the overhead luggage compartment. I sat back and let out an almighty sigh. Being around a tense Egan had rubbed off on me and I was feeling edgy. I planned on having a strong drink during the short flight home to help me relax. I closed my eyes and puffed out my cheeks.

It was over!

Whatever Egan had in store for Leon had nothing to do with me. I was out of it. I had escaped his world and could live to tell the tale.

Pretty much as soon as we were up in the air and the seatbelt light went off, the air stewards started coming around with drinks, snacks and the option to buy perfume, aftershaves and alcohol.

I still had a wad of Euros leftover so decided to treat Zoe to a bottle of perfume. As the stewardess approached, I ordered a double rum and Coke, a bottle of whisky for Grandad and a hundred millilitres of Miss Dior. Once the trolley had passed, I decided to put the perfume and whisky safely in my luggage rather than stow it in the pocket in front of me and predictably forget about it as I departed the plane.

I popped open the flap of the overhead, opened my bag and pushed in the perfume and whisky. As I did, I felt the crinkle of a strange material on my hand. I pulled my bag a little way out of the compartment and unzipped it further to establish what it was. To my horror, there were three, maybe four medium-sized silver sealed bags. I grabbed the contents and lightly squeezed one of them – pills! Unmistakably fucking pills! I had been done up like a kipper. I was going to be re-entering the UK in possession of a large consignment of MDMA.

Fuck!

I quickly zipped up the bag, pushed it back into the compartment and slammed shut the overhead door.

I turned and looked up and down the cabin for Egan. I couldn't see him anywhere.

I went cold. I needed to think. Maybe I could dump them at the airport when I arrived? I'm sure there must be a toilet at the baggage reclaim. I could flush them down the bog or could come clean and tell British customs that someone had planted them? I needed to do something. I walked up the aisle of the airplane looking for Egan but couldn't spot him.

I walked back towards the rear, where I was feverishly looking from left to right. There he was! He was in the rear row, sat in the window seat. I defied his orders, strolled over to him and stood at his row of seats.

"Sean, do you have a minute?" I called out.

He turned and looked daggers at me.

"Just a quick word," I said, pointing at the small, unoccupied area at the rear of the aircraft.

He squeezed past the two seated passengers and we stepped into the available space.

I whispered as softly as I could, trying to keep my cool. "There's a load of fucking pills in my bag!"

"What are you on about?" he replied, looking genuinely surprised.

"Pills, Egan. MDMA. Thousands of them and they are in my fucking bag! We had a deal, now what the fuck is going on?"

"I offered him the chance to take it, he needed the extra money and he agreed. He took the pills and put them in his holdall. I went to the toilet because you were messing around so long with the coffees and when I returned he grabbed his things and left."

"Well, he must have very kindly dumped the pills you gave him into my bag. What am I going to do?"

"Nothing. You'll do absolutely nothing. You'll have to take them through," he demanded.

"You what?"

"What else are you going to with them?"

"Can't I dump them?" I suggested.

"Dump them! Are you a fucking idiot? As soon as you walk into the airport there's CCTV and security everywhere. You'll blow the cover on this whole fucking operation. I need this gear; I need the whole lot taken through."

"I'm not doing it."

He grabbed me around the throat. "Oh yes you are! You'll do as you're fucking told. You've got the pills in your bag and that's bad luck, but you're not getting rid of them. I have a buy set up as soon as we get back to Leicester and he's expecting the whole lot, so you're taking them through, end of story."

"But—"

"End of story," he interrupted. "And if you don't, then I swear to God you'll regret it!"

He shoved me to one side and made his way back to his seat.

CHAPTER 26

I could feel the sweat gathering on the back of my neck as the plane began its descent into East Midlands airport. The fear that I believed had disappeared had returned with a vengeance. What had possessed me to leave my fucking bag with them? If I had taken it to the coffee bar then this wouldn't have happened. I sat shaking my head in disbelief. I had seen Egan's rage and it was clear there was no way out of this now. It had been decided. The pills were being taken through British customs and I was to be the smuggler. That was how this episode was to conclude and I felt like my whole life was riding on the outcome.

The plane landed and passengers were slowly getting off. I took my bag out of the overhead compartment and stood in the aisle waiting for my turn to climb down the temporary steps. The Dutch air steward was bidding goodbye to passengers. Those from her own country were receiving a traditional farewell in their native tongue. Her 'goodbye's were getting changed intermittently to 'vaarwel'.

I had heard this word somewhere before. "Vaarwel," she said to the next man leaving the aircraft. Someone had recently said this to me when I was not expecting it. "Vaarwel" – where the hell had I heard this before? She said it again to a businessman who was in front of me.

BOOM!

I then remembered who said it and when it was. It was Bod's mum during her last drunken visit to my house. "Vaarwel, Robbie, vaarwel," she had repeated. I wasn't exactly sure at the time what she was saying, but now it was clear. My head sank as I put two and two together and realised I was fucked.

She had obviously ear-wigged the conversation Bod and I had outside of her front door when I told him about the Amsterdam trip. I recalled mentioning precisely what I was going to do and where I would be doing it. Like an idiot, I had even told him I would be flying back into East Midlands airport. Once Mrs Bodwin had contacted the police, it would only take a check on the names of the people on the incoming flights to work out which one I was coming back on.

Mrs Bodwin saying 'vaarwel' to me was her way of letting me know, without giving it away, that she was to have the last word. I would be thrown in prison and she would go around telling everyone it was justice for what had happened to her son.

I walked dejectedly into the airport terminal. I stopped and pretended to tie my shoelaces whilst waiting for Egan to catch me up. I then followed him to the back of the queue for passport control. "They know I am here," I whispered.

"Who?"

"The feds, they know. I told Bod I was roped into a drug deal in Amsterdam and his mum has found out and grassed me up."

"How do you know that?"

"I just know. They'll be here. The second I walk through customs they'll nick me."

The queue was constantly moving forward as the immigration staff were fast-tracking entry for British nationals.

"Stick to the plan, it'll be okay," he said.

"How the fuck will it be okay? I'm going to get nicked!"

"Will you shut the fuck up!" he hissed.

"Why the fuck didn't you kill him in Amsterdam? Why go through this? He's a fucking scumbag. You might have guessed he'd do something to mess up the plan."

"We decided not to kill him because of you," he announced.

"What the fuck are you on about?"

"I was told from the outset you were a cocky little shit who needed to be taught a lesson and he was right."

"Who said that?"

"You know who said it. I bet it stings, doesn't it?"

"He said that about me?" I asked, a little shocked.

Egan turned and stared at me before he was called over to passport control. "Good luck, Robbie," he said as he walked away.

Tony had every right to describe me as a 'cocky little shit'. After all, that's what I was. I was forever making fun of him when he would tell me what was happening in the news and I always pretended everything was a joke. He was right about me back then, but I hoped his opinion had changed. It mattered. I cared now about how he viewed me as he was someone I valued. He had become a dear friend and, dare I say, unlikely father figure and, as a consequence, Egan's comment had hit a nerve.

I passed through passport control and into the baggage reclaim area. I was desperate to march into the toilet and dump these bags of pills, but I knew it would be pointless. There would be no escaping Egan. He would come after me and this would never finish. Maybe I would simply stroll through customs and out the other side? Maybe they had flagged up Egan on this flight and would focus all of their attention on him? Perhaps the feds had dismissed Mrs Bodwin's tip-off as nothing more than sour grapes and had ignored it.

There was nothing else for it; I was going to have to go through. I tried relaxing with five deep breaths, but my heart was pounding and I was physically shaking. I decided to walk slowly through the 'Green – Nothing to Declare' channel. I was to stroll through as if I didn't have a care in the world.

As I passed through, sure enough, Egan had been pulled over by a customs official who was looking through his passport. I continued walking slowly and saw the back of a red and black ski jacket. Leon had also been pulled over and three customs officials were gathered around him asking him questions. He was in deep shit. I tried not to look again at either Leon or Egan, but instead just to stare straight ahead.

I continued walking until I was able to see the exit. I could make out taxi drivers holding up signs and families who had come to collect love ones.

I then spotted Zoe, with Ollie in her arms.

She had come to meet me; she had dared to find out in real time whether I had made it through the trip. I could see she had spotted me and I began to wave. She was mouthing words to her son and pointing in my direction. The beaming smile on her face confirmed that she was every bit as pleased to see me as I was her.

It was then I received the call.

"Excuse me, sir!" he shouted. "Excuse me!" came the louder second command.

I stopped and slowly turned around. A male customs official was beckoning me towards his table.

"Would you mind coming over here for a minute?" he politely asked.

I turned and looked over at Zoe. She had seen me stop and would know something was wrong. I simply shook my head before turning my back on them both. My instructions to her had been clear: if I didn't make it through she was to forget about me.

Game over.

I wandered miserably over to him. The exit had been tantalisingly close, like a bad joke. I'd had a glimpse into my future, of what I could have won. I should have known this was going to be the outcome. Being on the same flight as Egan and Leon, along with the tip-off from Bod's mum, was always going to land me in trouble. I had walked the tightrope and lost my balance within a few feet of the end.

"Could you pop your bag on here for me, please?" he asked.

It was as if my life was unfolding in slow motion; a chronic nightmare finally revealing itself. I put my bag on the table and he started asking me questions about my trip. Behind him was a flurry of activity: an excitable bunch of customs officials and plainclothes staff. They were about to intercept a big score. There would be glasses raised in their favourite pub this evening. Amongst them, I spotted Brydges and Wood. Mrs Bodwin's plan for revenge had been completed. The cavalry had arrived and they had finally bagged their targets.

"I'm now going to open your bag. Before I do, may I ask whether I am going to find any illegal substances, weapons or firearms?" the official asked.

"Yes, you are," I replied. "You are going to find several bags of MDMA which I have been fucking stupid enough to try and smuggle in," I announced.

He looked at me surprised as I shrugged my shoulders. I knew any other line of defence would be futile. "You're going to need to follow me then, please, sir," he commanded, gesturing to a colleague that he needed assistance.

I was escorted through a labyrinth of corridors into an interview room where I was asked to take a seat. I provided an officer with my personal details which he recorded onto a computer.

"As we believe you may be in possession of illegal substances, I am authorised and entitled to carry out a full bodily search," said one of the officers.

I was then asked to strip naked before undergoing a thorough and humiliating intimate search. My clothes and mobile phone were placed in a bag and I was told they may be subject to forensic testing.

I was allocated a blue, faded sweatshirt and sweatpants to put on in the absence of my clothes, whilst a pair of flip flops replaced my trainers.

The contents of my sports bag were arranged onto the table. There were four silver bags, each with a few thousand pills in them. Everything was photographed and the pills were labelled. I noticed that my wash bag which was full of toiletry items was missing.

Presumably, that shithead Leon had removed it to counterbalance the additional weight that he'd added to my bag.

I had to prepare myself for a day of being searched, questioned and asked for personal details before eventually being charged and detained.

I was then escorted through to an interview office where I was told to take a seat.

I had been left in the room for what appeared to be an hour or so. I decided to play this with a straight bat. I would tell them I had bought the pills myself whilst in Amsterdam from an unknown dealer and I was to bring them back to sell in Leicester. To implicate Egan would be suicide.

A customs official walked in and sat down. "What on earth have you been doing?" he asked without any introductions.

"Making bad decisions, as usual."

"Who did you buy the pills from?"

"A fella in Amsterdam," I replied.

"Do you have his name?"

"No."

"Address?"

"No."

"How did you find out about him?" he asked.

"Look, as I understand it, I'm entitled to a solicitor, so I think it's best I don't talk to you until I have one here with me."

"You've not been charged with anything so we're just having a chat, nothing more."

"Not anymore we're not," I said.

"Okay, fine," he ended, shortly before leaving the interview room.

Ten minutes later, a second customs official, this time female, entered the room with my bag, clothes, phone and the rest of my stuff. She placed them on the table and, without saying a word, walked out.

As she left, DS Jem Langley walked in. "You can't say I didn't warn you," he stated.

"I knew all about the danger; that wasn't the issue."

"What was?"

"Wrestling myself free of Egan."

"Did he make you do this? If he did, you can give me a statement and I'll see what I can do," he said with a grin on his face as if he was toying with me.

"You'll never stop with your fucking offers, will you, Langley?"

"What do you think is going to happen to you?" he teased.

"I'm guessing an all-expenses-paid trip to Las Vegas with a couple of thousand-dollar-a-night hookers and several bottles of champagne, or will it be sharing a prison cell with some shit-stinking bloke for twenty-three hours a day? I sometimes get the two confused."

"Now wouldn't be a good time to get anything confused. You'll need to keep a clear head."

"I'd love to sit here and talk to you all day, but unfortunately I've decided to remain silent until I call my brief. So, unless you're going to make me a nice cup of tea, can I respectfully ask that you jog on."

"Guess what?" he asked.

"What?"

"You're free to go."

"That's a good one!" I replied.

"Leave your sweatshirt and bottoms on the chair, get your clothes on, collect up your stuff, and get the hell out of here."

"What the fuck is going on?" I queried.

"On this occasion, I'm not entirely sure. Sometimes Egan enjoys playing his little games."

"And you don't know what they are?"

"Well, not all of them. But maybe more than you think," he said, with a wink.

"You'll never catch him, will you?"

"That's a good one. Egan warned me that you were a bit wet behind the ears."

"What are you talking about?" I asked.

"I wasn't sure when he told me what he was going to do whether this was going too far."

"What's gone too far?" I asked.

"Take care, Robbie," he replied as he turned and walked out of the room.

I changed into my clothes and unzipped my bag. I checked my phone was working and made sure they hadn't taken any money out of my wallet.

The door to the room then opened and in walked Egan. "Come on, let's get you home," he announced.

"What the fuck has just gone on here?" I asked.

"Even the very best of British customs officers can't prosecute you for bringing back fizzers."

"Fizzers?"

"Sweets. Those horrible little coloured things you buy that tingle in your mouth. You were carrying nothing more than that."

"Why?" I asked, feeling more than a little irritated that he had put me through this.

"I wanted you to know how he felt about you. I told him I was with you and made him an offer. He could either take all of the pills through himself or dump half in your bag. He decided to dump half in your bag, I'm afraid. He wasn't prepared to do the right thing, even though they were, as you now know, only sweets."

A customs official then walked in and made it clear we needed to leave the area as soon as possible. I quickly gathered my things up and we walked out of the room.

"I've never met the fella, plus I'm seeing his ex-girlfriend, so why did you ever think he would take them all and do me a favour?" I challenged.

"You're seeing his ex-girlfriend?" he asked, confused. "But I thought you were seeing Zoe?"

"I am."

"Who are you on about then?" he queried as we walked down the corridor.

"Who do you think? Leon, of course!"

He stopped and turned around. "Leon – who the fuck's Leon?"

"Tony's daughter's ex-boyfriend, the fella Tony wants you to kill, the reason I'm here! Fucking hell, Egan, isn't it obvious!"

"Shit!" he replied with a shake of his head. "I get it now. You've totally got the wrong end of the stick, haven't you?"

"Wrong end of what stick? What do you mean?"

"And there was me thinking you had sussed me out! Fucking hell, I must be getting old."

"What do you mean, 'sussed me out'? What's been going here?"

"Me being in Leicester, everything you've been through, every challenge, every drug deal, the volunteering, the job you've landed, this trip; it was all put together by me, but signed off by someone much closer to you than Tony."

"Who then?"

"Your grandad."

I stood in total shock. The enormity of what Egan had told me had rendered me speechless. Grandad was behind all of this? A man who knew he was terminally ill had arranged for the most elaborate boot camp-style personal development programme imaginable.

"You're fucking kidding me?" I finally said.

"He was the captain who ordered the troops into the safehouse and brought me out alive. He's the one who called in the favour."

"Grandad! Why?"

"To teach you a lesson."

"So, if it's not Leon who took the drugs through, who was it?"

He carried on walking in front of me until he stopped at a window where Brydges and Wood were having a conversation with a man wearing a distinct red and black ski jacket. As we appeared in the man's peripheral vision, he turned and looked over to me.

It was my father.

CHAPTER 27

I was in the passenger seat of Egan's car desperately trying to piece together what had happened and attempt to discover the full story of his time in Leicester.

"Your grandad contacted me about six months ago. We had stayed in touch since Northern Ireland, but we hadn't seen much of each other, beyond the odd reunion drink. He told me he was ill and he had a grandson who needed straightening out."

"'Straightening out' – fucking hell!"

"He knew all about the lies, I'm afraid. He knew your story about the job at Coopers was bullshit. He used to laugh to himself every day when you used to go off to work."

"Oh no," I commented, realising the awfulness of what I had been told. So, the conversations we had had about Ismail, Des, Sally, Big Linda; all the time he knew I had been making them up. I suddenly felt very stupid and ashamed in equal measure.

"He called me around to your house one day and told me he needed to cash in the favour. Actually, by the time he had finished with all of his requests, it was three favours. Having said that, all three rolled into one didn't come close to what he had done for me."

"I can't believe my grandad was okay with me working with you and dealing drugs?"

"Are you kidding? Once I told him how I made my living it

was his suggestion! He wanted you to feel some pain, experience proper fear; he was convinced in the long run it would do you good. I took leave of my London operation and moved up to Leicester for a while."

"So, the Ethel story, how did that come about?" I asked.

"I needed a way in; I needed a hook. As you've probably worked out, I was tracking your mobile phone. I'd seen the messages between you and Bod about the charity shop. Once you had done the job I was always going to find something I could reel you in with. As soon as I discovered Ethel had resigned because of the robbery, it was too good an opportunity to miss."

"But, I could have been killed during the stuff you made me do; how could you be sure I didn't?"

"Yeah, well, let's just say not all of it was *real* danger."

"Meaning?"

"Take today: you were never going to bring pills in; it was only ever going to be sweets."

"What about Corey and his boys nearly injecting me with heroin?"

"They did it for a grand each. He was never going to plunge it into you. I reckon he enjoyed the play-acting."

"And Khally?"

"What about him?"

"He wasn't in on it on account of you blowing his brains out. So, the two occasions I went onto the estate, how did you have me covered?"

"That was trickier, and I'll be honest, there was a chance things could have turned nasty. But your grandad was happy for me to go through with it. The first time you went in I had a spotter covering you whilst you were on the streets."

"What spotter?"

"The black fella on the street corner who you made not quite so polite conversation with."

"He was with you?"

"Yes. He wouldn't have helped you if you'd had any trouble whilst on the estate."

"What about in the flat? Who would have watched my back then?" I asked.

"Shayan, the fella who had joined my team. He was packing an automatic weapon I'd given him just in case Khally got out of hand."

"What about the second time, when I did the deal with Khally at the park – who was around then?"

"Jem Langley."

"Don't tell me he's on your payroll as well?"

"That's how the game is played, Robbie. It took some convincing with his superiors that it was worth him being in Leicester, but once sanctioned he became a most useful asset. I'm not sure he wanted to come here but as he will be buying a new car with what he's made out of me, he shouldn't complain too much."

"And the business with my dad?"

"Ah, yes favour two, your dad. Your grandfather doesn't think much of him, does he?"

"So why not kill him?"

"In case you ever wake up one day and decide to forgive him, that's why. Your grandad was happy enough with the thought he'll be getting some more jail time. I tracked him down, befriended him and asked him if he wanted to do some work for me. Sorry to have to say this, but he really is a scumbag and will do anything for a dime. When I explained it was his son waiting to buy him a coffee, he just didn't give a shit. He was only interested in covering his own back. Bear this in mind if ever you have a moment of weakness in the future and feel compelled to reach out to him."

"What's he's looking at? Three to five years for the pills?"

"Plus, another six to eight years for the pure cocaine which was sewn into the lining of the bag I gave him. He'll be lucky if he serves much less than seven years, even if he behaves himself."

"What if he grasses you up?"

"The only witness who can corroborate anything he says is sitting next to me in the car right now. He also knows only too well if he opens his mouth too far open then I'll have a shotgun pressed against his tonsils."

He drove the car into my street and pulled over outside my house.

"What's next for you?" I asked.

"Back to the smoke. My time here is finished. I know it's been tough, but I don't ever want you to hold what has happened against your grandad. He only wanted what was best for you. If you're going to bear a grudge with anyone then let it be me. But when I look at you now, I see an altogether smarter, more streetwise person. I'm inclined to think the gamble your grandad took has paid off."

"Just wait until I see him," I said with a smile. "He'll have some explaining to do."

I waited for a second to see if he would say goodbye, maybe offer to shake my hand or even wish me luck – but there was nothing. I picked my bag out of the footwell, jumped out of the car and closed the door.

I then heard the passenger window open.

"Hey, Robbie, remember the story about my pet dog?" he asked.

"The one you found in Cornwall? Yeah, of course, I do."

"Fowey, that was his name. I forgave my dad in the end, you know."

"Did you?"

"I came to realise that sometimes living things have had enough; they don't want to suffer anymore, and when that day comes you have to have the courage to do the right thing."

"What's this got to do with anything?" I asked.

"Nothing. It's just part of the story."

I watched as he turned his car around and drove off. That was to be the last time we would ever speak to one another.

I walked into the house and called out to Grandad, announcing I was home. I dumped my bag on the kitchen table and walked into the lounge. I could see the top of his head in his chair.

"Do you want a cup of tea, Grandad?"

There was no answer. I walked around to his chair and could see from his pale, lifeless face that he had passed away. I lifted his hand, which was stone cold. With tears welling in my eyes, I wrapped my arms around his body and held him tight one last time. I whispered in his ear that I was sorry: sorry for the lies I had told him and sorry he had been so ashamed of me that he had resorted to summoning Egan to straighten me out.

At the side of his chair, on the little table where I would always place his cup of tea, was a small jar. Its lid was removed and I could see a few pills sitting at the bottom. I was guessing the rest had been taken by Grandad. Next to the jar was a yellow jiffy bag. I picked it up to examine it for clues as to where it had come from. As I did, a note dropped out and floated to the ground. I scooped it up and then realised there was some writing on it:

Favour three – like Fowey, he didn't want to suffer any longer, so I gave him these pills to take away the pain. Take care, Robbie. And remember, no more lies.

Egan.

17 MONTHS LATER

CHAPTER 28

I stood in front of the mirror making sure my shirt, tie and, indeed, my whole attire was immaculate. Nothing else would be acceptable.

I opened my drawer for the final time and removed Grandad's six military medals. I placed three in my left jacket pocket and three in my right. I wouldn't be able to display them but would ensure they were on my person.

"Robbie, how am I looking?"

I turned around to where Steve Parish, who had struggled as much as anyone on the fourteen-week basic training we had completed at the Army Training Regiment in Winchester, stood in front of me. As I had been older than most of the recruits, I had become somewhat of a mentor.

I tweaked his tie to ensure his knot was tight against his collar.

"You're looking just fine," I said.

I slowly and carefully put on my hat before carrying out one final check that everything I had brought to the barracks had been packed ready for me to depart.

We had been rehearsing the Passing Out parade until we could do it in our sleep, but each of us knew there was always the chance you could get it wrong, especially in front of the watchful, proud eyes of friends and family.

My relationship with Zoe had not been without its challenges, and my decision to join the army probably hadn't helped. But I had stuck to the promise I made and turned my back on anything resembling a criminal life. I was expecting her to attend today and to bring Ollie, with whom I had grown very fond of.

Since Grandad's death, I had moved on significantly with my life, but one issue remained unresolved: I had not been able to force a reconciliation between Tony and Zoe. I had invited them both here today to share my proud moment. I had told them that the other was invited and I was, to some extent, forcing a resolution. My understanding was they would both be in attendance. I hoped so.

My thoughts jumped back to the Grasshopper bar in Amsterdam when I incorrectly concluded Tony was behind the Egan episode. Realising he wasn't, the thought he may do something stupid to Leon played heavy on my mind. After much persuasion, Zoe gave me Leon's mobile phone number and I contacted him under the pretence of being a drug user to establish if he was still dealing. Of course, he still was. I set up a decent-sized buy with him before notifying Messrs Wood and Brydges, who were more than happy to gatecrash the deal and arrest Leon red-handed. As a dealer with previous convictions, the courts weren't kind to him and he was sentenced to five years. Who knows, by the time he's released, I might even be Tony's son-in-law and hopefully in a position to offer sensible counsel regarding burying his pledge of revenge.

As well as Passing Out, I would also receive the award of 'Best Recruit'. The other lads didn't seem surprised by this, but I was. I think it's the only award I had ever received and I was determined to relish the moment.

We were under strict orders not to try and locate where our friends and family were seated. It was a strict 'eyes front' message which had to be obeyed.

With the band playing we marched over to where the gathering people were seated and then went through the routine. I could hear the gasps from the crowd as our synchronised movements were admired.

There were breaks during the parade as presentations were made. I cast my eye into the crowd where there were rows of taken seats placed before us.

My eyes danced around until I spotted Zoe. Sitting next to her was Tony. I watched as he whispered something to her and she laughed. As I looked closer I could see young Ollie was sat on his grandad's knee. I could hardly contain a smile.

My thoughts then swung to Grandad. What I would have given to have him sat in front of me today. My bottom lip started to quiver and I needed to quickly snap out of it. Blubbering shortly before receiving my 'Best Recruit' award would only present me with a lifetime of stick from my fellow soldiers.

At the end of the ceremony, we mixed openly with our visiting guests, but not as men; rather, as soldiers. I greeted Zoe with a kiss and gave Tony a big hug. I then lifted young Ollie onto my shoulders and carried him around. Once he had become too heavy, I slowly put him down, crouched and pinned on his little coat one of Grandad's medals.

Beyond Ollie, about thirty yards away in the distance, I caught sight of a figure in sunglasses staring at me. As I moved Ollie out of the way to get a better look at who it was, he had turned and walked away. He knew I had spotted him and he wouldn't much care. I also knew that coming over and offering his congratulations wasn't what he was about.

I had never resented what he had put me through or, moreover, the tablets he had supplied Grandad. I could never deny that from the time I had spent with him I had learnt much. I carried his spirit, his planning, his cunning and his cold decision-making with me during the basic training I had completed so successfully.

And I would forever obey the last challenge he had presented me, a challenge which I knew would last a lifetime – I would never tell another lie.